GLENMILL

# ONE MAN'S MEAT

Having limped through a History degree at Cambridge; Mark Frankland spent several years importing and hawking goods from India. He then helped build a multi-million pound family business manufacturing cattle and sheep feed. The firm was wiped out by the BSE crisis. He now writes and works as a Marketing Consultant. He lives with his family in the Galloway region of Scotland. One Man's Meat is the author's first novel.

# One Man's Meat

## Mark Frankland

**Glenmill**

# A Glenmill Publication

First published in 1999

**Glenmill**
Dumfries
Scotland
DG2 8PX

**tel: 01387 730 655**
**http://www.glenmill.freeserve.co.uk**

British Library Cataloguing in Publication Data.
A catalogue record of this book is available from the British Library.

**ISBN 0 9535944 0 8**

*Design, Layout & Typesetting* by Ψasmin
*email:* nomad@cableinet.co.uk

*"Everyone gets everything that they want.
I wanted a mission and for my sins they gave me one.
Brought it up like room service. It was a real choice mission.
Weeks away and hundreds of miles up a river
that snaked through the war like a maimed circuit cable
plugged straight into Kurtz, and when it was all over. . .
I'd never want another."*

**Apocalypse Now**

# Acknowledgements

To all of my family
for their support and encouragement.

To Peter Stuart for helping to make it happen.

To Alex for keeping my chin up
despite lots of setbacks.

To Ollie for guidance.

To Robert Atkins for helping out
with the political stuff.

To Kevin, Mike and Adam for reading it
as I wrote it and persuading me to keep going.

To George for his intro's
into the Merseyside printing world.

To Yasmin and Jon for patiently
guiding me into cyberspace.

. . . and to hundreds of farmers whose stoicism
and decency in the face of such nightmarish times
have made this book worth writing.

# CONTENTS

# CONTENTS

# CHAPTER ONE

## PRELIMINARIES

It was a Friday night in November 1997. Cornelius St John and Vincent Allenby were sitting quietly at a corner table in a pub in Covent Garden. It was a typical British Friday night.

Secretaries and young men from the city were pouring down drinks in celebration of the weekend. The pub was filling up fast and music throbbed through a haze of smoke.

Vince took a sip of his flat beer and glanced impatiently at his watch.

"Is he coming?" His voice was low and from the Scottish Borders.

"My dearest Vincent, how I look forward to the day when you learn the art of patience." Cornelius had a voice that was crisp and clipped. It was all Oxbridge and an Empire upon which the sun never set.

Two slightly drunk women in their late twenties emerged from the crowd around the bar and meandered across to their table. They wore dresses that were designed more for June in Spain than for November in London.

"Mind if we join you gentlemen?"

"Join us?" Mused Cornelius "Join is something of an imprecise concept wouldn't you say?"

"How do you mean?" The girls looked at each other and giggled nervously.

"Well, in this particular situation the word 'join' could indicate many things. It could indicate that your legs are weary after a long week at work and you would like to rest them by joining us in the use of the seating facilities provided at this table."

He raised an eyebrow. They giggled. He continued. "In which

case the answer to your question is 'no'. We are endeavouring to save these seats for a visitor who we expect to arrive imminently. On the other hand the word 'join' could have an altogether different and more implicated meaning, whereby you are suggesting that you 'join' us for the evening. The evening would start with drinks, move on to dinner and possibly conclude with a 'joining' of a thoroughly Biblical kind." He paused to light a cigarette.

"If it is indeed this kind of 'joining' that you have in mind, I am mortified to inform you that we also have something of a problem. You see, we are both as queer as coots."

At this point Cornelius smiled radiantly and took a sip of his gin and tonic. For a moment the women were stunned, then the shock wore off, handbags were grasped and a fast escape was made.

Vince chuckled. It was a performance he had witnessed several times before.

"You're such an idiot Cornelius. I just wish that you wouldn't always rope me in as being queer as well."

"You never know, one sunny day . . . "

Vince grinned. "Do you remember when we first met? I do. It was our first day at Cambridge. I was unpacking my cases and you knocked on the door. 'Morning, I'm your neighbour, Cornelius St John, I don't suppose that you're gay by any chance?' To which I replied, 'Not a chance.' 'Pity,' you said, 'let's have a drink anyway.' We got drunk, I forgave you for being an upper-class git and the rest is history. That was the only time you ever attempted to seduce me. I thought that you had quite given up."

"That wasn't seduction. I was merely gathering background information."

Vince went to the bar and bought another round. Bitter for him and double gin for Cornelius. As ever they were the subject of interested glances. They were the archetypal odd couple.

Vincent Allenby was thirty-three. He was just over six feet tall and stockily built. His face was square and functional. It was a face to which a razor was a relative stranger. His colour was neither tanned nor pale, merely well worn. He had always spent a lot of his time outdoors. His eyes were a washed-out grey and his hair was longish and unruly. He wore an old army jacket, a check shirt and faded jeans. On his feet were a pair of desert boots that had obviously been around a bit. A plumber, a builder, a mercenary/poet, a farmer – he was essentially nondescript. He just looked like anyone.

Cornelius St John didn't.

He was a man who was beautiful rather than handsome.

He was about five foot ten and very lean. He had a mop of blond hair that he wore swept back. His skin was permanently tanned. He wore his usual attire: a baggy tweed suit that had cost as much as a decent second-hand car, a striped button-down shirt, a college tie with pin, and gleaming brown brogues. He could have walked onto the set of any period drama about the 1920's and never needed to change. Wherever he went he always stood out.

Suddenly his face lit up and he stood up and waved in the general direction of the bar.

"Reggie! Over here old chap."

A miserable-looking man in a regulation City suit manoeuvred his way across the pub with his drink. Cornelius was at his most effusive.

"Reggie, my dear chap, and how the bloody hell are you? You're looking marvellous, must say. And the delicious Cynthia?"

Vince struggled to keep a straight face. He thought back to the briefing about the meeting that he had received from Cornelius some hours before.

"Who is he?" Vince had asked.

"He was at Eton with me. He was in the year below. I've met him here and there since. The man's an absolute reptile. He has an I.Q. of about three. I nearly fell off the chair when I realised it was him on the phone. He gets hideously boorish when he is drunk, which is most of the time. Not the kind of chap to exhibit deep wells of sympathy for those of us with my particular sexual persuasion. Absolute bloody homophobe, though he no doubt buggered the blazes out of umpteen wretched ten year olds at school.

"His family owns half of Norfolk and they have done so for half of history. They farm grain and get enough subsidy from Brussels every year to fund the NHS. He got some City job out of pure patronage and generally swans around being ghastly.

"His wife is lovely, Cynthia. She came from Norfolk somewhere. She is a local village girl. there was a bit of a stink from father I believe. You know the sort of thing, can't wed the bloody staff and all that. Her mother was the cleaner at the house. Lord alone knows how Cynthia landed herself with Reggie Stevenson. Money I suppose.

"Just wait till you see his chin, or should I say, the space in front of his lizardy face where his chin should be."

Now the beaming Cornelius had risen and was pumping Reggie Stevenson's hand as if he was being reunited with a brother who had returned from Somalia after years of missionary work. Vince had to admit that Reggie's lack of chin was spectacular.

Reggie was in his early thirties and his thin blond hair was receding fast. His face was sulky, sullen, red, and blotchy. This, coupled with heavy bags under the eyes, suggested late nights with the bottle. Obviously he was a man with problems, but that of course was why he had called Vince and Cornelius – people who could sort problems out.

At a price of course, and Vince very much doubted that the price to a homophobe like Reggie would be remotely cheap. He contentedly took a swig at his beer and lit a cigarette as Cornelius got to work.

"Now Reggie, do sit down. This is my colleague Vincent Allenby."

Reggie shook hands with Vince with extreme reluctance and said to Cornelius, "I thought it would just be you. I don't know if I want to talk in front of anyone else."

The way he said "anyone else" was a clear reference to the old army jacket and the desert boots and the Scottish voice. Whatever crisis in which Reggie was immersed, it was one which he only felt comfortable in sharing with a proper chap from a proper school. Cornelius never missed a stride.

"Don't let it worry you in the slightest my dear chap. You see, Vincent and I are partners and we have been so for the last thirteen years. We are umbilically bound so to speak. Our operation simply wouldn't work if one or the other was not involved. I am sure that whoever recommended that you should seek our services must have made it eminently clear that absolute discretion is our by-word. So let's have no coyness old chap. Have a drink and tell us all your problems, and we will solve them."

Reggie looked morose and downed his large scotch.

"OK Cornelius, fair enough. Let me get another drink. What will you chaps have?"

Reggie headed off to the bar. Once he was out of earshot Vince leaned across to Cornelius.

"My God you were right. He's awful. I do presume, Cornelius, that you are going to rip him off big style."

Cornelius flashed a brilliant smile. "Why of course, Vincent, of course. The likes of Reggie Stevenson were born onto the planet for the sole purpose of being ripped off. It will be an absolute pleasure."

Reggie arrived back and plonked the drinks down on the table. His scotch seemed to have been upgraded to a treble. He took a deep swig and started his story.

"It's Cynthia. She's having an affair. I don't know who he is. I've seen pictures and he's nobody from our circle."

"Let me just stop you a moment there Reggie," Cornelius interjected. "Pictures, you say, what pictures are these?"

"I hired a detective. She had grown very cold. I couldn't understand it. She wouldn't let me touch her. She insisted on separate rooms. I knew something was going on. I could feel it. I have to travel to Frankfurt every week for two days. Whenever I got home she was cold. I just knew it. So I hired a detective a month ago and he's been taking pictures. The bastard comes to the house every time that I am away. The detective has pictures of him going in the evening and leaving in the morning. He's there every time that I go. And you should see her face. It's glowing, beaming, radiant, like the cat that got the bloody cream. I tell you Cornelius, I could kill the bastard, I could get my shotgun and blow the bastard's bollocks . . . "

Reggie's voice was rising. People at the bar were glancing over. Cornelius spoke soothingly. "Now Reggie, try and stay calm. You have done the right thing. You've come to the right place."

Tears were now building up in Reggie's bloodshot eyes. "I love her Cornelius you see, I adore her. I always have. Father never wanted me to marry her. She's from Norfolk, from the village, her mother cleans at the house. I've known her since I was a kid. I've always loved her. And now . . . I can't sleep, I can't stand it Cornelius, I just can't stand it."

Tears rolled down his face. He tipped back the remainder of his scotch. Cornelius looked over to Vince.

"I think another drink for Reggie is in order Vincent. I think rather a large one."

When Vince duly delivered a quadruple scotch, Cornelius began speaking in a matter-of-fact tone.

"The problem that you face seems reasonably clear to me Reggie. Please interrupt if I in any way have grasped the wrong end of the stick.

"Cynthia is having an affair with someone that you don't know. From the pictorial evidence and her behaviour at home you feel that this liaison has gone beyond a mere sexual coupling, and moved onto something altogether more serious.

"Not withstanding this, your love for Cynthia remains undiminished. You want more than anything that the unknown lover should disappear from her life and thereby give you a chance to start over. Am I hitting the mark so far?"

Reggie nodded and a faint ray of hope was beginning to light up in his eyes.

"If we assume that her feelings are reciprocated by the unknown lover," Cornelius continued, "then it will not be easy for him to be persuaded to disappear. If he were to do so as a result of any dubious means it would merely arouse suspicion from Cynthia. No. The answer to your problem Reggie is that Cynthia must suddenly find her lover is someone who is quite abhorrent and orders him out of her life never to return. In the light of this traumatic turnaround in her amorous fortunes she will feel wary of any similar entanglements in the future, and thereby view you in a new and kinder light. Correct Reggie?"

The hope was now shining out of Reggie's eyes as if someone had rammed a lighthouse through the top of his thinning skull.

"Why yes, Cornelius, absolutely, but surely this couldn't possibly be done."

"We don't run our little operation on the basis of 'couldn't possibly' Reggie. You are fortunate that we are here to resolve your little problem. I can assure you that Vincent has a brain that is both brilliant and unorthodox. He will find the solution to your difficulties and we will execute it. I can assure you that we have frequently dealt with problems far more intractable than yours.

"However, let me continue. I believe that you have been somewhat less than frank with us on one aspect of this affair. It was common knowledge that your father disapproved most vigorously of your marriage to Cynthia. Indeed, I myself once heard him having a drunken rail at your wedlock to, as he put it, 'some tart from the village'. Be calm Reggie please. I think that I am right in assuming that should divorce raise its ugly head, your father would not only remove you from his will, but also cut your not inconsiderable allowance, without which it would be somewhat difficult for you to continue to live to the standard that you have always been accustomed. I am quite certain that he simply would not allow a single penny of the Stevenson fortune to find its way into the hands of the fair Cynthia. Correct Reggie?"

"You bastard Cornelius."

"No Reggie. I am simply stating the facts as I see them. Have you any questions Vincent?"

"Two. You said that you didn't know who he was. Clarify that please."

Reggie straightened himself and made an effort to pull himself together.

"Well, I don't know his name. The detective followed him. I know that he works in the delicatessen shop a couple of streets away. I suppose she must have met him in the shop. The bastard must have chatted her up."

"Fine," said Vince. "Secondly, what time does he leave in the mornings. Is it consistent?"

"Yes. Six a.m. Every time."

"Excellent. I can see no problem with this Cornelius. When are you next over in Frankfurt?"

"Next Tuesday."

Vince smiled a reassuring smile. "Then we shall have your problem solved by the time that you return Mr Stevenson, assuming of course, that you agree to whatever terms Cornelius has in mind."

"Ah yes," said Cornelius, "Terms. Pricing up solutions to these problems is never easy. At stake here of course is an inheritance of 25,000 acres of prime grain-growing East Anglian land with a current market value of £4,000 per acre. A very significant sum indeed Reggie.

"Vincent's plans, though brilliant, inevitably involve a high degree of expense. We would therefore require a down payment of £5,000 to be payable to me personally in cash tomorrow. Following the execution of our operation next week, I would like you to carry on using the services of your private detective for a further month, without, of course, saying a word to him. Assuming that he reports that Cynthia has made no further contact with her lover, or at least that she has not allowed him over the threshold of your property during the intervening period, you will make a further cash payment of £15,000 to me on Wednesday, December 7."

"But . . . " Reggie spluttered.

"Please don't interrupt Reggie, I have yet to finish outlining our terms. If at the end of this summary you feel that our terms are inappropriate we can conclude our business right away. I can assure you that we are quite non-negotiable."

At this point Cornelius reached into his breast pocket and removed a small tape recorder and placed it on the table. Reggie tensed. Cornelius continued.

"I of course have no doubts that you are a thoroughly good chap and that you will pay up your second instalment like a gentleman. However, should you be tempted to indulge yourself in any ungentlemanly conduct by not paying the second instalment, I would have absolutely no compunction in sending a copy of this tape to both Cynthia and to your father. Should you decline our terms I will of course give you the tape here and now and we will go our separate ways."

Reggie looked utterly stunned. He played with his drink and

looked down assuming a rather beaten air. Cornelius smiled and lit a cigarette. Vince leaned back and hummed. No words were spoken for some moments. Reggie knew it was make the mind up time. He straightened himself and said, "All right Cornelius, we have a deal. But I want to know what you are going to do."

"Can't help you there Reggie. It is one of our rules. We never divulge our plans. You will simply have to trust us. I'm sure we came highly recommended."

"Bloody hell. OK. Sod it, I'll do it. I'll call round with the money tomorrow. Just don't let me down."

With this he got up and stalked out without a backward glance. As he slammed through the door and into the night Vince erupted into laughter.

"Christ Cornelius, you really do have a thing about chinless wonders who hate gays."

"Vincent there are few things in life that can compare with having an absolute shit like Reggie backed right into a corner with absolutely nowhere to go. Will it be easy?"

"Piece of cake. The time is good. She sounds gullible – insecure in the city and all that. She probably doesn't know that much about the target and his past. It should be like shelling peas."

"Come on Vincent. Our next appointment beckons. Marcus Dalrymple will be an altogether more formidable prospect. I'll tell you about him in the car."

Outside, Cornelius quickly hailed a taxi and they headed for Kensington.

"OK," said Vince. "Tell me all about it."

Cornelius lit up thoughtfully. "I must admit that I am somewhat in the dark about this one. Dalrymple rang a couple of nights ago. I know we never expect any of our phone calls, but somehow I would never have anticipated a call from Marcus Dalrymple. He's something of a dark horse. I've only ever met him briefly on a couple of occasions. He puts on a real Rolls Royce, old buffer act. You know the type, full of bonhomie and banging on about the bloody Germans kind of thing. I can't say he ever much of an impression on me.

"After he called I asked around a bit. I didn't find out much.

Surprisingly little in fact. Nobody seems to know very much at all about him."

"He's 72 and very robust. The family come from Yorkshire. His father started a textile business just after the Great War. It did well enough to survive the depression. Marcus went to the local Grammar school and would have gone to university but for the war. I received a strong whiff of the cloak and dagger when I have asked about the war. You know the kind of thing, knowing winks and wistful sighs from the old buffers in his club. Apparently he had a very good war but a very hard war – he was mainly in Yugoslavia; behind the lines stuff. He was 18 when he went out there. Must have been going on 80 when he got back.

"After the war he threw himself into the business. His older brother had been killed in North Africa and his father never really got over it. His dad died in 1952 and Marcus took the reins. And very successfully he took them too. As most of the Yorkshire mills closed down, Dalrymple's bucked the trend and flourished. Initially it seems that someone at the M.O.D. remembered him and threw him some juicy uniform contracts. Then he got into making high class tweedie stuff and exported it to the States by the shipload.

"He married in 1960 and had a son in 1962. Nothing out of the way happened for years. He ran his business, got pretty rich, bought a couple of thousand acres in North Cumbria and settled into being a low profile country squire.

"Then in 1982 his son Jeremy was killed in the Falklands and things changed. Within months he had sold his business to the Japanese and had gone semi-reclusive. His wife died of cancer in 1989 and nobody seems to have seen much of him since.

"And that, my dear Vincent, is that. We're off into the great Kensington unknown."

"Fine by me Cornelius. All of your aristocratic cronies are a jump into the unknown for me."

"I don't think that we should underestimate Marcus Dalrymple. Everything that I have learnt about this gentleman leads me to believe that he is anything but an old buffer. Sharp as a tack I should say. We must be on our very best form."

The cab pulled up outside a fine three-storey town house in a quiet cul-de-sac. Cornelius paid up, tipped the driver and jauntily bounded up the steps. A short time from the ringing of the polished brass bell the big ornate door was thrown open.

"Ah, Cornelius my boy, do come in. How the hell are you? Looking resplendent as ever I must say. Such a pleasure to find a young man with some appreciation of decent cloth. Very decent cloth indeed. We Yorkshire chaps always have an eye for a bit of decent cloth you know. Bred into us. Washed in with the rain. Bloody good show I must say."

Whilst maintaining this enthusiastic banter Marcus, in a flurry of energy, relieved them of their coats, and led the way into the drawing room.

"Sit down, sit down, no need to stand on ceremony here chaps, sit down and make yourselves at home."

For Vince, the room was love at first sight. It was a chaotic clutter of books, old papers, and obscure mementos. Unmatching pictures were thrown around the panelled walls in a completely haphazard fashion. There were watercolours, oils and old photos, all depicting scenes of smoking mills, terraced streets, and images of old industry. The furniture was leather and ancient and a host of bizarre ornaments occupied every available surface - mining lamps, looms, tools, even an old anchor. A fire was burning in the old grate and logs were heaped up on either side. Marcus noticed the direction of Vince's gaze.

"Ah, yes. Real fire. Real smoke. Not quite environmentally the thing I suppose. The buggers keep fining me. I keep paying the fines. I send them a letter with the cheque you know. Use this money to knobble some real polluters, I say. Fat bloody chance of course. The money will probably go to the Council holiday fund to send some pinko off on a jolly to Nicaragua or Cuba or somewhere . . . Who the hell are you anyway?"

Vince smiled. "Vincent Allenby. I am Cornelius's partner."

Marcus chuckled. "A bloody Jock eh. What's the accent? South somewhere. Borders?"

"Not bad Mr Dalrymple. Kelso."

"Don't Mr Dalrymple me for Christ's sake. It's Marcus. Now if you're a Jock you'll drink whisky. And if you're a proper Jock you'll appreciate a bit of decent whisky. Have a bash at this little bastard. Cornelius?"

"Actually, gin for me, if it wouldn't be too much trouble, Marcus."

"Trouble! Good God man, the day it's too much trouble to pour a decent chap a decent drink is the day that you should consider shoving a twelve-bore down the throat and popping off."

He bounced across the room and started throwing copious measures of alcohol into thick, chunky tumblers. Cornelius looked over and rolled his eyes comically. Marcus was a very vigorous seventy-two year old indeed. He stood a little under six feet, but very straight. He had lost none of his hair, and it sat atop his head like a wild white hedge. His clothing was unconventional, bordering on the eccentric. He wore shredded leather slippers, tweed trousers, a heavily frayed check shirt, and a thick ethnic type cardigan that looked to have hailed from somewhere in the back end of Afghanistan. His features were a mix of a drinker's red and an outdoor type's brown. He was well wrinkled, but the wrinkles spoke of a lifetime of smiling rather than being miserable. It seemed to Vince that the permanent twinkle of mischief in his eyes somewhat belied the impression of the reclusive, grieving father that Cornelius had painted in the cab. Marcus thrust a tumblerful of whisky into Vince's hand.

"Now then young chap, get a bit of that down your neck and tell me what you think."

The whisky's light colour had given Vince a pretty good clue, but nowhere near a good enough clue to prepare him.

"Bloody Hell Marcus, this is marvellous."

"Isn't it," Marcus beamed, "Isn't it bloody just that."

He took a generous swig from his own glass then sat down and clapped his hands.

"Now then, I'm sure that there are things that a couple of likely young chaps like you would rather be doing with your Friday evening rather than listening to a dreary old bugger like me."

"Worry not sir," said Vince, "you keep pouring this out and I'll listen to you all night."

Cornelius raised an eyebrow at this. It was rare for Vince to say much at these meetings.

"That's the spirit my boy, top notch, even if you do look like something that's been dragged in by an American cat." Marcus eyed Vince's ancient combat jacket mischievously.

"You mean, rather than a Persian one?" Vince smiled, looking equally mischievously at the old man's Afghan cardigan. For a moment Marcus was confused, then the penny dropped and he erupted into merriment.

"Bloody marvellous. Persian cat. That's me told good style. Persian bloody cat." It took him a little while to gather his thoughts as he brought his amusement under control.

"Right. To business. I've heard a bit about you chaps. Only a bit, nobody seems to know much about you. Quite right too I should say. Need to know and all that. But tell me if I have hold of the right end of the stick. You apparently claim to be able to provide solutions to otherwise seemingly insoluble problems. Correct?"

"Quite correct Marcus." Cornelius assumed his normal front man role.

"And from what I can gather, the solutions that you provide are, shall we say, unorthodox."

"We find that some problems can indeed lend themselves to an unorthodox approach, yes."

"And the Law?"

"Mind if I smoke? Thanks." Cornelius paused to inhale. "The Law. Well, we would like to feel that we work within the spirit of the Law if not necessarily within its strictest of bounds."

"That's Politician talk. Talk straight man."

Cornelius smiled, quite unabashed. "We have been known to break laws from time to time. We would never implicate a client however. That would be most unprofessional. We are, by the way completely professional; we don't have other jobs."

Marcus paused for a while.

"Didn't know how you would answer that. But I'm happy enough with the answer that you have given. The law's an ass a lot of the time. Sometimes it deserves breaking. Yes, I'm happy enough. I gather that your success rate is high?"

"Extremely high Marcus. It has to be. We only get paid on results."

"I heard about that too." Marcus was all of a sudden businesslike. "Yes, it attracted me. I can't stand people that want paying whether they succeed or not. Lawyer types. Bloody leeches the lot of them."

"We pride ourselves on our absolute lack of any resemblance to leeches."

Marcus sat a while thinking, leaving a not unpleasant silence to wash over the room. The logs quietly hissed and crackled and an occasional car brushed by outside. Eventually he stood up and, without a word, relieved them of their glasses and refreshed them.

"OK chaps, it's time to come out with it and tell all I suppose. You will know that I have a bit of a spot up in Cumbria."

"I thought it was only Americans and Australians that considered 2,000 acres to be a bit of a spot," Vince murmured. Once again Cornelius seemed surprised. Vince was positively garrulous tonight. Marcus merely chuckled.

"Forgive me. English-speak I'm afraid. I learnt it in the war. I once saw a chap who had stood on a mine and lost both his legs. He apologised that he might hold us a bit up due to a spot of bother with the old pegs.

"Anyway, to continue. I have a large upland estate in Northern Cumbria. I bought it several years ago. I would be a liar if I claimed that it was a purely commercial venture. No, definitely not commercial.

"After years of living in the crowded valleys I felt ready for some air and some real weather. You have obviously done your homework. You'll know I'm not short of a few bob. To start with it was a weekend place. Most of it was tenanted out and all I did was use the house. Then when Jeremy was killed I sold up and moved there. That was in 1982. Things started going wrong for agriculture about that time and got steadily worse. Within five years I had lost five of my tenants.

"I soon decided not to replace them. Instead I decided to try to learn to become a farmer myself. It was bloody hard going I'll tell you. Even with no mortgage and lots of capital behind me I've had to struggle like mad.

"Land is a funny thing you know. Every day I spend up there it kind of grows into me. I feel as if I'm being slowly absorbed into the landscape. It must be old age and loneliness I suppose. I probably spend too many days not seeing a soul and tramping around the moors in the rain. The thing is, I have developed a muddled mixed up view of the world. I was brought up as the son of a Yorkshire miller, all profit and thrift. Then I went to war. Then I lost a son and a wife. Now I struggle to farm in a hard place.

"Humour an old man. Words have never been a strong point for me, yet for you to understand my problem I need to give it some life. My farm up at High Glen has become everything to me. I love it with passion and one day soon I shall die there. It is financially immaterial whether or not I farm it for a profit, I have far more in the bank than I could ever hope to spend and not a soul in the world to leave it to. But that isn't the point you see. Every one of my neighbours has to fight the battle for survival every day of their lives. They have no fall back. I enjoy their company. I enjoy the bar at the auction mart and the Friday crack in the pub. We talk about sheep and farming and everything. I know that I will always be something of an impostor, but I could never settle with myself if I only played at farming and let my savings simply bale out the losses at the end of each year. Not the Yorkshire way lads. Not the Yorkshire way at all.

"During the last couple of years since the BSE crisis things have got really hard. Making a profit is well nigh impossible even for the best of farmers, and when all is said and done, I'm still just a beginner. It became apparent to me a couple of years ago that High Glen desperately needed another source of income. I thought and pondered and came up with the idea of Wind Farming. You'll have seen these new wind farms up and down the country. Marvellous idea. They take the energy of the never-ending gales off the Irish Sea and turn them into power which can be used to make a cup of tea in Halifax. No fumes, no punctures in the ozone layer, no burning of the world's resources. It is a fine project for an old man, a fine legacy, and gentlemen, it will generate sufficient profit and return on capital to put High Glen firmly back into the black.

"I decided to create a new limited company to run the wind

15

farm. My idea was that if I could create a successful wind farm then others among my neighbours would be interested in doing likewise. In exchange for shares in the new company they would allocate land and the company would finance and build more windmills. I have had all kind of feasibility studies conducted and it will be possible to pool all the electricity that we produce and shoot it into the grid in one go. It may be possible to generate enough power from our hills to look after a town of some size.

"As you can see, I have become something of an enthusiast. Anyway, I set up the company, did the surveys, came to a deal to buy eighty windmills from a company in Denmark and entered the dreaded maze of planning permission. To start with it seemed as if things were going to be fine. I have some experience with planning people, and my suggested trade off, a new wing on the local school, seemed to have done the trick. The project rattled through the preliminary stages and all was bang on course.

"Then I made my mistake. I'm afraid it was the mistake of an over-confident old man. One weekend I had a visit from the Managing Director of the Danish company who are going to build my windmills. He told me that they had hit a cash flow crisis and that their bank had given them a fortnight to come up with some funds or they were for the liquidator. I had agreed a price of £70,000 per windmill giving a total contract value of £5,600,000. He proposed that if I were willing to give him a 10% deposit up front he would do the job for five million. Half a million pounds was sufficient to help him over his cash flow hurdle and the guarantee of a five million contract to follow was more than enough to satisfy his bankers. I got the plane out to Copenhagen with him the next day and met with his bankers. They gave me an undertaking that the £500,000 would be lodged with them and that they would support the company for at least the time it would take for them to fill my order.

"Fine. A nice £600,000 discount for the new company. A heck of a deal I thought. I happily released a slug of funds into High Glen Windpower Ltd which in turn had them transferred to Denmark. Then the bloody demonstrations started. Demonstrations is probably too strong a word. There is a gang of about ten new-age idiots who come up from Keswick at the weekends to rant on and smoke dope. To be honest, they have been no great bother to me. They shout and yell as I drive in and out of the farm and that is about it. To be honest they're not bad types. They haven't done any damage and they don't leave a mess. In the summer I suppose it was a bit of a lark for them to drive up into hills, stick up a few tents, and do their bit to save the planet. As soon as a bit of rain fell they were nowhere to be seen.

"So all in all, they were a bloody nuisance but no real problem, certainly nothing to necessitate my calling on you chaps. However I received a call last Saturday which has rather changed things. They had been up for a couple of hours in the afternoon, but it was a cold day and they soon got fed up and scarpered off down to the local pub. Alf, the landlord, is a good friend and he rang to tell me about a conversation that he had overheard. Apparently, Channel 4 are doing a documentary about Windfarming and how it is causing all kinds of confrontations between the so-called money grubbing landowners and the country-loving British public. The main item on the agenda is a big planned development up in Scotland where there is a hell of a little war going on. To be honest the protesters up there have a bit of a point. The planned development is right on top of the hill that overlooks the town and it will do little for postcard sales. Mine, by the way, isn't visible from a single house barring my own. The producer wanted a quick slot from another dispute and had been put in touch with my demonstrators via Friends of the Earth. Apparently the crew need to be up in Scotland ready to film by lunchtime on Saturday, November 17. Their plan is to stay in Keswick and do a dawn shoot of my heroic eco-warriors before heading on up the motorway. They are scheduled to arrive at my place at 6.30 a.m. and they need to be back on the road by no later than 7.30. It seems obvious that they can only be putting together a couple of minutes of footage, five minutes at most.

"However, there is a chance that those five minutes could cost me £100,000 a minute. Cumbria puts huge emphasis on its environment and the authorities fight a running battle to convince tourists and investors alike that it is a wonderfully clean place to come, regardless of Sellafield. As the crow flies, Sellafield is a mere 30 miles from High Glen. There is a chance that a five-minute slot on National television could well be enough to give the planners a dose of cold feet. I had a quiet chat with one of them and he said as much to me. Don't get me wrong, it isn't absolutely cut and dried, it simply raises a big doubt.

"So gentlemen, you are now acquainted with my problem. If the programme to be filmed on November 17, i.e. a week tomorrow, goes ahead, there is a distinct possibility that I will lose £500,000 and the last dream of an old man will die. If it doesn't go ahead, then I have the nod that planning permission is more or less guaranteed at the meeting to be held on December J.

"I'll pour more drinks."

And pour more drinks he did. Cornelius took his gin and tonic and started to weigh up what his response should be. It was, without any shadow of a doubt, an interesting problem. Particularly interesting. The sort of problem which he felt could easily turn into a bite-off-more-than-you-can-chew sort of problem. He had had this feeling many times before only to be pleasantly surprised by Vincent's eventual solution. But this one was tough. How to start? What to say? He was thinking these kind of thoughts when he noticed Vince start to gently shake. The gentle shaking turned into a violent shaking which turned into a chuckle which turned into a guffaw. After a few seconds Vince was rocking up and down in his chair and laughing quite uncontrollably. Marcus looked on with open astonishment. Cornelius was similarly dumbfounded.

"Vincent, what the bloody hell is the matter?"

It seemed to take Vince a great personal effort to get a grip on himself, and when he did he was only able to blurt out the word "Prawns!" before once again relapsing into helpless hysterics.

Cornelius was starting to feel a twinge of alarm. Over the years he had come to know all of Vince's quirks, and having hysterics over the weirdest of things was not all that unusual. Not, however, in the company of a potential client. Christ, Marcus must take him for an absolute nutter. Time to ease the situation.

"Marcus, I simply must apologise. I could say that Vincent is unused to fortified liquor but that wouldn't be entirely truthful, possibly . . . "

"Oh do shut up Cornelius." Vince was regaining some control. "I'm sure Marcus has seen blokes crack up in his time. Marcus, are you aware of the definition of the word 'imputation'?"

Marcus thought for a while then responded, "Revelation, blinding light, Paul on the road to Damascus sort of thing?"

"That's it." Vince was still battling to hold back another bout of laughter. "Well I've just had one. A real blinding road to Damascus ripsnorter and it all revolves around prawns. Pour me another slug of that marvellous scotch and we'll talk terms. The solution to your problem is at hand my friend."

By now Cornelius's eyes were on the verge of popping out and he almost lost his studied cool as he clawed for another cigarette. He damn nearly lit it off the butt of the one he had been smoking. Deep breath.

"Ahhm, Vincent, I . . . "

"It's all right Cornelius, don't panic, I've not completely lost it. Marcus, I'm afraid my behaviour has come as something of a shock to my partner. You see, he usually gets us business with the very essence of the chinless upper-class pratt. I can't abide them, so I tend to sit quietly looking savagely working class whilst Cornelius does his stuff. I'm ever so sorry Cornelius, telling you to shut up was inexcusable."

Cornelius relaxed. "My dear Vincent, you know only too well that I would forgive you anything."

"Then I should like to ask a favour."

"Of course, ask and thy wish shall be granted."

Vince grinned. "Just this once I would like us to break with custom, and I would like to conduct the negotiations."

Cornelius rolled his eyes theatrically. "Oh Lord save us from the willing amateur. We are served up with one of the most difficult and intractable problems that we have ever faced and my partner chooses this very moment to assume duties in which he has no experience. The result of course will be a gross case of underpricing influenced by too much exquisite scotch and a wholly misplaced working-class sense of ethics." Cornelius grinned ruefully and addressed Marcus, "You must understand my concern for the profitability of this venture sir. Over the last few years I have been bored to the brink of oblivion by this man on numerous occasions. The topic that Vincent has been so boring about has been noneother than windfarming. It is, I hate to say, one of Vincent's great passions."

It was the turn of Marcus to laugh. "By Christ chaps, I don't know how good you are at solving problems, but I must say that you are damned entertaining. Bloody good value. Come on then Vincent, embark on the negotiations. I must caution that you've picked a rum bugger to make your debut on. I'm a mean hard-nosed Yorkshireman. A thoroughly bad 'un to get the best side of."

Vince, quite returned to normal now, smiled happily. "Oh, I don't know. I have a strong feeling that you are a fair man who will pay for what he gets. We can ensure that when the camera crew arrives at High Glen at 6.30 on the morning of November 17 there will be no bugger in sight. In fact to be on the safe side, we will ensure that there is no bugger there from 5.45 a.m. The result of this is that we will save you £500,000 and allow you to proceed with your commendable plans to build windfarms. I know it is worth a lot to you and I respect it. It would be worth a lot to me too. So make us an offer."

Marcus beamed with appreciation. "You'll bloody do me Mr Allenby. Well spoken sir. Now let me think." He took a slow ponderous swig of his whisky and came to a conclusion quickly. "OK You ensure that the demonstrators are nowhere to be seen at the appointed time and date and I'll pay 5% of what I save to any account you please. £25,000." He paused with studied drama. "On one condition. You tell me the plan."

Cornelius looked at Vince with interest. It was Vince who was always adamant that clients should never know of a plan, and should only learn it after the problem was solved.

Vince weighed it. "That is a big ask. It is a rule that we have never broken before. However, rules are made to be broken, but only for a price. I have a proposal therefore for both of you. I accept the fee of £25,000 on behalf of our operation. The plan that I have in mind is a three-man job, probably four. This would give us shares of £6,250 each. I will offer to pay the other three members of the team £8,333 each from my own funds should Marcus agree to give me 10% of the shares in High Glen Windpower Ltd by way of payment should we be successful. Cornelius?"

"Fine by me."

"Marcus?"

"Delighted. Young man, we have a deal." At which point they all shook hands. Marcus sat down eagerly. "And so, the plan. Tell all."

And Vincent told all. At the end of it Cornelius was in similar controlled hysterics to the ones suffered by Vince earlier. Marcus wasn't far behind. When the general laughter died down Marcus spoke.

"Now lads, I know that a deal is a deal and we shook on it, but I'm going to be a bugger and move the goalposts and add a further condition. The good news for you Cornelius and for your friend Victor is that it will raise your stake up to £12,500 each. When you said that your plan would require three maybe four I can see your dilemma. Ideally you would have a driver, but for the sake of an extra share you could conceivably do without a driver and you could do the driver job yourself Vincent. Am I correct?"

"Unerringly so," Vince agreed.

"Then my final condition is that I shall be your driver. And before you dare say a word I will let you know that once upon a time I parachuted into the mountains of Croatia in darkness when they were crawling with Germans. With that on my C.V. I will get mighty upset if you make any nonsensical noises about me being too old. Conditions have a price of course. Let me drive Vincent, and you can have 15%."

Vince smiled in delight. "Marcus, it will be a pleasure to have you involved. There is no need to pay any more for the privilege."

"Oh I'll pay chaps. Pay with a song in the heart. I felt that the time for me to be involved in a caper such as this had passed me by many, many years ago. Now, so long as you chaps have nothing better to do, I suggest that we get seriously drunk to celebrate."

And get seriously drunk they did. It was well after midnight when Cornelius and Vince staggered out of the Kensington house. Fond, slurred farewells were wished and arrangements made. All of a sudden they had a particularly busy fortnight ahead of them.

They eventually found a taxi and headed up to Notting Hill

Gate. As they rang the bell at the door of a nondescript four-storey apartment building Vince dug in his pocket for a coin. He tossed it, missed the catch, scratched around the floor for it, tossed it again and said "Heads or tails old boy?"

"Heads." Vince peered at the coin on the back of his hand. "Bastard. Heads it is. Sod it."

"What exactly are we tossing for Vincent?"

Vince looked vaguely miserable. "For who gets to tell Victor about the prawns."

Cornelius hooted with delight. "And heads it was. Have no fear Vincent, I promise to put fresh flowers on your grave every Sunday."

The speaker on the door frame crackled with a deep and angry voice. "Who's that?"

"Cornelius St John and Vincent Allenby require an audience with the chief on a mission of the greatest gravity."

The microphone spoke. "Ah for God's sake Cornelius, does it have to be now? I've got company."

"Victor, now it simply has to be. Open the door, tell the dear lady that we are hale and hearty fellows all, and that we will require you only briefly after which you can return to an evening of vigorous coupling."

The door clicked open. As they made their unsteady way up the stairs Cornelius hummed 'The Last Post'.

Victor Gama stood in the doorway on the second floor. Some guys are big. Some guys are really big. And some guys are really, really big. Victor Gama was a colossus. Victor was of the Ibo tribe of southern Nigeria. He stood six feet three tall and more or less the same across. He wore only a white towel around his waist which emphasised his shining coal-black skin. He had a high African forehead and ferocious burning eyes. When he smiled the great ebony face split apart to reveal two rows of huge dazzling teeth. Right now the teeth were well hidden by a brooding scowl.

"This had better be good guys."

Cornelius ran his eyes appreciatively across the massive chest.

"My God Victor, if I was into the macho type I would scratch the little strumpet's eyes out and attack you."

Victor's teeth shone out like a toothpaste advert and the hall was filled with a rumbling laugh.

"Come in wankers. Sit down. I'll go and settle the lovely lady."

The rented sitting room was decidedly Spartan. Victor had added little to the basic threadbare furniture supplied by his Lebanese landlord. It was always the same with Victor. No ties. No possessions much. Nothing that couldn't be dropped and left quickly. They had all met at Cambridge. Victor was doing a degree in English before heading for Sandhurst and a three-year commission with the Marines. On completing his stint with the British army the family plan had been for him to return to take up a post in the Nigerian forces. However, when that time came, the Nigerian army had wrested power in his homeland and was covering itself in little glory. Victor had no stomach for the idea of sacking villages and torturing those considered to be politically incorrect and so he had become an exile. His impressive stature ensured that he had no shortage of work as an actor or bouncer, but these occupations merely filled in the gaps between problem-solving exploits with Vince and Cornelius. They had been partners for years, and quite naturally Victor handled the military side of their operations.

After a few minutes Victor emerged from the bedroom wearing a T-shirt and tracksuit bottoms.

"If there are any difficulties Victor," said Cornelius with a slight slur to his voice, "I would be more than happy to go in there and make representations on your behalf."

"You can bugger right off. She'd take one look at you, turn to jelly and then reach for the Valium when she found out the shattering truth that you're a raging poof."

"You exhibit all the cruelty of the savage land that bore you Victor. Anyway, for Christ's sake, get us a drink or the horrors will set in."

The three of them sat for two hours going over the plans and requirements for the next fortnight. It was after an hour and forty-five minutes that Vince had to break the news about the prawns. The great black face drained of colour and turned a sickly grey.

"Oh come on Vince there has to be another way. Any way. Not prawns surely."

Vince assumed a grim air. "Victor, prawns it simply has to be. For a man with three tours of Northern Ireland under his belt surely a lousy dish of prawns can hold little fear. Besides, think of the payback. Twelve and a half grand – about £700 a prawn."

"Bastards. And Cornelius, if that little smirk grows any bigger I might just knock it through the back of your pretty boy skull."

Cornelius rolled his eyes in horror. "It is at times like these that I could almost cry for those poor heroic missionaries who fought so hard to civilise your ferocious race."

Vince continued. "So Victor, prawns apart, any problems?"

"None that I can see. If you pick up the van tomorrow I'll get the other stuff. He'll want a fair deposit, how are we for cash?"

"No bother," said Vince. "Cornelius is picking up a five grand deposit for the first job tomorrow. You two meet up at lunchtime and sort it out. When will you have the gear?"

"By the evening."

"OK We'll meet up about eight and drive the van up to my place. A day should be plenty for rehearsals. We'll come back down Monday morning ready to be in place early doors Wednesday."

Victor smiled happily. He loved these capers. "You know Vince, prawns apart, these are real beauties. You're a clever bastard at times."

"Come on," Cornelius said. "We best get to bed. Try not to wear yourself out Victor."

"Baas, it would take more than that skinny white-assed gal next door to wear out a big Ibo boy like me."

And with that they parted. Two operations were under way.

# CHAPTER TWO

## OPERATIONAL

Nobody in Elm Avenue saw the black van as it pulled up outside number 74 at 5.30 a.m. on the morning of November 12. Elm Avenue was in Belgravia and constituted one of the most outrageously expensive places to live in the United Kingdom. It was highly unlikely that there would be anybody up and about to notice the van at that time in the morning. People who could afford to live in Elm Avenue were well past the stage in life where they had to be up and on the road for 5.30 in the morning to make their way up the ladder.

The van was really rather sinister. They had used it for several operations because it looked the part so well. Vince had spotted it on the forecourt of a van-hire agency in Cricklewood several months before. It had shiny black paintwork and opaque, mirrored glass windows. Nobody on the outside could see a thing inside the van, whilst those on the inside could watch without anyone knowing.

A thin winter drizzle was leaking down from the dark skies above. The pavement gleamed a doleful orange in the light that spilt down from the street lamps. It was very quiet indeed. There were no paperboys, no insomniac dog walkers. There wasn't even a breath of wind. It was all particularly film noir.

As Cornelius sat smoking in the driver's seat he felt in a particularly film noir mood. This was largely because of his outfit. It consisted of a grey three-piece suit, a white shirt and an Irish Guards tie. Over this he wore a baggy raincoat and a grey gangsterish hat. He had gazed at himself critically in the mirror at 3.30 that morning. As he had pulled hard on a cigarette he had decided that Bogart himself would have been impressed.

Vince and Victor were sitting on wooden bench seats in the back of the van. Their attire was rather different. They wore black jump suits cut from a heavy canvas type cloth. Over these they wore black bullet-proof vests and complicated webbing belts which were draped with an array of menacing weaponry. The bottoms of the jump suits were tucked into shiny black boots. To cap it all off they wore black berets and communication headsets. The uniform was not a copy of any real-life outfit. It was in fact a product of Cornelius's imagination and a number of high octane action films that he had watched.

Victor had scoffed. He had said that the outfits were ridiculous and that any self-respecting special serviceman wouldn't be seen dead in one. Vince told him not to worry. Cornelius moodily explained that their goal was not to storm a Hezbollah stronghold in the Bekaa valley, merely to make a devastating impression on an impressionable girl from the backwoods of Norfolk.

As the clock ticked slowly towards 6.00 a.m. the tension in the van grew steadily. It wasn't an unpleasant tension. It was a feeling that they all enjoyed. At one minute after six the front door of number 12 eased open. An attractive young woman in a dressing gown stepped out gingerly and looked carefully up and down the deserted street. Once she was happy that no neighbours were up and about she ducked back inside and a moment later a young man in a bomber jacket stepped out. He turned to kiss the woman briefly and then headed off down the pavement. As he passed the van Cornelius got a good view of him and decided that he didn't much like what he saw. The man had a hard, thin face and as he strode down the pavement he never looked back whilst Cynthia shivered on the doorstep.

Once he was away around the corner she closed the door. Cornelius leaned back over his seat. "OK chaps. Showtime."

Cornelieus got out of the van and bounded up the steps and knocked the door. Cynthia answered almost immediately. Her pretty face underwent a rapid change of emotions. First there was astonishment at the sight of the strangely clad Cornelius on her doorstep at six in the morning. Then there was the beginnings of pleasure for she had always liked Cornelius. Then there was confusion as he turned and waved to the sinister black van which was parked outside the house. Then there was blind terror as two monstrous black military figures leapt out of the back of the van and barged past her into the house. Cornelius could sense a scream coming on and acted swiftly. He took Cynthia firmly by the arm and led her inside whilst Vince and Victor crashed from room to room with murderous intent.

"Cynthia darling, it really is very, very important that you try to stay calm. Why don't we pop through to the kitchen whilst these chaps do their stuff."

His voice seemed to soothe the terrified young woman and she meekly led him through to the kitchen at the back of the house whilst the sound of stampeding boots was to be heard from the upstairs rooms.

Once in the kitchen she started the process of making tea, looking for all the world like an automaton. The kettle was just about to boil when Vince and Victor came in to the room breathing heavily. Cynthia shuddered at the sight of them.

"Don't worry, Cynthia, you are in no danger. These are my men." Cornelius turned and looked up at the towering figure of Victor. "Well?"

"Nothing sir. He's gone. There's no stash either."

"You're sure?"

Victor's massive face registered resentment at the question.

"Quite sure, sir."

"OK then. You two can pop off then. I'll meet you later."

This agitated Victor even further. "But sir, what about the woman . . . "

"I said pop off."

"But sir . . . "

Cornelius's voice suddenly cracked like a rifle shot on a crisp February morning. "If I have to repeat this order one more time Sergeant I'll have you cleaning the toilets in Londonderry HQ for the next five years. Now get the hell out here of right now. Is that clear?"

The big man was utterly chastised. He and Vince dug into a holdall and dragged out two large raincoats. When they pulled these on and buttoned them right up they completely covered their military gear. Victor muttered a brief "Sir," and they were gone.

Cornelius pulled a small mobile phone out of his breast pocket. "Tango One this is Beartrap. The cuckoo has flown the nest. There are no eggs. I repeat. There are no eggs. Over."

He flicked the cover of the phone down with something of a flourish and popped it back into his pocket.

"Do you smoke, Cynthia?"

"No. I've given up."

"Then I would suggest that this is a particularly apt moment to start again." He lit two cigarettes and passed her one. "May I say that you have conducted yourself magnificently. It is clear that you are a lady of great strength and depth as well as a great beauty."

She gave him a small sad smile. "Thank you Cornelius."

"Cynthia, I must tell you that you are facing a situation of great gravity. By staying back to talk to you like this I have also put myself in some jeopardy as you may have guessed from the reactions of my associates. I know that we don't know each other well, but I must say that you have always made a particularly favourable impression on me. In fact it would be fair to say that should my amorous inclinations have led in a different direction I may well have fallen head over heels in love with you."

He gave her his most dazzling smile and she blushed chronically all the way to her toenails.

"I know that you have no knowledge of this business and I will ensure that your life is not ruined by your association in it. Tell me, what name do you know your friend by?"

"Kevin. Kevin Backhouse."

"I know him by a different name Cynthia. Sean Rearden. He was born in 1973 on the Ballymurphy estate in West Belfast. By the time he was 19 he had served two sentences for minor terrorist crimes. We lost him then. Intelligence suggests that he probably spent some time training in Libya. We have strong suspicions that he has become one of the slickest operators in the Provisional IRA. We believe that he played a major part in the Manchester bombing. I'm afraid we know very little about him. Rumours from Belfast say that his technique is to enter into relationships with respectable ladies in his target city. He then uses their homes to store explosives and weapons. That is why the chaps searched the house. Thank God it is clean.

"We picked him up at the weekend when he met with another glory boy that we have under 24-hour surveillance. From there we were able to follow him to the deli, to his rented flat and to the house of another married lady in Chelsea. He obviously likes to keep his options open. I'm sure that you can see that this man is extremely dangerous. You should feel no guilt at falling under his spell.

"Now, there are no weapons in the house and there is no need for you to be implicated in this tawdry business. My position enjoys some seniority and I will be able to bury the necessary files.

"I understand Cynthia, I really do. Remember, I was at Eton with Reggie. I know what he is like. I can quite understand why this has happened. But look, I know that everything must seem impossibly black right now, but you are still young and there is plenty of time to turn your life around, believe me."

Big tears rolled down her cheeks as she stubbed out her cigarette. He handed her another which she took eagerly with a wan smile.

"Have I made everything clear?"

"Yes Cornelius. All clear."

"Good. So now we must tie up the loose ends and get you out of this. When are you next due to see Kevin?"

"Next Tuesday night."

"Fine. Find some writing paper and an envelope and we'll write him a letter. We'll say that you've had a sudden and overwhelming realisation that you love your husband, that you want to have his children and that this madness must end. You'll send it to Kevin care of the Deli this morning. We will finish the letter by imploring him never to come again and with luck he never will. If he does come it will be on Tuesday night. I will come round and sit with you. I will pretend to be your trusted cousin for the night and help get rid of him. I don't, however, believe that you will ever see him again. You will, of course, have to find an alternative supplier for this wonderful coffee."

Her wretched eyes shone with tears. "How can I ever thank you for this Cornelius?"

"No need Cynthia. There is nothing that gives us Brits more pleasure than helping a damsel in distress."

She found paper and pen and they concocted the letter of disengagement. He promised to come to her the following Tuesday evening and she promised to be brave. As he rose from the table she suddenly hugged him fiercely and unexpectedly.

"You'll always be my very most trusted cousin for this Cornelius." She released him and looked embarrassed.

"I shall be honoured fair Cynthia. Now I must depart and start the process of manipulating the grinding cogs of my secret world."

He put on his gangster hat and carefully set it to a rakish angle. He grinned. "Till Tuesday then."

"Yes, Tuesday."

He strode jauntily down Elm Avenue and found a cab. Half an hour later he met the others in a favourite early morning cafe. They looked up from their plates of bacon and eggs.

"All OK?" asked Vince.

"In the bag dear boy, in the bag."

And so the first operation was complete. Next, thought Victor ruefully, next come the bloody prawns.

They headed back to their various flats and packed bags. Victor visited an ex-marine gunrunner friend to cash in the Belgravia gear and pick up some more. They met up at just after one in the afternoon and pointed the black van north. It was dark, windy and bone cold when they eventually reached the impressive entrance to High Glen, the wild country seat of Marcus Dalrymple. They had picked their way along numerous tiny single-track country lanes and had risen up well over a thousand feet. The gates were simple in design, two ten-foot-high cairns of cemented stone topped by bronze buzzard statues. They were given a sparse shelter by a thin copse of bent and twisted trees. The sky was crystal clear, and a bright wash of moonlight lit up the track as it stretched across the back of the fell. The stars were spectacular; diamonds sparkling on a black velvet cloth, outrageous in their clarity compared to the sad, pollution-dulled firmament that hung over London.

The track ran over the moor for a mile and a half then it dropped into a shallow valley where the house was situated by a small stream. Like the gateway, the house was afforded a limited amount of shelter by a small wood. It was by no means a mansion. The steading was built in a square. The house ran along the banks of a stream on one side of the square whilst stone barns made up the other three sides. It was typical of hundreds of similar upland farms in Northern Britain. However, as they drew the van up in the cobbled yard, Vince soon noticed what wasn't typical; it was far too well preserved. All the slates were new, all the pointing was recent, and there were new doors and shutters on the barns. Even the cobbled yard had been lovingly restored. He smiled as he saw more evidence of the real Marcus. He hadn't bought an ostentatious Manor house. He had bought a working farm and spent a fortune in returning it to its original condition.

The low oak door swung open and a beaming Marcus strode out to greet them.

"Welcome to High Glen gentlemen. Always a pleasure. Come on in. Chuck your bags in the hall and we'll have a drink before I show you to your rooms." His eyes sparkled wickedly as Victor entered the hall. "And here he is. The prawn man himself. Heard a lot about you sir. let me introduce myself, Marcus Dalrymple."

Victor shook hands and resisted the temptation to indulge himself with a real bone crusher. The old bugger was a cheeky sod but he was also 72.

The lounge was low-ceilinged and flag-floored. Frighteningly expensive Persian rugs were dotted around carelessly. The furniture was old, leather and well worn. At the end of the room a huge open fire roared out heat.

They sat down and Marcus filled thick glasses with hefty measures of drink and passed them round. He stood in front of the fire and smiled with all the happiness of an eight year old on his birthday.

"A toast my friends. Everybody goes home."

They repeated the toast solemnly. It meant little to Vince and Cornelius, but Victor gave a small nod  before drinking as one old soldier recognised the other. Then, with almost uncontrolled enthusiasm, Marcus continued.

"I can report a major development gentlemen. I was going to wait till dinner but I can't. I only have one true friend left in the world, but he is the truest of friends. We have shared this friendship for over fifty years since he carried me on his shoulder over a mountain in Bosnia with a bullet in my leg. You'll understand that you can trust a man after that kind of thing. I have always shared everything with him and I had told him all about my problems with the windmills.

"In fact it was he who came up with your number Cornelius. He had promised to ask around and see if he could come up with anything. I must admit I expected some sort of extortionate lawyer rather than you lot. Anyway, I met up with him on Sunday and brought him up to speed. I can tell you that his opinion of the operation was the very mirror image of my own. Genius, he said. The essence of genius. However he had a suggestion which he felt could offer us a bit of icing on the cake. It will involve us in no cost, and will be supplied by him as a favour. My view is that we take him up, but I accept that the final decision must be yours Vincent."

He told them. They were stunned, but they all accepted that the addition was indeed the icing on the cake. Marcus picked up the phone and dialled. He didn't have to wait long for an answer.

"Liontamer one to Liontamer two. We are operational."

He gently replaced the receiver and his old weathered face was suddenly lost in a distant expression.

"It was many, many years ago since I last spoke those words. There were many who never got the chance to speak them again. I never would have thought that I would have wanted to. But time passes and time heals, and now it gives me the greatest of joy. I must thank you my friends. You have given two old men the chance to be young again; if only for a little while."

The next day, Friday, they carefully scouted all of the ground. Opposite the main gate was a flat field that ran a hundred yards to the edge of the moor before sweeping down into a deep valley. Marcus pointed out the area where the tussocky grass had been flattened by tents and a circle of ash marked the spot where a campfire had been burning. As Marcus had previously mentioned, the demonstrators had left little mess. His friend Alf, the landlord at the village pub, had again come good with his intelligence. His son had been shopping at the supermarket in Keswick and had met one of the demonstrators who worked there as a checkout assistant. She had told him that they were all going to camp up at High Glen for the weekend just in case any other members of the press should come. They were going to drive up after work on Friday and head back down on Sunday afternoon with a few drinks in Alf's pub on the way. She had giggled at the prospect of the cold and how the only way around it would be for her to find someone to share a sleeping bag with.

They agreed that this was all that could have been hoped for. They spent the afternoon rehearsing their lines and timings. After this there was little for Cornelius and Vince to do. Ahead of them stretched a lazy week. Cornelius spent long days huddled in front of the blazing fire reading classics that he had neglected for years. In the evenings he spoke effusively about Charlotte Bronte and Thomas Hardy. Vince spent his days roaming the estate on a quad bike with Marcus. They spent hours studying the plans for the windfarm, and ways and means that the idea could be sold to the other farmers who shared the fell. On the Tuesday morning Vince dropped Cornelius at Carlisle station to catch the train to London to share the evening with Cynthia. He returned the next day to report that nothing had been heard from the lover from the Deli and that he had failed to show up. Cynthia had recovered well from the shock and would be OK He was quite confident that there would be no hitch and that they would collect their £15,000 on the seventh of December.

For Victor, work started on Friday night. He was lolling in his room in a small hotel about ten miles from High Glen when his mobile phone rang. It was 6.45 p.m. and it was Vince.

"They're just arriving," he said. "There are ten of them so far. Four couples and two singles. Six tents. All busy, busy. I reckon that if you give them a couple of hours they should be all set up."

"No bother," said Victor and disconnected the line.

The mood among the demonstrators was one of apprehension. They had camped in the field opposite the gates on several occasions during the summer, but this was rather different – it was nearly December and the twinkling stars threatened a cold night.

They were an oddly assorted bunch. Bill and Janet Freeman were the unspoken leaders. They were in their late thirties and veterans of many marches and causes over the years. They had learned to be flexible, always on the look-out for a new torch to grasp as one was taken away. Over the years they had seen Mandela released, nuclear weapons scrapped and disappear from the news, and Thatcher reduced to a grumpy old granny scrapping for ever-diminishing rays of the limelight. Green issues were their natural next move. However green issues offered few mass rallies or big days out at Wembley. Green issues tended to be local and required a lot of do-it-yourself. For a couple of years they had been increasingly frustrated at their inability to find a really juicy green issue to get their teeth into. Every Thursday night they staged meetings for Friends of the Earth in the Black Dog. They had seen new members come and go, but mainly go. Their meetings tended to attract lonely people who were desperate to escape their cheerless bedsits, and when these lonely people found partners they seldom kept up their attendance at the Keswick Green Action Group. The ten shivering wretched souls round the struggling campfire constituted the whole of their current membership.

There were three other couples. Arthur and Janet Sherwood – early forties, quiet and keen: he was a junior customer services clerk at a small bank whilst she worked in a newsagents. Jeremy Hyde and Susan Wilson – 19, students, fighting acne and mad keen to save the world. Esther Wade and Jean Bennet, mid-thirties, hearty, one a florist, one with the council, lesbians looking for a sympathetic circle of friends in a community of unsympathetic rural types. Then there were the two singles. Angela Richards, a smiling 19-year-old checkout girl from a local supermarket who was on the look-out for love and adventure. And Jimmy Denham, a chronically shy 20-year-old trainee mechanic who was desperately trying to summon up the courage to leap all over Angela Richards who he loved more than anyone in the world and thought about through all his waking hours.

By 9.00 p.m. the frontline eco-warriors were cold and fed up.

The fire was struggling, the food was eaten, and endless long hours of cold boredom were stretched ahead of them. In truth, none of them really had a burning anti-windmill passion to keep them warm and give their cold vigil purpose. They followed their cause for company, laughs, and the hope of excitement. Although nobody said it, they were all having severe doubts at the original idea of doing this for two whole nights and the weekend following. At their meeting the night before it had seemed really sensible. Maybe in the light of their forthcoming moment of fame on Channel 4, other members of the media could well come up to cover their story. After all, the *Cumberland News* had run a small story a couple of weeks before. Small was something of an overstatement: it was three lines on page 7 in the 'Country Matters' section. Now it seemed ridiculous, instead they all knew that they would waste yet another weekend shivering in the now familiar field where they would be lucky to see a single soul. As a cause it stank. But for the prospect of the upcoming documentary, they would have certainly dumped it.

Angela cocked her ear and listened intently.

"What's that?"

They all listened to the sound of an engine coming closer as it wound up the small lanes. Soon it was clear that it was a motor bike. Who could it be? They never saw traffic on the small lane in the evenings except on the very rare occasions when Marcus Dalrymple spent an evening out. The sound grew and boomed in the still winter air. They could now see where the headlights lit up the bent gorse bushes that flanked the lane. It was obviously a big motor bike. Finally the bright headlamp sprang into view as the 1250 Honda roared around the last corner and drove into the field. Their field. Who in God's name was it?

The rider stood the bike up and stretched. He seemed huge in the jumping light of the inadequate flames of the fire. His boots crackled the frosty grass as he strode vigorously to the huddled group. When he reached the fire he heaved off the helmet to reveal a huge coal-black face and about a million impossibly white teeth. When he spoke his voice was deep, rich and all-consuming.

"Yo guys, allow me to introduce my good self to y'all. Marvin Hammerhead, all the way from Springtown, Alabama. Read all about you in the *Cumberland News*. Thought I'd ride on down to give a bit of support." He brandished a bottle of bourbon and chuckled. His voice had all the steamy, tropical warmth of the American Deep South and he exuded warmth and bonhomie.

"May the good Lord have mercy, but there ain't enough in that fire to warm a skinny cat. My years in the Marine Corps taught me many a wicked way, but they most surely taught old Marvin how to raise a real mother of a fire." He turned his beaming face to Angela. "Now my lovely lady, may I prevail upon you to furnish these good people with some of this warming liquor whilst I give this fire's ass a good old Alabama kick."

As they sat stunned he pounded over to his bike, heaved a diabolical-looking machete from one of the paniers, and proceeded to attack a dead gorse bush at the edge of the field with great gusto. Within minutes the flames of the fire were reaching for the stars and after half an hour an impressive pile of hacked wood was stacked on the edge of the group. Hammerhead sighed with pleasure as he sat down next to the blaze and took a long pull of bourbon from his tin mug.

Bill Freeman, rather taken aback by this startling visitor, felt that the onus was on him to speak.

"I can only agree that you can indeed make a hell of a fire Marvin. But I simply must ask, who on earth are you?"

Hammerhead beamed. "Of course, of course. I can fully see that a big 'ole boy like me riding out of the night must come as bit of a shock. I'm with Friends of the Earth. We have a few full-time operators who deal with the wilder side of conservation. They like ex-soldier boys like me. We don't get threatened too bad you see. We work on a need-to-know basis when we are operational so I can't tell you too much. I figure that you folks can take a two and put it with another two and make a four. I'm sure that if you look at the map and see what lies thirty miles away on the West Coast you can guess what kind of business brings me to Cumbria. We have a friend on the inside at Sellafield and that friend has told us that they are about to do some really very naughty things indeed. I really can't tell you any more than that, but I've been sent over to keep an eye on developments. Been here two months now and I can tell you that I've been getting just a little bit lonesome. I've had a ride up a couple of times to see you but without success. So as you can see, it makes me real happy to find some friendly faces to spend a bit of time with."

Bill was delighted. "You are more than welcome. We are merely on the fringes of the fight. We do what we can. Sometimes we forget that we are part of something that is worldwide. To meet someone like you from the front lines, well, it makes it all worthwhile."

"Sir." Hammerhead was suddenly grave. "Don't ever underestimate what you are doing. We are fighting a war. A war that we have to win. The war has many battlefields and we have many enemies. Powerful enemies. Rich enemies. Right now we are few. Every new recruit is vital. Every sentence in every paper is vital. It takes special people to come up here on a cold night to fight for our planet. Without special people like you, what kind of polluted hell of a world will be left for our children in the years to come? You must be proud. Always proud."

The speech awed them. Made their shoulders lift and the cold inch away. They felt special and vital. Cogs in a global machine that would one day keep the planet beautiful and clean.

Freeman was ecstatic. All the meetings, all the photocopies, all the cold nights up at High Glen, all of a sudden it was all worthwhile. "Goodness me, how remiss, I must make some introductions." In turn, Hammerhead shook hands with each of then, swallowing their cold fingers in his massive bearlike paw. The bourbon flowed and the conversation was animated. As the bottle was emptied Marvin produced three more. The strong liquor quickly fizzed their heads.

And Marvin told stories.

He told them in a deep rolling voice as the fire spat and crackled and the stars sparkled above. He told of his childhood on the small farm in America. Of how he had helped his father eke out a bare living from scratching meagre cops of corn and soya from tired and weary land. Of how when he was eight the Ku Klux Klan had come to the house and killed his dog. Of how his father had been broken by the rocky soil and had died when he was seventeen. About the Marines and the brutal training he had endured.

He told them of the landing craft as he had headed into the beaches of Grenada. He told them of the great assault of the Marines as they had crashed through Saddam Hussein's fortified lines on the first day of Desert Storm. The smoke, the noise, the piles of wrecked Iraqi bodies as the 'First of the First' had rampaged through like demented bulls. His voice grew quiet as he told them of the flaming oil wells, and the endless clouds of choking black smoke that blotted out the sun for days on end. Then he told them of the Basra highway and the mangled and shattered vehicles that had been blown apart and shredded by the American planes as they had spat hell itself onto the choked road. Flames. Carnage. And silence. The awful silence of a mass grave, broken only by the humming of millions of flies that feasted on the carrion.

It had been enough for Hammerhead. His dreams were broken. He was under no illusion that Saddam was a demon who had to be stopped, but the price had been too high. The wasted landscapes and the mutilated charred corpses of the highway had been too much. He had no longer wished to be a soldier for politicians who could do these terrible things for the sake of sound-bites and opinion polls.

For a while Marvin was silent. They were all silent as they gazed deep into the flames. He had brought the stench and the noise and the choking smoke of that most high tech of battles into the still of the Cumbrian night. They were in awe.

He broke from his reverie and once again grinned. "Hell, I'm sorry guys. I'm getting all morbid. Y'all wait right there, I've got a bit of something in my bag to lighten the mood."

He returned to the fire brandishing a spectacular bag of marijuana. "Hope y'all approve of this. This mother is all the way from Zimbabwe, Africa, and it's the Goddam finest grass to be found on the whole Goddam planet." He rolled an enormous joint, and in turn the happy group felt their brains nearly erupt through the top of their skulls in a way that they had never dreamed possible. The deep voice was now mesmeric.

He continued his wondrous story. Of how he had left the Marines and drifted around America meeting other veterans from other wars with faraway eyes and broken souls. And then, by chance, he had found a new cause. The Environment. The memory of the boiling, black skies of Kuwait had left a deep scar. It had made him look on the planet with new eyes, eyes that were more open, eyes that couldn't bear to see any more beauty destroyed and ravaged in the name of progress.

After a year or so he was recruited as a full-time soldier by Friends of the Earth. His work had taken him all over the world, to dangerous places where faceless corporations wreaked their havoc.

Which led him to the present, and a small field high up in the Cumbrian fells. It was well past three in the morning and one by one the group wished each other goodnight and crawled into their tents.

When Jimmy the mechanic reluctantly retired Marvin was left alone with the young Angela. She was enthralled by this strange man. Drunk, stoned, flying with excitement, emboldened.

"Marvin," she said in a small voice. "You seem to have all kind of stuff in that bag of yours, but what about a tent?"

"Nope. No tent. But I've got one helluva sleeping bag which I'll roll out by the fire right here."

"There's lots of room in my tent."

"Well my oh my, there's an offer that I simply cannot refuse. Thank you kindly young lady, thank you kindly."

And so they crawled into her tent. She unzipped her bag and laid it on the floor and he laid his fifty-tog special over them. She disappeared into his bear-like grasp and felt liquefied with anticipation about what was going to happen next. She only experienced a mild disappointment when what happened next was deep and even breathing. She snuggled happily into the massive body and drifted off to sleep as the dope spun soothingly round her mind.

She awoke about ten to find that she was alone. Outside, the camp was slowly coming to life. Tent zips were coming down and hungover groans were uttered.

The air was filled with the smell of cooking. She pushed her head out to be greeted by a beautiful clear day. The sun hung low in the sky, and over the crest of the hill the view was superb.

The fire was blazing merrily and next to it was a new

construction. It was a kind of stone trench made from pieces of slate and granite. Inside was a fire and atop were pans of bacon, sausages and eggs.

Presiding over the whole remarkable scene was Marvin in jeans and a T-shirt, quite oblivious to the chill in the air.

"Mow'nin Miss Angie. I see the beauty sleep has worked well."

"Marvin." She said quite astonished, " How on earth . . . "

"Oh my Daddy taught me to get up early and tardiness was never allowed among Uncle Sam's finest. I was up at six as usual, and I made me a little trip down to the local butchers to get us some of this breakfast. This morning you will see how well Uncle Sam taught me to make a breakfast. This evening you will see how well my Mama taught me to make Alabama chicken."

And so began a joyous, never to be forgotten day. They wolfed down Marvin's breakfast, then spent all morning and afternoon putting the world to rights around the fire. In the evening they gasped in wonder at his Alabama chicken. Once again copious amounts of dope and booze were consumed and once again Angela drifted off to sleep in the giant Marvin's warm embrace. Only Jimmy was quiet and miserable as he saw the look of adoration on his dream girl's face. On Sunday morning Marvin again produced breakfast and the weekend reached a happy conclusion over several beers at Alf's pub. They parted on the car park and Marvin promised to try and make their meeting the following Thursday evening. As his bike roared away down the small lane they looked on with wonder. It had been a wonderful weekend and they felt part of things. Really part of things.

The days of the week dragged. The Thursday meeting and the Saturday documentary filled their thoughts every waking hour. The other girls in the supermarket tittered at the dreamy look in Angela's eyes as she scanned eggs, and apples and bottles of own-brand bleach.

By 9.30 on Thursday evening the mood among the group was sombre. They had met for an hour and a half and Marvin hadn't arrived. Angela in particular felt tragic. Then the door swung open and he was there, his leather motorcycle suit gleaming and drenched from the rain. He bought a pint of lager and joined them at the table.

However his smile was tight and he was distant and far away. He only stayed for forty minutes and then rose to leave.

"I'm sorry to have to leave so soon but things are starting to happen. Bad things. Real bad things." His eyes became focused on a far horizon. He spoke very quietly, almost to himself. "Bastards." Then, as if with a huge effort, he brightened. "Anyway I promise that I will really try to be there with y'all tomorrow night. I don't know. I really don't know. It all depends. But if I can be there, I will. If not, y'all know I'll be thinking of you. Give 'em hell."

And with that he was gone. He left them in sombre mood. What nightmare things were going on in the vast nuclear reprocessing plant out on the coast? What terrible dangers were lined up against Marvin? The world that had seemed so bright and full of hope the weekend before all of a sudden seemed dark and bleak and filled with the forbidding forces of evil.

When they arrived at High Glen the next evening their mood was still sombre. The spell of clear bright weather had broken that morning to be replaced by a mild, drizzling warm front. They cursed as they struggled to erect their tents in the gusting breeze. There were few high spirits as they sat around the fire. Even the fire seemed to miss Marvin as it hissed and fizzled in the rain. By 11.00 p.m. they had given up on him and each felt the chill of dread at what he was doing. The wet was taking its toll and the subdued talk turned to turning in. The tents were cold and they all felt damp. Sleep, when it came, was fitful. They all tossed and turned as the rain drummed down onto the flysheets of their tents. Angela was cold and miserable and shivered almost uncontrollably.

By 5.24 she still hadn't slept a wink when she heard the sound. It was a distant sound which thumped and vibrated. She suddenly realised that the sound was familiar, it was the sound of a helicopter. Immediately it seemed threatening. She pulled on her coat and boots and climbed out of the tent.

Outside the evening had cleared and the stars were out. It was still pitch black. The noise was louder now and the others were starting to wake up. Zips came down and anxious faces peered out of the tents.

"What is it?" asked Bill Freeman.

"A helicopter," Angela answered. "Look. There, there, I can see it. It's over the valley and it has a searchlight."

Soon they were all outside, shivering and watching the sweeping light of the helicopter as it crept nearer. And then they became aware of another sound, a more familiar sound, the sound of a motor bike. The engine was straining as it was being driven at full, flat-out speed. It came nearer and louder until the light exploded over the brow of the hill and Marvin's Honda screamed down the road.

He skidded into the field, leapt off and ran over to them. He had only covered half the distance when he convulsed and vomited. He seemed barely able to stand as the violent retches shook his whole body.

They rushed to him. They gasped when Bill switched on his torch. Marvin's eyes were ringed red and wild. Vomit covered the front of his jacket and trousers. He was shaking, desperately trying to keep control. He tried to speak but was stopped as another fit of vomiting took hold. At last it passed and he managed to speak. The voice was little more than a whisper.

"Oh Jesus, the bastards, the bastards." He took deep shallow breaths. "The tip-off came through this morning. They were moving a load of hot plutonium rods out tonight. In a van. A transit van for Christ's sake. Breaking every rule in the fucking book. I picked them up and followed them and . . . " More vomiting. "Ah shit, Oh God, they came off the road. A load of hot rods on board and the stupid bastard came off the road and crashed. The driver was dead. His mate was all broken up. I didn't know what to do. Then I heard the chopper. I grabbed one of the rods and scarpered. It was in a case. That's why I thought it would be OK I had to get it out. It's proof you see, proof of what we've known all along, proof that they . . . "

This time the vomiting was too much and it threw him to the ground where he thrashed and squirmed.

They were in a state of shock. Paralysed. Unable to move or think. At last Angela fell to the floor and cradled Marvin's head. His voice was getting weaker now.

"No Angie, for Christ's sake keep away from me. Get away!

The box! The box must have been cracked. I'm hot. Irradiated. Contaminated. Don't touch me." He summoned strength and pushed her away. She tripped and fell, then stood with tears pouring down her face.

All of a sudden the helicopter swooped up out of the valley and bathed them all in the harsh light of its search light. They stood there like rabbits, frozen in an absolute terror. A hard metallic voice cracked out of a tannoy and across the night.

"Move away. I repeat, move away. This man is contaminated. Move away."

They backed away from the desperate figure sprawled on the floor in the mud. More noise. More lights. A black van hurtled into the field and skidded to a halt. Two figures straight out of a science fiction film leaped out and and approached the terrified group. The men were dressed in full nuclear protection suits. One strode to the edge of the group whilst the other hung back, covering them all with a machine gun.

Hammerhead writhed on the ground and made to get up.

The first figure drew out a pistol and levelled it at him. Marvin sat back, face stretched with pain and tension. The helicopter came down and landed fifty yards away on the other side of the field. Someone adjusted the searchlight to ensure that it still held them in its glare.

The robot figure spoke. Inside the cumbersome suit Cornelius used his most military voice.

"Don't be a bloody fool Hammerhead. It's over can't you see." He threw a metal case onto the floor by Marvin. "Put the bloody rod in there for Christ's sake. You're putting these people in danger. Now do it man before I shoot you."

Marvin's whole body seemed to sag. He reached into his jacket and pulled out a small metal case, not much bigger than a steel glasses case. He dropped it into the box and fastened it shut. The second soldier sprang forward, retrieved the box and ran to put it in the back of the van before returning to cover them with his gun.

"Oh Jesus guys, I'm sorry, I shouldn't have come. I should never have put you in danger. Do as he says and you'll be OK. Just do as he says."

Angela's voice was high with grief and fear, "Oh God Marvin, oh you rotten stinking bastards . . . "

"Shut up !" Cornelius slammed her into silence. "Can you walk Hammerhead?"

"Yeah, I guess so."

"Then get over to the helicopter and we'll see if we can get you scrubbed. Now move."

Marvin dragged himself to his feet and staggered drunkenly to the helicopter where he was half dragged inside. The chopper lifted away from the ground and disappeared west at high speed.

Suddenly there was silence. The second soldier quickly swept around the area with a small geiger counter which spat out a frightening static sound.

"Now listen up." Cornelius's voice was lower now that he didn't have to shout over the sound of the chopper. "You're all in some danger but not grave danger. Marvin Hammmerhead stole Government property and became contaminated with radiation. In turn he may have contaminated you to a certain extent. It is highly unlikely – I repeat – highly unlikely – that you will have received any dangerous dosage. However we need to be sure. You must therefore drive to Sellafield immediately to undergo decontamination. I will make arrangements. We cannot accompany you. We need to secure the area here. I will answer no questions. It is of course your own choice whether or not you go to Sellafield, I can only recommend that you do so. However I am now deeming this a military zone and must insist that you leave. Will you go?"

There was a stunned silence before Bill Freeman said, "Yes, we'll go."

"Good. Very sensible." Cornelius spoke quickly into a small radio. "This is Alpha One. We have retrieved, repeat, retrieved all material. There are ten, repeat ten, civilians who will require decontamination treatment. Please make preparations for their arrival. They will be with you in about an hour. Over."

He slipped the radio away. "Right that's arranged. Please wait in your vehicles. My corporal will pack up your gear." As they sat silent in the three cars Vince, the second soldier, quickly stuffed all the camping gear into large plastic bags and stowed it away in the car boots.

"Now listen up. I repeat, you are only likely to have suffered mild contamination. There is no need to drive to Sellafield like maniacs. Go easy and take your time. They are waiting for you."

With this, Cornelius banged the bonnet of the first car and the small convoy moved away. Their lights meandered away down the fell and into the valley.

It was 5.50 am. The whole operation had lasted twenty six minutes. Without a word they checked the field, then Cornelius jumped into the van with Marcus. They did a three-point turn and quietly headed through the gates to High Glen. Vince rode up on the motor bike. In the yard they parked the van and bike in one of the barns. They then walked quickly back down the track to take up station in a hide that they had made in a small copse overlooking the main gates fifty yards away.

At 6.35 a van drove up in the breaking dawn and pulled to a halt outside the gates. It had a 'Channel 4' sign written boldly on the side. For a minute nothing happened as the engine idled. Then the doors opened and two men and a woman got out. They looked about hopefully and kept checking their map. One of the men pointed to the gates and the sign that said 'High Glen' and shrugged. They could hear snatches of conversation, particularly from the woman whose voice was strident and angry.

"Try the bastard on mobile," she yelled.

One of the men dialled a number then strode around in frustration as he awaited an answer. There was none. He put the phone back in his pocket and shrugged.

They talked a for while longer before the woman split the early morning air with a mighty cry of "Bastards!!!!"

Then they heard further snatches of her angry voice "Five o'clock in the bloody morning . . . Godforsaken northern hellhole . . . lazy bastards can't even get out of bed . . . " culminating with, "Come on, there's nothing going to happen here, let's piss off."

Doors slammed. The van reversed, turned around, then headed sedately away down the lane. As the sound of the engine faded to nothing, the three figures in the hide started to laugh. Their laughter grew and grew and became quite uncontrolled. Finally they calmed down.

"Well Vincent my boy, I think that there is a fair chance that you have just become a 15% shareholder in a windfarm. Let's go take these space suits off and open a bottle of bubbly to celebrate," said a gleeful Marcus.

As the sky slowly lighted up for another day the three strangely clad figures strolled companionably back to the fine old house and its blazing fire.

Back in his hotel room Victor lay on the bed and wondered if he would ever feel well again. The first time that he had ever eaten prawns was at a dinner at Cambridge with Cornelius and Vince many years before. The ensuing fits of uncontrolled vomiting had made him swear that nothing would ever induce him to eat another prawn in his life again. Camaraderie and £12,500 had caused him to break this vow. But now as he rushed to the bathroom he made it all over again.

At the main gates of the Sellafield Reprocessing Plant, first the guard, then his duty officer, then one of the plant managers struggled in vain to calm the wild crowd that had landed at the plant at 6.50 a.m. that morning. At last, after an hour and a half, they persuaded the indignant demonstrators to move on.

Over the days that followed several reporters and the producer of a Channel 4 documentary received wild calls telling a tale of 'hot plutonium rods', and helicopters, and soldiers in space suits and a huge, black eco-warrior called Marvin Hammerhead. The reporters dismissed the calls as the fantasies of cranks. The TV presenter answered the call with a stream of expletive-filled invective that would have come as a great surprise to viewers of her caring, politically correct programme to be seen weekly on Tuesdays at 8.30 p.m.

Slowly, as the weeks passed, the members of the Keswick Green Action Group came to realise that they had been had, particularly when they read that planning permission was granted to High Glen Windpower Ltd at the meeting of December 7.

The group never recovered from the events of the night of November 14. The Freemans decided that enough was enough and joined the local badminton club. Angela and Jimmy went out on one date to the pictures in Penrith but it wasn't a success.

As time passed it was all forgotten. Except for Angela Richards. Even years later when she was married to a postman with two children she would lie awake some nights and remember two clear winter evenings up at High Glen when she had lain in the arms of a man who called himself Marvin Hammerhead. And nothing had happened.

Some days later when Vince and Marcus were going over plans, Vince looked up and said. "I never did say thanks for the helicopter. You were right, it was brilliant."

"Wasn't it just," chuckled Marcus.

"Who was it?"

"Can't tell you that. Need to know and all that. But I'm sure you'll meet one day. In fact, I think you will be hearing from the pilot pretty soon. Could be more work for you methinks."

"The pilot. Why the pilot?"

"Just wait and see." Marcus smiled mysteriously. It was clear to Vince that he would get no more out of him, so they went back to the plans.

One December 7, Cornelius collected the £15,000 balance from Reggie Stevenson and announced that he was going to spend his ill-gotten gains on taking his new boyfriend to the Caribbean. The new boyfriend was a Jamaican called Montgomery who managed several Reggae bands in London. Cornelius was head over heels about him and the two of them headed off to Heathrow one morning gleefully singing Bob Marley songs. Victor, now fully recovered from the prawns, headed back to Africa to meet some of his family in Ghana for Christmas – he wasn't a welcome guest in Nigeria. Vince finally left High Glen on December 20 and drove north to his small-holding in the hills above Kelso to spend a quiet Christmas alone.

# CHAPTER THREE

## INTERLUDE

Vince had bought Cragside in 1992. He had seen it advertised at £17,000 and after a successful summer of operations he had gathered together enough to bid £15,000. The bid was accepted and he became the proud owner of a hopelessly derelict Scottish croft and 23 wild moorland acres.

Even a Saharan Bedouin would have considered Cragside to be a little isolated. To reach it involved a ten-mile drive up into the Cheviot hills from Kelso, and then, having spotted the semi-demolished gateway in a dry stone wall, a winding three-mile 600-foot climb up a rutted, treacherous track. Hence access to Cragside was only possible by foot, donkey or a 4x4 vehicle.

It had taken the proceeds from many more operations to make the house habitable, but by 1997 it was more or less complete.

A further £20,000 had bought a new roof, new doors and windows, a septic tank, an oil generator to send power through the new wiring, as well as a thorough sandblasting inside and out. It was a single storey building that crouched back into the jagged crag that skimmed across the top of the fell. It faced east and enjoyed a fine view over the rocky moors to the rich arable fields of Northumberland that lay in the far distance. Inside there were four rooms. The front door opened into the large open lounge. The floor was flagged and the walls were open stone. At one end of the room a huge open fire could soon drive out the chill, and the thick walls and low beamed ceiling easily held in the heat. At the back of the house was a small kitchen dominated by an oil-powered Aga. The other two rooms were a bathroom and a reasonably sized bedroom.

Cragside had taken time, patience and money, but it had all been worth it. Vince's life with Cornelius was forever fast and furious and complicated. He needed Cragside to clean out the brain and the smog of the city. He had always been comfortable with solitude, and in the spaces that sometimes opened up between their ventures he would happily climb back into his lonely hermit life like it was a favourite old dressing gown.

On the afternoon of December 23 he was returning from a long tramp over the moors in the cold blustery rain. It was just before four and the light was fading fast. As was so often the case high up in the hills, the weather was choosing the very last gasp of the day to clear. The solid banks of cloud were breaking apart and little by little the long view to the plains was opening up. He sat for a while on the top of the crag watching the dramatic shafts of red and orange sunlight carve their way through the breaking cloud to vividly light up patches of moorland below. At last the light faded from yellow to red to grey to night, and he picked his way down between the rocks to the kitchen door.

He plonked the kettle on the Aga and hung his wet coat on the door. In the lounge his word processor seemed to stare at him reproachfully. Yet again he had made all kinds of vows to really make a start on his writing and yet again it hadn't happened. Maybe tonight could be the night, Lord alone knew he had little else to do. Well, maybe he thought, first a coffee, then a fag, a bit of cooking and . . . well maybe not. Maybe he'd have a read instead and listen to the play on the radio. He smiled at the usual list of all-too-familiar excuses as they rattled through his mind. The kettle whistled and he decided to put the decision off for a little while.

In the kitchen he glanced down at his mobile phone on the table and noticed that it said '1 Call Missed' and a small envelope sign denoted that a message was waiting. He frowned slightly as he picked it up. With Cornelius in Jamaica and Victor in Africa he couldn't think who it could be. This was mainly a business mobile, and he couldn't think who else had the number. Possibly Gideon, but he couldn't for the life of him think why Gideon would call. Then he realised that he had given the number to Marcus Dalrymple, his new partner.

The bland recorded voice informed him that he had one new

message. Once again he frowned when the recorded voice was anything but the buccaneering bouncing voice of Marcus. It was deep, it was lightly Scottish, it carried an easy air of amusement and it was very much female. He listened to it five times then poured a whisky and smoked thoughtfully.

"Hi. I presume that this is the office of Vincent Allenby. This is your pilot speaking. I do hope that you enjoyed using our services and I can assure you that our woefully ill passenger did not get that way from eating any of our airline food. I rather hope that your business doesn't close down over Christmas as I am in need of your services. Please call me on the following number any time after seven tonight. Ciao till then."

The number was carefully written on a pad in front of him. He rang directory enquiries who told him that the area code was Perth, Scotland. He found himself nearly chain smoking as he considered the call. He considered ringing up Marcus but dumped the idea quickly. The old bugger would only laugh and give him a lecture on the need-to-know principle. There was nothing for it but to wait till seven that evening and ring back. He soaked in a hot bath, cooked a chicken stew, smoked too much and worked his way through several tumblers of Marcus's whisky.

And to his horror he listened to the message a further three times. Eventually at about half past six the alcohol that was lightly swimming round his brain forced him to admit that he was behaving like a panic-stricken sixteen year old. The voice had hooked him just as surely as a big fat salmon from the river Tweed down on the Northumbrian plain below. He and Cornelius had once had a long drunken evening pondering the likelihood and reality of love at first sight. It had been brought on by Cornelius spotting a handsome, blond student steering a punt down the River Cam one gorgeous evening in May. Their deliberations had been inconclusive and the next morning had brought hangovers, rain and the news that the object of Cornelius's desire was straight as a die and happy dating a second year female chemistry student from Girton.

Love at first sight was one thing. Love at first listening to a message on a mobile phone was bloody ridiculous. Vince decided that he was losing it – too many lonely walks on lonely moors and getting back in to drink whisky and reading fat Victorian romances.

He was a near-gibbering wreck when he dialled the Perth number a little after seven.

"Hello." The voice dropped the pit of his stomach like trap door.

"Good evening, is this the, urm, pilot?" Oh yeah Vince, terrific, who the hell else is it going to be, Eva Braun?

"Why yes, and you must therefore be Mr Vincent Allenby of problem solving fame."

"Absolutely." Keep it short Vince. Professional. Don't act pissed.

"Splendid. May I ask, does your operation close down for Christmas or are you still available for hire?"

"Well, we don't close down as such, but 66% of our available forces are currently out of the country which rather limits our options."

"Leaving 34% which is in fact you."

"Leaving 34% which is in fact me." And with that she laughed a low soft laugh that more or less threw him on the stone floor and dragged him round the room.

She continued. "Well, I have a feeling that my particular problem could quite easily only be of the 34% variety."

"Really." Oh Christ Vince, get a bloody grip, where are you when I need you Cornelius!

"Yes, really. Marcus tells me that you live in Scotland."

"Yes, I'm about ten miles from Kelso; up in the Cheviots."

"Oh, that's not so far. I live near Perth. Would it be possible for me to drive down tomorrow for us to have a bit of a chat. I really would be most grateful."

"Yeah, sure, no bother, it's just . . . "

"I know, it's just that Mr St John usually undertakes the negotiations for your venture. But I am reliably informed that that little rule has been broken rather recently."

"Well, yes, that's true. So, urm, fine. Do come down. I'll meet you in Kelso and show you the way."

"No need, I'll find you all right."

"Maybe not, I'm rather isolated up here, it's not the easiest place to get to." Again the stomach-churning chuckle.

"Don't trouble yourself so. I'm a country girl. Just give me the grid reference from the ordnance survey map."

"And then there's the track. It's three miles long and rough as hell, I . . . "

"Country girls drive Land Rovers and know how to use them. May I be bold and suggest that negotiating a difficult track in a vehicle designed for that very purpose should be marginally less difficult than landing a helicopter in a Cumbrian field at night."

This time he laughed. "Touché. That's me told. OK we're on. I'll get you the co-ordinates." It took him a couple of minutes to dig out the map. He gave her the grid reference and a few landmarks to look out for.

"What sort of time should I expect you?"

"About noon?"

"Fine. I'll make lunch. You're not vegetarian are you?"

Again the throaty laugh. "Absolutely not. I'm a beef farmer."

"Oh, right, fine." Jesus Vince, oh, right, fine, can you come to the pictures on Friday, get a bloody grip.

"Noon it is then?" He felt sure from the amusement in her voice that she knew what a terrible effect she was having on him.

"Yes noon it is, and by the way, who are you?"

"Helen McIntyre."

"Well I look forward to seeing you tomorrow Miss McIntyre, oh sorry, it is Miss is it?"

"Yes, Miss is correct, I'm just a little old Scottish spinster sat firmly on the shelf. See you tomorrow Mr Allenby." And the line was dead.

Vince stared at the phone in wonder. Who the hell was this woman? She flew helicopters, drove Land Rovers, was a beef farmer, had the most wonderfully sexy voice on God's planet and was coming to see him tomorrow with a 34% problem to solve.

He knew with a horrible certainty that the intervening hours would drag by with the tortured slowness of a physics lesson.

And how they did drag.

On and on endlessly.

He awoke the next day to an awesomely beautiful morning. The sky had stayed clear and a hard covering of frost coated the moors making them sparkle in the winter sun. On days like this the view from Cragside was astonishing as the plains stretched out for miles east until they spilt into the North Sea. He had a walk, did some shopping, put the beef in the oven and was digging carrots, potatoes and a swede out of the vegetable store in a small outhouse when he heard the distant noise of an approaching engine. From a small outcrop a few yards from the front door he was able to watch the Land Rover pick its way up the last mile and a half of his track. With every yard he was intensely annoyed to find that his nerves were getting more out of control. At last the wheels crunched the icy frozen puddles on the flattened parking area.

The door opened and she jumped out.

His first impression was one of energy. He guessed that she was in her mid-thirties. She was quite tall and obviously lean under her baggy clothing. She wore wellingtons, jeans, a well-worn wax jacket and a thick Arran jumper. Her hair was black, cut very short and not remotely styled. Somehow he sensed a strength and vibrancy as she walked toward him. Her face wasn't pretty in the slightest, it was far too severely boned. It was a strong face; demanding, appealing, full of expression. And as she got closer she became beautiful; beautiful because of her easy genuine smile and startlingly blue eyes. He realised that he was standing as frozen as a lump of suet on a butcher's counter and snapped himself out of his reverie.

She spoke first. "Vincent Allenby I presume." And she held out her hand. He took it and shook, feeling a strong dry grip.

Her smile broadened as she took in the surroundings.

"So where's Man Friday?"

"Oh, he buggered off back to Fiji for Christmas. Never could stand the Scottish winters."

They gazed down over the endless view.

"I must say Mr Allenby that you live in a very beautiful place."

"Ever read any Raymond Chandler?"

She raised an eyebrow. "Some."

"There's a bit at the end of one of his books, I can't remember which. It was about a woman called Velma I think. She was a Femme Fatale who had strung all the guys along and got most of them killed. Old Marlowe had got mixed up with her, but she got killed as well and he had to square things with the cops. He got his normal ticking off and eventually they let him go. The book ends as he stands at the top of the steps of the police station looking out over the bay. It says something like 'It was a clear day and you could see a long, long way. But not as far as Velma had gone.' "

"Is that what you tell all the girls when you lure them up to your hideaway in the sky."

"I bloody well would if I could find any with Land Rovers and an affinity for map reading. Anyway, come on in."

They went inside and he poured coffee. She poked about the house whilst he peeled vegetables. She quizzed him about how he had found the place and how long it had taken him to carry out all the work. Once the pans were boiling merrily away he opened the Aga and checked the beef. She said, "I sincerely hope that isn't Argentinian Mr Allenby or I may have to consider boycotting the use of your services on ethical grounds."

"I can assure you that if anyone suggested to my butcher that he was stocking Argentinian beef he would run them out of his shop with a claymore. Even though this is a professional meeting I do think it might be better if you call me Vince."

"Certainly, and you must call me Helen."

"Could I ask you a personal question Helen?"

"I suppose so."

"Do you ever stop smiling?"

"Only when I absolutely have to, and I must admit that driving up to this wonderfully mysterious place does make me particularly inclined to smile. For goodness sake, I feel like I've walked into an Enid Blyton book."

They laughed and it occurred to him that from the very moment she had spoken to him his nerves had disappeared.

"Tell you what. Lunch is a bit off if I turn the veg down. Why don't we have a stroll to build up an appetite and you can familiarise me with your 34% problem."

They headed up over the crag and onto the moor. Even though

there was frost everywhere, there wasn't a breath of wind to make it feel cold. Her stride was strong. High above them a lone buzzard circled round and round in the spectacular blue sky.

They stopped after half an hour and sat on an outcrop. He pulled a hip flask from his pocket and passed it. She took a swig and chuckled. "Now I know exactly where you got that from. A new business partner I believe."

"Yes, Marcus, great old boy isn't he."

"Oh he's a lovely man. My Godfather you know, and no girl could wish for a better one."

They fell into a happy silence as a curlew flew by, briefly filling the air with its haunting call.

Vince decided it was time to do a bit of a Cornelius.

"Anyway lass, let's be having it. What can we do for you?"

"Ah yes, to business. Right. I know this chap called Donald Fearnley. He has a large estate down in Northumberland, in fact you could probably see it from your front door. I've known him for years and to be entirely frank he has always carried a bit of a torch for me. He's into beef farming as well you see, and I suppose that he sees me as his dream soulmate. Unfortunately I have never carried any kind of a torch for Donald. Don't get me wrong, he's an absolutely lovely man and we can talk Angus talk all night . . . "

"What on earth is Angus talk?"

"Aberdeen Angus. Beef cattle. We both breed pedigree Aberdeen Angus."

"I see."

"Well this has been going on for years, since we were both teenagers. I have tried everything but he's so single mindedly, doggedly persistent. I haven't been really nasty or anything because I would hate to hurt him. I just wish he would realise that I am never going to be his happy ending and get on with finding somebody else. To be honest I had pretty well become resigned to the fact that this would go on for ever when I got roped in to a crazy exploit driving a helicopter around Northern Cumbria. And then it occurred that you might be just the sort of guy to sort out my particular problem. Now Donald's family are going to be throwing a particularly lavish New Year's Eve party and it seemed that it could present something of an opportunity."

Vince took another sip of whisky and passed it to Helen.

"Mind if I ask a few questions?"

"Of course not."

"Well, it is clear that he really loves you, the question is how."

"What do you mean?"

"You share interests, you've known each other for years, you get on well, which all means that he obviously has great affection for you as a friend."

"Yes, I'll go with that."

"The complication is that you really should be a bloke. But you're not, you're rather a beautiful woman." She blushed a little.

"Therefore his mind is forced to work in other ways. The only thing to aspire to with a beautiful friend who shares all his interests is love and marriage. Got to be, it's the dream ticket. Is this psycho baloney or do I have a point?"

"It is utter psycho baloney but I think that you possibly do have a point, so do continue."

"Well I reckon that you're probably up there on a pedestal. You're an icon. You're his dream girl. And he can never give up hoping for the happy ending whilst you remain his dream girl."

"Carry on."

"Other stuff. You say it is a big estate. Do you mean big estate as in manor house, and local hunt, and dad's the magistrate kind of thing?"

"Oh absolutely. Five thousand acres, six generations of Scots Guards and dad is in fact the magistrate."

"And the whole family would absolutely approve of Donald finally landing his prize catch?"

Blushes again. "Yes, I do believe they would."

"Good. Then I don't see too much of a difficulty."

"Just like that?"

"Just like that."

She smiled. "You mean that I've struggled with this for nearly twenty years of my life and you can glibly sit there drinking from a hip flask and say that it will go away just like that?"

"Well I can say it."

"But can you be sure?"

"Nope."

"Well tell me for goodness sake and we'll see."

"I normally don't divulge plans Miss Macintyre but on this occasion I fear that I will have to. You see with all of my normal accomplices overseas I will need your active co-operation. So here goes."

He told her. It didn't take long. It really was a very straightforward plan. The lovely blue eyes widened a couple of times but otherwise she took it in her stride. Finally when he was done she said, "For God's sake give me another drink. I can't believe that you haven't actually met Donald. You've got it nailed right on the head. Oh, it will work, no doubt about that, I had just hoped that I might not be so thoroughly implicated. But, what the hell, we only live once. So go on, what's the cost you miserable bastard?"

"Oh it's miserable bastard now is it? Well in the light of that I'm going to have to take my time in dreaming up some suitably wicked terms. After all, I don't want Cornelius coming home to find that I have been a soft touch. Come on, this miserable bastard better get on and cook your lunch you grumpy old cow."

With that she gave him a vigorous shove which tipped him off the rock and left him sprawling on the deck in an undignified heap.

Lunch flew by and along with it two bottles of red wine that he had secured the day before at diabolical cost. They talked and talked about anything and everything. By 7.00 p.m. they were sat in front of the raging fire working their way through tumblers of Marcus's whisky.

"Vince, I think we have a bit of a problem. I don't want to get all girly or anything, but the truth is that I'm becoming increasingly pissed, and should I successfully negotiate your track I fear there will be denizens of Christmas coppers lying in wait between here and Perth."

"No bother. The bed is all yours. I am more than familiar with the couch. I'm forever giving up the bed for Cornelius and Victor and their varied companions. I am afraid they have both fallen into the habit of using Cragside as a pulling pad."

"You're sure?"

"Of course, quite sure."

"Then that's brilliant. My turn to cook."

The evening rolled on with more wine, more food and lots more talk. By 11.00 p.m. they were both well the worse for wear. She came back from the bathroom and sat next to him on the old heavy settee that had once emerged heroically from a house clearance in Jedburgh. She lay her head on his shoulder and he put his arm around her as they watched the logs spit and crackle.

"Tell me Vince, how the hell did you get into this extraordinary line of work?"

He smiled at the memory. "Long story with a sad bit and a funny bit."

"Fine by me, we've all night." She snuggled into him and he started to recount the events of thirteen years before.

"Cornelius and I became very close almost straight away at Cambridge. We were the original odd couple: the quiet Scotsman and the outrageous Etonian queen. We cut a dash in those days, quite a dash. It's funny to think now, but Cornelius only came out of the closet when he arrived at college. His father was an old Etonian and kept tabs with lots of the teachers at old boy reunions and things. So for years Cornelius kept his sexuality under wraps in terror of what his father would say. At Cambridge he obviously vowed to make up for lost time and did he ever.

"In the third term he met a lad called Jamie and I tell you it was real love. Never seen him like it since. They were inseparable and they lived out the Cambridge dream in punts and gardens and little country pubs with thatched roofs. After the end of term Cornelius invited me and Jamie to come and stay with him at his parent's place in Dorset.

"It was a brilliant time until disaster struck. One night his father caught him in bed with Jamie. It was horrible, awful, an absolute nightmare in every way. His dad's a real top of the league, first rank bastard. He went absolutely berserk, I mean really berserk, lost it completely. I was sleeping down the hall and by the time I got to the room he had hauled them out of the bed. Jamie was a really sensitive lad and he had become quite hysterical, screaming and crying. Cornelius was crouched in a corner trying to protect himself as his dad was laying into him, kicking him over and over again.

"I pulled his father off and punched him harder than I've ever punched anyone in my life. I did a bit of boxing at the time and it knocked him into next week for a while. Cornelius was covered in blood and trying to console Jamie. We threw our stuff into bags and got out. Just before we got to the car his father was on the steps. It was a really massive old house and there he was framed in the moonlight with a shotgun. He was totally out of control by this time, screaming and cursing, telling Cornelius never ever to come back as lights started going on in windows all over the house. Then he fired, deliberately high, but it scared the hell out of us and we tore off down the long straight drive doing about ninety.

"We took Jamie home and he never saw Cornelius again. We drove to his Auntie Esther's house in Hertfordshire. What a bloody woman she is. She lives alone in this huge old Victorian pile and is more mortgaged than anyone on the planet. God help the poor bankers who are given the job to go and try to call it in. Well, she loved Cornelius and took him in without a second thought. The next week a solicitor's letter arrived telling him that he was disinherited and that he should never attempt to visit the house again. It all hit him really hard for a while and it was months before he was himself again.

"When he came back from the Christmas break of our second year he told us that some batty cousin of Esther's had landed up from New Zealand. She had taken up residence at the house and showed no intention of leaving. After a few weeks it was driving Aunt Esther to distraction. Cornelius was fuming and felt that there must be something he could do to help out.

"One morning we were sat in my room after a bit of a wild night. We were watching kiddies television, and what should be on but 'Scooby Doo'. God knows why, but I came up with this idea that we should haunt out the unwelcome cousin. The next Easter holidays we put the plan into action. At breakfast every morning Cornelius would complain that he hadn't been able to sleep again because of the ghost. Esther would tell him off, and insist that he didn't talk about the silly old story in front of their cousin. Sure enough the cousin couldn't contain herself and she quizzed Cornelius about it. He told her of how a past owner had once owned an African slave who he had abused and tortured mercilessly until one day he had beaten him to death with a club. Ever since, the tormented soul had wandered the empty corridors howling a lament for his lost home and family. And then it started. Me and Victor camped out in the grounds and at night Victor would sneak in and howl and sing all kinds of sad old tribal songs. After a few days of this the cousin was beginning to lose it, and then one night Victor burst into her room wearing a loincloth. We had made him up to look as if half his head had been smashed in. He howled an babbled in Ibo, that's his tribal language from Nigeria, then ran screaming down the corridor. Early the next morning the dreaded cousin packed her bags and has never been seen since.

"Aunt Esther thought it was brilliant, and every time she was thick end of a few gins she would tell the tale to anyone who cared to listen to her. And then, little by little, we started getting enquiries from others in her circle and of course we started charging for our particular method of sorting out people's problems. And the rest is history."

He grinned and chuckled at the memory. She spoke in a sad, quiet voice.

"Poor Cornelius, did he get over it?"

"Not really. Oh, he pretends that he has, but it all left a hell of a scar. He always has a boyfriend, but since Jamie it has never been love, poor old lad."

"You'd never think it. But who knows what goes on behind the masks we all wear."

"What, do you know Cornelius?"

"I wouldn't say I know him, I've met him from time to time at parties and things. He's so beautiful, he's bound to leave an impression isn't he?"

"What on earth is a Scottish beef farmer doing going to the type of parties that are frequented by the dreaded Cornelius St John?"

She smiled. "Oh, for a simple country girl I do have the odd hidden depth you know. And you Vincent, I'm going to call you Vincent, Vince is so bloody Australian somehow. That alright?"

"Fine, Cornelius always calls me Vincent."

"Good. Now tell me," her voice was becoming lower as it got ever so slightly slurred. "What on earth is a fine handsome chap like you doing living up here all alone in the howling wilderness?"

"My, now that is late-night talk."

"Whisky and a big fire and a shoulder to lay my head on, sure, why not? Wait a minute, let me get something from the car."

She returned a couple of minutes later clutching a cassette. "Where's your stereo?"

"Over there, under the window."

She switched on the music and the mellow voice of Sinatra filled the room as she snuggled happily back onto the sofa.

"There you go, old blue eyes is playing, so tell me all about why you are home alone." She laughed lightly but he didn't, and when he didn't she looked up with concern. "Oh, I am sorry. I'm being unforgivable, please forget I said that."

"No it's fine." He gave her a reassuring squeeze. "Absolutely fine. I just don't talk about it much. Taciturn Scotsman and all that. I've talked to Cornelius of course, but otherwise it all stays buried. But I don't mind talking to you – fire and whisky and a head on the shoulder and all that." He was quiet for a few moments as yet another song of lost love and late-night American bars floated around the room. "I was once really, really in love. It was a girl that I grew up with. She was my first girlfriend and I was her first boyfriend when we were both sixteen. My parents both died when I was young and I lived with an uncle. He was good enough to me but we were never close. So I spent all my time with her, we were quite inseparable. Then one day when we were eighteen she got hit by a truck that ran out of control. It smashed all her brain to pieces. She was on a life support machine for nine months and I sat with her every night. She died just before I went to Cambridge. I didn't know how I would ever get over the loss, and I turned into a thoroughly weird, miserable sod. If I hadn't met Cornelius on my first day I would have probably been a recluse right through college, maybe for the rest of my life.

As it is, I ration my reclusion to the time that I spend up here."

She was very still and very quiet. When he looked down he saw that tears were easing down her cheeks. "Hey, sorry, are you OK?"

Her voice came from a long way away. "No I'm not very OK, but it's fine, not your fault, not at all. I'm the same you see. For me it was Jeremy. Marcus will have told you about Jeremy, his son who was killed in the Falklands. He was my fiancé. We were to be married and instead he came back in a body bag. So I can promise you Vincent, I understand. I understand only too well."

With that they fell into silence. There was no need to talk. They huddled together in their sad memories as the fire burned and Sinatra sang. Eventually they fell asleep.

When Vince awoke the next morning he found that she was cradling his head in her lap and stroking his hair. She smiled down warmly as his eyes opened.

"I'm really rather glad that I drove that helicopter Mr Allenby."

He grinned. "And I'm really rather glad that you didn't crash it."

They very nearly kissed but didn't. Somehow there was no hurry. Somehow they both knew there was all the time in the world. He cooked bacon and eggs and they took another stroll in the cold wind that had blown up during the night. At last she climbed into the Land Rover ready to head back to Perth for Christmas Eve with her father. They smiled at each other.

"So," she said, "the next time we meet is at Donald's party on Hogmanay. You still haven't quoted me a price yet. So come on, name the terms of the contract."

"Ah yes, of course, the terms. Well they are indeed harsh, as promised. Since you will be leaving your first New Year's engagement in a hurry, the terms are that you come and see in 1998 with a miserable bastard of a hermit who lives hidden away in the hills."

"I find those terms quite acceptable."

"And . . . "

"There's always an and."

"And one day you will owe me a ride in your helicopter, assuming of course that the operation is a success. I've never been in a helicopter."

"That is also acceptable. I just hope you find the experience rather more pleasurable than your big Ibo friend did. Till New Year's Eve then."

"Till New Year's Eve."

He watched the Land Rover as it picked its way down the valley and eventually disappear out of view. Life was seriously looking up and to celebrate he threw his head back and howled into the wind like a wolf.

By 10 p.m. on New Year's Eve the Fearnley party was in full swing. Helen as a rule found these occasions to be a severe trial. They were evenings of red-faced, boorish aristocratic louts banging on drunkenly about fox hunting or kicking the unions where it hurt most. They were evenings of empty-headed, over-dressed, bleach blonde women giggling about being bonked whilst on cocaine in St Moritz and dropping hints about absolutely super salons in town who could work wonders with Helen's hair. They were evenings of being pushed next to dreary souls out of the backwoods of Norfolk somewhere by well-meaning old buffers attempting to make a match. They were evenings of sheer, unrelenting hell which only got worse when she became cornered by her adoring Donald.

And now at 10.03 pm, as 1997 breathed its last gasp, she was very much cornered by her fervent suitor. As usual he was being ever so nice, considerate to a point, and doing absolutely everything in his strictly limited powers to try and make her happy. And as usual his mother was looking on with a yearning hope that her son would either win her over or finally grow out of his puppy love.

A string quartet was droning on hideously in the drawing room whilst at the back of the house the younger guests were gallivanting to the techno music of the nineties. Helen was firmly cornered in the large reception room amidst the cigar-smoking, brandy-swilling older guests.

There was no avoiding it; it was time. She surreptitiously reached into her handbag and pressed the 'Send' button on her mobile phone whilst smiling enthusiastically at Donald's description of the new calf units he was planning for the New Year.

She counted mentally to twenty, then pressed the 'End' button.

Within seconds her mobile phone rang in her bag. She apologised as she pulled it out and answered it, oblivious to the frowns of disapproval from nearby revellers.

"Oh Wolf, hi, . . . where are you . . . you're what !!! . . . what outside here? . . . Yes, here, . . . Donald's house, . . . oh my God . . . "

Donald's brow was furrowing. She placed her hand over the mouthpiece and tried her best smile. "I'm awfully sorry Donald, it's Wolf, he's a, well, urm, well he's a friend of mine and he's outside. I'll just be a moment. Sorry." She went back to the phone. "Hi, yes Wolf, I'm here . . . well I can't . . . well of course I can't, I'm at the party . . . well I suppose I could . . . it really is rather difficult,  I know . . . yes, I know it would be great but . . . look calm down, . . . just give me a minute . . . "

Again she covered the mouthpiece. "Sorry Donald. He wants me to go to another party and it's in Glasgow and if I don't go now we will miss all his mates because they are riding up to the Isle of Skye and . . . I really am ever so sorry Donald, just a moment."

Once again she spoke into the phone, "OK Wolf, I'm going to come, yes, . . . yes, brilliant . . . now you wait outside whilst I get my coat and I'll be out in a couple of minutes . . . no, I'll come out, . . . no please Wolf . . . no, I really don't think that is a good idea . . . no, you stay there . . . no please Wolf don't come in . . . don't . . . "

She stared frantically at the phone in her hand and then looked solemnly at Donald. "Oh my God Donald, he's coming in, you must forgive me but . . . " At this moment every face for thirty feet was trained at them. Five seconds later every face was glued to the huge front door as it was hurled open.

Every guest gasped at the totally unexpected sight of Vince clad from head to toe in the imposing black leather uniform of a Hell's Angel. He wore a long black wig and a patch over one eye. Rain water streamed down him. He looked wildly piratical.

Very quietly Helen muttered to herself. "Oh my God."

Utter silence descended on the throng for what seemed like an eternity. Vince met the silence and the astonished glares with a wicked grin, then all of a sudden threw back his sopping mane of hair and bellowed at the top of his voice, "Where's the fair Helen

McIntyre! May she step forward and make herself known." Again he froze his audience with a menacing grin.

With the utmost sheepishness Helen stepped forward and said. "I'm over here Wolf."

"Ahh!!!!" he bellowed. "A veritable swan amidst a pen of sows." And he bounded across the room, picked her up like a doll and snogged her furiously. To Helen it seemed to go on forever. To everyone in the room it seemed to go on forever. For 32 seconds exactly time stood still before the Wolf broke off and howled his delight as if to a full moon. The quiet Borders accent had totally disappeared without trace as Vince had turned into Wolf and it had become pure, rough-edged booming East side of Glasgow.

"What a bloody woman, aye, what a bloody, one hell of a woman you are Helen McIntyre." With this he snatched a bottle of champagne from the hapless and utterly bemused Donald. "I think we'll liberate this drop of pop and be on our way. Enjoy your New Year you over-indulged, exploiting rich bastards! Let's hope it's your last!! Up the bloody revolution!!!"

He grasped the sheet-white Helen by the hand and bounded through the door and into the night waving the bottle of champagne like a trophy. The shocked silence lasted several seconds longer. Then, all of a sudden, a hubbub of outrage and horror broke out. Huge brandies were poured and there was much talk of bringing back the birch. Brows were furrowed with anger and voices were raised. And yet one man who stood quietly and for the moment quite unnoticed at the back of the room didn't have a furrowed brow at all. He was a fine-looking man, tall and unbowed even though he was 73 years old. He looked resplendent in his white tie and tails and his hard, bony features were framed with a small smile. His deep blue eyes twinkled with amusement in much the same way as his daughter's were prone to do. He was Sir Alistair McIntyre, Helen's father. He nodded briefly to himself, as if finally making a decision that he had brooded on for some time. He then made his way with great dignity to the wretched figure of Donald who was still staring at the front door like a shell-shock victim.

When he spoke, his voice was deep and commanding and

rollingly Scottish. "Never mind Donald lad. I always told you she was too wild for you, but you never listened. Give it up now, find someone else. I hope you forgive her though. She would always want to be your friend. Come on, have a bloody drink lad."

Outside Vince and Helen roared away in his Land Rover. They laughed until tears poured down their cheeks as the adrenaline coursed through their veins.

She shouted over the roar of the diesel engine. "You're a rotten stinking bastard Allenby. What happened to the plan then? I don't remember anything about a bloody eye patch, I don't remember anything about 'up the revolution' and I certainly, absolutely don't remember anything about snogging!!"

"Well, you see you're new to this Helen. A plan has to have fluidity and you have to make snap decisions in order to ensure it is executed to its maximum effect. I took an instant judgement under the fiercest of pressure that snogging was vital to the success of the mission."

"Well if it is your opinion that it was imperative that you snog me for about six and a half hours wearing a bloody Blackbeard eye patch in front of every gossip queen in the country, then it is my opinion that you can just bloody well pull up this Land Rover and do it again."

Their embrace lasted a long time and when they came apart she was smiling. "Something tells me that I am really glad to have met you Mr Vincent Allenby. Very glad indeed."

"Ditto Miss McIntyre. Come on, let's head for the hills."

An hour later they were once again sat in front of the roaring fire at Cragside. The clock was ticking slowly round to 1998 but they were taking little notice. They had just started their second bottle of Champagne and they had at last calmed down as the rush and excitement of the operation slowly faded away. Helen seemed to take a deep breath and then spoke,

"Vincent, I need to tell you something."

"Oh Lord, please don't hit me with some bad news. I really can't deal with it."

She laughed and hugged him. "No, no, calm down, it's nothing dreadful, I promise."

"Really promise?"

"Yes, really promise."

"All right then, let's hear it."

"Well I haven't been entirely truthful. Everything about me coming to see you and the operation tonight wasn't absolutely as it seemed. Well it was, but then again it wasn't, if you see."

"No, I can't say that I do see to be honest."

"No, of course not. How could you? Let me start again. Almost everything is indeed as it seems. I did fly the helicopter. I did want something done about poor old Donald. But I wasn't alone in the helicopter you see. Daddy was there as well. He's the old wartime pal that Marcus told you about. When it was over he talked to me about you guys doing something for him. Something really big. I didn't know. Part of me thought the whole thing was really crazy, and yet, another part said that it might just work. I told him that I needed to know more about you before I made up my mind. I decided to kill two birds with one stone and not only learn a bit more about the mysterious Mr Allenby, but also to rid myself of the tragic Mr Fearnley."

"I see, a double game you scheming woman."

She smiled with relief that he hadn't taken it badly.

"What wasn't part of the plan at all was that you would sweep me off my feet and leave me as smitten as a teenager."

"And how has the assessment gone?"

"Oh, if anyone is mad enough to make it happen I'm sure that it is you. As you dragged me out of the party I caught Daddy's eye."

Vince was horrified. "Oh Jesus, you mean he was there! I must have made a hell of a first impression."

"He winked at me. A wink was the signal. The signal to say that I should ask you all to Black Loch next week. Are Cornelius and Victor back by then?"

"Yes, they are back this weekend."

"And will you come?"

"Of course. After all, we are guns for hire. Will you tell me about it?"

"No. I promised Daddy that I would leave that to him."

"Fine by me. I'll get the others to meet me here and we'll travel up. When?"

"Wednesday morning. About 11.00 a.m."

"We'll be there in force. Now how about you young lady? Do you have anything planned for the next few days?"

"Well I called up Man Friday in Fiji and asked whether or not he would mind me filling in for a while."

"And?"

"He was rather pleased actually, he's met a typist in a grass skirt and they are thinking of settling down."

"Always was a bit of a dark horse, Man Friday."


Vince eventually got hold of Cornelius by phone on Sunday evening. Helen had left that morning after a three-day stay.

"Hello."

"Ah, the Caribbean venturer returns to us at last."

"Why it's my old chum Vincent, and may I ask, how was your festive season? Unimaginable bleakness in the wilds?"

"Fine. Unlike some I've been working."

"Good God, you're not telling me that you have actually written something."

Vince smiled. Cornelius couldn't have shown more amazement had he said he'd found a Yeti in his outhouse. He hadn't realised his failed writing dream was so painfully obvious. "No not writing, an operation."

Now Cornelius really was amazed. "An operation. What operation? We had nothing in the pipeline."

"No, it just turned up out of the blue. It was fairly urgent and it only needed one person so I knocked it off."

"Just like that?"

"Yup, just like that."

"And are we rich?"

"Indescribably."

Cornelius laughed. "Nice lawyer's answer old chap, indescribably, i.e. something that is not describable, and of course one cannot describe riches if in fact there are none of the aforesaid riches to describe. Is that somewhere near the mark my dear?"

Vince chuckled. "In the ball park. Near enough for me to send you a fifty-quid bill for the lawyer's answer."

He sensed Cornelius lighting up and sitting back. "So tell me all about it."

"Not now. Tomorrow. It would appear that my little solo job might well have been a sprat to catch a mackerel. We have an appointment at 11.00 in the morning on Wednesday."

"Good Lord, I slip off on a quiet break and return to find myself standing at the very gates of redundancy. Any clues?"

"Nope, just pitch up here for tomorrow. Bring Victor as well."

"Yes, that's fine by me. Prepare the hideaway for three by the way, Montgomery will be coming. I'm in love Vince."

"You're always in love Cornelius."

"I mean really in love."

Vince knew the difference between truth and jest in his friend's voice, and now there was no trace of jest. He heard a certainty that had been missing for very many years. There was no need for comment, but Cornelius felt the warmth of his voice. "Fine then. Three it is. Will you make it for the evening?"

"Sure. See you then."


Dusk had all but fallen when Victor parked up his battered 4x4 at the top of the long track.

The three of them hopped out and banged the door. Their mood was light as drinks were poured and Cornelius launched into a series of tales about their tropical Christmas. Vince had only met Montgomery briefly on a couple of occasions and took rather more notice of him in the light of Cornelius's disclosure. He was about 25 and five feet ten inches tall. He was lithe and lean and looked very fit with the build of a gymnast. His hair was tied into medium-length dreadlocks and his voice rolled melodically with a deep Jamaican accent. He was relaxed and easy and he soon fitted in. Vince was hugely encouraged by the look in his eyes whenever he glanced at Cornelius. When Vince rose to cook some supper Montgomery volunteered to help. As they peeled vegetables he told Vince of how he had joined a Reggae band when he was 17. The band had never got very far but he had got the bug for the music business. He had gone through a variety of jobs until going solo and becoming a promoter/manager. He had recently managed to raise enough capital to start his own record label and things were going well. They were about to carry food into the lounge when Vince lightly touched him on the shoulder. He smiled but his voice was grim.

"Hurt him and I'll break your neck. No offence meant."

Montgomery returned his gaze easily. "Man, if I hurt him, you're more than welcome. No offence taken."

As they sat down to eat, Cornelius finally could stand it no longer. "Oh, for God's sake Vince, the suspense is killing me, tell us, tell us all of it, and tell us with passion."

Vince worked through the story methodically. Victor's eyes widened in amazement with the news that the mystery pilot had been a woman. They roared with laughter as Vince acted out the role of Wolf with gusto. He finished by confirming that the operation had been successful and that their reputation was still in tact. Cornelius spoke.

"OK Mr Allenby. There is much evidence to suggest that your operation was indeed something of a success. However I must now put some questions to you by way of a debriefing. Number one, you rather skated over the issue of remuneration. As partners, Victor and I would obviously like to know to what extent our personal fortunes have been swelled."

Vince became somewhat awkward. "Now that's a complicated issue. Remuneration wasn't made in a moneyish kind of way."

"Not a moneyish kind of way?"

"No."

Cornelius raised an eyebrow and looked stern. "So may I ask, if remuneration was not moneyish, in what form was it made?"

Vince squirmed. He had come to the moment that he had been dreading. "She agreed to see the New Year in with me up here at Cragside."

Cornelius never missed a stride. "An evening up at Cragside. And when, prey, did your client depart Cragside?"

"Yesterday morning."

Cornelius lit a cigarette and weighed his words with care. "The method of payment is indeed rather unusual, and compelling evidence that our little business must immediately revert back to its accustomed practice of leaving all matters of pricing and negotiation in my hands. There are details of this story which trouble me somewhat. To undertake an operation in return for an evening with a young lady is quite within character for you my dear Vincent. It is simply more evidence of your irretrievably romantic Scottish soul. However there are other facets of your behaviour which are wholly out of normal character. You were cagey with me on the phone and this evening you have hopped and fidgeted like a teenager. In the light of this, I simply must ask you one further question to which I demand a truthful answer. Vincent Allenby, I do believe that you are in love."

"Guilty as charged. Head over bloody heels."

Cornelius leapt to his feet and embraced him fiercely. "About time too, about time too." He stepped back and held his old friend by the shoulders and gazed deeply into his eyes. After a moment he seemed to be satisfied with what he saw, nodded and smiled hugely. "Well, so long as you and the new lady haven't consumed all of our stocks, I believe that champagne is in order and lots of it."

Bottles were popped and toasts were raised. Eventually Cornelius said, "Anyway, you mentioned that your little solo effort had maybe led us to more business. What can you tell us?"

"Nothing really. As I said, Helen's dad is an old wartime comrade of Marcus's. He was in the helicopter and he watched me at the party. Apparently he has been weighing us up for something big. Helen wouldn't tell me anything, except that her father wanted to know if she thought we were up to it, and that she had given us her vote of confidence. It was funny really, she didn't seem all that delighted about it. It was as if she was committing us all to something rather daunting. I don't know, I may just be getting paranoid."

"Who is she?"

Vince was slightly embarrassed. "It is crazy, but I hardly know anything about her at all. She is called Helen McIntyre. She is a beef farmer from Perth, she's in her mid-thirties and she says she knows you from parties."

Cornelius's eyes widened to full Walt Disney size and his mouth fell open. Vince was quite shocked by the effect that he had had on his partner. "What's up?" he asked.

"Confirm that please. Your lady is Helen McIntyre of Perth and her father was in the helicopter up at High Glen?"

"Yes."

"Jesus." Cornelius grabbed a cigarette and lit it. "My God Vince, you really don't know do you? There are times when I wonder what planet you live on." He noticed the look of rising panic on his friend's face, and smiled to calm him. "No, it's all right, she's not an axe murderer or anything. Christ, where do I start?" He paused for a moment.

"Sir Alistair McIntyre is the Chairman and majority shareholder of McIntyre Holdings. The McIntyre Holdings group of companies is a worldwide conglomerate, they are into everything – shipping, commodities, timber, transport, everything. The company has a share capital value of in excess of two billion. It is blue chip, and the family retains a majority stake. As well as being one of the country's ten richest men, Sir Alistair McIntyre is a decorated war hero, a Knight of the Realm and one of the biggest movers and shakers in the field of charity. Once upon a time, long, long ago, the McIntyres were in fact farmers, scratching a meagre living out of 15,000 acres of the Perthshire countryside. Strangely enough Helen has in a way been rather honest with you. For years she has shunned the limelight and quietly looked after the pedigree Aberdeen Angus cattle that the family has bred since the late eighteenth century. She has always been a something of a mystery. Sir Alistair has no sons, which makes your Helen the sole heir to a fortune of about a billion pounds, and, by a process of deduction, one of the most eligible ladies in the world. And you go and win her heart by doing a Hell's Angel act and whisking her up here to the wilds."

Cornelius could stand it no longer and exploded into laughter which soon infected Montgomery and Victor. Vince merely smiled and looked completely lost. Cornelius noticed this and immediately calmed down. "Hey don't worry Vincent. I do know Helen a bit, like she said. She's one of her own. You wouldn't think it was possible to be unaffected by being that rich, but if anyone is, it's her. Don't let me faze you, but my God Vincent, you really are a dark horse."

"Just like Man Friday."

"Just like who?"

"Never mind."

"Bloody Hell." There had been many times in his life when Vince knew that he had been rather more articulate, but the sheer magnificence of the gates to Black Loch meant that this was not one of them. The fact that the gates were built twelve feet high out of granite with stone statues of rampant lions on top spoke volumes of old money. The fact that the gates were immaculately maintained in every way and that entry could only be gained by announcing yourself to an electronic box spoke volumes about new money. The fact that they had just driven for at least three miles along a perfectly maintained ten foot high stone wall before even reaching the gates simply spoke of masses and masses of money that had been there for ever and were still there.

The electronic box must have been happy with them because the huge wrought iron gates suddenly swung open to allow them access.

Montgomery's voice sang out from the back seat. "You know Vincent man, I once had a bit of a 'ting with a boy from Dorking. His parents had a big fine detached house and it seemed mighty posh to a Kingstown boy like me. But this is somtin' else man."

Victor guided his old Land Rover quietly down the drive as it twisted between ancient Scots pines and vast great banks of rhododendron bushes. The tarmac was new and smooth. After about a mile they came out of the forest to the edge of the Loch. At the far side of the Loch was a steep, treeless hill of black granite. The day was still and the skies bright and clear. There wasn't a single ripple on the surface of the lake and the sheer black cliffs were reflected in the mirror of the still waters, making them appear inky black and endlessly deep. Victor stopped and allowed the engine to idle as they gazed on the view with awe. A few crows flapped aimlessly across the sky, and way up above them a pair of buzzards drifted about in lazy circles. There wasn't a sound. From where they were parked the drive picked its way around the rocky edges of the Loch for about a mile and a half before it reached the house. Except it wasn't a house. It wasn't even a mansion. It was very much a castle. Its black walls seemed to climb straight out of the ebony waters like sheer mythical cliffs until they split and shaped into several towers. The towers were topped with slender cone-shaped turrets with tiny windows and the promise of a princess hidden in every one. It was awesome, beautiful, staggering, mind-boggling. Montgomery let out a low whistle.

"Wow man, we's talking Hans Christian Andersen here."

Cornelius chuckled. "Nonsense Montgomery. I told you, we only ever deal with the better class of client. Now let's all get a bit of a grip shall we, we've all got to make a favourable impression on Vince's new in-laws."

As they pulled up in the cobbled yard at the front of the castle the huge oak front door swung open and Helen strode down the steps to meet them. As soon as Vince stepped out of the passenger door she embraced him and murmured quietly. "I suppose you know all about me now."

"Well, some of it," Vince squeezed her, taking in the view with a smile, "The funny thing is that I was under the impression that the beef industry was struggling."

She released him and turned to the others. "So who have we here? I seem to recall you from somewhere sir, not perhaps looking quite as hearty as you seem today." She shook Victor's hand.

"And Cornelius of course, may I say that you are looking as beautiful as ever, which means that you must be Montgomery, Hi I'm Helen."

Within a matter of seconds she had taken them out of their reverie and put them at ease.

"Now then, Daddy's a bit tied up for an hour or so. So, if it's OK with you, I'm going to spend the time doing a bit of showing off. We can all squeeze in this vehicle."

They drove back down the drive for half a mile then turned off left into the forest of pine. The track was rougher now as it wound upwards for a few hundred feet and cut the brow of a forested hill.

"Stop here a sec Victor."

From the viewing point they could see the rolling countryside unfold below them for several miles. It was mixed country, with a patchwork of small fields defined by well-kept dry stone walls. About three miles ahead, sitting by a small river, were a cluster of buildings.

"This is our farm. Do any of you know anything about beef farming?" Her question was answered by shrugged shoulders. "OK, I'll give you a bit of a crash course."

As they made their way down the valley she explained that the mother cows lived outside for most of the year. They would give birth in the spring when the fresh green grass had enough goodness to enable them to produce enough milk to rear their calves. Mother and calf would stay out in the fields until the weather became too cold. They would then be moved down to the farm.

When they arrived at the farm she marched them round the various buildings. The old stone courtyards were immaculately maintained in every way. The walls were freshly pointed, every slate was in place on every roof and the cobbled yards were carefully weeded. As they entered each shed the cattle came across the straw-bedded floors for her to pat and fuss them.

"They're like big soft dogs," mused Vince.

"The angry, unsocial bull is a bit of a myth." She smiled. "They do get pissed off at times of course, well don't we all, but by and large they are lovely affectionate animals." She nodded towards Montgomery who was fussing the shining black head of a particularly inquisitive heifer. He grinned when he noticed their attention.

"Hey, stay out of this you guys. This is a black thing."

Their colour was indeed the most striking feature of the magnificent cattle. Their coats were an inky, jet black and they shone with health. Helen went on to explain the difference between the pedigree and commercial animals. The pedigree bulls were kept to be either used on the farm or sold. These were the best-bred and the best-looking animals that had been chosen to pass the highly thought-of Black Loch bloodline onwards down the generations. The commercial bulls were kept in separate sheds to be fattened ready for the dinner table.

Victor was the one who asked the most questions as his instinctive African love of cattle shone through. It took them three quarters of an hour to make their way around the various units. They were introduced to Hamish Mclean, a young man in his early twenties, who helped Helen on the farm. "Hamish's family have managed the cattle here for well over a hundred years. His dad retired a couple of years ago, so now it's just the two of us."

"Only two?" Cornelius was astonished.

"Yes, that's it, the business won't stand any more I'm afraid. We are relatively lucky here, the Black Loch name is well established which means that we can make fairly good premiums for our stock, but even so the farm has seen income fall by over 40% over the last year. Times are hard gentlemen, but we're not about to go under, I can assure you. Ah, I note your look of confusion. I will explain. I have been looking after the farm since I was 22. In that time the farm has never taken a penny from any of the other McIntyre businesses and it never will. Daddy does his thing and I do mine. Daddy's side has been somewhat more successful over the last few years, but we struggle on. Come on, let's get some coffee."

They went into a large room at the edge of the main courtyard. A woodburner belted out heat. A large mahogany desk dominated the room and a line of filing cabinets ran along one wall. Another wall was covered by large-scale maps of the farm. The long wall facing the small windows was spectacular. Every spare inch was filled with rosettes, certificates and photographs of Angus cattle being awarded prizes. The more recent photos showed Helen or Hamish standing proudly by their beasts. Other photos went back years, maybe even a hundred years, to show earnest-looking men in kilts or tweed suits picking up trophies. The trophies were displayed in a large mahogany cabinet which was discreetly back-lit to emphasise their gleaming sparkle. "I'm afraid that I can't take any credit for the polishing. That's down to Hamish's mum. She comes in every Friday rain or shine."

Helen pulled chairs out for them and poured coffee.

"We don't really know how long there have been Angus cattle here. There is evidence that the breed has been present in these parts since the sixteenth century. We are certainly to be found in the first breeder's handbook which was published in 1862. Whatever, it has been a long time and many, many generations of my family have been beef farmers. I doubt whether any of them ever saw a time like this though."

"You do your ancestors great credit." Cornelius spoke with a grave respect. When they had finished their coffee, she glanced at the clock on the wall and said, "Well, I think daddy should be ready for us now. We best head back."

As they once again crossed the brow of the hill that separated the loch from the farm, Cornelius said,

"I don't suppose you feel like giving us any clues about what your father wants by any chance?"

"No, not a chance. You are just going to have to wait. There is only one thing that I want to say, and that is that you must not feel bad if you say no. You in particular Vince." She laid her hand over his, "You must say no if that is what you really feel. I promise it won't change anything. I promise."

"Stranger and stranger," mused Cornelius.

They entered the castle with a vague sense of foreboding. Inside it was dark and gothic. Suits of armour and wicked-looking medieval weaponry mingled with grainy old oil paintings of McIntyre ancestors in the high-ceilinged entrance hall. "Come on, this way, we're meeting in the twentieth century!"

She led the way down three corridors which took them to a modern extension at the back of the castle. They filed into a large room which had so many windows that it felt like a conservatory. It was built right up against the loch and the view was wonderful. The only furniture in the room was a long teak table lined with high-backed leather chairs. Sir Alistair McIntyre sat at the far end, and much to their collective surprise, Marcus Dalrymple sat next to him. As soon as they entered, Marcus leapt to his feet and began speaking effusively.

"Ah, they're here. Bloody good show as well." He pumped their hands until he came to Montgomery, "And who the bloody hell's this then, new member?"

"I'm still on trial I think. Montgomery Headley, pleased to meet you." As Marcus shook hands a gleam appeared in his eyes.

"That accent my boy is pure Jamaica, know it well, I'm always listening to Michael Holding on the cricket commentary. Now tell me, is George Headley a relative of yours? I saw him get a hundred at Headingly years ago, wonderful batsman, quick feet, lovely off driver."

"No relative man, but my granddaddy always did say that he was the finest batsman ever to walk out to the wicket."

"Well I could mention Sir Len Hutton but I don't suppose everyone would be best amused. Come on chaps, let me introduce you to Sir Alistair. They shook hands in turn. Vince was in the grip of chronic nerves as he met the old man's firm dry grip.

"A pleasure sir."

"Good day Vincent, or should I call you Wolf?"

"Oh, Vincent is fine I think."

"Young man, you have generated more gossip in these circles than Bonnie Prince Charlie ever managed." Vince was massively relieved to hear the unmistakable amusement in the deep commanding voice. Alistair clapped him on the back. "Come on gentlemen, sit yourselves down and we'll get down to business. Pour these fellows some whisky Marcus, they'll need it having been dragged around my daughter's beloved cattle. Young St John will have gin, and you Montgomery?"

"I've already sampled the famous Marcus whisky and it will do me just fine. In fact I took a bottle out to Kingstown for my Grandma and she says you can drop by for spicy chicken any time you like Mr Marcus."

Drinks were poured and they waited on Sir Alistair. He sat for a few moments gazing out onto the black waters of the loch as he collected his thoughts. At last he began to talk. He commanded their attention easily, just as he had dominated many board meetings over the years.

"I am sure that you will have done some homework and that you will know a little bit about us. My family owns 53% of McIntyre Holdings as well as 15,000 acres of the Perthshire countryside. We are very lucky and privileged people who have seen our wealth and influence grow over many generations. I like to think that we have never abused these privileges but that is not for me to judge. My father tried to instill into me a sense of duty and I hope that I haven't let him down. I fought against Hitler many years ago, I have served as a Member of Parliament and I have spent a great deal of time and energy with my involvement in various charities. For better or worse, these efforts were recognised some years ago with a knighthood. I have also been a successful businessman and during my twenty-six years as Chairman of McIntyre Holdings I have seen our family business become one of the largest and strongest of its kind. I hope you don't take this speech as an old man's boast, I am merely stating facts as they stand.

"My wife died several years ago and so the McIntyre family is all that you see around this table – Helen and myself. Everything that I own and everything that I have achieved is entirely secondary to my daughter Helen. You will have realised I'm sure that my daughter is a wilful young lady and will do exactly what she feels she wants to do with her life. She will no doubt have told you that the global activities of McIntyre Holdings hold little fascination for her. She has inherited the family's love of the land and cattle. A farmer she is and a farmer she will always be. Of course I respect that.

"Two months ago I received bad news. I have been suffering poor health for some time and it was finally diagnosed as cancer. The doctors say that I may live for several years yet, on the other hand I may not see 1999. I hold no bitterness, after all, both Marcus and myself were damn lucky to see 1944 – in my book 45 years of borrowed time is hardly bad."

Vince glanced to Helen who was sitting next to him. Her eyes were bright with tears and he took her hand and squeezed. Sir Alistair continued.

"This kind of news has a great impact. Once you know that your life has started to ebb away like sand through an egg timer you start to look at things differently. I have no wish to go out with a whimper gentlemen, no wish at all."

Again he stared out over the loch where a heron flapped slowly across the blue sky.

"I believe there is time for me to try for one last campaign, one last fight, something worthwhile. Something important.

"I have already said that the most important thing in my life is Helen. And after this morning I am sure that you all know what is the most important thing in hers, although I have a feeling that that may be changing a little." He smiled at Vince. "And when all is said and done, I, like all the McIntyres before me, am a farmer at heart. What is going on at the moment is a great tragedy. This ludicrous BSE crisis is destroying the livings of thousands upon thousands of upright, honest and hard-working farmers.

"We have farmed beef cattle here for hundreds of years. We have never had a single case of BSE and yet the idiots in London now tell me that it is illegal for me to eat a T-bone steak from one of my own animals. We have many problems in our society – drugs, crime, unemployment, and more than all this, cancer, the disease that is eating me away and spreading through us all like a plague. Any sane society would have spent four billion pounds on finding a cure for this mass murderer of a disease. Instead we are spending it on a disease that is an invention of media-mad scientists which just might have killed twenty people last year. Our government has lost the ability to see what is important. All the politicians are capable of is pandering to the gutter press without any regard for cost or consequence.

"I will soon be dead. I even have a timescale now. As any father approaches his last days he begins to think about his legacy. Over the last few months I have spent many hours pondering mine. Until December my thoughts were vague and undefined. Then my oldest friend Marcus here co-opted me into a wild crazy night of flying the company helicopter around Cumbria.

"I must say that I was inspired. Your solution to the windfarm problem was both incisive and brilliant and it got me thinking. Finally, I talked to Helen about my thoughts and she thought I had gone senile. At last I persuaded her to make contact with you on the pretext of her ridding herself of the unfortunate Donald. I was able to witness the exploits of Wolf at first hand and once again I was impressed.

"Gentlemen, it is time to stop beating about the bush. I have decided on what my legacy to my daughter should be. I want to see the BSE crisis over. I want to see the madness stopped. The beef crisis is my problem and I want you to solve it."

There was a stunned silence in the room. This time it was Helen's turn to squeeze Vince's hand. Marcus beamed with delight.

"Please open the folders in front of you gentlemen. The publication inside is *Farmers Weekly*. It's not a bad magazine. Turn to page 27 . This is the 'Markets' section. At the top right-hand corner you will see the title 'Trends'. Underneath we have the livestock prices that were paid in auctions all over the country. This is last week's edition. You can see that the average price that was paid for finished steers last week was 88.6 pence per kilogramme. The price during the corresponding week three years ago in 1995 was 126.2 pence per kilo. At 126.2 pence, beef farmers were able to make a profit which was just reward for the hard work and long hours that they put in. With the price at 88.6 pence many farmers have actually been driven to suicide as their businesses have collapsed. There will be many more farmers commit suicide this year than victims that die of CJD."

"The doctors tell me that I have at least a year to live but I have never much trusted doctors. To play safe I will give myself nine months. Which leads me to my terms. If the price for finished steers that is reported in the first edition of *Farmers Weekly* to be published next September equals or exceeds 126.2 pence per kilo I will consider the problem to be solved. If you accept the contract and successfully deal with the problem I will make a payment to your operation of £20 million in any currency to any bank account anywhere in the world. Furthermore, should you accept this commission for the next nine months to the exclusion of all other work I will immediately transfer the sum of £500,000 to remunerate you for your efforts. All expenses will be over and above this figure. Should you accept the contract you will have all of the assets and amenities of McIntyre Holdings at your disposal. All of these assets of course will soon belong to Helen and she has convinced me that she is more than happy to put them at risk in order to beat the beef crisis.

"I will insist on a full personal involvement in the operation. I will also insist that Marcus is also involved. I believe that my daughter will also wish to be a player.

"Regardless of money, I am convinced that there is no conventional solution to the beef crisis. Your solutions to problems however are anything but conventional, and with the assets that I can put behind you, I really believe that you can do it.

"Let me tell you a little story.

"In the spring of 1940 I was with my regiment in France. Conventional wisdom had taught us that the only way that the Germans could attack us with tanks was out on the open plains. We had no worries. We had laid the might of the Maginot Line down in their path and we outnumbered them by at least four to one in every sector. We didn't need to protect the area in front of the Ardennes forest because everyone knew it was impossible to drive a tank army through it. It was considered to be impenetrable. The tanks could manage the small, muddy roads, but the petrol tankers would never be able to keep up. You can't drive a tank without petrol and the task of invading France through the Ardennes was quite impossible. Or so we thought. Two generals called Rommel and Guderain thought otherwise. They simply dropped paratroopers on top of petrol stations and as the Panzers rolled through they filled up from the pump. Within six weeks the German Sixth Army marched into Paris.

"It was supposed to be impossible, but it wasn't. I think that you can be my General Rommel Vincent. Find me the Ardennes and I'll give you tanks enough to crash through it."

He fixed Vince with a long, level stare. Their eyes locked and Helen squeezed his hand hard under the table. The room was deadly quiet and time stopped. At last Cornelius spoke.

"It seems that there is rather a lovely path along the side of the loch down there and the weather outside is quite agreeable for the time of year. I hope that it wouldn't be considered terribly rude if Vincent and I were to take a little stroll for a few minutes."

Sir Alistair smiled. "Not at all, but make sure you're back by 1.30 for lunch. Go on, off you go. We'll have another drink. There's a door over there. The steps lead down to the path."

As Vince stood up like a man in a dream Helen waited for a while before releasing his hand. "Remember, you can say no. I promise, everything will still be fine if you say no."

He briefly touched her cheek, then followed Cornelius outside.

Once outside Cornelius lit up two cigarettes and passed one to Vince. They strolled in silence for a few hundred yards until they came to a bench where they sat down. A small wind had blown up to raise gentle ripples on the surface of the loch vaguely distorting the reflected image of the black cliffs.

At last Cornelius spoke. "So?"

"Big bucks."

"Very big bucks indeed Vincent, very big bucks even if we fail."

"But we've never failed yet have we Cornelius."

"No."

"And we've never entered into a contract without feeling at least a 90% certainty of delivering the required result."

"No."

"Basically, Cornelius, we've just been offered exclusive membership of the club they call the Big Time. Are we up to it?"

Cornelius lit another cigarette and smiled a distant smile."I rather liked the bit about Rommel you know. It rather focused things. On the surface of things what Sir Alistair is asking is frankly ridiculous. On the other hand he may just have a point. We are being asked to influence the buying habits of fifty million people in a very short period of time. Hell, that's what it boils down to. No matter how we try and do this, to do it successfully will cost an absolute fortune. No problem; we've had one of the country's greatest fortunes put at our disposal. More importantly, to achieve something like this, regardless of money, will require inspiration bordering on genius. For what it's worth, I sincerely believe that you have it my friend. No bullshit, that's the truth.

"But there is another issue. I have watched you struggle through many stony years and now at last you have found someone special. Unfortunately she is all tied up with this venture. So what do you do? Only you can decide, and I promise that I will go along with you 100% no matter what your decision may be.

"As for my own penn'orth of salt, I will say two things. My own, hopelessly romantic nature tells me that if Helen is going to love you, she will love you whether we do this or not, and whether we are successful or not. Secondly, I believe that if you walk away from this you will regret it for the rest of your life. You will never have another opportunity like this, they come around but once in a lifetime.

"So my view, my dearest Vincent, is that we bloody well do it. You find that good old Ardennes forest and I'll drive a bloody tank. To be honest, I always found that Waffen SS Panzer uniform hellish fetching."

Vince looked long and hard at his friend until he was satisfied that he had spoken in earnest. He smiled.

"I presume that I am right in thinking that you really want to have a crack at this?"

"Too bloody right I do."

Vince held out a hand and Cornelius shook it. They laughed.

"I don't suppose," said Cornelius, "that you have the first clue about how we're going to go about this?"

"Not the bloody foggiest."

"Good. Neither have I."

They strolled back along the loch without speaking. When they re-entered the room the look of childish glee on their faces immediately gave them away. They resumed their seats and Cornelius adopted a formal air.

"Sir Alistair, having given the matter due consideration, Vincent and I have decided to accept your offer. The scope of the operation, the timescale and the terms are all in order. I shall furnish you with full details of our account in Geneva and we shall hereby cancel all of our other obligations. May I take this opportunity to say thank you on behalf of my partners for selecting our services, and that with a haircut and the right uniform I am confident that Vincent here can produce a more than passable impersonation of Field Marshall Erwin Rommel."

"Bravo!!!" boomed Marcus. "Bloody Bravo and twice again. This is going to be one hell of a caper and I for one can't wait. A toast please. I propose a toast to 126.2 pence per kilo for finished steers."

They toasted. They shook hands, and when Sir Alistair came up with champagne they toasted again. When Victor took the floor he fixed them all with a murderous look. "I propose a toast to our successfully completing this mission without ever once resorting to the use of prawns or any other shellfish."

Amidst the general euphoria Vince led Helen to the doorway and they stepped outside.

"Cornelius said that you would still love me whether we did this or not you know."

"I don't recall ever saying anything about love Mr Allenby."

"Oh, I'm speaking entirely hypothetically of course Miss McIntyre."

"Well if by any hypothetical chance I did love you, then I think it would be fair to say that I would be cock-a-hoop at you giving it a bash. And what's more, I believe that you are just crazy enough to pull it off." She pulled him to her and they kissed for a long time." Come on. Let's get back in. Lunch will be ready."

"Not for me."

"Why?" She was surprised.

"I need to get started. I'm heading straight back to Cragside. I want at least three clear days of brainstorming on my own. We have a mere 236 days to change the world my dear. Come and see me on Sunday. I'll tell the others to come at the same time."

They went back inside and Vince announced his departure. He suggested that they reconvene back at Black Loch in a week's time at 9.00 a.m. for a full day of planning. He took Victor's keys and was about to leave when a final thought struck him. "Cornelius."

"Yes?"

"See if you can bring Gideon along on Sunday. Whatever we do, we're going to need Gideon."

"Sure, we'll dig him out. See you on Sunday."

"You bet."

As Vince drove back along the loch his brain was already racing in top gear. Helen and Cornelius stood together on the steps and watched the Land Rover disappear around the last rocky bend.

"By the way Helen, you do know that if you hurt him I'll drown you in that loch of yours."

She smiled. "My word Cornelius, that's unusually macho talk coming from you."

He grinned back. "Well, to be honest, I'd probably get Victor to do it."

"Now that," she said gravely, "is a warning that a girl would be very foolish indeed to ignore. I promise that I will do my very best." She looked thoughtfully at his handsome face. "He's very lucky to have someone who loves him as much as you do you know."

"Yes, isn't he just?" He chuckled. "Come on, let's go eat."

# CHAPTER FOUR

## THE GHOST OF MZILIKAZI

On the same morning in January that the crowd had gathered at Black Loch, Oliver Hamilton's alarm clock buzzed him awake at 5.30 a.m. In one movement he killed the sound and threw himself into a sitting position. He rubbed his eyes vigorously to drive himself awake. He was about to stand up when an arm reached up from under the covers and wrapped itself around his waist. A muffled, sleepy voice came from somewhere under the duvet.

"Come on Oliver darling. There's no need to be up so early. Let's enjoy a little longer in bed."

"Sorry Alice. Things to do. Places to go. Big, big day coming up."

As her face emerged from its hiding place he switched on the light, causing her to groan and blink.

"Oh you bastard Oliver. Switch it off."

"In a minute, stick your head back under the covers if it bothers you." He heard his own voice. It was harsh and impatient. As he looked down at her early-morning pouting face he thought that she looked at least ten years older than she had looked the night before. And she hadn't looked so bloody young the night before, he thought ruefully. But he still needed her, at least for a little while longer, so he moderated his voice carefully, "Sorry Darling. I'm just a bit tense, you know, the Board Meeting and all that, I didn't mean to be short. Here, I'll switch the light off."

He cut the light and leaned over to kiss her and didn't move when her eager hand reached between his legs. He gave it thirty seconds before gently pulling away. "Hey, cool it baby, plenty of time later you know, I need an early start."

He got up and left the room feeling his normal sense of vague self-disgust. His weekly evenings with the widowed Alice

Fairclough had been going on for three years now. When they had first started seeing each other he had been 32 and she had been 46. Nobody had ever found out. He had met her at an annual management conference. At the time he was one of the youngest men ever to reach the position of Senior Store Manager in the history of the Shawfield Supermarket chain.

Such a fast climb up the ladder would have suited most aspiring young executives hammering their way down the fast lane of the Thatcherite dream. Not so Oliver Hamilton. Nothing could come too quickly for Oliver Hamilton.

When he had found out that the over made-up and rather drunk lady that was making flirtatious advances towards him in the late night bar was none other than Simon Shawfield's personal secretary, he had made a snap decision. Four large brandies later she was in his bed, and she had been there once a week ever since.

Hindsight had taught him that his snap decision had been truly inspired. Pillow talk gave him the kind of critical insight that he needed to turn his fast track rise in the company into a meteoric one.

Alice Fairclough was the mother ant of a whole underground network of secretaries and under secretaries throughout the sprawling mass that was Shawfields Plc. The company boasted 1,547 supermarkets nationwide with a further 43 in the pipeline. These megastores were fed by several huge distribution warehouses and a growing fleet of wagons. The business employed a staff that ran into the thousands and over the years it had become a darling of the City due to its ability to generate terrific profits whilst sitting on an ever-growing pile of cash.

Alice had thoroughly enjoyed the task of propelling her toy boy to the very highest echelons of the Shawfield Empire. She had found ways of ensuring that his file mysteriously popped up when promotions were in the air. Whenever Oliver had hit the logjam of a more senior manager looking to block his progress she had worked the secretary network to dig up dirt on them. It was seldom that they wouldn't be able to sniff out evidence of an affair or minor embezzlement. It was always enough for Oliver to blast them aside at quiet meetings on the car parks of motorway service stations.

When she had first happily allowed herself to be seduced she had believed that she held a maternal-type passion for the young executive. But as she had seen the brutal side of his nature as he bullied and blackmailed his way to the top, she had been ashamed to find that her passion had become that of a hungry animal. She knew only too well that Oliver Hamilton was a cold-hearted predator who would dump her without so much as a second thought. But the realisation did her no good whatsoever. She was hooked and helpless. One day he would most surely break her heart, but until then she would do anything, quite literally anything, that he asked of her.

As soon as he left the bedroom Oliver erased all thoughts of Alice Fairclough from his mind. The box room of his expensive apartment had been laid out as a gym. For forty minutes he worked his naked body without mercy. Finally he stood in front of the wall-sized mirror and gazed at himself with appreciation. At 35 he felt close to his peak. His sunbed ensured that he was tanned from head to toe. His body was hard and lean from regular work-outs and games of squash. His face was square and attractive in a cartoonish kind of way. When he grinned at himself his teeth were agreeably white and even. His hair was always short, just long enough to avoid looking too military. His was the style favoured by hard, young American executives. He gazed at himself for a whole two minutes then spoke quietly to his reflection.

"OK Ollie. Let's go do the bastards."

He dressed in the living area. He put on each item of his wardrobe with meticulous care. As ever, he couldn't help totting up the total value of the day's outfit. Today it was £1,050. Four figures, quite right too, for today was a real four-figure day. He had come to appreciate clothes at the age of sixteen when he had become a member of the ICF. The ICF stood for the 'Inter City Firm', a notorious group of East End boys made good who followed West Ham United all over the country. They always travelled first class on the train, hence their name. They prided themselves on the expense of their dress and the viciousness of their fighting. They would stand in caged terraces from Grimsby to Cardiff waving fifty-pound notes above their heads to enrage the locals. He had loved the ICF. He loved the camaraderie, and the danger, and most of all, the violence. He had had to give it up once he became a manager at Shawfieds, but he had soon found that the corporate battlefield was every bit as exhilarating as any Saturday afternoon back street.

It took him a full ten minutes to dress. He wore an Italian suit over a silk button-down shirt with no tie. It was the kind of outfit that enraged the more conservative elements of the Shawfield senior staff. But he knew that it made him stand out. It marked him down as the coming man.

One day during the previous July, Oliver and Alice had achieved new and dizzy heights when he had been appointed to the main Board of Shawfields. He was the youngest non-family member ever to become a director. He was appointed Fresh Produce Director, and given the job of filling the 1,547 superstores with fresh fruit, vegetables, meat, eggs and fish and to achieve the maximum profit for the company by doing so.

Most young men would have taken a year or two to tread water and ease their way into this new level. Not so Oliver Hamilton. He wanted to show that he could make a radical impact on profitability within a year. Like most of the UK supermarkets, Shawfields had been sitting on the fence with regard to the Beef Crisis. They had been buying enough British beef so as not to appear totally unsupportive whilst enjoying a pleasant rise in profits as farm prices collapsed. They had also bought a modest amount of imported beef at a particularly cheap rate in order to be able to claim that they were being careful and sensible. Once again, this did no harm to profits.

Oliver had chosen his third Board Meeting to make himself known. He had carefully collated several pieces of market research which had demonstrated that the great British public were becoming increasingly bored with the beef crisis. The rather disappointing lack of good, grisly casualty stories had switched people off. The tedious scientists in corduroy jackets who occasionally appeared on TV put people more in mind of their old chemistry teacher than the Grim Reaper. With every month that went by the people were happily falling back into their old beef-eating habits. Sales of burgers, sausages and mince were all steadily rising, whilst the sales of prime cuts had never taken a serious fall.

Oliver pointed out the fact that the buying public had hit their boredom threshold over the beef crisis. He promised that this offered a major profit opportunity for Shawfields. For whilst the British public had more or less shrugged off its terror of eating beef, other populations, particularly those over the water in Europe, were still in the grip of fear. This fact, coupled with an unusually strong currency, meant that there was a vast surplus of beef on the world market which could be imported at a substantial discount to the price of British beef.

It was Oliver's belief that public support for the plight of the British farmer was luke-warm at best and maybe even non-existent. If there was indeed no general support for the farmer's plight it was quite frankly ridiculous for Shawfields to be paying a high premium for what was at best a very dubious brand. He had therefore proposed that Shawfields should quickly move as much of their retail sales as possible into imported beef for as long as it remained significantly more competitive. They should market these products under their own label whilst undertaking their usual rigorous quality control audits. By maintaining the current retail price and drastically reducing the purchase price, he promised his fellow directors an additional 10% net profit on all beef sales.

The board's reaction had been mixed. Several older directors were annoyed by their cocky new colleague who was throwing his weight about with such arrogance. They highlighted the dangers of Shawfields going out on a limb whilst their competitors maintained a compromise situation. Others were more supportive, and pointed out that the company's next half-year figures were critical and that the City was impatient for success. Competition in the sector was getting tougher all the time and it was going to be increasingly difficult to keep shareholders happy by maintaining profits by grabbing an ever-growing market share. Ideas such as Oliver's, where the company could find significant extra profits from existing sales without losing custom, were vital to the next phase in Shawfields' development.

The meeting became gridlocked, and eventually the Chairman, Simon Shawfield, came up with a compromise proposal which was accepted. Fifty stores would quietly be moved over to 100% imported beef sold under the company's own label. Sales and customer comment would be monitored for the two months of November and December with a view to an extension of the policy being assessed at the Board meeting of January 7.

As Oliver was leaving the boardroom at the end of the meeting he felt a hand on his shoulder. He turned to find Simon Shawfield smiling an avuncular smile at him.

"Jolly well done Hamilton. You held your ground manfully. Most impressive. Would you be available for a spot of lunch tomorrow?"

Lunch had gone well. In fact everything had gone well. For two months the sales of the imported beef in the fifty selected stores never wavered. They simply mirrored the sales figures achieved at the other 1,497 stores. The only difference was that they left an extra 17% profit. Even better news came at the beginning of December when the Minister of Agriculture made the astonishing move of banning T-bone steak. Rather than generating new levels of fear, this move simply made the whole crisis appear to be more of a joke to the general public. Then in the third week of December the really big news came for Oliver.

He was driving eastwards along the M25 when his mobile phone rang.

"Is that Mr Oliver Hamilton?" The voice was a deep rich Irish.

"Yes."

"Well, good evening to you sir. My name is Rearden, Patrick Rearden, and I would like to buy you dinner tonight."

"Oh really?"

"Yes, really. The place that I had in mind was voted as the best restaurant in London for the month of September and I can assure you that I won't receive a penny of change out of £250 when I pay our bill."

"Well, that's all very well but . . . "

"Furthermore, I'll be bringing an envelope with £1,000 in nice used notes which I would be delighted to give you in return for having the pleasure of your company tonight."

"What do you want?"

"I'm in the business of selling beef Mr Hamilton, and I believe that you are rather a large buyer."

Oliver thought briefly. What had he to lose? He was intrigued. "OK I'll be there. What time?"

"Shall we say 8.00 p.m?"

"Fine. How will I know you?"

"Oh don't worry yourself about that Mr Hamilton, I'll most surely know you."

Oliver entered the lavish French restaurant at a little after eight. As soon as he arrived at the bar he was accosted by a jovial, red-faced man of about 45. "Well now Oliver Hamilton, you're a mighty punctual chap to be sure. Let me sort you out with a drink, I hope you've not come out in a silly thing such as a car."

"No. I'm on the tube."

"Then that's marvellous, we'll be able to share in some of the wonderful wine that they keep here without worrying about blowing in bags or any such like."

They took their drinks to a small table in the corner and Rearden discreetly passed over an envelope. Oliver equally discreetly peeped inside and found that it was indeed filled with ten-pound notes. "You're a lucky man Mr Hamilton, it's usually only famous models and film stars that get paid so handsomely for enjoying a spot of fine wine and food."

They sipped their drinks. Rearden immediately took up the conversation with his sing-song Irish voice.

"Now then Oliver, I hope you don't mind me calling you Oliver?"

"Oliver is just fine Patrick."

"Well, that's splendid then. You see, Oliver, I've been making some very discreet enquiries about your good self. And I've been mighty impressed with what I've found out. The youngest non-family man ever to make the Board at Shawfields no less. Quite an achievement Oliver. Quite an achievement indeed."

"Well, thank you Patrick."

"Oh, but it's a great pleasure to see a young man getting on through nothing else but his own dedication and merit. Truly it does the heart good. I've been looking about for a man like you, because I think that there are certain areas where we can work together and maybe make some serious money. Would you be the sort of fellow who might just be interested in making a bit of pretty serious money?"

"I might be. It would all depend on what was involved."

"Well that's splendid then, we'll order some food and talk a little. If at the end of the evening you don't feel that we have any common ground, then we'll go our separate ways."

Over dinner Rearden spent most of the time quizzing Oliver about his life, his work and his aspirations. Oliver answered his questions politely but guardedly, and patiently waited for him to come to the point. The point eventually came as they retired back to the corner table to smoke cigars that cost £54 each and drink vintage port at £33 a glass.

"So did you enjoy the meal Oliver?"

"It was truly outstanding."

"Splendid. Now let me tell you a bit about myself. I'm the Managing Director for a company called Emerald Meats. We're based in Cork, in the South of Ireland. We handle a fair amount of Irish beef, but do a lot more on the trading side shall we say. We have found that there have been plenty of customers who have been interested in buying a bit of competitively priced meat over the last couple of years, but they wouldn't particularly want the country of origin to be shown on the invoice, if you can follow my drift. So what we tend to do is to buy a bit of imported meat and slip it into Cork docks where we have a fine understanding with some of the officials. Then we mix this beef up with a bit of Irish beef and sell it on to our customers with a nice Irish name on the invoice.

"Now there's some who might say that what we do isn't entirely ethical, but to be sure it's a hungry world that we live in, and there's a lot out there without a great deal in the pocket to spend on the dinner table.

"Now I might have things all wrong Oliver, but you strike me as a man of the world, and not the kind of fellow to miss out on quite an opportunity for both your company and your good self for the sake of a few silly old ethics. But then again I could be wrong."

"I'm not walking out Patrick."

"Well there you are then. Now would I be right in thinking that when you buy a bit of imported beef, you'll be paying somewhere around 85p a pound, instead of about a pound a pound for the British stuff? Would that be somewhere near the truth?"

"You certainly wouldn't be a million miles out."

"No, I didn't think I would be. And a little dicky bird has told me that you have run a bit of a trial in 50 of your stores to see whether anyone noticed that all the beef was imported."

Oliver was shocked. "Your little dicky bird has it about right."

"And even though you're managing to buy this beef at a particularly attractive price you have made the wise decision not to pass on the savings to the customer. And why not, we all need to make a few shillings extra to help us through these difficult times."

"Every penny counts."

Rearden smiled as Oliver continued to give off all the right signs. "My little dicky bird tells me that there is rather an impressive profit at the 50 trial stores, and that you have had the rather inspired idea of switching every one of the 1,547 Shawfield stores onto imported beef should the Board agree with you."

Oliver smiled. "I hope you never stint on the sunflower seeds when you feed your song bird."

"Why of course not. You'll never be finding Patrick Rearden stint on anything in his life. It seems that I have all of my facts pretty well right. And that being so, I think that I can offer you something that will be of the greatest of interest to you. Now I'm going to tell you some things which you wouldn't even want to think of telling anyone else about. It pains me to say it, but I do know where you live, and I know of lots of chaps who would do the most dreadful things to your kneecaps for a bit of Friday night beer money, if you get my drift."

Oliver's stomach dropped but he kept his face neutral. "I have always been aware of the importance of discretion."

Rearden beamed as he saw Oliver take a long look at the big fence, then jump straight over without touching the top.

"Well I have a hell of a potential client. He would like you to buy 15,000 tonnes of his beef through my little company over the next six months. By my reckoning that would be just about the amount that you would need if you persuade your Board to adopt your inspired new policy. Amazingly enough, he is happy to sell you this first-class beef for the knock down price of 60p a pound. Yes, you heard right, 60p a pound delivered to your cold stores. Furthermore, my client is so keen to secure this order that he is willing to pay you a commission of 1p per pound should you swing it his way.

"So we're all winners Oliver. You can put an extra £6 million onto the Shawfields bottom line and at the same time my client will pay £300,000 into a nice little bank account in Geneva just for your good self."

Oliver was thunderstruck. He just managed to keep his cool. "Continue."

Rearden beamed. "Now I know exactly what you are going to say and you'd be quite right to say it. How the bloody hell can my client sell his beef at such a crazy price? Well let me tell you how it works. My client sells his beef to a little trading company that he owns in Luxembourg for £1 a pound. This company then sells the beef on, without handling it at all, to Emerald Meats for 55p a pound, and we in turn sell it on to Shawfields at 60p a pound. So how does the Luxembourg company ever pay its bills? How the hell does it stay afloat? Well, this is where my client does a bit of a clever thing. Firstly, if the truth were to be known, my client owns all three of the companies although he doesn't advertise the fact. Secondly, the trading company in Luxembourg has another source of income. It receives quite a bit of revenue from another of my client's export commodities. This is a rather more unofficial export commodity than the beef, its the sort of thing that you might have smoked at parties from time to time. We've always found that a beef carcass is a handy place to hide away the odd other material which isn't quite as bulky as the beef itself, if you see what I mean.

"So as you can see, my client has something of a two-way trade.

On the one hand he can use the beef as a way of moving his other product into Europe via Cork docks where, as I said before, we have a lot of friends. And secondly, he uses his Luxembourg company to send home excellent payments for the beef in nice, clean, hard currency. Right now my client has rather a lot of cattle which are ready for shipping, and the Luxembourg company has rather a lot of money that it is itching to use for payment. He feels that the operation needs to be moved up a gear. We can't seem to move the volume through small outfits here and there, we need a nice new big customer to take a nice big order of 15,000 tonnes. And we feel that Shawfields could just be the customer that we are looking for." Rearden puffed on his cigar. "Now I'll tell you what I have in mind. I'm going to extend you an official invitation to come on over to Cork and have a look at Emerald Meats. You'll come over on December 23 and stay for a couple of days. What the hell, since you're in Ireland for Christmas, why not stay a few days more and enjoy our famous hospitality. So you'll take the Monday after Christmas off and have a nice five-day break. The thing is that we won't stay in Ireland. We'll take a flight out on Christmas Eve with you on a false passport and we'll go and pay a visit to my client. We'll pay you £10,000 in advance for your troubles and if at the end of the visit you're not happy, then we'll call it quits and head off in our different ways. If on the other hand you are happy, then we'll return to Ireland via Geneva to sort you out with a nice little bank account to salt away your little nest egg."

Oliver still managed to keep his voice steady although it took a Herculean effort. "And where, may I ask, does your client operate from?"

"Zimbabwe. Lovely country at this time of year. Even more lovely than the Emerald Isle itself. So what have you got to say about it all then Mr Hamilton?"

"Oh, I think the idea of Christmas in Africa has a certain appeal. I'll come and see your client on those terms. What arrangements need to be made?"

"Hardly any. Your secretary will receive an invitation to Ireland with plane tickets and bookings in the next couple of days. We'll just take a stroll down to the photo kiosk at the tube station right now, and I'll sort you out an identity ready for our trip to Africa."

"Very thorough Patrick."

"You'll find we're very professional people Oliver. Good to work for, and we pay really very well indeed. But we're not very good people to get the wrong side of, not very good at all."

For a moment Oliver felt an icy chill of fear run down his spine, like when he had stood with the ICF in the away end at the notorious home of West Ham's arch rivals Millwall. Then he felt the surge of adrenaline run through his body and he raised his glass with a smile.

"Oh I don't think that there will be any need for me to get the wrong side of you Patrick. No need at all."

They clinked glasses and headed into the frosty night.

Having left Dublin at 4.30 a.m. on Christmas Eve they had landed at Bulawayo late in the afternoon. A large, shiny black Mercedes was waiting for them and they were soon out of the town and heading south across the gently rolling grasslands of Matabeleland. To their right the sun was setting over some distant hills in the fast explosive colours of the African dusk. The road was in poor repair, and the car was seldom able to exceed fifty as it constantly had to slow and swerve to avoid deep potholes. They drove through small, meagre villages where groups of old men sat on rickety verandas smoking, whilst their women pounded maize meal in large wooden bowls. Children in ragged clothes bounded along by the big car yelling with excitement, their faces beaming with joy.

It took them over an hour to cover the forty miles to a turn-off onto a small dirt road. A quarter of a mile further on they came to a road block where a group of five young men flagged the car down. They wore denims, baseball caps and the ubiquitous mirror sunglasses of Africa. They exchanged a brief word with the driver before waving him past with smiles. Each of them held AK 47 assault rifles with a casually practiced air. The vast fields were now dotted with hundreds of brown, hump-backed cattle tended by groups of small boys wrapped in torn old blankets to fend off the evening chill. After a further two roadblocks they came to a gateway. Hung over the gateway was a large sign reading "Clearwater Ranch". The corner had been torn away years before by a burst of rifle fire which meant that instead of reading "Proprietor – A. Jackson" it now read "Proprietor A Jac ". To one side of the gateway a rather gaudy sign was nailed onto the fence posts saying "Matabele Meat Company".

Seven miles after they had entered the ranch, the Mercedes drove over a low hill and the main house could be seen by a small stream that wound along the bottom of a shallow valley. The house was a large single-storey structure with a corrugated iron roof. As they drew up in front, Oliver could see that unlike so many of the old colonial buildings that he had seen during his brief first sight of Zimbabwe, this house was in fine repair. It was built in wood and had obviously been freshly painted. To the side there was a well-stocked vegetable garden and all around the house there were beautifully manicured lawns which were being gently sprayed by irrigation pumps. Two young black men in starched white uniforms bounded out of the house as soon as the car pulled up. They took Oliver and Patrick's bags from the boot and hurried inside. A third, rather older servant met them on the steps. He greeted them formally in a deep and rolling voice.

"Gentlemen, you are most welcome here at Clearwaters. Please come inside. Mr Kumalo awaits you in the lounge."

Inside, the house was polished from top to bottom. The ceilings, walls and floors were all made from old and seasoned African hardwoods. Numerous stuffed animal heads stared glassily from the walls and a variety of skins adorned the floors. Their footsteps echoed as they were led along a corridor to the back of the house. At the end of the panelled corridor the old servant ushered them into a large room with a long picture window that looked out onto the stream below. The furniture was old and orderly and a fire burned merrily. As they entered, a tall man stood up from a leather chair by the fire and turned to face them.

He was a striking man in every respect. He was 6 feet 2 inches tall with broad shoulders. His body was lean and gave off an impression of coiled power. He was dressed simply in black slacks and a crisp white shirt with the cuffs neatly folded back. It was, however, his face that immediately grabbed and held the attention. He was ebony black and his features were carved in sharp, straight lines. His hair was cropped to the bone and he wore an equally tightly trimmed beard. A huge scar ran from just above his left eye, down across his cheek, over the side of his mouth and on down to his chin. When he smiled his grin was twisted by the gash to give off an overwhelming menace.

He ate up the space between them in four long, easy strides with his hand extended. When he spoke his voice was quiet but immensely commanding.

"My friends, welcome to Clearwaters. Welcome to Matabeleland. Welcome to Africa. Come, please sit down, let me get you a drink. But first I must introduce myself. I am Julius Kumalo, and you must be Mr Oliver Hamilton. Patrick has told me much about you."

Oliver was shocked by the power of his grip as they shook hands. He felt the dark eyes burn into him and concurred with everything that Rearden told him about staying on the right side of his new friends.

"Is this your first visit to Africa Oliver?"

"Yes."

"Then it is all the sadder that it is to be so short. I will ensure that your days are filled so that you will return with a fair impression of Matabeleland."

It struck Oliver that he seemed to purposefully avoid any mention of Zimbabwe; it was always Matabeleland. "Tomorrow we shall show you the ranch and the facilities of the Matabele Meat Company. Then on Boxing Day I will take you to my hunting ranch. Tell me, do you shoot?"

"A little, I have been out a few times."

Kumalo laughed. "No doubt you have shot pigeons and pheasants and silly little birds. We will find you something real to shoot. Out here it isn't seen as fitting for a man to spend time hunting little birds. It is a habit for the dirt-eating Shona bastards from the North."

As they drank, Kumalo grilled Oliver about Shawfields and the UK beef market. Unlike his dinner with Rearden, there was no small talk. A little after nine, the servant came in and announced that dinner was ready. They made their way into a beautifully panelled dining room and sat down round a vast mahogany table. Candles flickered from antique silver holders, and their softly jumping light lit up a huge steaming roast of beef.

"Now Oliver, you can sample our goods. Unlike your beef, we keep our cattle until they are four years old so that the meat has a proper flavour. Our Matabele cattle are the finest in the world. You will soon see what a treat your customers have in store."

The meat was indeed truly delicious. Oliver noticed that Kumalo ignored his silver cutlery and ate with his fingers. He tore off pieces of the joint, and ignored the selection of vegetables, preferring to wipe up the juices of the meat with maize cakes. Oliver soon put his cutlery to one side and used his fingers as well. Kumalo smiled with approval. They swigged down four bottles of fine red wine as they talked.

When they had eaten they wandered out onto the veranda where they sat around a brazier. The moon was now high in the sky and Oliver admired a firmament of stars unlike any he had ever seen before. Beyond the quietly bubbling waters of the stream there were several small fires flickering out in the fields.

"Who are they?" asked Oliver.

"Guards," replied Kumalo simply. "I have many enemies. Security is always vital. Let me tell you the story of my family, my people and this land of ours."

As his mesmeric voice unfolded his story, Oliver became entranced by the stars, the moon, and the endless plains of grass that stretched away into the night. The distant lowing of the cattle and the almost imperceptible breeze that softly brushed over the veranda were the night's only sounds.

"Nearly two hundred years ago an ancestor of mine was a lieutenant of King Chaka of the Zulus. Chaka's empire stretched all over Southern Africa and nobody dared to stand in his path. My ancestor, Mzilikazi, grew tired of living in the shadow of Chaka. He decided that he was unwilling to hand over the proceeds of a cattle raid, and instead of returning to the Kraal of the king, he led his people, the Kumalo tribe, into the lands of the north. They marched for hundreds of miles, conquering all the tribes who dared to stand before them. When they came to a land of endless sweet grass fit for their herds of cattle they stopped and formed the Matabele nation. They took the land easily, throwing out the weak, dirt-eating Shona people who had no men to fight.

"When Mzilikazi died, his son Lobengula took the throne and my ancestors always lived in the kraal of the king. When Rhodes and his thieves came, we fought many times to defend our land, but we found that our spears could not fight the Maxim guns of the white men. In 1895 our great rebellion was broken and for 85 years we lived under the heel of the white man. My family lived here at Clearwaters, the ranch of the Jackson family. We lived over there in the village." He pointed to a cluster of small fires that twinkled about a mile up the valley. "We looked after their cattle and waited on them in the house, but we always waited for the day when the land would again be ours. When our people started to fight back in the sixties and seventies we always helped and supported the forces of Zipra – the Matabele freedom fighters. My oldest brother left home when he was 16 to join the fighters and he became a great warrior. One night a Land Rover came into the village. Young Jackson came with eight of his men. Jackson was a dangerous warrior and fought with the Selous Scouts, the most terrible and murderous of all the white forces. They threw my brother onto the floor in front of us. My mother tried to run to him but one of the soldiers beat her to the ground. Jackson gloated that we could never win. My brother was nearly dead. He had been tortured and beaten and he could hardly move. Jackson cut his throat with his hunting knife whilst we all watched and he told us that we should be warned.

"The next day I left to join up with the Zipra forces in Zambia. I fought for two years. One day we were ambushed by the Scouts and Jackson made this scar on my face with the same knife that he had used to kill my bother. I stabbed him in the stomach and escaped. Three of us got away and it took us two months to make it to safety. Jackson was many months in hospital before he recovered. Before he got out we had won. At the Lancaster House Conference we were given our freedom and the new land of Zimbabwe was born.

"And yet so-called democracy brought only more misery for the Matabele people. For every two Matabele there are eight Shona. We had been promised land and cattle. Instead the Shona bastard Mugabe allowed the white farmers to stay, and my family still had to work for Jackson. The police were all Shona, the Government were all Shona, the courts were all Shona. They started to take our young men away to camps where they were tortured and killed. When we tried to fight back they sent their Fifth Brigade into Matabeleland. As the world turned its back, they came with their bastard North Korean friends and they killed us by the thousand. I fled over the border to Botswana with two hundred of my old Zipra comrades. We heard that they had come to our village in the night. They killed my mother and all my sisters. They raped them and they killed them. They killed all the babies too.

"For months we were trapped, living wild like bushmen in the empty wilderness of Botswana. Then we started to adjust. We had weapons and we were soldiers. We poached the game parks, we smuggled goods into South Africa to break the sanctions, we moved drugs. As a member of the Kumalo family I became the leader. Our band grew to over a thousand strong and I copied the methods of the Cosa Nostra family of Sicily, for they too were exiles and bandits. Soon we were able to bribe anyone we wanted in Botswana, and dispose of any who dared to cross us. We became rich on the proceeds of smuggling drugs and selling weapons all over Africa.

"In the late 1980s the world finally forced the Shona bastard Mugabe give up his persecution of the Matabele nation and we were able to return. When I came back, Clearwaters was all run down. Jackson had never been able to work properly again after his wound. Cattle prices had collapsed, and he couldn't find any good Matabele men to tend the cattle. He had become an alcoholic and the land was going to waste. I made him an offer. A tiny price to be paid in Zimbabwe, and a bigger price to be paid into a bank account in Switzerland. He couldn't say no, and for the first time in 100 years the lands of Clearwaters came back to the sons of Mzilikazi. We have bought many farms over the last few years. The Matabele Meat Company has more than 150,000 cattle, as many as

King Chaka all those years ago. In the carcasses of the cattle we can send drugs and weapons all over the world.

"You see we need the money and the power, so that the next time the Shona dogs come barking round our villages we will drown them in blood. One day the Colonial joke that is Zimbabwe will be over and once again Matabeleland will be free for the peoples of Mzilikazi.

"I tell you all this Oliver so that you know me as a man. I have seen my mother, my brother and all of my sisters killed. I have killed many times myself. I have killed white men and I have killed black men. For me it makes no difference. Those who have crossed me are all dead, and if you cross me, you too will be dead. We are a people who know what it is to kill. And yet we do not kill for pleasure and fun like the Shona dogs in the North. Jackson lives in Bulawayo now. He lives all of his days in a bar and at the bottom of a bottle. I could have him killed tomorrow but I do not. I do not because I see him as he is a man. When he killed my brother he was fighting for his own people. I would have done the same. After the war he lost half his stomach and my face will forever bear the mark of his knife. We are even, there is no need to kill him.

"When Rhodes was buried my people turned out at his funeral to give our respect. He had stolen our land and murdered thousands of our children but we saw him as a man. We called him 'Bayete'. We called him king.

"I tell you this Oliver so that you know. If you work with us I will be your brother. You will earn much money, and I will stand beside you when you need me. If you betray me I will kill you. This is what you must know. This is our way."

He was silent as the soft sounds of the African night whispered over the long, rolling fields of grass. Oliver felt a long way out of his depth and a long way from home. And yet he also felt the power and the spell of the man. He felt the proximity to ultimate danger and it chilled his body and made it tingle with excitement. Just as the corporate jungle had superseded the short, vicious excitement of Saturday afternoons, he now knew that the world that had been shown to him by Julius Kumalo would supersede the pitiful back stabbing and ladder climbing of Shawfields. With this man he would move onto another level. With this man he too would one day learn to kill. He racked his brain for something to say that would be right. At last he looked Kumalo long in the face then said,

"One day you will tell me that I have been true to the memory of Mzilikazi."

Kumalo nodded gravely. "Then one day you will be a man."

When Oliver and Kumalo shook hands Rearden found that he shuddered. All of a sudden it was as if he had ceased to exist. He was with them on the veranda but in reality they were all alone. At last Kumalo broke the stare and said, "Come. We will retire. Tomorrow we get up early and I will show you our lands."

It was still dark when Daniel, the old servant, awoke Oliver with a cup of tea. He had to almost peel his eyes open to read the clock: 5.15 a.m.

"Good morning Daniel."

"Good morning sir. Merry Christmas. Mr Kumalo says you will leave at 5.30. You will meet him at the front." After a hurried wash and shower, Oliver just made it. There was no sign of either the Mercedes or Rearden when Oliver walked outside. Kumalo sat at the wheel of an open-topped Land Rover. He waved as Oliver emerged. The back of the vehicle was full of bags and two of the denim-clad guards were perched on top.

A thin, blood-red band of colour was slowly thickening in the east as the first light of Christmas Day grew stronger. The dawn air was filled with exotic bird calls.

"Good morning, Oliver, and Merry Christmas."

"Merry Christmas to you too Julius."

Kumalo chuckled. "I'm afraid there is little chance that it will be white. From a weather point of view, snow is unheard of here and we gave up the other kind of white Christmas in 1980 when we kicked out Smithy and the rest." He started the engine and they pulled away.

"No Patrick this morning?"

"No, Patrick isn't much of an outdoor man. He's going to have a lie-in and take it easy. I have rather taken the liberty of deciding that you made up your mind to join us last night Oliver."

Oliver saw little point in hedging and he certainly wasn't going to barter the man. "I'm in."

Kumalo grinned. "Excellent. Then I'm afraid that your visit will be even shorter. You will need to leave tomorrow afternoon to get to Geneva to open an account and deposit your money. That means our tour will have to be brief."

They headed away from the dirt track that they had travelled in on. After a few hundred yards they came upon the first cluster of guards whose small fire Oliver had spotted the night before. Kumalo stopped the Land Rover and spoke to them briefly. Then they headed out across country. All morning they drove over the low hills of grassland, passing thousand upon thousand of the brown cattle. Progress was slow as Kumalo constantly stopped to talk to guards and the young boys that tended the beasts. Eventually they came onto a tarmac road and headed north towards Bulawayo.

On the outskirts of the town they came to an industrial unit which bore a sign: "Matabele Meat Company. Head office and Abattoir". It was a fairly new set-up built on a three-acre site. It was completely surrounded by a ten-foot wire fence, and a number of guards sat around the front gate.

"I'm afraid we won't be able to go inside," said Kumalo. "We don't work on Christmas Day of course. There isn't much to see really. The building on the right is our Head Office. The large shed in the middle is the abattoir and the sheds on the left are the cold stores where we freeze, store and containerise the meat. I'll be honest with you Oliver, standards inside aren't up to those demanded in your country these days. That's why we decided to buy an Irish company to label the goods and find someone like you who would turn his back on traceability."

"That's no problem to me Julius. Most of our traceability rules are bullshit anyway, it's just an excuse to drive down prices from our suppliers."

They skirted the edge of the town and headed west. After an hour they came to a range of hills and Julius skilfully drove the Land Rover up a steep track that climbed sharply. Eventually they came to the summit and got out. Ahead of them the plains of

Matabeleland were spread out in the haze. As Julius and Oliver stared out into the view, the two guards from the back quickly made a fire and brewed tea and made maize cakes.

Oliver felt almost overwhelmed by the majesty of the scene.

"Your country is very beautiful Julius."

" It is why we have always fought so hard. Nobody is ever going to take it from us again. Not while there is breath in my body."

After lunch, they drove back down to the plain and headed east. Gradually the land got drier, and the grassland thinned. Soon it was quite arid and broken by low rocky hills. After several hours they stopped and the two guards busied themselves with making camp. Kumalo dug a rifle, a pair of desert boots and a slouch hat out of the back and tossed them to Oliver. "Come. We will hunt now."

They picked their way through the bush for three hours until the sun set. They saw a variety of animals but Kumalo explained that he had bought a permit for Oliver to shoot a buffalo. He explained that when he was in exile he had no qualms about hunting all manner of game. But now Matabeleland had been returned, it was vital to restock the game parks in order to attract tourists and their hard currency.

They sat by the fire in the night and talked. All around, the air was filled with the sound of animals, each of which Kumalo identified. Once again they awoke before dawn. A stranger had arrived in the night who knew where they could find buffalo. They walked for four hours until the guide picked up the trail. By ten they had found the small herd of buffalo and they moved closer with patience.

Oliver made his kill just before noon. He made it with one shot to the neck just as Kumalo had recommended. As he stood over the great beast he felt a primitive sense of joy wash through his body. Kumalo watched him with interest, and without Oliver seeing, he nodded to himself with satisfaction.

"I think it feels good Oliver."

"Yes. It feels good."

"Then I am happy for you. I have seen how it goes for white men when they kill in Africa for the first time. Some are sick with sadness and remorse. Others allow their souls to accept the reality of Africa. Here we live in a hard place and we play by hard rules. We don't cover things up with lies."

Oliver was quiet on the drive back to Bulawayo. The kill had changed him. He knew that it had opened up the door to another era of his life. Things would once again be different now.

He shook hands with Kumalo when they met the Mercedes on the road a few miles from Bulawayo.

"I think that you can do this job Oliver Hamilton."

"I know that I can."

"Then go well. We will meet again."

He said little to Rearden either on the flight or during their brief stay in Geneva. When they parted at Dublin Airport two days later Rearden had promised to have a full legal tender for 15,000 tonnes of beef on Oliver's desk by the end of the week.

That had been less than a fortnight ago, although it felt like much longer. When he had returned to Shawfields he had thrown all of his energy into preparing for the big Board Meeting. Alice Fairclough had gently spread the news of Oliver's successful lunch date with Simon Shawfield to the secretaries of his fellow directors. He had arranged quiet meetings with three of the ten who he knew to be having affairs. It wasn't difficult to win the promise of their support in the vote in return for his silence. As he drove through the early morning traffic he knew that he had a guarantee of four votes including his own. He therefore needed two more and felt confident that he would win these from some of the more go-ahead directors who had given him support at the last meeting. All of Rearden's documentation was impressive and it painted a convincing picture of Emerald Meats as a buoyant and fast-growing business. He rehearsed his own presentation in his head until he knew that it was perfect.

He was on his feet at 11 a.m. to present item 3 of the agenda. At 11.40 it was voted through with a 10 – 0 majority. Alice's rumour-spreading had had a powerful effect. None of the board wanted to appear to be gratuitously blocking the progress of Simon Shawfield's new favourite. It was agreed that they would take delivery of 625 tonnes of Irish beef every week for six months commencing in the first week of February.

As the meeting broke up Oliver's head was spinning. Within a matter of months he had come to the brink of both power and wealth. He took a deep breath and remembered the feeling of the kill as he had stood over the great bleeding body of the buffalo. A hand touched his arm. Simon Shawfield was all smiles. "That really was more than impressive Hamilton. You have your project now. If you can make it happen like you have promised, well, I must say that great things are in store for you, not least at the next salary review. If on the other hand things go wrong, you must be aware that you have crawled to the end of a long, high branch and there are several men who would take the greatest pleasure in sawing it off."

"It will work Simon. Of that I have no doubt."

"I can see that. You are one of those men who simply don't allow doubt. I wish you well."

After the Director's lunch he ordered his secretary to hold all calls and rang Kumalo on his personal mobile.

"Kumalo."

"Good afternoon Julius, Oliver Hamilton here."

"And?"

"Mzilikazi smiles."

There was a brief pause. "You have done well Oliver. We will speak."

" Yes, we will speak." He pressed the "End" button and allowed himself a small smile of satisfaction.

Shawfields had become the first major British retailer to sell 100% imported meat.

# CHAPTER FIVE
## PLANNING

Everybody reconvened in the meeting room at Black Loch at 9.00 a.m. on the morning of January 14. Outside a gale force wind was blowing thick rain almost horizontally across the choppy waters of the loch. The weather had been wild for days as they had sat huddled round the fire at Cragside throwing ideas at each other. There was one new face at the table, Gideon Rosenberg, who Cornelius introduced to Marcus and Sir Alistair. Gideon was the last regular member of their group, and in a way he had been responsible for its foundation.

He was a small man of slight build and delicate features. He was very pale and always wore a small black skull cap over his straight black hair. He was chronically short-sighted, a problem that he rectified by wearing outrageously thick, heavy glasses. No-one had ever let him know that glasses could be a fashion item. No matter what clothes he wore or what they cost they always seemed to drown him and make him look rather ridiculous.

He had always been shy and his first few months at university had been a prolonged misery. One evening he was returning to his college a little after ten when he had been accosted by some dinner suit-wearing drunks who had recently emerged from a dining club. One particularly sozzled student called Rupert Appleyard had decided that it would be hysterically funny to steal Gideon's skull cap. He had wrenched it from his head and they had embarked on a joyous game of piggy in the middle as they tossed the cap to each other whilst Gideon had miserably tried to recover it. The mocking cries of, "Come on, come and get it Yiddo!" had drawn Vince and Cornelius to the scene. Vince had stepped into the middle of the melée and Cornelius had followed with some reluctance.

Vince had spoken in a perfectly reasonable manner.

"Come on lads, enough's enough, give the lad his cap back. You've had your bit of fun."

But Appleyard's blood was now well and truly up. His public-school voice was loud and slurred. "And may I ask, what the fuck do you think you are going to do about it then? A Jock and a poof. What you going to do then?"

Vince's answer was fairly clear as he sent the taller man crashing backwards into the wall of the bridge with a particularly well-timed punch. He was about to hit him again when he was grabbed by two of the other revellers and they held him down whilst the enraged Appleyard started to pummel him. Cornelius's hopeless attempted intervention had merely resulted in the other two members of Appleyard's group starting to hammer him black and blue. Gideon made Herculean efforts to intervene, only to have his frail frame brushed off with contempt. Vince was aware that he was drifting off as the blows rained down on him when all of a sudden the punches stopped. He heard screams and then a splashing sound. As he dragged himself to his feet he was just in time to see the last of Appleyard's group being hurled over the bridge by an enormous black man.

He hauled Cornelius to his feet and the giant strode over to them beaming his spectacular smile. "Hi guys, allow me to introduce myself, Victor Gama."

Cornelius spat out a mouthful of blood with disdain. "Whoever you are you're a bloody Godsend. May I offer our fondest gratitude."

"Oh, none needed man. If there's one sport I love it's throwing racists in rivers."

A small quiet voice spoke up. "Urm, could I also introduce myself. I'm Gideon Rosenberg and I'd like to buy you all a drink."

And so it was that the unlikely foursome came together. Gideon was full of mischief and humour once he overcame his shyness, and he and Victor soon became great friends. He studied Maths at university and came out with a Starred First without breaking sweat. When he left his studies he took up his appointed position with his father's merchant bank, 'Rosenberg and Bloom'. It was, however, always accepted that he could have periods of leave as and when he was required to join in any capers with the others. Within their small organisation he always handled the accounts and worked their earnings through a tortuous worldwide web before returning them back to the UK in a form that the tax-man wouldn't suspect. He also controlled any of their ventures which entered into the corporate field.

As he sat gazing myopically around the room his brain ached from the long hours of planning that had filled the last few days. As soon as he had heard about the new project he had called his father and informed him that he would be unavailable for work until at least the first of September. His father hadn't questioned it, he treasured the relationship that his strange and lonely only son had built up over the years with his odd friends.

Helen put a coffee in front of him and waved her hand in front of his face mockingly. "Come on Gideon, wakey, wakey, business is at hand." She had taken wholeheartedly to the strange young man and found it hard to resist the maternal urge to look after him.

They all sat down and were ready to start. Sir Alistair naturally assumed the role of Chairman.

"Right then, let us get kicked off. The floor is yours Vincent. May I assume that you have the beginnings of a plan?"

Vince smiled. "Rather more than the beginnings."

"And will it work?"

"I reckon it will."

"Then fire away."

Vince paused to light a cigarette. He then stood up and started.

"Before I outline any of our ideas I want to go through the broad outlines of our task and the main method we need to use to achieve success. Let's look at the crisis first.

"BSE was first discovered in cattle in the early 1980s and steadily grew in the perception of the public. However, the fact that cattle were suffering from the disease had little impact on the sales and consumption of beef for several years.

"The problem became chronic in early 1996 when the Health Minister announced that there was indeed some evidence that there was a link between BSE and the human equivalent disease,

CJD. However at this point something really crucial happened. The supermarkets panicked at the thought that they were going to be left stranded with large stocks of beef that nobody dared to eat. They immediately took the decision to offer massive discounts on all beef products, and what happened? The shelves were empty within hours.

"This is vital, and it gives a critical insight into the mood of the public. A bunch of boffins were warning that by eating beef we were in danger of contracting a chronic brain disease and dying a slow and horrible death. They even hinted at a new plague. Now if you're seriously worried about this you're not going to eat beef whatever it costs. If someone comes up to you and offers you heroin at £5 even though it usually costs £15 you're not going to buy it.

"The conclusion that we can draw is that even when the scare was all over the front pages there still wasn't enough fear generated to stop the British public buying beef when it was cheap.

"This is really, really good news. If there was a real fear of the product, our job would be much more difficult, maybe even impossible.

"So. What is the task? We have to move the price of beef up by about 35% in about eight and a half months. How do we do this? How do you move any price up? Simple. Supply and demand. The oldest rule in the book of capitalism.

"In the very simplest of terms we either have to reduce the supply of beef into the United Kingdom or increase the demand. The supply issue is twofold. To stay within the spirit of our engagement, there is obviously no way that we can look to up the price of beef by damaging and reducing the supply of the British product. The whole idea of our operation is to influence the market to ensure that more British beef is sold at a higher price.

"This of course leads to the question of the supply of imported beef. Clearly it is the volume of imported beef that is now pouring into the country that has pushed our home beef industry to the brink. Unfortunately, the news of BSE in Britain very quickly reverberated around the rest of the world. Where the British public, by and large are now eating more or less as much beef as they did before the crisis, this certainly is not the case in other countries where demand has collapsed. This has meant that many countries have a huge surplus of beef, and the current strength of our currency has meant that they have been able to pour huge volumes of heavily discounted beef into Britain.

"Can we stop this supply? The answer, in short, is no. We are looking at literally thousands of wagons coming into the country at umpteen different entry points. To attempt to stem this flow is totally unrealistic and, more to the point, illegal. The very fact of it being illegal wouldn't necessarily put us off. The key fact is that the Government has clearly demonstrated that it will deploy the police force, regardless of cost, to ensure that the movement of goods into the country is uninterrupted. There are many precedents that suggest that it is almost impossible to stop goods entering the country, whether it be the Government's failure to stem the drug trade or the miners' failure to stop coal imports in 1984. We can learn much from the failure of French farmers to stop British exports of lamb, and they tried every trick in the book.

"There is nothing that can be done to move the price of beef by artificially attempting to restrict supply. That we believe is final. Which means that the scope of our operation has a single focus. We must radically affect demand.

"Now as we all know, there is currently and export ban in place which means that British farmers are not allowed to sell their product to anyone else in the world. They are not even allowed to give it away. Furthermore, there seems little possibility that this ban will be lifted within the foreseeable future. We cannot therefore stimulate extra demand by helping to promote sales of British Beef to other countries.

"This of course simplifies our operation even further.

"We need to affect the buying habits of fifty million Britons. That is all that we can do.

"We need to look at effecting these buying habits in two ways. Firstly we obviously need to make British beef seem more attractive. Secondly, we need to make imported beef seem much less attractive. We have come up with numerous ideas and schemes that we believe will achieve both these aims. However, simply making people want to buy British beef rather than imported beef is only half the battle. It is no good simply wanting to buy something if you are unable to find anywhere to buy it.

"The vast majority of beef sales in the UK are controlled by the large supermarket chains. It has become clear that the prime objective of these organisations is to drive down the prices that they pay their suppliers whilst maximising their own profits. Very, very few suppliers are able to compete with supermarkets on equal terms, even giants such as Heinz are fighting a rearguard action against their biggest customers' own label brands. We might well be able to stimulate demand significantly, and even achieve the specified target price for beef by September 1. However it would only ever be half a job.

"So long as the major supermarket chains enjoy more or less complete control of food retailing, anything that we achieve will be transient at best.

"How do we get round this problem? Well gentlemen, I'm afraid that it is time to take a deep breath. I believe that we need to create our own marketing outlet. We need to ensure that the customers have guaranteed access to British beef. Our proposal is that we should create a new company that will sell and market British beef both vigorously and permanently.

"We believe that the key to the success of this concept is vertical integration. The company will need to employ people to source the beef animals at cattle auctions. It will need abattoirs to slaughter and butcher the meat. It will need processing companies to wrap and pack it. It will need a cold distribution to deliver the products nationwide. Finally it will need retail outlets to sell to the public either in the High Street or delivered to their homes.

"Gideon has come up with several models and sets of figures. He believes that it will be vital for the new company to achieve a 10% market share within six months. It will do so by blanket advertising and marketing. The aim will be to create a branded range of 100% British products. Once the brands have been successfully launched we believe that other major retailers will be keen to market them.

"Gentlemen, this is our main aim. Our operation will radically lift the profile of British beef and damage the image of imported beef. As each phase of the operation comes into play it will coincide with a major marketing campaign from the new company.

"As you can imagine, this is a huge project. Gideon has spent hours on it and he has come up with some pretty good basic stuff. He has spent time scanning through sets of accounts that are lodged at Companies House and he has been able to identify many companies in the sector which are weak and vulnerable. He believes that we should be able to acquire businesses to cover all of our logistical and retailing needs for £400 million. We feel that a further £100 million will be required for the marketing campaign.

"In Gideon's opinion, the investment should be fairly secure due to the fact that the majority of the acquisitions will be made at rock-bottom prices, and if things went radically wrong, they could be asset stripped for at least the purchase price.

"So guys, half a billion quid. It is a great sum of money. Where does it come from? Well, Gideon has also undertaken detailed research into McIntyre Holdings, and he has told us that there has been constant City speculation about a takeover bid from a major American outfit. Apparently these overtures have been consistently rejected, but not with sufficient vigour to put the ardent suitor off. Gideon estimates that should negotiations begin in earnest, the conclusion would be a sell-out deal for somewhere in the region of £1.7 billion, which of course would put a sum of upwards of £900 million into the family coffers.

"Following our original discussions, I have taken the liberty of outlining these plans to Helen and she assures me that she would wholeheartedly support such an investment. However, takeovers of this magnitude take time, and it would be well after our September 1 deadline that the cash would become available. There is a solution to this timing problem. Gideon has talked with his father, and 'Rosenberg and Bloom' are willing to furnish the new company with a bridging facility of £500 million.

"Initially it would be a private limited company with Sir Alistair as Chairman, Marcus as Vice Chairman, Gideon as Financial Director, and other Directors to be appointed as you feel fit. However we would make it known that our intention would be to publicly float the company sometime next year, offering a preferential share price to farmers who have sold their animals to us.

"And the name? We have all thought long and hard about it. We like the idea of 'Matador'.

"In a nutshell, that is the framework upon which the whole operation will hang. I don't want any response whatsoever yet. Gideon and I will now go through our various planned operations in some detail. I hope that you all had lots of sleep last night because this is going to take a while."

And it did take a while. The room was soon filled with smoke, and the table became a litter of plates and cups and paperwork. Sir Alistair and Marcus attacked every detail of Vince's operations. When it was Gideon's turn, he too was grilled without mercy. By the time that Gideon had finally worked his way through his dossier it was well after midnight. His pale face seemed to have hollowed out and behind the thick glasses his eyes were red-rimmed. Helen leaned over and gave him a squeeze.

"Gideon, that was quite heroic. It was like trying to persuade wolves to turn vegetarian."

He smiled rather wanly. "Do you think that it was OK?"

"Of course it was. You were wonderful."

Ties had been loosened and everyone had a rather threadbare look. Everyone bar Sir Alistair, who still sat erect and commandingly alert. Vince stared into his eyes and said, "So that's it boss. Well, not quite, there is one other small detail that you might not particularly like, but it will have to be done."

Sir Alistair lifted an eyebrow. "Which is?"

"We are going to make you a media star."

"A what?"

"You heard me. A media star." Vince explained. Before he was halfway finished the room was filled with the joyous sound of Marcus laughing. It was an infectious laugh and soon they had all joined in. Sir Alistair looked desperately to his daughter for support, but she too was quite engulfed in hysterics.

"Come on Daddy, don't be soft. I promise not to make fun of you when they put the make-up on . . . "

More laughter until Marcus squeezed out the words, "You might promise that Helen, but I bloody don't!"

Eventually the hilarity subsided and an air of expectancy filled the room as the gale outside howled and wobbled the double-glazed windows. Sir Alistair looked to his daughter. She nodded firmly. He then looked to his oldest friend who nodded equally firmly.

He stared down at the table for what seemed like a long time and then he looked up. His hard, craggy face slowly broke into a smile.

"I believe that Chicago is about seven hours behind us. I will make the call now and tell Mr Tanner that he has a deal. Marcus, you and I will travel to London tomorrow to meet Gideon's father and form a new company. We are going to be busier than men in their seventies really should be, but I feel that we are going to rather enjoy it.

"Gentlemen, Matador will be a reality next week. Come Hell or high water we will be open to trade by no later than March 1. Vincent, this is quite the most outlandishly daring scheme that I have ever heard of. You know what? It might just work. It is time for a drink, a toast and then bed."

He fetched champagne and filled glasses. They all stood rather formally. Sir Alistair looked around the table and raised his glass.

"To Matador."

# CHAPTER SIX

## AUNT ESTHER'S PARTY

"Hello."

"Aunt Esther, it's Cornelius."

"Cornelius St John, you're an absolute monster. You have neglected your old Auntie for weeks on end. I'm tempted to bang the phone down right here and now." Her words were full of bluster but huge affection shone through every syllable. She was one of those people who had never learned the meaning of talking quietly. Her booming horsey voice could always be heard across any gathering in almost any size of room. Like many such loudly-spoken people, she felt the necessity to double the volume level when speaking on the phone.

"Now, now, Aunt Esther. I don't believe a word of it. You know only too well what a busy boy I am. Work keeps me going from dawn to the very dusk and makes me neglect calling even my very nearest and dearest."

"Bullshit Cornelius. I met Beatrice Webster last week who told me that she had bumped into you in Montego Bay with a spectacularly beautiful young man on your arm, now don't you dare tell me that you were working so hard that you couldn't even come and see your old loyal Aunt at Christmas."

Cornelius laughed. "I'll never get past you will I? Talk about having a spy in every camp. Anyway, I have great tidings to bear."

"And what might they be. The thought of your good tidings makes me shudder."

"You are going to have a fiftieth birthday party the likes of which Hampshire has never seen."

"In case you had forgotten young man, I am fifty-five."

"Well in that case better late than never. We both know that you would have put on the most almighty bash for your fiftieth if you had had the money. So what I say is let's do it now."

"I still haven't got any money. I never have any money."

"Don't you worry about that even for a single second, because my dearest Auntie Esther, I'm paying."

This made her cough out a bark of a laugh. "You're paying! Don't be so ridiculous Cornelius. The day I manage to have a party at this house again I promise you that it will be a proper party, not some half hearted-effort to please the weird and wonderful crowd that you'll no doubt bring down from London on a day pass from the zoo."

"Ooh, that's a dreadfully hurtful thing to say Auntie. The truth is that I will only be inviting four people. I will help with all the arrangements and I will throw £7,500 into the kitty. Now how bad do you feel about all those wicked things you've been saying? Day passes from the zoo indeed."

The line went quiet for several seconds. "What's the catch Cornelius?"

"Hardly anything really, just a couple of very minor details."

"Like?"

"Well, firstly it will have to be two weeks on Saturday."

"Good Lord. That's out of the question, I couldn't possibly . . . "

"My £7,500 cheque has a sell-by date I'm afraid."

"Go on. The second minor detail."

"I need you to invite Dwight Forrester."

"Dwight Forrester! Absolutely not! There is no way that I would entertain having that boorish Colonial lout anywhere near my house, it's quite out of the question."

"Don't be such a snob Esther. I didn't notice the local hunt showing too many reservations when he offered to come up with enough sponsorship money to keep them afloat."

"Well that was different, it was a matter of life and death. Anyway, that man's a multi-millionaire tycoon. There is no way that he would be available at such short notice."

"Oh, but he is Auntie. I've already checked. He's due to be out with the hunt the very next morning. We both know that the poor man is desperate to gain entry into local society, and there is no way that he would miss the opportunity to hob-nob it with the true blue locals at such a major event as your fiftieth birthday party. Hell, he may even pay off one of your mortgages as a present."

"Oh, please don't be vulgar Cornelius. I dare say you will insist that I ring this dreadful man first to make sure that he is indeed free to come before making any other arrangements?"

"My goodness Aunt Esther. How very perceptive of you."

"And how do you suggest that a stone-broke country warhorse like me could possibly fight my way through the switchboard at Forrester International and get put through to the main man in charge?"

"I have the number for his private line. You will simply have to get by his personal secretary and that I have no doubt will be quite within your considerable powers."

She sighed in defeat. "As usual Cornelius, you have covered all of your bases. You are of course quite right in all of your assumptions. I certainly cannot possibly miss out on the chance to put on a good thumping £7,500 bash, and from what I know of the awful Mr Forrester, I very much doubt that he will be able to resist an invitation from one of the good and the great of the shire. I don't suppose you would even consider telling me anything about what this is all about?"

"Quite right. I wouldn't even consider it."

"But I don't suppose you want me to invite Mr Forrester so that you can give him a bunch of daffodils."

Cornelius chuckled. "Not quite."

"Good. That makes me feel a little better. Now give me the wretched man's number and I'll call him right away."

Dwight Forrester's personal secretary was indeed no match for such an experienced battle-axe as Aunt Esther. Within five minutes a seething Dwight Forrester stormed out of one of his daily big meetings to rip the phone from the terrified secretary's grasp.

"Who the bloody hell is this? You better have a bloody good reason for hood-winking my secretary into getting me out of a bloody important bloody meeting." His Australian accent always became more pronounced when he was angry.

"Oh do calm down Mr Forrester, nothing could possibly be so important. You men do become awfully vulgar when you wrap yourselves up in your tedious commercial matters." She piled on her most aristocratic voice and poured it down the phone.

He frowned. "May I ask who I am speaking to?"

"Of course you may ask you silly man. We enjoy the luxury of free speech in this country. I am Esther St John, we are more or less neighbours in Hampshire. My modest little holding runs up against the western border of your ranch."

Forrester's face drained of colour as he mouthed the words "Shit, shit, shit!!" to his shuddering secretary. "Mrs St John, may I . . . "

"It's Miss actually."

"Ah, well yes, well Miss St John. May I please apologise for that unforgivable outburst. If I had been given any inkling that I was addressing a neighbour and a lady, well . . . "

"Good Lord man. There is no need to apologise . No need at all. I worked in a munitions factory in Coventry during the war and I learnt enough ribald language to last me a lifetime. If I fell out with every male friend who swore like a soldier I would surely have none left."

Dwight grinned with relief. "So what can I do for you Miss St John?"

"I'm having a fiftieth birthday party two weeks on Saturday. Like an old fool I left the sending of invitations to my oafish nephew Cornelius and I have only just discovered that he hasn't sent you one. You may be assured that I have given him the most fearful earful about it. I have phoned immediately to invite you in person and to apologise for my wretched nephew's oversight."

Now Dwight grinned with happiness. "Why please, there is no need to apologise. I'm only glad that you even thought of me at all, what with my being rather new to the area."

"New maybe, but very important none the less. I shudder to think what would have happened to the hunt without your generous support."

"Well it's nice that you feel that way. We Aussies like to be neighbourly you know. As it happens I'm out hunting the next day so I would be delighted to come to your party."

"Well that's splendid. I will of course ensure that you receive a formal invitation by post but there is no need for you to RSVP now that we've had this little chat."

"Two weeks on Saturday Miss St John."

"Yes indeed Mr Forrester. I look forward to seeing you."

Esther smiled wickedly as she replaced the receiver. She lit a cigarette and dialled.

"Hello."

"It's you your old bag of an Aunt."

"Good Lord that was quick."

"I make an effort not to mess about young man."

"And . . . ?"

"Oh, I had the poor devil eating out of my hand. He will be available for you to do to him what you will. Now I expect you to be in my kitchen by no later than 7.30 tomorrow morning. We have a great deal of work to do. Will you be alone?"

"Actually no."

"Will you be arriving with the ravishing friend from Jamaica?"

"Yes."

"And should I approve?"

"He'll organise you a steel band for the party."

"In which case I approve. I shall just have to conveniently forget to send an invitation to your father."

"You're a brick Auntie Esther."

"Aren't I just."


A little over two weeks later Dwight Forrester was carefully tying his black tie. Once it was done he stepped back to admire himself. Even though his stomach was a good six inches too large he felt that he didn't look bad for a fifty-two year old. He had a round face which had enjoyed a lifelong tan. When he smiled his eyes sparkled and his easy charm seldom let him down. When he scowled he quickly became murderous. He was a passionate man, a man filled with boundless energy. His charm, energy, ruthlessness and a Rhino hide had enabled him to take the small-town newspaper business in Queensland that he had inherited from his father and grow it into one of the world's largest media empires. He had married at 23 years old and divorced at 27. He had always felt that this had been one of his greatest pieces of luck. When he had divorced his wife he had only had to give her half of not a lot, and he had made the decision never to marry again. It was a decision that he had never regretted as he had seen many of his contemporaries torn to pieces by bloody divorce battles fought by armies of bloodsucking lawyers. For a quarter of a century he had basked in his reputation as an untrammelled and unashamed womaniser, and being single, well, why not?

He had come to England ten years before when he had borrowed himself up to his eyeballs and bought *The Globe. The Globe* had been a slowly failing tabloid that was quietly going bust whilst still hanging on to a few old-fashioned scruples. Dwight had soon put a stop to that. He had sacked almost everyone and within weeks *The Globe* was out tabloiding all the other tabloids. Nobody was safe from his voracious reporters – sportsmen, royals, politicians, vicars, teachers, TV personalities, it seemed that when anyone of any standing lowered their trousers in the wrong place there was always a *Globe* reporter waiting in the cupboard. His paper was now the third best-selling in the country, his overdrafts were all cleared and profits grew every year.

For eight years it had all been enough for him. The constant buzz of the newsroom, the race for every scoop, the constant round of sacking and poaching. Then, to his horror, a year after he turned fifty, he found that he was slowly catching the British disease. He had bought a vast country estate in Hampshire and bailed the local hunt out of financial trouble. He suddenly had a yearning for acceptance in his adopted country, and every now and then when he couldn't sleep at night he allowed the thought of a Knighthood to drift around his mind.

So it had been the cause of great delight to him when he had received his invitation from Esther St John. It had been the first sign of real thaw from the local community, the first hint that one day they may lower their drawbridges and let him in.

He sipped thoughtfully at his scotch and decided that he would give his chauffeur a night off and drive himself the three miles to the party. If push came to shove he could always ring to be picked up if he had one too many.

Esther met him at the door.

"Mr Forrester. How good of you to come."

"The pleasure is all mine." He smiled his most charming smile and noted that it seemed to have hit home to a certain extent.

"Now then, do come and have a drink. We Brits have a rather caricature impression that Australians drink more or less constantly, is it such a caricature Mr Forrester?"

"To be honest there is a new health-loving breed who drink herb tea and eat low cholesterol stuff, but I must admit to being of the old school. I do drink like a bloody fish I'm afraid. For God's sake call me Dwight will you."

"Of course. I'm Esther, and I must admit that I rather drink like a fish too. Now you will find that there are a few fearfully stuffy types here tonight but don't let them cramp your style. I believe that parties are for letting your hair down and enjoying yourself, how about you?"

He grinned. "On the bloody button Esther, tell you what, if anyone spoils your night by being over stuffy, you give me their name and number, and I'll expose them on page 5."

"My, what a simply marvellous idea. Come on, this way."

She led the way through the fine old entrance hall where Montgomery's steel band were banging merrily away and into the drawing room where drinks were being served. Esther marched over to a long table which was weighed down with copious quantities of all manner of alcohol.

"Champagne, or something stronger?"

"Ah bugger it, if we're not standing on ceremony I'll have a scotch." She poured two thumping great tumblers full and raised her glass to him. They chatted for a while and despite herself she found herself laughing at his stories. When he suggested that she join him "over the fence" at his place one day she was happy to accept. Then she spotted Cornelius and waved him over.

"Dwight, this is my wretched nephew Cornelius, remember, the clot who forgot to invite you."

Cornelius was looking utterly resplendent in full white tie and tails. He beamed at Dwight and extended a hand. "Why Mr Forrester, it is indeed a great pleasure. Please forgive my oversight, in truth I have spent a lot of time away of late and I'm not particularly up to speed with local matters. Well Auntie Esther, who would ever have thought that one so powerful and influential would come to one of your parties."

Dwight scowled a little. "Don't be so silly mate. I'm just an Aussie out for a good time."

Esther beamed. "And quite right to. Cornelius, I expect you to look after Dwight this evening. He has told me that he likes a drink, so ensure that his glass stays full. Introduce him to people but don't you dare lumber him with any tedious stuffed shirts. Now I best get on with being a hostess."

As Cornelius worked his way from room to room, and from group to group, he was impressed with Dwight's unaffected charm. He had no airs and graces about him, and had the rare knack of being able to put everyone at ease instantly and get them to talk. His capacity for whisky was spectacular as tumbler after tumbler disappeared without any marked effect. All around them the oceans of booze were beginning to take a toll. Voices got louder and ties disappeared as guests headed for the throbbing calypso sounds rolling out from the back of the house. It was a little after eleven when the group that they were mingling with was broken into by two extraordinary-looking twins. They were dressed identically in long black dresses with towering stiletto heels. They had bleached wild hair and they were made up to kill. When they spoke they had light London accents.

"Good evening Mr Forrester, I'm Kip."

"And I'm Kim, Mr Forrester."

"And nobody can ever tell us apart," said Kip.

"At least not with our clothes on," said Kim.

"Which isn't always the case," said Kip.

"Oh, not always the case at all," said Kim.

"You see we do have one or two small distinguishing marks on our bodies," said Kip.

"If you know where to look of course," said Kim.

"We're model girls you see," said Kip.

"And we would like to take this photo opportunity," said Kim. With this they both threw their arms around Dwight, pressed their cheeks against his, and cast seductive, provocative looks to a black, dreadlocked cameraman who had appeared out of nowhere. He hit the motor setting on his expensive Japanese camera, and within a second had fired off seventeen shots. The girls broke away giggling. Cornelius, along with the rest of the group, was agape.

"Well, Good Lord, I must confess Dwight that I haven't the first clue who these guests are."

Dwight laughed heartily. "Nor will you have my old mate, nor will you have." He gave Montgomery a slap on the back which almost knocked him off his feet. "Bloody good effort mate, I like your style. Here," he handed him a card, "ring this bloke up. We'll always find work for photographers with a bit of initiative. And you two lovelies, well, if you present yourselves at Forrester International we'll find a slot to put you in the paper I'm sure, though I figure that our readers will want a bit of a look at the old birthmarks, what do you say?"

"Enchanted," said Kip.

"Delighted," said Kim.

And then, as quickly as they had materialised, they were gone as if they had never been there at all.

"Dwight, I really must apologise, I have no idea how . . . "

"Don't be so bloody silly Cornelius. No need to apologise. I don't mind one of my rivals printing my picture with that pair, Jesus, it will do my reputation no harm at all."

Cornelius beamed with relief. "Oh well that's fine then. Splendid. Another drink?"

By midnight the whisky was at last having an impact on Dwight. His charm was still absolute but there were a few signs of wear and tear. Cornelius took him by the arm.

"Tell you what old boy, I don't know about you, but I'm beginning to feel a bit pissed. Esther would kill me if I didn't show you the garden. It's her pride and joy you know. Let's go get a bit of air and clear the heads a bit."

They strolled out of the back of the house and down the old steps of the terrace. A path cut a line across a huge lawn which shimmered in the winter moonlight. A manicured hedge at the end of a path had been shaped carefully to make a natural arch. As they

131

strolled through Dwight suddenly felt himself grasped by a vice-like grip and something was held over his mouth. He tried to struggle, but the arms that held him were far too powerful, and very quickly he found that he was floating slowly down a moonlit sky on a cotton wool cloud into an endless black void.

When he awoke he felt great hammer blows crashing away at the inside of his head. He was utterly shattered and was consumed by an overwhelming sense of depression. He peeled his eyes open to find himself in a strange room. He made to sit up, but the top of his throat seemed to want to lift off through the top of his head and he fell back and groaned.

"Good morning Dwight."

The sound of the voice persuaded him to once again peel his eyes open. He saw that Cornelius was sitting by his bed doing a crossword. He had changed out of his tails into a Harris Tweed jacket with baggy corduroy trousers. He smiled encouragingly. He held out a glass of water.

"Here, drink some of this. You'll need it."

Dwight slurped the water greedily then looked around again. "Where the hell are we Cornelius? And what the hell happened? Where's my bloody clothes?"

Cornelius spoke in a soothing voice. "It's all right Dwight, everything is OK. We're in London." Memory started to crawl back into Dwight's addled brain. Moonlight, an arch in a hedge, a vice-like grip, and fading away . . .

"Wait a minute, some bastard jumped me, they grabbed me in the bloody garden . . . "

"Try not to excite yourself too much Dwight. You really will be very weak."

Realisation now slowly began to dawn. "Why you rotten bastard, it was you wasn't it, you set me up, I'll bloody . . . "

He started to raise himself up but Cornelius gently pushed him back. His body seemed oddly detached and he could do nothing to fight.

"Now, now. You're in such a bad state Dwight that I sincerely doubt that you could manage to bother even me. But I know for certain that you couldn't do a damn thing to Victor here. Say hello to Dwight, Victor."

"Hello Dwight," said Victor as he stepped forward from the back of the room.

"Hello Victor," said Dwight with resignation. "Something tells me that this is going to be a really, really bad day."

Cornelius carefully lit a cigarette. "I can't pretend that it will be the best day that you've ever had, but it is important that you try and keep a positive outlook on things. Now, sit up, drink some more water and we're going to watch a little film together."

Dwight gingerly sat up and sipped at his glass whilst Victor activated a video machine that sat on a small table at the end of the bed. When the picture came on it showed Dwight lying flat out on the same bed as he now occupied in his dinner trousers and shirt. He was asleep but slowly coming awake. He slowly sat up and looked about with a glazed expression, then he smiled as he saw something. Kip and Kim then came into the camera's view. One of them leant down and started to kiss him passionately as his arms were drawn around her. The other sat at the end of the bed and took off first his shoes, then his socks, then his trousers and then his underpants. She started to arouse him whilst casting smiles at the camera.

Dwight groaned. "Oh for God's sake guys, this is way over the top, nobody would dare use it, even I wouldn't dare use it, you can't print it, and in case you didn't know, I haven't got a bloody wife."

"A little patience Dwight. A little patience," said Cornelius.

On the screen the hugely aroused Dwight was tearing at one of the girl's dresses. As it came off to reveal her underwear the watching Dwight squinted at the screen with concern. First the bra was torn off and then the knickers. As the knickers slipped over the long smooth legs he groaned as the realisation sank home. "Ah for Christ's sake it's a bloody bloke."

At the front of the bed the second twin peeled off her dress to reveal her manhood to the camera with a smile. The camera now zoomed to show Dwight's face. Lust was momentarily replaced with confusion only to be once again overtaken by lust. He watched with astonished horror as the film showed him indulging in an array of sexual activities that he would never have believed himself capable of.

"Oh Jesus Christ switch it off. I can't believe it. Look at my face! I'm enjoying every minute!"

Victor stopped the video and Cornelius chuckled. "Don't look so horrified at yourself Dwight. The Ancient Greeks swore by it. You should count yourself rather lucky to have had such a skilled introduction. Do you realise that Arab visitors pay upwards of £15,000 for a night like the one you've just had with Kip and Kim and it hasn't cost you a penny."

"You mean this little caper cost you fifteen grand?"

"Good Lord no, I go back a long way with Kip and Kim. We help each other out every now and then. I get discount rates."

"You mean that you're . . . "

"Oh yes I'm . . . "

"Well I'll be buggered."

"You just were Dwight." Dwight cast him a murderous look then his features softened and miraculously he started to laugh.

"OK lads, fair cop. You live by the sword and all that. It's still far too explicit. Nobody could even think of printing this."

Cornelius smiled. "Oh I'm absolutely sure that they wouldn't, but, my oh my, wouldn't a few of your business competitors enjoy watching it."

Dwight pondered this for a moment then slowly nodded.

"You're right enough there. They'd bloody love it, the bastards. I'd be getting snide comments for ever. No, that's a nightmare. How much do you want?"

"Good God Dwight, you don't think we would set up something like this for money do you? Whatever do you take us for? That would be unforgivably vulgar. No, not money, in fact I believe that we will actually make you money. I really do."

"If not money, then what?"

"We want your paper to start a new campaign. A campaign that you will pursue with passion, zeal and ingenuity. It is just the kind of thing to give you added credibility which can only lead to a higher readership."

"What is it?"

"It is a thumpingly good patriotic campaign, you'll love it. Dwight, as of next week *The Globe* will become the champion of the

British Beef Industry."

Dwight exploded. "The British fucking beef industry! You must be bloody kidding. That's not our kind of story."

"Oh I think that you will find that it is. We have some splendid stories that you are going to cover. Real front-line investigative journalism. You're going to really love it, and there are extra perks as well."

"Like what?"

"Well firstly, I know that you are keen to make a bit of a mark in Hampshire and I must say that everyone was most taken with you last night. Just think how much affection everyone will hold for you when you embark on a lone and heroic campaign to save the countryside. There are a lot of beef farmers around Hampshire you know, and they will be ever so grateful."

Dwight nodded thoughtfully. "Yeah, all right, I can see that, go on."

Cornelius smiled. "Very soon we are going to see a new company formed to vigorously promote the sales of British beef. It is going to be a particularly well capitalised company, and it would be perfectly natural for it to place lots and lots of full-page advertisements in a paper that showed such unwavering support. Without haggling about rates of course."

It was Dwight's turn to smile. "Who the bloody hell are you guys?"

"Oh we're just hired hands doing our bit."

"Hired by who?"

"You'll find out in due course. May I assume that you're on board?"

"You may. Answer me one question. What the hell was the Micky Finn that you slipped me?"

"Lord knows. I got it from a friend of mine. He promised that it would have dramatic effects, you know, loosen reserve and raise libido. It seemed to work rather well didn't it. All I know is that it cost £200 and I reckon you'd get six months suspended if you were caught in possession of."

"So what next?"

"We'll run you back to Hampshire. We parked your car near the house. Then we need an appointment with you at nine o'clock sharp on Monday morning. You have an excellent young reporter called Ricky Myers on your books. Make sure that he is there too. He's the one we would like to cover the stories that we have in mind."

"And the video tape?"

"I have placed a copy somewhere safe. So long as you give us your best efforts I will return it on September 1. Believe it or not, you can trust my word, and you have it."

Cornelius held out his hand and Dwight shook. "For some strange bloody reason I do trust your word. I'll do my best. Can't say fairer than that. I actually believe that working with you guys could be a laugh."

Cornelius gave a mischievous smile. "And after last night, do you think you'll . . . "

"No I bloody won't. I'm an Aussie for Christ's sake. And no more bloody jokes about it."

"OK. No more jokes." Cornelius agreed.

"Promise?"

"Promise."

"Good. Well let's get back to Hampshire then. I'm supposed to be going hunting."

# CHAPTER SEVEN

## MOBILISATION

On the evening of January 25 Vince and Helen sat together in a near empty pub in Dolgellau, mid-Wales. It was a tired, dismal place with lots of scuffed plastic surfaces and faded pictures of forgotten places. A rather ugly 1950s fire was making a half-hearted effort to burn. It did little to take the damp chill out of the musty air. The landlord sat behind the bar watching a game show on the TV whilst his only other customer, a yellow-skinned pensioner, sat looking reproachfully at his half-pint glass.

"You stick with me babe, and I'll show you a life of real glamour." Vince winced as he sipped at his tepid beer and gave a rueful smile.

They were both tired. They had been on the road constantly for nine days and had driven nearly three thousand miles up and down Britain. Hopefully their task was nearly complete. They had set out to recruit twenty men. They had seen thirty-two and had signed up nineteen. What was encouraging was that they had only offered their proposal to nineteen and all of them had accepted with alacrity. The other thirteen hadn't seemed to be right.

"What time is it?" asked Helen.

"7.25. He said 7.30. Could I have another quick look at the file?" She reached into her case and passed it to him. "David Williams. Age 32. Pentre Isa farm, Dolgellau, Wales. 350 acres. Tenant. Farms 50 suckler cows and 400 ewes. Served in the Welsh Guards from 1980 to 1995. Two tours in Ulster, Falklands War and Gulf War. Rose to the rank of sergeant. Came out of the army to help on the farm when his father took ill with angina. He looks good."

"Yes," she agreed. "Very good."

At precisely 7.30 the door swung open and a man walked in

wearing a soaking wax jacket. He scanned the pub, spotted Vince and Helen, and walked over to their table. When he spoke he had a sing-song Welsh voice.

"I dare say you are the people I'm looking for."

"David is it?" asked Helen.

"It is indeed."

"Hi, I'm Helen McIntyre and this is Vincent Allenby."

"Oh my word. Things are looking up. I'm getting names now am I?"

Helen smiled warmly. "Yes, sorry about all the cloak and dagger stuff. You'll understand why I think. Let me get you a drink."

"Good lord no. Don't get up. I'll get these. What will you have?"

He returned back from the bar and sat down at the table. He tossed his sodden jacket onto the bench seat and pushed his fingers through his hair. "Bugger of a day out there. Been out on the fell all afternoon lambing sheep. I lost three bloody lambs, though it might work out cheaper losing them rather than keeping them this year." He smiled and gave a sad shake of the head. He was under six feet tall but he was powerfully built, even though he seemed rather shapeless under his thick sweater. His hair was wild and red and his features were bold and coarse. Many punches must have landed on his fighter's nose over the years and he obviously hadn't bothered shaving for several days. He yawned and uncoiled his body into a mighty stretch.

"Sorry about that. Bloody lambing time. I can't remember when I last had a decent night's sleep. It seems all the harder when you are working all hours that God sends only to lose money. Anyway, I'm sure you've had enough of farmers moaning. I rang Donald after we spoke last night. I couldn't get a thing out of him. He just told me to wait and see."

They had visited Donald Atkinson in Somerset the day before. Atkinson had served as a Lieutenant in the Welsh Guards for three years in the late eighties and had passed on the name of his old sergeant, David Williams. Unlike Williams, he was a gentleman farmer with 500 acres of prime West Country land. He hadn't hesitated when they had put their proposition to him.

Williams took a long swig at his beer. "So come on, what's it all about then?"

"Donald was sure that you would be able to keep a confidence," said Vince.

"That was big of him. Yes, I have always had a fair control of my mouth."

"Good. If what we have to tell you is of no interest we would be obliged if you kept it to yourself."

"No problem."

"OK then." Vince felt very conscious of the fact that this was the thirty-third time that he had embarked on this pitch in nine days. "We have been hired to try and end the Beef Crisis." As with all the others, he noted David's sudden look of amazement, but he hadn't been able to come up with a better way of broaching the topic and had decided that the direct approach was best. "I know, I know, it sounds like an impossibility, but hear me out. Within a month there is going to be a major new company formed to promote and sell British beef. The people who are starting up this business are injecting £500 million, i.e. they are not messing about. There is going to be a massive advertising and marketing campaign which we believe will have a positive effect. However we are also going to be running several more covert operations alongside the official campaign. I will go into more detail about this later. In short, these operations will be unconventional, risky, possibly illegal and maybe even dangerous. The operations will be aimed at destabilising and damaging anyone who is a perceived enemy to the British beef industry. We are looking for twenty men to sign up to help us to undertake these operations. Over the last nine days we have recruited nineteen. We have been recommended men with an army background and a strong vested interest in the British beef industry. Each one has been put forward by someone who has served with them in the past and has signed up themselves. Obviously your name was put forward by Donald Atkinson.

"We will need you to be able to come and join us full time from February 1st and you will not finish until September 1. The pay is £5,000 per month and you will be enrolled as a consultant for the new company. We will pay three months in advance to enable you to find someone to come and cover for you on the farm whilst you are away. You must have an up-to-date passport and a moderately clean driving licence. If you are experiencing any problems with your mortgage or bank in the light of the current crisis we can arrange for all of your borrowings to be transferred to a friendly bank at a subsidised rate of 6%. Should our operations be a success, I will tell you of the terms under which we are working in due course, then a bonus of £20,000 will be payable on September 1. Should you agree to join us we would insist that you say nothing about your activities to anyone other than immediate family.

"We know the pressure that you are under and we know how much anger you must feel. We can offer you a real chance to use all the training that you received in the army to kick the bastards back hard; right where it hurts. How am I sounding?"

"Like the bloody Messiah boy. Where do I sign?"

Helen smiled. "The signing bit is metaphorical. Welcome aboard."

They talked through plans with David for three hours. He gave them all of his bank details and it was agreed that an accountant would him visit in a few days time to organise the wrapping up of his mortgage and overdraft. They gave him the address of a cafe in Glasgow and asked him to be there for eight in the morning sharp on February 1. As he drove his old Land Rover through the rainy night, David's head was spinning. The sense of misery and despair that he had tried so hard to stave off on the windswept fell that afternoon had now completely evaporated. He felt like an old gun that had been left discarded and forgotten in a cupboard for years until being retrieved, oiled, loaded and pointed ready to shoot. Now the rotten bastards would feel what it was like to be at the sharp end. For the first time in ages he started to sing loudly as he threw his vehicle around the tight corners of the road home.

At the same time that David Williams sang his way home, Marcus was staring hard across the table at Bill Bamford. He had spent ten hours sitting in the boardroom of Bamfords Ltd the day before and he had now been there for over thirteen hours. Old man Bamford was a twenty-two stone sixty year old and hard as Sheffield nails. His two sons were in their thirties and must have weighed an aggregate of over thirty-five stones. Mrs Bamford, incredibly enough, would have weighed no more than six stones dripping wet and she perched at the end of the boardroom table like a nervous sparrow. All three of the Bamford men had Marcus fixed with ferocious stares. They shared the same red faces and piggy eyes and seemed to act and think as one.

When he had arrived for his nine o'clock appointment the day before to announce that he wanted to buy the company, he had worried for a minute that they would hang him up on a hook and butcher him. The boardroom had been in instant uproar. Old man Bamford had told him in no uncertain terms that the Wakefield abattoir had been in the family for over a hundred years and in the bloody family it was bloody well staying.

When they calmed down a bit, Marcus pointed out some of the points that he and Gideon had been able to glean from the Bamford accounts. Even though the company had managed to avoid overdraft for a full century, the spectre of the need for a bank was clearly on the horizon. The lean years since the BSE crisis had stripped the company of much of its lovingly built up cash reserves, and heavy borrowing was inevitable as the company was going to have to invest large sums of money to conform with onerous new EEC regulations.

By the afternoon they were talking terms. Unbelievably enough, after a solid nineteen hours they were still talking terms. Marcus rued the fact that the last of his target abattoirs happened to be in Yorkshire. Throughout the day they had left the heating deliberately high and he had doggedly refused to either remove his jacket or loosen his tie. At last it was time for the angry approach. He crashed his file down on the table and drew some heart from the fact that all three of them flinched. He allowed more than the usual dose of Yorkshire to filter into his raised voice. "Right. That's it. You've pissed me about for long enough. Now listen up. This is the final offer and if you don't like it, I'm off to see Blenkinsops first thing in the morning. Five million for the business and that's your lot. For you Mr Bamford, I'll extend your contract to five years, six weeks a year holiday, £50,000 a year and I'll throw in a new Jag. For you Mrs Bamford, three years at £25,000, same holidays and a £15,000 car. For the lads, five years at £30,000, Land Rover

Discoveries, three weeks holiday. And that is bloody that. Here's my hand Bamford, for the love of God shake it."

Bamford stared long and hard at Marcus's hand, then with agonising slowness he hauled his vast bulk out of his chair and stood up. For a further moment he looked daggers at Marcus, then his beetroot face split into a grin and he took the proffered hand.

"Mr Dalrymple, I do believe that we have deal."

"Wonderful. Now for the love of God, why don't you pour us all a drink."

"Aye, well why not, now that business is concluded it would seem more than proper for us to indulge in a tipple. Mavis, go fetch some bottles of ale and some glasses. And ring the Crown and tell 'em we'll be wanting food for five and that Mr Dalrymple will be staying another night." Mavis soon scuttled in with bottles of brown ale and the four men drank thirstily. Marcus grinned through the froth that had collected around his lips.

"I'd have gone to six million you know."

"Aye, and I'd a taken four."

They both roared with laughter. Matador had secured a large abattoir in Wakefield to go along with the ones Marcus had already bought in Glasgow, Birmingham and Reading. The four plants they believed were capable of butchering sufficient beasts to supply 10% of the country's beef market.

The day after, there were twenty men sat around the table at the Black Loch meeting room. They were all young, none of them were older than thirty. They wore smart suits and lovingly pressed shirts. Their attention was latched onto the figure of Sir Alistair who was standing with his back to them staring out across the black waters of the loch. At last he turned and gave them a craggy smile.

"Welcome gentlemen. You're all sat there wondering what the hell is going on and I'm going to tell you. What I'm going to tell you is highly confidential and if one of you breathes a word I promise that I will seek you out and personally crucify you. Is that understood?"

They all nodded earnestly.

"Now, I have spent a week scouring the personnel records for the company and I have concluded that you gentlemen are the best and brightest that we have in our ranks. You have all done well. You all have it in you to do better.

"Last week I agreed terms to sell McIntyre holdings to an American consortium. The City will probably get the news next week unless the lawyers get in a muddle. Most of the McIntyre family money will be going straight into a new company which wrote its articles of association last week. Initially it will be a private limited company but our intention will be to float within two years. Our core activity will be the retail of British beef. We are going to launch British beef on the population with more razzmatazz and vigour than anyone has ever even dreamed of. The company will start life with £500 million in capital and we're going to give it a real go. We are currently building up our infrastructure by acquisition and over the last three weeks we have bought four major abattoirs, a distribution fleet of 130 chilled wagons, three processing companies and five chilled distribution warehouses. We already have the structure to source, kill, butcher, pack and deliver 10% of the country's beef needs. Our next phase is to acquire retail outlets.

"As yet our new company, Matador, has no executives. The board at the moment consists of myself as Chairman, Marcus Dalrymple as Vice Chairman and Gideon Rosenberg as Financial Director. There will be slots for a Sales Director, an Operations Director, a Distribution Director, a Personnel Director and a Marketing Director. I intend to make these appointments on April 1, 1999 and I would like to make them from those of you who are sitting around the table. I want a young company. I want a vibrant company. I want an aggressive company. And I want you gentlemen to be my executives. In front of you you will find an envelope which contains a contract of employment. Take it away, have a think, and come back if you want to sign it. If not, please leave the envelope by the front door when you leave. You have 'til eleven o'clock. It's hard I know, but I want men who can make a decision. Off you go."

He watched with amusement as they scuttled out of the door

clutching their envelopes and felt a tinge of sadness at the thought that his own part in the new Company would probably only be a brief one. The terms in the contracts were particularly generous, and meant a substantial rise for all of them. Generous share options when the company floated offered a huge incentive. He wasn't in the least surprised when all of the young men were sat back at the table within an hour with every contract signed.

"Welcome to Matador, gentlemen. I have agreed with our American friends that you may be released from your notice obligations to McIntyre Holdings so you can all start more or less immediately. Take two days to clear your desks. Head office will be here at Black Loch but you will be on the road most of the time. Most of the company's management structure is already in place at the companies that we have acquired. You will report back here in two days time to collect your new cars, phones, faxes and computers."

Sir Alistair pulled a cloth away from a an easel-mounted map of Britain. "Here is our market. We have divided the map up into ten equal population zones with five million people in each. You will work in pairs. One pair for each zone. Our target is to supply half a million people with their beef in each of these zones. We intend to do it in two ways. Firstly you need to get out there and buy butchers' shops, and lots of them. Wherever possible we want to leave the current staff in place on reasonable contracts. We then intend to recruit a doorstep sales force to knock on every door to inform the public who we are, where we are and to offer our home delivery service. This will be backed up by a massive nationwide advertising campaign that will commence on March 1.

"Think momentum. Think profile. We have a wonderful product to sell which nobody has seriously gone out to sell before. We will have all kinds of promotions and offers. It's going to be your show." He pointed at the map. "These are your territories. You hold the cards. Come to me with every idea and I'll look at it. We've got plenty of budget. I want energy. I want initiative. I want results.

"Matador is going to pick one hell of a fight, but I tell you what Gentlemen, we're going to win it."

144

Cornelius arrived at the impressive head office of Forrester International a little before nine in the morning. His name rang all the right bells at the front desk and he was soon in the lift heading for the 14th floor with some regulation canned music in his ears. He was met at the door by Dwight's personal secretary who led him down the corridor to the office.

The interior of the office came as something of a surprise to Cornelius. He had been expecting something gaudy and brash in line with the style of *The Globe* and the flamboyant image that Dwight Forrester had created for himself. Instead the room was merely functional. One half of the room was filled by a basic meeting table whilst a desk and some visiting chairs filled the half by the window. The walls were filled with cuttings from back issues and a large cheese plant was working its way doggedly up the wall from its place by the window.

As Cornelius entered Dwight rose from behind his desk. As he stood up he cursed roundly. "Bloody sodding bastards." He clutched at his back. "Tell you what mate, I'm not sure I'm cut out for this hunting lark. I'm a bloody stiff old cripple for days after. Sit down will you. Jean, get Mr St John some coffee, and no bloody calls either, even if it's his wretched Auntie."

Cornelius sat and pulled out his cigarettes with a raised eyebrow.

"Yeah, sure, no problem." Dwight slid an ashtray over. "So, no big minder today, you're feeling confident are you?"

Cornelius smiled "By the look of the state your in I don't think that I have too much to fear. Kip and Kim do a lovely massage you know . . . "

"Now look. We had a deal. No bloody jokes you pommie bastard."

"Quite right. I'm sorry. No more jokes."

Dwight shook his head ruefully. "I still don't believe it. Anyway, before we get started I've got a condition and if you don't like it you can get stuffed."

"Go on." Cornelius felt a mild twinge of concern.

"I got in early and I've done a bit of homework on this beef business. Now I've no idea what you have in mind but I figure that you're going to have a go at imported beef, which is why you need *The Globe*, yeah?"

"Could be."

"Well, that's fair dinkum. I've no great problem with that. We've played the patriotic card enough times in the past. It sells papers, particularly when there's a war on. But look here, there's no way this paper is saying anything bad about Australian beef and that's final. My uncle Ted's a beef farmer and he'd never forgive me. Now if that's not on you can bugger right off."

Cornelius grinned with relief. "Absolutely Dwight. We would simply never dream of doing anything against our friends from the Antipodes. You need have no fears on that front."

"Good. Shall I get Ricky Myers in then?"

"Not just yet. There is something we need to discuss first. Your company owns a record label, Sunshine Records, you purchased it four years ago."

"Correct."

"And over the last year its shares have soared somewhat due to the success of one of its bands."

"Yeah, The Orange Boys."

Cornelius nodded. "The Orange Boys. A wonderful story. Two young lads from the streets of Liverpool come from nowhere to adorn the bedroom walls of half of the teenagers of Britain. Talented boys too, it seems that they are carrying the dreaded 'new Beatles' tag rather well. They have a fiercely anti-establishment stance and are really rather articulate beneath the Scouse accents. You must be rather pleased with them."

Dwight nodded. "Yeah, they're great. Mind you, it's all bollocks you know. They don't speak like that at all in real life. It's all a sham. They have a real sharp bastard as an agent. If he says smash up a hotel room, they smash it up. If he says kick a bouncer whilst on stage, they kick him. It's all out of a handbook. Things you need to do to sucker the press into giving you free publicity and turning you into mega-stars. The only thing that those boys are interested in is money I tell you."

Cornelius leaned back in his chair. "Good. That exactly confirms everything that I've heard. I would like you to arrange a photo shoot. The kind of thing that you've done before, in fact it has been a couple of months since you last used them in the paper."

A sly look came on to Dwight's face. "What kind of photo shoot?"

"Oh a low-key discreet kind of affair. A hotel suite. No roadies. Just the lads, the photographer and a couple of pretty girls. I thought Kip and Kim would do rather well, don't you think?"

A slow grin spread across Dwight's face. "Oh you bastard Cornelius. The biggest problem will be their agent. He won't let them go anywhere without him."

"Yes I heard that. I don't see too much problem there. I'm sure if you were to suggest lunch, he would be quite happy to let the lads get on with things."

"OK, I'll set it up. When?"

"Next Wednesday. I have the hotel all arranged."

"Next Wednesday! Impossible, they have a massive schedule. I couldn't possibly . . . "

"Of course you could Dwight, you own them, remember?"

Dwight chuckled. "Yeah, fair enough, you really don't piss about do you."

Cornelius handed him a sheet of paper. Dwight dialled a number. "Ray, it's Dwight Forrester . . . yeah, I'm good. Look, I need you to have the Orange Boys at the Caledonia Hotel in Mayfair at 11.00 a.m. on Wednesday morning . . . I don't give a damn what they are supposed to be doing, cancel it and get them there . . . oh piss off Ray, go and read the contract . . . I need a feature and I'm going to do it and you can't do a bloody thing about it, so get them there or I'm going to sue your arse for default of contract. See you there . . . yeah I'm coming, I want to buy you lunch, there's a few things we need to chat about . . . fine . . . 11.00 on Wednesday. See you."

He put the receiver down with evident satisfaction. "He's one hell of a jumped-up little git that one. It's just lucky he doesn't know how to read a contract." He chuckled contentedly. "I don't suppose you're going to tell me what you plan to do with them. I figure that I can guess the first bit."

"I thought that you might. Why don't you do a little more

147

research. Get one of your people to dig out some background on a chap called Ignatious Loyola. You'll soon get a clue."

Dwight dutifully wrote the name down. "You want Ricky in now?"

"Yes please."

Dwight hit the intercom. "Jean, get Ricky Myers up here please and hurry up with the coffee."

Five minutes later there was a tap on the door and Ricky Myers walked in. He cast rather a shabby, skinny figure in jeans, jacket and collarless shirt. His face was thin and bony, and the stubble on his chin exaggerated his pasty complexion. When he spoke, his voice was hard, flat and straight from East London.

"Morning boss."

"Morning Ricky. I've a chap here I want you to meet. Now he's a real toff so you're going to hate him at first sight. Well, that's just bloody tough because he's sold me on a big new concept and we're going to be launching *The Globe* on a major new crusade. So shake hands, sit down and listen up. This is Mr Cornelius St John."

Cornelius shook Ricky's small bony hand. Ricky sat down and lit up. He shook with an impressive morning cough then spoke.

"OK then boss, so what's the big crusade? Even more tits by page 5? Take the lid off the 'Princess murdered by Corgi hit squad' story?"

Forrester laughed. "No mate. Nothing so mucky and crude. No this is a proper, fine crusade for a blue-chip paper like ours to embark on. We're going to become the champions of the British beef industry, defenders of the salt-of-the-earth farmers against the scheming politicos and the the devious wiles of Johnny Foreigner. Don't you worry mate, you're going to love it."

Ricky's face was a picture of astonishment. "Farmers? Beef? Are you sure you're feeling OK Guv?"

"Never better Ricky boy. Sure it sounds a bit dull on the surface, but once we get into it it will stick at least 5% on the circulation figures and fetch us a whole new breed of advertisers. Go on Cornelius, tell him where we start."

"Certainly Dwight."

Forrester felt a wholly unfamiliar nervousness as Cornelius

started to speak. The ruthlessly efficient nature of his own entrapment had led him to assume that the stories they would want in his paper would be of a similarly high standard. However if they were not, he would be doomed to printing successive agricultural pieces which would cause his circulation to collapse. However, as Cornelius spoke in a clipped voice he found himself relaxing. The first story was nice. Easy to understand, easy to present, with a nice easy message, good classic tabloid fare. It led on to an even better story, one that would cause outrage and, best of all, it nailed an archetypal villain who couldn't possibly sue.

"I think that takes care of February. I'll brief you up on more later." Cornelius concluded.

Forrester jumped in. "Now hold on. You obviously only know half the job here. These stories are sweethearts Cornelius, they're right on the button. Beauties. The first one is no bother, but the second will need preparation. You can't just waltz into a country like that, do your stuff and bugger off. No way. I need to find someone on the ground to case it all out and have things ready for when you get out there. Now if there are more stories like this you better tell us now so we can case everything out in advance ."

Cornelius nodded. "Of course. Good point. Can I . . . ?" He lifted an eyebrow and glanced over at Ricky.

"Yeah, no worries. Rick's my main man. My right hand. You can talk about anything with Ricky. He's been with me a long time and he knows me well; well enough to know that I would personally chew his bollocks off if he ever crossed me."

"Good."

It was after four in the afternoon when Cornelius at last stood up to leave. "OK Ricky. Get yourself to the Highland Hotel in Perth tomorrow night and Helen will meet up with you. Say eight o'clock in the bar?"

"Lovely job. Will she know me?"

"Just carry a copy of tomorrow's *Globe*."

"Good. See you around, Cornelius." Ricky left the room with a grin of approval. Cornelius shrugged and spoke to Forrester.

"You seem happy Dwight."

"I am. Whoever is calling the shots is no mug. These stories are

sweet. The whole campaign is sweet. You should just have come
and seen me and talked about it, I might have been keen without
having to stick my dick up any bums."

"I doubt it Dwight."

"Yeah, you're right. I'd just have told you to piss off. I'm going
to print on Friday, is that OK with you?"

"Splendid. We'll want a hard-hitting editorial as well."

"I'll write it myself."

"See you on Wednesday Dwight."

"See you then."


On the same Monday morning David Williams got off the train
at Glasgow Central Station and made his way across town for half
a mile to the appointed cafe. He had tidied up all his affairs, and
hired a neighbour's teenage son to help his father out with lambing
the sheep. The day when he had transferred all of his borrowings
over to Vince's friendly bank he had felt a huge weight lifted off his
back. Now, as he strode through the thin Glaswegian drizzle he felt
as excited as a child heading off on holiday.

The Cafe was a mean affair in a street where most of the shops
were up for sale. He ordered coffee and scanned the room for
somewhere to sit. He spotted his old Lieutenant, Donald Atkinson,
at a table at the back of the room. He was reading the paper, and
gave a delighted hoot when David joined him.

Atkinson beamed with delight. "Bloody Hell sarge, so you went
for it?"

"Did you seriously think I wouldn't?"

"No, not at all. So how's things."

They were early. Contact wasn't due for another hour, and they
talked about old times and new problems over several cups of
coffee. At nine o'clock the cafe door opened and Helen stepped in
and scanned the room. She spotted the two men at the back, smiled
and left. They paid up and stepped out to find a coach waiting a
little way down the road. Helen waved them over and they
climbed on board. As they made their way to a seat at the back she
spoke into the tour guide microphone.

"OK gentlemen. This is David Williams and Donald Atkinson.

They are our last pick-up. We are now going to head for the hills."

It was an hour's drive to the farm in the hills above Stirling. The farm belonged to the McIntyre estate and was run by Jimmy Sloan who was a wiry, hard swearing sixty-eight year old who refused point blank to even consider retirement.

A long track wound round the edge of a hill and down into a secluded valley where the main steading was built. The coach dropped them off in the yard and Helen led them away. They walked two miles further into the tight valley until they came to an encampment by a small copse of trees. The valley had turned a slow corner from the farm, which meant that the camp was quite invisible from the yard.

There were fourteen small sleeping tents, three latrine tents and a large green command tent. All of the gear was from army surplus auctions and was instantly familiar to all of them. As they looked about the scene laughing and exchanging jokes a fierce voice split the mountain air.

"Come on you horrible bastards, stop gossiping like a bunch of washer women and see if you can remember how to fall in. Come on!! Move!!!"

The command came from a squat, tough-looking man with cropped hair and huge shoulders. Instinct took hold of all of them, and more or less immediately they stood to attention in two ranks.

The flap on the command tent opened and Victor stepped out looking gigantic in his combat fatigues. With him he had another man in uniform who looked less familiar with his attire and surroundings. Victor stood in front of them and spoke.

"Good afternoon gentlemen. Welcome to your new home. You will be here for three weeks and you will probably hate it. I am Victor and this is Sergeant Major Atkins. We are both from the Royal Marines. The third gentleman is Bob, and the most recent institution that he has frequented is Wormwood Scrubs prison. Now I have reviewed all of your service records and unfortunately myself and Sergeant Major Atkins are the only Royal Marines on the team. This is unfortunate because it means that the rest of you are ponces.

"Our main job over the next three weeks is to try and get you out of the poncy habits that your old poncy regiments taught you and to mould you into the kind of outfit that the extortionate amounts of money that we are paying you warrants. I am now going to split you into pairs. You will then go to your tents which are numbered from one to ten. Inside the tent you will find your kit. You will take five minutes to put it on and then report back here. You will be chuffed to bits to hear that my friend sergeant major Atkins here will be taking us for a little jog. We will start with five miles today and go up by half a mile a day from then on."

He read out a list of pairs and the men darted off to the tents. Helen came over.

"Well my goodness Victor, I never guessed what a horrid fierce man you really are."

He beamed. "I'm wicked. Seventeen and a half stone of pure Nigerian wicked. Are you staying a bit?"

"No. I best move it. See you on Friday."

"Sure. Ciao."

As Donald and David changed they spoke.

"Bloody Hell David, how fit are you?"

"Not bad I suppose. I'm up and down the hills with the sheep, but I figure it will be tough going keeping up with those two hard buggers."

And it was. An hour and a half later the twenty recruits were sprawled on the floor coughing and groaning. Victor and his sergeant major stood over them with contemptuous expressions.

Victor, who was barely out of breath, spoke. "OK ladies, you've done yourselves proud. There's tea in the main tent. In you go. We'll make a start." Wednesday morning.

Helen and Ricky had been on the road for two hours. She had picked him up from the hotel a little after eight and they had driven north. They were headed for a farm six miles to the west of Inverness. At first she had taken rather a dislike to the brash reporter, but slowly she had peeled away the hard front to find the interesting man behind. He had grilled her about farming and the state of the industry for the whole duration of their journey. He picked up quickly and had a receptive mind. As they drove out of

Inverness and started to wind around small country lanes he fell silent for a while. At last he spoke.

"It's a proper bastard isn't it. I hadn't realised at all. I don't suppose many will have realised. City folk have nothing to do with farmers. We just see rich bastards in big 4x4's who tell us to piss off when we walk on their land. I like this though. All of us hacks dream of doing something good you know. We all pretend we like the exposing the rich and famous bit, but it stinks really. The bosses want it, the bosses pay through the nose for it, and we provide it or we get fired. But this is more like it. I think you might just have a convert on your hands."

She smiled. This was something of a bonus. "Brilliant. I'm sure your stories will be all the better if they can come from the heart."

He laughed. "Oh I'll have the grannies in tears and their husbands frothing at the mouth with righteous indignation, just you wait and see."

She adopted a serious air. "Now don't be too upset if they are a bit off with you. I am afraid that Billy isn't over-keen on the idea at all, but I have persuaded him that it is for the best. He hasn't any great love for the tabloid press."

Ricky looked rueful. "He's not on his own. Mine is the kind of job that makes you want to fudge when people at a party ask you what you do. Don't worry, I'm used to it. I've got a hide like a buffalo."

They pulled into the yard just after half past ten. It was a hill farm and all the buildings were very run down. Two sorry looking cannibalised tractors stood at the end of the yard. A cold north wind was gently lifting the corrugated iron sheets that had been used to patch the roofs, making them groan and creak. The farm seemed very silent as they stepped out; the feeling of isolation and decay was all-pervading.

Helen walked over to the house and tapped on the peeled back door. Presently it was answered by a happy-looking lady in her sixties. Her face lit up when she saw her visitor.

"Och, Helen, I was so chuffed when I heard you were coming. Will you come in and have a cup of tea or do you want to find the men first?"

"We'll have a look for the men, Mary. Now don't you trouble yourself, we'll dig them out." She cocked an ear. "Listen, that sounds like a quad bike."

From the yard they could see the distant figure of a man on a four-wheeler motor bike making his way down the side of the moor. He was driving fast and bouncing over the tussocky grass. Soon the bike roared into the yard and skidded to halt in front of Helen and Ricky.

The man on the bike was in his early thirties. He was clad in a thick waterproof jacket that was splattered with mud that had been sprayed up by the wheels of the bike. His face was remarkably striking. It was lean to the stage where it was gaunt. His skin was stretched tight over the protruding bones. He had no colour at all and fierce dark eyes burned with permanent anger. He looked hard and fit. He didn't get up from the bike to greet them. He couldn't. He had no legs.

Helen bent down and hugged him warmly. "How are you Billy?"

A small smile. "Nae bad."

"This is Ricky, the reporter."

"Aye, so it is." He turned the dark eyes to Ricky and held him in a brooding gaze before looking back at Helen. "Dad's coming down on the tractor. He'll be a while. Come and see this."

They followed the bike around the back of the sheds. Billy pulled a sliding door that opened on to a straw filled pen containing three black bullocks. He tapped the backside of one with his stick until it reluctantly heaved itself to its feet. "There you go Helen. What d'ya think of him. I might just make you work for your money a bit at Perth in a couple of years."

Helen walked all around the young beast giving him a thorough once-over. At last she spoke. "He's a beauty Billy. You should be proud."

They fell into conversation about Angus breeding and the pedigree market. Ricky stood in the doorway, a rather forgotten figure. The sound of a tractor in the yard stopped the conversation.

A tall man climbed down and marched over. He had the same hard, gaunt face as his son. It was wreathed in a leathery smile as he shook hands with Helen. The smile vanished when he was introduced to Ricky.

"Come on, we'll go in." He ordered.

There was a metal frame at the back door. Billy parked the bike under a bar, then reached up his arms and lifted himself off the bike and into a wheelchair. Inside they took seats in the small lounge and Mary served tea. Billy eventually broke the small talk.

"I don't like this Helen. I don't want any charity."

"Listen Billy, I keep telling you, this isn't about charity. We're going to start fighting back, and we have persuaded *The Globe* to help us. Now they are not in the business of writing stories that say 'Oh dear, the beef crisis is a bit of a shame isn't it', they need more. They need stories to catch the public mood. Surely you must see that?"

"Aye I ken Helen. I ken well enough." Once again he fixed Ricky with his hard eyes. "But you listen up. I won't have any rubbish looking for sympathy right. You can make me angry, that's fair enough, but I won't have you make me pathetic. If you do, I'll break your scrawny neck."

Ricky held his gaze. "Fair enough."

Billy's expression softened a degree. "What can I tell you then?"

"Tell me what you like. Tell me the story."

"Not much to tell. I was in the Paras. I was eighteen when they sent us to the Falklands. We fought our way all the way to Port Stanley. It was a night attack. I heard my mate get hit when we got collared by a mortar bombardment and had to fall back. He was screaming. I ran back out to get him. I was pulling him back when another mortar round hit us. It killed him and took both my legs. That was the end of me as a soldier."

"You were decorated I believe."

"Aye, Military Cross."

Ricky looked over to Billy's father. "I believe you also have the Military Cross."

"Aye."

"When did you win yours?"

"Anzio, 1943. I've still got a piece of German metal in my shoulder."

Silence fell on the room. Helen began to feel miserably uncomfortable and was seriously regretting ever suggesting the idea to Vince in the first place. She was about to speak, but Ricky beat her to it. He had reached into his bag and came out with a bottle of whisky.

"OK chaps, you can't abide me because I'm a cocky little bastard from London writing crappy stories for a crappy newspaper. Well, fair enough, but if I'm going to do this I might as well do it right. Now if you don't want to help me and you don't want to help your industry, well, why not do it for Helen here, because she deserves it." He took a long pull at the bottle and held it out to Billy. Slowly he took it, drank and passed it to his father. Ricky smiled, "That's more like it. So come on, tell me properly, and give me colour and sound and smell for Christ's sake."

As the bottle was passed round they painted Ricky his pictures. The Hellish, murderous firework display on the Falkland hills and the burning, blood-soaked beachhead on the Italian coast. He then took them outside and took pictures. They posed in front of the open shed with the three young bulls. They wore their medals and stared into the lens with burning pride. As he operated the camera Ricky felt the hairs on his neck stand up. The pictures were special, he knew it. The story was also special. When he shook hands before leaving he promised that he would be true to their wishes.

Helen glanced across to him as they drove back down the track.

"They are very special people."

He nodded thoughtfully. "Yes. It's humbling really."

"Will the story be good?"

"Oh, the story will be bloody fantastic. Fan-bloody-tastic."

A little before midnight on the same evening, Cornelius and Victor were sitting in an opulent suite in the Caledonia Hotel in Mayfair. Two young men were spark out on the vast bed. They lay in a messy heap amidst a chaos of rumpled sheets. Cornelius glanced at his watch.

"Shouldn't be long now."

Half an hour later there were small signs of movement on the bed. Finally there was a pained groan. One of the men sat up slowly and fought to focus his glazed eyes. As his vision cleared, the figures of Victor and Cornelius emerged from the fog. He shook his head angrily and groaned again.

His voice was pure Liverpool. "Who the fuck are you then?"

Cornelius smiled. "Well good evening Malcolm. How are you feeling."

Malcolm Lyle and Pete Swan were the 'Orange Boys', the biggest pop phenomenon of 1997. It was a year that had seen them hit the top of the charts four times and complete a sell out nationwide tour. Their brooding adolescent faces stared out petulantly from the walls of millions of teenagers, mostly girls. They had the angry pose of many such young men who had gone before them. As the world slowly came back into some kind of order, Malcolm's face took on a look of rage.

"Don't you good evening me you twat. What's going on?" He reached across the bed and started to shake the sleeping body of his friend. Quickly he managed to raise groans and Pete Swan dragged himself awake. "Come on Pete, we're getting out of here. I don't know who these perverted twats are but we're off."

"Actually, I'm afraid that you're not off just yet chaps. We need to have a little talk first."

Lyle leapt to his feet and lunged at Cornelius. He wasn't even half-way towards him when Victor stepped forward and slapped him hard across the face. The blow rocked him back and he fell on the bed. He sat up shakily with tears of humiliation in his eyes. His friend asked anxiously. "You all right there?"

His voice was quiet. "I'm fine."

"And I'm extremely glad to hear it," said Cornelius. "Now why don't you put your clothes on and I'm sure you'll feel better."

They obliged moodily. At one stage Lyle pitched into a litany of vicious threats, but when Victor merely laughed, he gave up. Eventually they sat on the settee whilst Cornelius showed them the video. For the most part they were silent, they just groaned miserably at a couple of the more explicit close-ups. When the tape finished Cornelius switched off the set and lit up a cigarette.

"Oh dear boys, oh deary, deary me."

"Oh yeah," spat Lyle, "So what then. Who's going to give a shit, this is 1998 in case you'd forgotten."

"I am actually well aware of the calendar thank you. By the way there is no need to put those Liverpool accents on quite so thick, we know full well that you don't really speak that way. You're from Heswall on the Wirral for goodness sake; it's all blue rinse and zimmer frames and nice pubs for retired bank managers."

This statement widened their eyes. When Swan spoke, his accent was much lighter. "Please tell us what this is all about. You can do what you like with the tape. Being bisexual is no big deal these days."

"Oh I agree wholeheartedly," said Cornelius. "Thankfully we live in enlightened times. I'm sure that lots of your fans will not mind in the very slightest when they see you having such a terrific time with Kip and Kim. But not all of them I'm afraid. I don't think those darling 13-year-old girls from Grimsby and Falkirk will share that enlightened view. I don't think they will have quite the sexual maturity to carry on putting your pictures on their walls when they see that you have popped your willies up another chap's bottom with such evident enthusiasm. Your record company will of course realise this rather quickly and all of those terrific royalties will dry up in the blink of an eye. You see, you can go on until you are blue in the face about your talent and artistic integrity, but in the end you are just pretty pin-up boys. The question is, do you want to be pretty pin-up boys raking in a fortune? Or do you want to disappear off the face of the planet to become another sad, has-been band with a small, but devoted gay following?"

The two young men exchanged a miserable glance, and the arrogance soon drained out of them. Lyle spoke, "OK. You win. What do you want?"

"That's better isn't it. We don't really want anything awful off you at all. Let me tell you how you are going to make a real splash when you start your new tour in March. And then come the spring, well, let's just say that come springtime you will be heroes, real heroes."

Cornelius told them. Their mouths were open with astonishment. But when they caught a taxi home later they agreed that it could have been worse.

Loads worse.

In fact when they thought about it they felt that it might actually be quite good.

Friday morning.

Sir Alistair looked up as the door to his office opened. Marcus Dalrymple strode in with a beaming smile. He tossed a copy of *The Globe* onto the desk. "Have a read of that then. I would rather say that the ball is rolling."

Sir Alistair picked up the paper and was amazed at the dramatic front page. It was dominated by a striking photograph of Billy Fraser and his father. Their proud, hard faces wore stares that bored into the camera. Behind them the interested faces of three young Angus bulls stared out of their pen. Both men wore medals on their dirty work-clothes. Billy sat on a four-wheel motor bike which emphasised the sad stumps of his legs. The photo was perfectly balanced and exuded power and passion.

"Bloody Hell," muttered Sir Alistair, "The boy knows how to take a picture."

The headline yelled out from under the haunting photo.

## 'BILLY'S RAGE AS ARMY BUYS ARGIE BEEF'

There wasn't much text on the front page, most of the article spread over onto the second page which showed two photos of the Fraser men in uniform from their days in the army.

Sir Alistair read carefully.

*There are no shortage of heroes at the Fraser farm near Inverness. Forty-five years ago Tom Fraser helped storm the beach at Anzio. Despite being shot in the leg, he was able to lift a wounded comrade off the beach and carry him to safety amidst a hail of machine-gun fire. He spent over a year in hospital and still walks with a limp. He was awarded the Military Cross.*

*Thirty-nine years later Billy Fraser followed in his father's footsteps and joined the Parachute Regiment. He was one of the ones who footslogged through the mud and rain to the hills over Port Stanley.*

*Victory was in sight when a vicious final battle was fought out on the windswept, muddy slopes.*

*As Billy's section was thrown back by a barrage of mortar fire one of his mates was hit. Just like his father all those years before, Billy didn't hesitate. As he dragged his wounded mate down the hill they were both hit by a mortar round. His friend was killed and Billy Fraser left both his legs on that lonely hillside twelve thousand miles away.*

*Like his father before him he won the Military Cross.*

*Today the Fraser men are angry men.*

*They are once again fighting for their very existence, this time on their farm in the hills above Inverness.*

*Due to the Beef Crisis their income is over 50% down and every day they wait for the bailiff to call. Their bank is threatening repossession.*

*" . . . Things like this make you feel rage towards the Government," says Billy. "Sixteen years ago they sent me halfway round the world to save a few hundred farmers in the Falkland Isles. They were told that it would cost thousands of lives but they still sent us. It cost me my legs.*

*"Now when thousands and thousands of British farmers are threatened, they refuse to take money from Brussels to help; money that has been paid by the British taxpayer."*

*His eyes become deeply sad. "I don't know. I can't say anything that the Government does surprises me much. It's what the army is doing that really hurts.*

*"When I was eighteen they told me to do my duty and I did. I paid the price. Now they won't even buy my beef. We've never had a single lousy case of BSE on this farm you know. But what do they care about that. They are buying Argentinian beef instead because it is cheaper. Argentinian for God's sake. How would you feel?"*

*Unless things change quickly the Frasers will lose their farm. A bank will take it and they will fall on the mercy of the state. They will exchange their lonely hills for a council house.*

*This is how the Government and the Army repays its heroes.*

Under the article the was a note that read 'Editor's comment, page 11.' Sir Alistair flicked through the paper and found it.

*Today we have featured the tragic story of the Fraser family. This paper supported the Labour Party through the election. We have supported them for their first months in power.*

*But enough is enough.*

*They are abusing their majority. They are going too far.*

*They did a U-turn on tobacco advertising for Formula 1. Fags cause cancer, it says so on the packet. Cancer kills almost one in three of us, it says so in the graveyard. But who cares, revenue is at stake.*

*They tell us that there is about a one in a billion chance that we just MIGHT get ill if we eat a T-bone steak. It is about a thousand times more dangerous to cross the road, have a bath, or boil a kettle. The risk makes driving or standing on a chair to change a light bulb look like Russian Roulette.*

*But they don't care. They doff their caps and do what the French and Germans tell them. Banning T-Bone steaks is a joke.*

*Thousands and thousands of British farmers are paying the price of this idiocy with their livelihoods.*

*Shame on you Mr Minister for Agriculture. You are a coward and a fool. If you have any guts, then go and visit the Fraser men and tell them why you have banned T-bone steaks.*

*This paper has had enough Minister. We are going to hound you and you deserve it.*

"Wow." Sir Alistair dropped the paper on his desk and shook his head. "This is amazing. It would appear that Dwight Forrester is showing a little more enthusiasm than a man simply driven by the demands of blackmail."

Marcus nodded. "Cornelius said as much. He seems to rather rate him."

Sir Alistair stared down at the paper with quiet amazement. "This makes it real doesn't it. Somehow it was just a game before, but now it is real."

"I bet you wouldn't swap it."

"God no. We're going to go all the way with this my old friend. All the way."

He read and reread the paper three more times.

The paper was being read with interest all over the country. Vince and Helen read it in bed at her house on the farm. Cornelius and Montgomery read it with their breakfast at Montgomery's flat in Brixton. Victor handed out copies to his recruits as they returned gasping from a seven-mile run in driving rain. Morale flew up as they read. Gideon took a copy to his father who smiled with delight.

"So it is our story next?"

"Yes, father."

"Fax this to Uncle Joshua in Tel Aviv. He'll appreciate it."

"Of course father."

Oliver Hamilton spotted the banner headline as he bought his morning paper at his local newsagents. He frowned deeply as he read the article whilst he sat in the front seat of his new Porsche. What the hell was going on? He felt a small icy chill of fear as he drove to one of the company's main distribution depots at Stevenage to supervise the first delivery of Kumalo's meat.

The Minister of State for Agriculture read the paper with open astonishment when he arrived at his office in the House of Commons. He had been under a degree of pressure from the farming industry but this was rather different. What on earth had got into Dwight Forrester? What on earth was happening?

His phone rang. It was the Prime Minister.

"Morning."

"Good morning Prime Minister."

"I should feel that your seat is a little warm this morning."

"Just a little."

"It seems odd to say the least. Don't worry, you're doing a fine job. I'll give Forrester a call, I'll try and straighten him out a bit."

"Thank you Prime Minister."

He sat staring at the paper for several minutes. He had known that he would make himself enemies by banning beef on the bone. He certainly hadn't expected Dwight Forrester and *The Globe* to be among them.

Ricky Myers called Billy Fraser.

"Billy. Ricky Myers here."

"Good morning."

"Have you seen it yet?"

"Aye I have."

"And?"

There was a pause. "It's fine Ricky. It's fine."

Ricky was amazed at how relieved he felt that the haunted young man had given his approval. "Thanks Billy."

"Nae bother. You write well."

It was three days later when a copy of the paper arrived at Julius Kumalo's office at Clearwaters. When he had read it he stared out of the window for a very long time.

# CHAPTER EIGHT

## OPENING SKIRMISHES

When Ricky Myers awoke at 5.30 a.m. on the morning of February 2 it was to a sensation of blind claustrophobic terror. He couldn't move and something was held over his mouth and nose. He was bound in a grip of iron. He struggled to find his bearings as the clouds of sleep were swiftly blown away.

After a few seconds which seemed like several hours it came back to him. He was lying in a ditch in Argentina under a tarpaulin sheet. He rolled his eyes to the side so that he could see Victor. Without releasing his hand from Ricky's mouth Victor nodded to the small line of daylight that was framed by the top of the drainage ditch and the tarpaulin sheet that covered them.

About twenty yards beyond the ditch were a pair of feet. The feet were shod in military-style boots and were facing away from them. The dawn silence was broken by a splashing sound as a vigorous cascade of urine fell to the dusty earth. Victor asked the question with his eyes and slightly released his grip enough for Ricky to nod. He then completely released the grip and the two men watched as the owner of the feet finished his business, buttoned up and walked away.

Ricky sagged back against the mud wall of the ditch and took several deep breaths to control his pounding heart. "What the am I doing here Victor?" he whispered shakily.

A big white-toothed smile. "Experiencing the thrills and spills of front-line journalism my boy. This could be the first step on the road to you becoming the next Hemmingway."

"Did Hemmingway need a pee at bad times too?"

Victor reached into his bag and passed Ricky a plastic bottle. When he had finished the awkward process of filling it, Ricky realised just how tired he was. The two-hour nap that he had just emerged from had merely scratched the edges of an overwhelming exhaustion. The last fifty hours had without doubt been the most tiring of his whole life.

They had taken the long red-eye flight from Heathrow and had landed in Buenos Aires at five in the morning. They had then driven their hire car for eight hours over the drab, featureless plains to a dreary motel a few miles out of the town of Pedrosa. They had slept for a few hours that afternoon until Sanchez had come to their room at eight in the evening to brief them. Sanchez worked for a detective agency in the capital and had been engaged by *The Globe* to find out as much as he could about Peter Haan, the reclusive Dutchman who kept 75,000 cattle on his 100,000-acre ranch.

Sanchez had told them that enquiries in the small town of Pedrosa had been far from easy. He told them that most people had immediately clammed up at the mention of Haan's name. Many people from the small town drew their living from the Haan estate and were suspicious of the man from the capital. At last he had met an unshaven alcoholic on a bench in the small park by the town hall. The drunk had agreed to talk for the price of a solid week's drinking but had insisted that Sanchez should pick him up at five the next morning on the edge of town. He had instructed Sanchez to drive ten miles out of town and to park well off the road before he was ready to talk.

He had been a mine of information. He had worked as a guard on the estate before he was sacked for being caught asleep on duty. Ever since he had scratched a living as best he could from odd jobs here and there. He told Sanchez that Haan had never once left his ranch since 1962. Haan was passionate about security and employed fifteen security men. Four of these manned the guardhouse at the perimeter of the ranch in two twelve-hour shifts. Six patrolled the perimeter of the main house in two similar shifts, whilst five worked the inside of the house. They were all heavily armed, well paid and generally alert. Their services were supplemented by an impressive array of electronic security systems. The house was ringed with cameras and security lights, and a pressure-pad alarm system ran in a circle around the house on a radius of 250 yards.

Even with all these systems in place, Haan never moved around his land without at least three guards in his vehicle. He had told Sanchez that it was impossible to get to the house without a small army. Sanchez had told him that he wasn't wanting to actually get into the house, just to get near it, near enough to take pictures.

The old drunk had considered this, then come up with the solution. If anyone wanted to get close they would have to walk in. It would be best to walk in from the northern boundary which was the opposite side to the road to the ranch. It was a twenty-two mile walk, but the going would be easy. There was a drainage ditch 350 yards from the house where a man could hide without having to worry about the pressure pads. This ditch gave a view onto the back of the house where Haan was accustomed to sit on the veranda for his morning coffee. Sanchez had then shown the old drunk the tape recorder that had been used to log their conversation and warned him that should he play a double game he would send it to Haan. The drunk promised him he wouldn't dream of it as he hated the bastard because he had ruined his life and caused him to lose everything. Sanchez had paid him treble what he had asked, and they had parted company.

Sanchez had brought detailed maps from Buenes Aires and they had spent the next day poring over them and planning. He had dropped Victor and Ricky on the northern perimeter an hour after darkness and they had reached the ditch a little after three in the morning. They stretched the sheet over their heads to hide them and had eaten.

Ricky had fallen asleep almost instantly and had been far, far away when Victor had awoken him with a hand clamped over the mouth. The guard had now walked the full distance back to the house.

Victor started to assemble the tripod for Ricky's camera. After a few minutes the camera was set up and Ricky worked on the focus. By 5.30 they were set, and Victor grunted his appreciation when he took a sighting through the long telephoto lens. The veranda seemed no more than fifteen yards away.

And so they waited as the sun slowly climbed into the sky and the flies started to buzz. Two hours later, at 7.30, there were signs of activity. Three guards came out of the house and strolled about fifty yards out in different directions. They spent a minute or so scanning the horizon before one talked into a small radio. The door to the veranda opened and an old man emerged leaning heavily on his stick. The camera whirred softly as Ricky took pictures as Haan moved across the veranda to a small table. He sat side-on to them, sipping coffee and reading a book.

"Any good?" whispered Victor.

"Not bad. Probably good enough," replied Ricky.

Haan sat peacefully for a further forty minutes and Ricky took several more shots. He clipped another longer lens quietly onto the camera. He explained to Victor "Bit risky this one. It's not always easy to keep steady, but we've already got quite a few decent shots."

He had only taken a couple more shots when Haan stood up. He turned fully towards them and leaned on the rail of the veranda to gaze out over his land. Through the lens Ricky brought his face into full focus and as he pressed the shutter a slow smile of satisfaction spread over his face. Seen close up, Haan's face wasn't frail at all; it was hard and cruel. Best of all, in the clean, bright morning light, the duelling scar on his right cheek stood out clear and strong.

"Got you you bastard," muttered Ricky as he took his final shot.

They sat and sweltered in the ditch all day until Victor was happy that they were safe to move out. They made the walk back to the perimeter without incident and Sanchez picked them up. Thirty-six hours later they were back in London.

On the morning of February 14 Sir Alistair had once again assembled his twenty young executives at Black Loch.

Each of the ten teams reported on their progress and all over Britain the Matador shopping spree was well on course. When the day to go public arrived, they would be offering British beef from 500 butchers shops backed up by a delivery service of 1000 vans.

Once the routine reports had been heard, Sir Alistair asked for ideas. He smiled as they came in thick and fast. What about freebies; baseball caps, pens, mugs? Vote. Do it. How? Go the loyalty card route. So many points per pound spent on Matador products. Who sorts it? The job went to the executive from Newcastle and Tyneside who had mooted the idea. London area suggested that once the sales force had been recruited there should be a national two-day launch in advance of March 1. Again agreed, again the job of finding a suitable venue and making all arrangements was given to the proposer.

"Do you think we could get John Cleese to do a bit of sales training?"

Sir Alistair grinned. "We can certainly try."

Another suggestion came from Greater Manchester. "On the subject of John Cleese, I have had a bit of an advertising idea." He went on to explain it, feeling nervous at first, but then happier as general laughter broke out around the table. As the hilarity subsided Sir Alistair said, "I'm sorry chaps, this is when democracy goes out of the window. We won't be voting on that proposal because I am personally insisting that it happens. I'll volunteer to try to get hold of Mr Cleese."

The meeting broke up after an hour and the executives rushed back to their territories. Sir Alistair phoned Vince.

"Morning Vince. Alistair here."

"How's tricks boss?"

"Couldn't be better. I've just had all the guys in and everything is bang on target. They're warming to things nicely. We've had some outstanding ideas come out this morning." Sir Alistair quickly gave an update on the various schemes that had been approved. Vince chortled with delight when he heard of the last one.

"Now that, Sir Alistair, is an absolute ripper. Christ, I hope you can get him. That will really get right up the nose of our beloved Minister for Agriculture."

The following Friday *The Globe* ran its second story. This time the front page was dominated by two striking photographs. The first was of a young German officer wearing the full uniform of the Gestapo. It was a head shot. From under the black peaked hat stared out a hard arrogant face. The man was bleakly handsome with high cheekbones and piercing eyes. At his throat the Knights Cross was worn with pride. A long duelling scar ran down his right cheek. The second photo was the long-range close-up that Ricky Myers had taken from the drainage ditch in Argentina a few days before.

Even though fifty years separated the two photos, the man carried his head in exactly the same way. The young handsome face had become worn and wrinkled over the years, but the eyes still burned with a cold cruelty, and the scar still dominated the right cheek.

Nobody would ever doubt that the pictures were of the same man.

Above the two photos ran the blazing headline

## 'BEEF FROM THE BUTCHER OF BUCHENWALD'

Once again the main text of the story was to be found on page 2.

*Many of you will have read our story of the Fraser family. We highlighted the shameful facts of how the British Army is buying Argentinean beef. Since then we have looked into the Argentinean beef market and found out some shocking facts. The old man in the photo goes by the name of Peter Haan, a Dutchman, who keeps 75,000 cattle on his 100,000-acre estate in Western Argentina. He is one of the richest beef farmers in the country and there is every possibility that in recent months you may well have eaten some of his meat without ever knowing it.*

*We have discovered that his name isn't really Peter Haan at all. We have discovered that he isn't a Dutchman at all. His real name is Heinrich Rolf and he was born a German. Rolf left the University of Heidelberg in 1938 and was immediately recruited into Himmler's Gestapo. Over the next seven years he was involved in numerous atrocities. For the last three years of the war he was a senior officer at the Buchenwald concentration camp where his savage, merciless cruelty earned him the title "Butcher of Buchenwald". At the end of the war he simply disappeared. We now know that he took off with a fortune in stolen gold and made his way to Argentina. He was able to buy his vast estate with the proceeds and has lived in luxury ever since.*

*In 1962, Israeli commandos captured Adolph Eichmann in Buenos Aires and took him back to Tel Aviv for trial and execution. This terrified*

*Rolf and since then he has never left his farm. He hides behind armed security guards and snarling dogs.*

*But he still sells his meat. Thousands and thousands of tonnes of it.*

*His vast fortune grows as the weeds grow on the unmarked graves of his thousands of forgotten victims.*

*And who are his customers? We are.*

*We don't deliberately buy his meat of course. How can we possibly know it is his? But those who sell his meat know. They know that by buying meat from this most filthy of murderers they will make thousands of British farmers bankrupt.*

*These people don't care for anything but profit.*

*We know that the British people are better than that. It was the British people who stood up to the Nazis all those years ago, and the same British people can help once again.*

*How?*

*Easy.*

*If it doesn't say British on the packet DON'T BUY IT.*

The *Globe's* first story had caused a mild stir. There had been much talk in press circles about what on earth Dwight Forrester, King of Sleaze, could possibly be up to. Circulation had without doubt risen slightly as farmers all over Britain bought the paper waiting for the next move in the new *Globe* campaign. The politicians had deployed politician-speak to talk all round the subject and a fearful bore from the army had issued a frightful statement promising to look at things. The price of finished steers in the *Farmers Weekly* eased up a penny.

The second story had rather more of an impact. Dwight had just got out of the shower when his phone rang a little after six that morning. He picked it up somewhat grumpily.

"Forrester."

"Oh good morning Mr Forrester, this is Sheila Hunt from the *Today* programme on Radio Four. We will be reviewing the papers at 7.15 as normal and your beef story rather stands out. Would you be willing to do an interview for us?"

"Of course. Would you like me to come to the studio."

"That would be wonderful."

"Give me half an hour."

Dwight had nearly finished dressing when the phone rang again.

"Good morning Mr Forrester. I am Leslie Greenhalgh. I am the producer for the Nicky Campbell show on *Radio Five Live*. We are all rather intrigued by your beef story. Have you ever listened to Nicky's phone-in show that runs from nine till ten?"

"Occasionally."

"Well we're considering featuring your thoughts on the beef crisis this morning. Of course the thing that would make it worth our running this is if you were willing to appear on the show yourself."

"Who else would be on?"

"We would try to get Professor Potter."

"OK I'll do it. I'm at the studios anyway for the *Today* programme. You're in the same building I presume?"

"Oh, absolutely."

"Well I'll see you later then."

As his chauffeur threw his Rolls through the thickening West End traffic, Dwight called Cornelius on his mobile phone.

"Morning Cornelius, I suggest you get your radio on this morning. I'm on the *Today* programme at 7.15 and on the *Five Live* phone-in at nine."

"Christ Dwight, are you feeling confident?"

"Course I am. I'm an Aussie."

Cornelius chuckled. "Give them Hell."

Mobile phones buzzed busily all around the country over the next few minutes and everyone was glued to their radio sets at 7.15.

"The time has just gone 7.15 and we're going to take a look at today's papers. The story that rather stands out this morning is the latest in *The Globe's* new campaign for British beef. The front page leads with the Headline "Beef from the butcher of Buchenwald" which is followed by a story which alleges that some of the Argentinean beef that is coming into Britain is supplied by a wanted ex-Nazi who fled Germany in 1945. In the studio with me is Dwight Forrester, the flamboyant owner of *The Globe*. Dwight, these stories are something of a new departure for your paper."

"Well you may say so, but I don't agree. *The Globe* always tries to feature any story that we feel is within the public's interest. This goes for buying beef from war criminals as much as the bedroom antics of our MPs."

"Your allegations against Mr Haan are rather explicit. How certain are you of their veracity?"

"Well we wouldn't have printed it if we hadn't been certain. Our information comes from excellent sources from within Israel. However, the *Globe* is bound by international law, and Mr Rolf is more than welcome to come over and try to sue me. He'll get my number in the paper. However, since he has hidden behind his fences and dogs for the last thirty-six years, I don't feel that he is about to get on a plane now."

"On a bigger issue, what has led you to take up the cause of the British beef industry?"

Dwight smiled inwardly at this. If you did but know, he thought.

"My paper has given its full support to this Government for almost a year now. By and large they have done quite well. However we feel that they are beginning to behave with unacceptable arrogance in certain areas and it is vital that a responsible media never allows any government the luxury of arrogance. We feel that what is being done to the farming industry at the moment is an absolute disgrace and we intend to expose it."

"So you feel that there is a deliberate attack being launched on the farming industry Mr Forrester?"

"No not an attack. This Government is more subtle than that. This isn't like Maggie flaying the miners in 1984. It is more that they are showing a complete indifference to the destruction of one of our vital industries. On the one hand they are willing to pass simply outrageously stupid legislation such as banning T-bone steaks and ram it down the necks of our farmers, whilst on the other hand they are content to see all kinds of dubious, products dumped from all over the world on our UK market.

"When I say dubious, I mean either morally dubious as is the case with our purchases of beef from the likes of the murderous Mr Rolf, or dubious in terms of safety and quality which is the case for a great deal of beef which is reared in inhumane and unhygienic conditions in certain Third World countries. *The Globe* believes that it has the right to look after the interests of its readers. That's what you get when you spend your 30p on our paper. If we find that one of your MPs who is happy to stand and preach high moral standards to you is having an affair with a 13 year old on the quiet, then we are going to find out and tell you. Similarly, if we discover that our readers are being sold unclean, morally unacceptable meat for their Sunday table, then we are going to find that out and tell them."

The presenter was somewhat taken aback at the vehemence of Dwight's attack. "You certainly seem to have taken rather strongly to this particular cause Mr Forrester."

"Absolutely right I have. Way back when, I came from farming stock in Queensland. My uncle is a beef farmer. I now live amongst farmers in Hampshire and I hate to see what is being done to them by Government and supermarkets alike. I will take this opportunity to warn anyone out there who is cutting corners on food hygiene in order to make a few extra quid out of imported meat, that you had better watch out, because the *Globe* is going to find you out and show you up for what you are. And my message for the Minister for Agriculture is that you may feel that the British farmer is a soft touch who will lie down and die quietly whilst you show off to your new friends in Brussels, but you had better start to tread carefully, because the British farmers have a big new friend in the playground. And the name of that big new friend is the *Globe*."

With a chuckle the presenter wound up the slot. "Well, we have certainly heard some forthright views on the beef issue from Mr Forrester and I'm sure that they will have livened up the Minister for Agriculture's breakfast should he be listening. Maybe we will get to speak to him later."

As Dwight pulled off the headset and left the recording studio the presenter grinned at him and give him a thumbs-up. Outside Dwight strode quickly down the corridor and bolted into the Gents. As he closed the door he leaned back on it heavily and took several long deep breaths.

It took him several minutes to realise quite what he had done.

As he had driven to the studio that morning he had not formulated any particular plan about what he was going to say. It was something that he hardly ever did. He had always been a firm believer in taking everything as it comes and relying on his instincts. Never before had his instincts carried him quite so far and so fast. He had declared war on just about everyone on the most listened-to morning show on British radio. He splashed cold water in his face whilst the consequences of what he had done started to sink in. As they did he relaxed. For once he was more than convinced that the cause was a just one. His personal wealth was quite secure and he was convinced that he had said nothing for which he could be sued. The knighthood was probably a gonner, but what the hell. His mobile phone rang.

"Forrester."

"Dwight, it's Cornelius. You are my number one hero and you will be for evermore. That was absolutely, totally, comprehensively bloody marvellous. Keep it up. Now watch the bastard Potter. He may seem like your typical unworldly boffin, but he is an absolute snake."

Dwight grinned. It seemed ridiculous to him that he was so gratified by the praise of the extraordinary young man who had blackmailed him so outrageously. "Thanks Cornelius. I'll watch my back."

"You do that. We're all rooting for you. By the way, are you busy this weekend? After this morning I think we have to accept that you are fully on the team. Why don't you come and meet the rest of the chaps?"

Dwight felt his smile grow even wider, again to his great surprise. "I'd love to Cornelius. Ring me later and we'll sort it."

The morning interview set off a chain reaction all over the country. Rearden heard the broadcast while he was shaving in his hotel room. He dressed quickly and darted out to buy a cassette player to record the nine o'clock show. The Minister of Agriculture was indeed at breakfast when Dwight's statements almost caused him to spit out his cornflakes in astonishment. His phone rang quickly. Firstly one of the spin doctors suggested that a brief interview was in order, but that he should stay cool and stand back from any kind of slanging match with Forrester. He proceeded to give a bland interview to the *Today* programme, where he indulged fully in politician-speak to assure everyone that everything was absolutely fine, no matter what certain sections of the media were saying. As he put the phone down, he had an uneasy feeling that Forrester had come out of the morning rather better than he had done himself. When he walked out of his front door, he was surprised to be met by a small group of reporters begging for comment. He smiled easily and climbed into his ministerial car. As the car picked its way through the early-morning traffic, he pondered on the strange turn that events had taken.

Initially the Ministry for Agriculture had seemed an ideal short term post which he could use to kick-start his rather stalled career. The almighty mess than the previous government had made of the beef crisis more or less guaranteed that he could shine modestly whilst enjoying a higher profile that most Ministers for Agriculture. He had been quite unconcerned when it had been made eminently clear to him that there would be absolutely no more funding made available for agriculture and that he would have to sort everything out on a shoestring. It hadn't seemed a problem. Certainly things would be hard on the farmers and they wouldn't like it, but in the end they didn't threaten many government seats, and they certainly didn't have any history for supporting his party. He fully agreed with the party line. There were far more pressing demands on the strained public purse than propping up agriculture. He would ensure that his Ministry would underspend its budget and do nothing to rock the boat in Brussels. These two things should ensure that his next Cabinet post would be a higher one.

It had all seemed to be going rather well despite his receiving a certain amount of personal ridicule over the T-bone steak affair. Yet all of a sudden things had changed out of all recognition. The owner of one of the nation's best-read papers which had offered his party critical support during their election victory, had very publicly declared war on him. As the car inched through the early-morning petrol fumes, he thanked his lucky stars that he hadn't any hideous personal skeletons stacked away in dusty cupboards.

Dwight Forrester was a formidable enemy. He would need all his wits about him.

Oliver Hamilton was in his car when he heard Dwight. He felt a cold sweat under his collar as he listened. He pulled his car into a lay-by whilst the interview ran. At eight-thirty he rang the office to tell his secretary that he would be in late, and he sat in his car watching huge wagons thunder past as he waited for the nine o'clock phone-in show.

Nicky Campbell, the presenter, was an easy-going Scot who had taken the show to a steadily higher listening audience. Dwight sat with him in the studio whilst his other guest, Professor Donald Potter, was plugged in up at the BBC's Pebble Mill studio. Before the BSE crisis, Potter had been a typically anonymous science Professor at a Midlands University. However, he had seen his career take off as the media scoured academic institutions for experts willing to comment on the progress of the new killer disease. The biggest problem that the media had found with BSE as a topic was that it was highly technical, highly complicated and nobody from the world of science was very willing to put their academic careers on the line by making any rash statements. Nobody, that was, except Professor Donald Potter, who took to the media game like a duck to water and indulged himself in issuing threats of a new plague to eclipse AIDS. Many of his colleagues found his doomsday preachings to be ill-founded and irresponsible, but Donald relished his new-found fame and would not be put off. When the phone rang that morning he had dropped everything and sped into Leeds for the programme. Unlike the Minister for Agriculture, he was delighted with the sudden upturn in public interest. For him it meant more excitement in front of the camera and behind the microphone.

The sports news and the weather were wound up and Nicky Campbell opened the show.

**Campbell.** "Morning everybody. Once again this morning's news is dominated by the story that just won't seem to go away. I refer of course to the Beef Crisis. In the past, it has been new scientific revelations that have made the news. This time things are rather different. With two extraordinary stories over the last fortnight, the country's fourth best-selling paper, the *Globe*, has very publicly grasped the torch of becoming the farmers' champion. In an interview on the *Today* programme two hours ago, the Globe's owner, Dwight Forrester, launched a withering attack on the Government and more or less declared a journalistic Jihad against the Minister of Agriculture.

"*The Globe's* owner claims that British retailers are exploiting the beef crisis to make extra profits by selling us all imported beef, which is sometimes morally unacceptable and often produced in unhygienic and inhumane conditions. Furthermore, it is claimed that the Government is more than happy to turn a blind eye to all this, and will allow the beef industry to be annihilated as a result. Dwight, is my summary a fair one?"

**Forrester.** "Yes I would say that is more than fair Nicky."

**Campbell.** "Our second guest this morning is Professor Donald Potter, who over the last two years has been the loudest scientific voice warning us all of the dangers of eating British beef and who has gone a long way to creating a new generation of vegetarians, such has been the strength of his doomsday warnings. Professor, what is your reaction to this morning's story?"

**Potter.** "I find it utterly appalling. We in the scientific community are desperately trying to avoid a massive risk to public health which has been caused entirely by the excesses of intensive farming, and it is quite irresponsible for a joke paper like the *Globe* to try to create an artificial bandwagon on the back of this huge potential crisis by printing silly stories simply to boost circulation figures."

**Campbell.** "How would you respond to that Mr Forrester?"

**Forrester.** "I will be charitable and assume that the Professor hasn't actually read this morning's edition. I had better bring him up to speed with what our story actually was. We have exposed the dreadful truth that beef is being imported into our country which has been sold to us by a wanted war criminal. His name is Rolf. He is hiding in Argentina living off the gold that he and his murdering cronies stole from the Jews they slaughtered. There are still a few survivors of his crimes who are alive, if not well, in Israel. We have shown them the photo of this man, which was printed on the front page of our paper today. They have all positively identified him as the man they called 'the Butcher of Buchenwald'. Now the good Professor here may consider exposing one of the men who was involved in the mass murder of five million of our fellow human beings to be a 'silly little story', but I don't agree, and I don't believe that our readers do either. If Professor Potter never learned about the Holocaust during his scientific studies, I would be more than happy to furnish him with some relevant reading material. Our claim is that buying meat from an animal like Rolf is morally unacceptable and I stand by that claim."

**Campbell.** "What is your response to that Professor? Surely the *Globe* has a point." Campbell was smiling broadly. He had never had much time for Potter.

**Potter.** (Feeling exceptionally flustered.) "It is not for me to comment on matters of historical morality. I am a scientist and I am only interested in practising science to help the public."

**Forrester.** "I seem to remember that there were scientists in the concentration camps who gave similar answers. What was it? We were only obeying orders. It wasn't our fault."

**Potter.** (Exploding) "Why, that is the most . . . "

**Campbell.** (Calming) "Now then, let's keep things cool, I think that it is time to take our first call, which is Mary from Redhill. Good morning Mary."

**Mary.** "Good morning Nicky. I would just like to say that I agree completely with the *Globe*. We must know if we are buying beef from someone like this dreadful man Rolf. Well done Mr Forrester. You have a new reader."

**Forrester.** "Thank you Mary. I hope you enjoy the paper."

**Campbell.** "We have Stuart from Walsall on line 3. Morning Stuart."

**Stuart.** "Morning Nicky. I won't disagree for a minute about it being morally wrong to buy beef from the war criminal, but I would like to refer back to some of the comments that Mr Forrester made this morning about the government. Now he says that his paper is going to defend the British farmer against imported meat as well as Government policy to look after the interests of his readers. What about the dangers that his readers face by eating

British beef which has proved to be dangerous to public health?"

**Campbell.** "Professor Potter?"

**Potter.** "I agree entirely Stuart. There is a risk to eating beef. The Government is absolutely right in responding to that risk and taking every step to protect public health by acting on the advice of the scientific community."

**Forrester.** "I am not qualified to comment on the scientific niceties of this issue. However I am perfectly qualified to comment on facts. Last December our Minister of Agriculture got himself on all the front pages and won lots of Brownie points with his pals in France and Germany by banning the T-bone steak. His reason was that the scientists had warned him that there might, I repeat might, be a one in a billion chance that eating T-bone steak might, I repeat might, cause CJD. Now I don't believe that we elected this Government to pass legislation to protect us from one in a billion chances of being in danger. If, however, they are going to be consistent about this, then they must get cracking and ban a few more things that are infinitely more statistically dangerous than eating a T-bone steak. Now let's see. There is driving, going on a train, flying, using electrical appliances, playing any sport other than snooker, bowls or tiddley-winks, having sex, drinking, having a bath, the list goes on and on. And then of course there is smoking. It is pretty well proven that smoking causes cancer and cancer kills about one in three of us and yet the Government is more than happy to allow us to buy cigarettes because they generate lots of tax and employ lots of their voters. I actually fully agree with this because this is a free country and we are all adults who are capable of making up our own minds about what risks we are willing to take in the way we live our lives.

"I would like to make a final point about CJD. We don't really know what it is yet, despite anything that our Professor says. What we do know is that about twenty people die from it every year and have done so for the last hundred years. So far it would appear that about twenty people will die from it this year. There is absolutely no evidence of the new plague that Professor Potter here has threatened, and yet, acting on his advice, the government has spent billions of pounds on killing and burning innocent animals to avert this mythical plague. I just wonder how much nearer we would now be to a cure for cancer had the government invested our hard-earned money in searching for a cure for a very real disease rather than chasing Professor Potter's shadows. One fact that the good Professor should know and may not be proud of, is that more farmers will commit suicide this year than people will die of his so-called plague."

And so it went on. The calls became increasingly favourable to Dwight, who warmed to his task and attacked the beleaguered Professor mercilessly. At ten to ten the best call of the lot came in for the *Globe* and the conspirators.

**Campbell.** "We have Ian on line 3. How are you Ian?"

**Ian.** "I'm fine Nicky. I'm calling from the barracks. I'm a soldier, a corporal, and I serve in the Scots Guards. We all read the story about Billy Fraser a couple of weeks ago, and we've read the story today. All the lads here are behind the *Globe* and we're behind Billy Fraser and his dad. We've all talked about it this morning and we are going to stop eating beef until the army assures us that it won't buy anything but British. We didn't go to the Falklands to eat Argentinian beef. We are pretty sure that we are not breaking any rules by refusing to eat beef, so I would just like to say to any other squaddies who are listening, come on lads, let's stick together on this and make a bit of a stand. The Scots Guards are on a beef hunger strike as of now until we know it is British. And I'd just like to say to Billy Fraser that if he fancies a ride down here one Friday night for a binge with the lads, we're buying Billy, and best of luck to you."

**Forrester.** "May I say Ian that this is brilliant news. We at the *Globe* always believe in people power and this is just the kind of thing that will make the army think again. For any other soldiers listening, please let us know at the paper when you join the Scots Guards in their stand, and we'll give you the publicity. I'll also say to young Billy Fraser if he is listening, if you want to take Ian here up on his offer tonight, we'll send our helicopter to your farm to take you there and back. You deserve it mate."

Ten minutes later Nicky Campbell wound up the phone-in. He was ecstatic. It had been one of the best ever. A poll taken later gave Dwight overwhelming approval. Ricky Myers rang Billy, who was more than happy to take his ride in the helicopter. He had his best night for many years, followed by one of the worst hangovers of his life. He was delighted for Ricky to take photos and his beaming smile dominated the front page of the Monday edition of the *Globe*. The story that followed listed many regiments of the British army, navy and airforce who had contacted the paper to announce their support for the Scots Guards. Two weeks later the army succumbed to the pressure and announced that it would in future buy only British beef. In order to avert a potential public relations disaster, it also announced that it would buy all the animals from the Fraser farm as a mark of respect for the heroics of the farm's two generations of soldiers. The Friday following Dwight's big morning, the price of finished steers in the *Farmers Weekly* had risen by 6 pence.

Oliver Hamilton had a wretched morning in the office as calls came in from depots all over the country from worried managers who were fielding difficult questions from customers who demanded to be assured that none of their beef was Argentinean. He had three snide calls from fellow directors pointedly asking for assurance that the imported beef that he had put into their stores was indeed not of South American origin. He had blustered his way through, but it had not been easy. The prospect of the next few weeks was suddenly a bleak one. Rearden posted the tape of the phone-in show to Kumalo and the two men talked at length when it had arrived. Kumalo recommended that Rearden stay as close as possible to Oliver to make sure that the young man held his nerve.

Cornelius, Montgomery and Dwight set out early the following morning and caught a flight up to Edinburgh where they were met by Helen and Vince. Dwight grilled Cornelius mercilessly on the plane for details about what was going on, but he was met with constantly evasive answers. Following Dwight's radio performances everybody had agreed unanimously that he should be brought fully onto the team. There was no real reason for Cornelius being so evasive, he just enjoyed winding up the eager

Australian. They headed over the Forth estuary and arrived at the farm near Stirling in the late morning. As they parked in the yard on an unusually mild winter morning, Dwight simply couldn't stand it any more.

"Jesus guys, give me a bloody clue. You've got me out of my bed and flown me up here. Surely we aren't just going to have a wander around a few fields. What's going on here?"

Vince decided to take pity. "Don't worry Dwight. All is about to be revealed. A mile or so down the valley we have established a training camp. There are twenty guys there and we have been putting them through their paces for three weeks. You will no doubt remember Victor, I believe the two of you met a little while ago."

"Too bloody right I remember him."

"Well the poor devils that you are about to meet have been under his gentle tutelage for the last twenty-one days. I can't say that I envy them."

Dwight shook his head. "Come on mate. Stop being so bloody obscure. Why the hell have you got twenty guys camped out in the Scottish wilds in the middle of winter? Lets have a few answers. Who are they? What are they doing?"

Vince grinned at Dwight's eagerness. "Cornelius has of course told you that we have been hired to solve the current Beef Crisis. We are a small partnership who specialise in solving people's problems in rather unorthodox ways. I must admit that this is the largest contract that we have yet undertaken. This operation will be made up of two separate campaigns which are in the process of being launched. On the one hand there is the overt campaign which will commence on March 1. A new company called Matador has been set up to vigorously promote, market and sell British beef products. The company is going to start life with a capital investment of half a billion pounds and it will aim to achieve a 10% market share of the British beef market within the next six months. You will be hearing all about what Matador will be up to over the next couple of days.

"On the other hand, we will be running a number of covert operations alongside Matador's activities. These have already started in a small way. I consider the recruiting of yourself and the

Orange Boys to have been covert operations.

"In normal circumstances we like to undertake all covert work ourselves. However, as you can well imagine, this is a rather bigger project than those we have been accustomed to in the past, and so we have had to extend our team. We have recruited twenty men who are beef farmers but who have also spent many years in the army. They are being well paid but their motivation to achieve the same goals as ourselves is obviously guaranteed. Over the last three weeks they have undergone some pretty intensive physical training, but they have also been involved in planning their various operations. We have also brought in specialists to train them in skills which they wouldn't have learned either in their army or farming careers."

"Such as?"

"Breaking and entering, disabling alarm systems, phone tapping, surveillance, that kind of thing."

Dwight shook his head and grinned as they strolled down the rough path by the stream. "The more I hear about you guys the more I can't believe you."

Cornelius chipped in. "We're not that bad you know. We have never hurt anyone and we rather pride ourselves on the fact that we tend to bend laws rather than break them. I don't suppose what we do is a million miles different to tabloid journalism."

"Fair enough, but I still can't really understand why I'm here," said Dwight.

Cornelius continued. "Simple. After yesterday I felt that you were showing rather more enthusiasm for this business than a man simply being pushed on by a rather naughty blackmail scam. I actually think that you are rather enjoying yourself. These were thoughts that my colleagues fully concurred with. Our operation revolves totally around the manipulation of public perception. If we are successful, then the good old British public will go out and buy our beef in droves. If not, well they won't. It seems to me that if one wanted to find a real expert in the field of manipulating public perceptions, one would surely look no further than the owner of one of the country's most successful tabloid newspapers. Basically, many of the missions that the lads here are going to get involved in will be designed to create stories which put people in the mood to buy our products. We will obviously be using the *Globe* to present these stories in the same way that you have already done. It now seems sensible to bring you fully on board to asses the operations before we actually launch them. Sensible?"

Dwight nodded thoughtfully. "Yes, I would say so."

"And I am right, am I not. You are really rather enjoying all of this."

"Yes Cornelius, you are absolutely right. I reckon this is a bloody riot."

As they walked into the camp men in army fatigues emerged from their various tents to greet them. Vince stuck his arms in the air to get everybody's attention.

"OK guys, listen up. I know that you have all been reading the *Globe* over the last three weeks and I know you all heard the radio yesterday. Well this here is the man himself. I would like to introduce you all to Dwight Forrester."

Dwight had his hand pumped and his back slapped and they made their way into the main tent. Lunch was served and washed down with beer. The tables were then cleared an the chairs laid out classroom style. Each pair then outlined the details of their operations whilst the rest of the men questioned and quizzed them. Dwight filled page after page of notes, and made numerous suggestions for small refinements. By 7.00 p.m. all the briefings were complete. At this point Sir Alistair and Marcus arrived with Gideon. Cornelius led Dwight over to make the introductions.

"Dwight, allow me to introduce the Matador Board. You have asked me on several occasions who is behind all of this. Well, this is he. Dwight Forrester, please meet Sir Alistair McIntyre."

Dwight felt all the pennies drop at once. "Now I get it. McIntyre Holdings right? You've just sold up for £1.7 billion to an American outfit. So that's where the bloody money is all coming from."

Alistair smiled and shook hands. He had had some reservations about bringing Dwight on board, but he had been happy enough to go along with Cornelius. Even though he had a natural aversion to the modern tabloid press, he had liked what he had heard of Dwight and had been particularly impressed with his radio efforts the day before. Now as he shook hands with the tanned Australian with the mischievous grin, he couldn't help but like him.

"Mr Forrester, it is indeed a pleasure. My young colleagues seem to have rather taken to you which is good enough for me. I feel that I should make something very clear before anything else. Launching this operation was my idea and I am paying the bills. The lads outlined many plans to me, most of which I approved. What I am really saying is that I gave the nod of approval for the operation to get you and your paper on board and I take full responsibility for it. It isn't something that I am very proud of, and I would like to offer my apologies."

Dwight gave him a meaty whack on the shoulder.

"No need mate, no need at all. Hell, I know the saying about live by the sword and die by the sword. It serves me bloody right and that is all there is to it. That said, I have a cast-iron deal with the lads that they don't mention it and they don't take the piss. So long as they stand by that, well everything is fine by me. I can assure you that if I had been in your shoes I would have done exactly the same thing. So let's forget it shall we?"

Alistair smiled. "Gladly."

Outside, some of the men had got a pit of charcoal burning and were starting to roast a huge side of Helen's beef. An end-of -term atmosphere now filled the camp and the drink flowed merrily. By ten they were all well drunk and stuffed full of beef. Sir Alistair stood up and banged his tin mug on the trestle table until he silenced the hubbub.

"Panic not gents, I am not intending to bore you to tears. Just humour an old man for a minute or two. I only met Victor here a few weeks ago but I think I can guess that he will have ensured that the last three weeks will not have been like Butlins. Anyway you've done it, and big as he is, I feel sure that if you all employ a bit of basic teamwork you should be able to throw him into the stream out there before the night is out.

"Next Wednesday is March 1; Our very own D-Day. Being here tonight with you all brings back a lot of memories for me and I know that there are several of you who sailed to the Falklands. We all have our reasons for doing what we are doing, but we can all know that what we are doing is absolutely right. I know that you have all suffered over the last few months and it is time that it stopped. I fought in a World War and I saw a lot of my friends give their lives for freedom and justice. Now these seem oddly old-fashioned words these days, but then again I am a bit of an antique myself.

"There has been nothing just about what has been done to the beef industry. We have all been exploited by politicians and big businesses who couldn't care less what happens to any of us so long as they get their way. They have done what they have done because they are quite convinced that we are a soft touch, and no matter how hard they kick us we will simply lie there and take it. Well, no more gentlemen. No more. The days of lying down and taking it end next Wednesday on March 1. Yes, some of the things that we will do will not be entirely legal, and yes, some people will get railroaded along the way. We know this and I believe we can accept this because in the end what we are doing is right. Not long ago I was in danger of feeling like a tired old man counting down the days to the grave. I was looking around our modern world with little more than sadness. I was lucky enough to meet some young chaps who helped me to persuade myself that it was worth having one last roll of the dice. Well the dice gets thrown in earnest next Wednesday and we all hope and pray that when it stops it will show a six. But even if it shows a one, and we don't achieve any of the goals that we have set ourselves, I for one will have no regrets.

"I am proud to be associated which each and every one of you. It is not everybody who will set out to the climb the mountain that everyone believes to be unclimbable. As I look round tonight I really, really feel that we are going to get to the top."

Alistair stopped briefly and took a slow look around the room. As ever his face was hard and craggy but his eyes were unmistakably moist. He raised his glass high. "Gentlemen. I give you victory."

They roared out the toast. The drinks flowed until the early hours of the morning. Well after midnight a beaming Dwight crashed into a chair next to Cornelius and draped his arm over his shoulder. "Tell you what mate, I haven't had such a good night for bloody years. By the way, I forgot to mention. I looked up your pal Ignatious Loyola. He was a big-time Jesuit about four hundred years ago. He had this theory that the best way to get a catholic for life was to get into the heads of kids as early as possible. He reckoned that people are kind of extra gullible when they are young. Now I reckon that you guys feel that with someone like the Orange Boys in tow that you will be able to dupe the gormless youths of this country to eat lots and lots of extra burgers."

Cornelius chuckled. "My, you are ever such a perceptive chap Dwight."

A little after two, Vince and Helen slipped outside and walked up the valley hand in hand. The night sky was stunningly clear and a full moon bathed the rocky ground in its silver light. They picked their way up the side of the stream for half a mile before sitting on a smooth rock which overhung the bubbling water below. For a while they were silent as they enjoyed the quiet gurgling of the water.

Then Helen took Vince's face between her hands and kissed him slowly. When she pulled away she tried to see deep into his eyes. "Are you scared?"

He nodded slowly. "Absolutely terrified. This has all suddenly become very, very important to me. I think it has for all of us. Damn it all, who wouldn't be swayed by your old man's Charge of the Light Brigade speech. He's a hell of a guy isn't he?"

"Oh yes, he's that all right. I can't bear the thought of how much I'm going to miss him."

The thought of the Sir Alistair's short lease on life pushed them both back into silence. Eventually Helen took Vince's hand and squeezed. "Well there is one thing that you should know before you enter this crazy adventure my dear Vincent. Win, lose or draw you get the girl. That is, if you want her."

He smiled. "Oh, I want her all right."

They sat in silence for several minutes more as the moon bathed the Scottish night in its clean light. Somewhere downstream an owl hooted softly and the icy waters of the stream made their patient way down over the rocks to the sea that lay waiting to receive them. There was no turning back, there was no room for second thoughts. Vince found that his mind was filled with the image of Kitchener's vast volunteer army counting down the hours before the Battle of the Somme. Each must have had their own private thoughts and dreams as they smoked or cleaned their weapons. What fate awaited him? He was about to find out.

# CHAPTER NINE

## OVER THE TOP

On the morning of March 1 the country woke up to Matador. In over ten million homes a large glossy brochure dropped through the letterbox. It was filled with idyllic photos of beef cattle in picture-postcard upland settings from all around the UK. Contained within were details of the new local Matador butchers shops as well as hotline numbers to be used for people to get more details. There was an impressive picture of a thousand chilled delivery vans, all newly painted with the distinctive Matador logo, all parked in a long staggered line with their drivers beside them. The text inside the brochure was easy and light, and words such as 'traceable', 'humane' and 'clean' recurred. Inside every brochure was a £5 voucher which could be redeemed at any Matador outlet against a purchase of £15 or more.

Large adverts were to be found in all of the main daily papers where the striking company logo of a bull's head stared out at its potential customers. Once again limited text accompanied a colour picture of a group of Angus bulls in a field of spring flowers framed by the backdrop of the Perthshire hills. Press releases had ensured that the launch of the new company was widely reported in the business pages. Here it was rightly assumed that Matador had overnight become the country's largest private business. The brochure also landed through the letterbox of every beef farmer in Britain accompanied by an information pack. This explained the company philosophy. There was a registration card for the farmer to fill in. Once that he had completed this and sent it back he would be allocated a supplier code for him to quote whenever he sold animals to Matador. The company made a written promise to pay a retrospective bonus to all of its suppliers in line with year-end profits. A pledge was made to try and always beat average market prices. Matador buyers would always be immediately recognisable at any auction mart as they would wear the company's distinctive red baseball jacket and cap. All suppliers were also promised that when the company was publicly floated at some stage in the future they would be offered a preferential share price. A personalised letter from Sir Alistair McIntyre promised that it was Matador's goal to market and promote British beef in a way that had never been done before. He promised that prices to the public would always be kept as low as possible. He promised that Matador products would only ever be sold anywhere under their own brand name. Finally he categorically guaranteed that Matador would only ever sell British beef, and so the brand name would always offer a secure home to all British produce.

All over Britain 500 butchers' shops were opened with razzmatazz. They had all been newly signwritten and extensively redecorated. Inside they not only carried the usual range of fresh meat but also an extensive selection of microwaveable ready meals. In the high streets of many towns, the newly recruited young salespeople in their Matador jackets and caps manned small kiosks where the passing public were given burgers and sausage sandwiches, and leaflets and balloons for the kids.

After the lunchtime news the first of many TV adverts was screened. The advert opened with a montage of achingly beautiful images of rural Britain. Classical music merged into a voice-over which promised the new company was about bring a very old product back to the people. A camera panned in from a hillside to slowly focus on Sir Alistair standing amongst a group of five of his Angus bulls. He was dressed casually in cord trousers, black wellingtons and an old woollen jumper. The young bulls were playfully chewing at his sleeves and he ruffled one of the heads fondly. After a moment he turned to the camera and smiled.

*"Hello. I would like to introduce myself. My name is Alistair McIntyre and these are my cattle. My family has raised these Aberdeen Angus cattle for well over a hundred years and we are all rather proud of them. We have*

never had a case of BSE on our farm, and you will probably be surprised to know that there have been remarkably few cases of BSE on any of our hill farms. And yet I have been told that my animals have become a danger to public health. I have been told that it is illegal for me to eat a T-bone steak from one of my own cattle. Like most farmers I have had to grit my teeth and see years of toil undone by crazy government policy driven by publicity-hungry scientists who have yet to categorically prove a thing. At the same time we have had to watch beef pour into our shops from countries where animals are treated appallingly, where they are filled with hormones and growth promoters, where no heed whatsoever is taken over cleanliness and hygiene.

"Well, enough is enough. Today we have launched a new company called Matador. You may well have had a letter from us through the post. Matador will offer you the finest beef in the world at a price which is fair and sensible. We have opened hundreds of butchers' shops all over the country and we have a fleet of delivery vans which can deliver our products to your door. We have employed hundreds of young people to come and visit you at home to tell you about ourselves and our products. Now when they come, give them a break, they are all just kids fresh out of school and college and I promise that they won't be exerting any pressure. I know for a fact that they are all terrified at the prospect of knocking at your doors;, I don't blame them, so try not to chase them away. I am afraid that my colleagues have press-ganged me into doing these adverts so I fear that you will be seeing more of me over the coming weeks. If you feel the urge to hit the mute button on your remote control, I for one don't blame you – I would no doubt do the same myself. All we ask is that you give British beef a proper chance and we know that you will find it to be the best in the world. Thanks for listening."

More music and pastoral views and the advert ended.

It didn't take long for the media to get excited and Sir Alistair and Marcus were fully booked making radio and TV appearances for several days. The burger kiosks stayed in the high streets for four days and over 200,000 burgers were given to the passing public.

Gideon had very little sleep indeed for the first week. A mountain of figures poured into his office at Black Loch which he laboriously fed into his computer. He had created a complex model which assessed a variety of factors to try and predict how the initial launch was proceeding. Sales from every shop were logged along with orders for deliveries. Wholesale enquiries were noted. The number of £5 vouchers redeemed within the first seven days indicated the extent to which the brochure had been read. Once the door knockers hit the streets, their day sheets logged, the number of calls that they had made, and they judged the warmth of their reception by a factor of one to four. These figures in turn gave an indication of the public's thoughts. The targets that had been set were steep, but it quickly became apparent that they were being exceeded on almost every front by about 4%. Predictably, the biggest problem that had to be tackled was distribution. Some shops exceeded all expectations and had to have emergency deliveries of new stock late at night. Luckily the decision to play very safe with opening stock levels had been made and the main delivery centres were able to cope.

On Thursday morning the *Globe* ran its third story under the simple headline

### 'MEAT AND BONE MEAL SHAME'

This time the leading photo was unrelated and showed the naked torso of an emerging starlet of a popular soap opera who had unwisely believed that she had been safe to sunbathe topless whilst on holiday in Turkey. There was the promise of more inside. Dwight had thought long and hard about this. He had no doubt that the meat and bone story had to run, but it was obvious that it wasn't visual and could easily be perceived as boring. In fact, it wasn't the sort of story that his paper would normally have run in a month of Sundays. With this in mind he had decided to rely on a favourite tabloid technique to draw attention to his front page: when in doubt, show them a pair of famous tits. He had kept the photos of this particular famous pair of tits up his sleeve for several weeks waiting for just such an occasion.

The story was fairly short and to the point.

*As you all know, the Globe is undertaking a new and in-depth*

*investigation into just what is really going on with the beef that we eat for our Sunday lunch.*

*The more we look into things, the more appalling are the facts that we unearth. Here is a bit of history.*

*In 1989 the scientists said that cows had been infected with BSE by eating food which contained contaminated meat and bone meal. The Government asked that the animal feed industry should stop using meat and bone meal in cow and sheep food and they did so. It is worth noting that nobody else in the world took the same step.*

*It was seven more years before the scientists decided that there was a link between BSE and the new CJD. At this point the government insisted that meat and bone meal should not only be banned from cow and sheep feed, but pig and chicken feed as well. Furthermore, they decided that every tonne of meat and bone meal was unsafe and should be burned.*

*Fair enough, or is it?*

*We looked at this and felt that there was a big unanswered question. Where did the meat and bone meal go for those seven years?*

*Well, some of it obviously went into pig and chicken food, but what about the rest? Where did all those thousands and thousands of tonnes actually go? Thousands of tonnes of a product that is so dangerous that it now must be burned at colossal cost to the British taxpayer.*

*The Globe has found out. We have talked to several people in the meat and bone industry who have felt the need to talk and come clean.*

*It was exported to our European partners. Thousands and thousands of tonnes were quietly exported to Ireland and France and Germany and Holland. And what happened to it then? Oh we can guess that easily enough. It was fed to cows.*

*These are the countries that now have the cheek to tell us that our beef is so unsafe that it is a criminal offence to send even one beef sausage out of this country. These are the countries who have the cheek to claim that they have no BSE in their beef herds. Well that is a lie and we are happy to go into print and say that it is a lie in big capital letters. **IT IS A LIE**.*

*We know that nobody will dare sue us because they would get the same judgement that the Texan farmers got when they tried to sue Oprah Winfrey when she told the American public that there was BSE in the United States – Oprah took them to the cleaners just as we will take anybody to the cleaners who dares to take us on.*

195

*The sad and tragic fact is that BSE is very much a worldwide disease, although the tragedy is for the cows. There is still just about no evidence at all to prove that it has any link with any human disease.*

*The big fact is this. There is only one country in all the world that has taken serious steps to get rid of BSE and has done so for the last ten years: Britain.*

*There is only one country where the number of cases of BSE in cattle falls every year: Britain.*

*There is only one country that has taken the trouble to ensure that its beef is absolutely safe: Britain.*

*And yet our Government allows thousands and thousands of tonnes of dodgy meat to be dumped in this country and turns a blind eye.*

*We would like to ask another question of our Minister of Agriculture and we demand an answer. His European cronies have told him that our meat is so dangerous that it must not be fed to anybody in the whole wide world. It is supposed to be so dangerous that we actually have to burn it rather than send it to the poor devils in Africa who are starving to death. So what about us Minister? If your EEC pals are so convinced that our beef is lethally dangerous, then how come they are happy for us to eat it?*

*Do we not matter? Is it OK if a few Brits die? It is a rather difficult question isn't it Minister, and we **WANT** an answer.*

*We **DEMAND** an answer.*

It was a cause of some personal annoyance to the Minister of Agriculture that he had become accustomed to turning to the *Globe* first as he reviewed the morning papers over his breakfast. He was even more annoyed at the fact that his stomach tended to tighten with nerves as he unfolded the paper to see what was on the front page. Over the last few weeks he had often felt a surging sense of relief to find that the space on the front page was filled with a run of the mill "Sex-mad vicar hounds choirboy" type story.

Wednesday had been a bad day for the Minister as the talk of the House had revolved around the story of the Matador launch. He had felt the prevailing mood strongly. Sir Alistair McIntyre had been a popular and respected MP, and there was no doubt that most of his fellow politicians were on McIntyre's side. This uncomfortable sensation had stayed with the Minister all day. He was on the wrong end of knowing glances and snide comments, and these were by no means exclusively coming from the opposition benches.

And now this. He read and reread the piece with amazement. This wasn't a *Globe* story. It was an *Independent* story aimed at a minority of thinking liberals and causing minimal damage. He shuddered as he thought of the millions of *Globe* readers who would wake up to this outrageous tirade once their eyes had been drawn to the tender breasts of the soap actress. Worst of all was the question. It was an awful question and one that he had never asked himself. It was a horribly logical question to which he could think of no easy answer. It was the sort of rotten, difficult question that all MP's anticipate from a TV interviewer or in a pre-election debate. It was not the sort of question that you expected to be posed in writing to you personally on the front page of the third best selling paper in the land.

Predictably enough the phone started to ring soon after seven. He hated fielding the journalist enquiries with the "No comment" routine, but he could think of little else to do.

The Prime Minister called a little after 7.30.

"Things don't get easier for you do they?"

"No, I am afraid that they don't Prime Minister."

"I fear that you are going to have to come up with an answer to Mr Forrester's question and I think that it will have to be pretty good." The minister's heart sank when he registered that his boss had used the word "you" instead of the more comforting "we".

"Of course Prime Minister."

The voice on the end of the line became a fraction warmer. "May I ask, have you ever looked at the issue in these terms?"

"No, I can't say that I have."

"I haven't either. It is rather a sobering thought, wouldn't you say?"

"Extremely sobering."

There was a pause on the line. "May I venture a suggestion. I personally do not believe that there is an adequate answer that you can give on this matter. I feel that the best response is to make it clear that we as a Government inherited these policies from our predecessors, that we have been bound by their decisions, and that we are of course working with all efforts to solve the current crisis. I know it is weak and horrible, but I really cannot think of any way round it."

The Minister's heart sank. He had been edged into a corner where he had no choice but to make the kind of mealy-mouthed politician statement that the public hated so much. He would come out looking weak and ineffectual and it would not be forgotten. He could think of nothing to say other than "Of course Prime Minister. I will do my best."

"Good. I'm sure that you will. I have put off calling Mr Forrester but I think that it is now rather pressing. I cannot think what has got into the wretched man. Unfortunately I gather that this little campaign of his has put his circulation figures up rather than down, so I can't say that I am wildly optimistic about persuading him to change his tune. I suppose that his allegations about BSE being a Europe-wide problem are correct?"

"I'm afraid so Prime Minister. The others are simply covering it all up. Typical really."

"Yes, typical. They are not going to like this one little bit of course. Anyway, we shall simply have to try and make the best of things. Make your statements and I will call the dreaded Australian."

With a sense of great weariness the Minister rang his secretary and instructed her to agree to an appearance on the *Today* show. It went absolutely awfully as the presenter badgered him to give his own thoughts rather than harping back to what his opposite number had done in the past. His only solace was that he had kept his temper and hadn't made an absolute fool of himself. As he climbed into his car and headed for the Commons he felt resigned to another uncomfortable day of sarcasm and innuendo from his fellow MPs.

Dwight got into the office for 7.45 and a little after eight his secretary excitedly informed him that he had the Prime Minister on the line. He smiled eagerly to himself and took the call.

"Good morning Prime Minister, and how are you on this fine sunny morning."

"Well, to be honest Dwight, I have had better mornings. What on earth is going on?"

The aggressive tone annoyed Dwight. "I don't know, you tell me."

"I would like to know why you have suddenly started to pose difficult questions to my Minister for Agriculture and why you seem intent on hounding the poor man as if he had been caught with his trousers down."

"May I say Prime Minister that I feel that you do the *Globe* an injustice. Our commitment to the defence of our readers' interests does not end with exposing the sexual peccadilloes of their leaders. We feel that there has been a great injustice done to the British farming industry and that our readers are being sold sub-standard food by unscrupulous retailers."

The Prime Minister sighed with exasperation. "OK, OK, enough of the publicity-speak. Let's talk straight shall we?"

"That is something that we Australians pride ourselves on."

"In that case cut the bullshit. What's happening?" There was now an edge to the PM's voice.

Dwight sat back in his chair and swung his feet up onto his desk. "What is happening Prime Minister is just the same thing that has happened in my life for the last thirty-odd years. I am a journalist and a newspaper man. I print stories that my readers like and that sell papers. Since we took up this campaign of ours our circulation figures have risen by 2%. Just so long as that is the case we will continue to indulge ourselves in running a campaign that is just and right and fun. Even I get fed up with always having to come up with a new pair of tits every day to sell my paper."

The Prime Minister was aghast. "Please don't tell me that you have got a crusade hat on."

"You bet I have, and it feels pretty good too. So I am sorry to say that I have no plans to call off the dogs, no matter what you say."

There was a long silence on the line. Eventually the Prime Minister spoke again, this time in rather a more conciliatory tone.

"We of course always appreciate it when one of our newspapers takes up a cause which is bold and just, particularly when it is so clearly aimed at promoting the interests of one of our industries.

Should your campaign not be quite so aggressive towards my government I am sure that we would view such a praiseworthy campaign in a very positive light when it comes to issuing our list of New Year's honours. It would be interesting to have Sir Dwight Forrester on the same list as Sir Donald Bradman don't you think?"

Dwight sighed to himself. It had only been a few short weeks ago that he had caught himself daydreaming about such an offer. He had felt that the best way to achieve such an offer was to offer his paper's unqualified support for the new Government in order to be granted such a reward. Now he felt mildly depressed to be at the receiving end of the kind of cynicism that had dominated British policy for hundreds of years. "Your offer is very kind Prime Minister, but once again you misjudge me. I am not some jumped-up little colonial who can be bought off by a trip to the Palace. There is a much easier way for you to ensure that my paper stops attacking your agricultural policies. Stop doffing your cap to the French and bloody Germans and do the right thing for your people. Now if there is nothing more, I have things to attend to."

The Prime Minister's voice was thoughtful. "No Dwight, there is nothing more. May I say that I didn't enjoy making you that particular offer and I am not displeased that you threw it back in my face. It is what I deserved. You should be commended for what you are doing, although I wouldn't dream of saying so publicly. However it is obviously our destiny that we must fight, let's keep the fight clean shall we?"

"I am happy to give you my word on that Prime Minister. You've just made sure that your Government shall continue to enjoy the full support of the *Globe* on all issues other than your agricultural policy."

"Well thank you for that. Goodbye."

"Goodbye Prime Minister."

Dwight put the phone down and suddenly felt about twenty years younger. He immediately picked the phone back up and called Cornelius on his mobile.

"Hello."

"G'day Cornelius, it's Dwight."

"Morning Dwight. Nice story again. We were all rather

concerned that it could be a bit boring. How very clever of you to use that poor young girl's bosoms to draw the eye of the readers to the front page. You really are a rather dreadful man I must say."

Dwight chuckled happily. "Oh I'm just an out and out Aussie bastard. Anyway we've hit a nerve this time. I've just had the bloody Prime Minister on the line."

"Good Lord. What did he have to say?"

"He tried to bully me first and when that got him nowhere he offered me a gong to back off."

"And?"

"I politely told him where to stick it. Actually he was pretty good about it. He apologised and came over a bit guilty about acting so typically bloody British. We're still friends."

"Well I'll be damned. A knighthood. Well, you will always be Sir Dwight to me old chap."

"That's big of you. How is the launch going?"

"Great. I've just come off the phone with Gideon. His fancy programme says that we are 4.37% ahead of target in all areas, although I don't pretend to understand how he works that out."

"Ahead is ahead and that is all that matters. I would say that things are really rather well set for the concert, wouldn't you."

"Oh, absolutely Dwight, absolutely."

"Have no fears, the *Globe* will be there to tell it hard and straight to the great British public."

"Brilliant. Speak to you soon."


On the evening of Friday March 3 Cornelius, Vince, Montgomery, Victor, Helen and several of the ex army farmers met up at Ringway Airport on the outskirts of Manchester. After a couple of drinks they drove to the Nynex Centre in the middle of the city where the Orange Boys were due to kick off their latest UK tour that evening.

Outside the huge hall the atmosphere was frenzied even though the concert wasn't due to start for two hours. Ticket touts and T-shirt sellers alike were doing a booming trade and harried policemen were trying vainly to control the seething crowds. Helen headed off backstage with David Williams, Donald Atkinson and two other farmers. The rest of the team used their newly issued press passes and headed for the VIP lounge. As they swapped tales of their most recent activities, Cornelius noticed that Victor seemed rather quiet. He sat down next to him.

"Penny for them big guy?"

Victor smiled ruefully. "Oh I'm OK, just tired."

"Well that is what the Ritzy globetrotting life does for you my friend. Argentina, Brazil, it just seems a shame that there isn't a burgeoning beef industry in Tahiti. I do believe that some dusky Copacabana girl has stolen that big vulnerable heart of yours."

"Brazil wasn't very good Cornelius."

Cornelius frowned with concern. "Did things go wrong? What happened?"

"Oh things went fine, no problems, it was just . . . I don't know. Let's leave it hey. Check out the paper on Monday. Read all about it." His eyes caught sight of Ricky Myers who had just got himself a drink at the bar and was scanning the room. "Yo, Ricky! Over here!"

Ricky sat down with Cornelius and Victor. His thin face seemed more drawn than ever and black bags hung under his eyes.

"Jesus guys, I'm shagged."

"Have you done the story?" Asked Victor.

"Yeah, all filed. Boss seems happy. How's the launch gone Cornelius? I reckon you guys are slacking, there wasn't a word about it in the papers in Rio."

"Absolutely Ricky, we've all been spending most of our time having our nails done and reading Proust. Actually, things have gone better than we could have expected. I suppose Dwight told you about all the hullabaloo over the meat and bone story?"

Ricky's eyes gleamed with pride and the tiredness fell off him. "Did he ever. How about it. Phone call from the PM no less. I think we are really getting to them." Victor stood up and ambled into the Gents. Cornelius watched him go then said to Ricky. "Is he OK?"

"Yeah he's fine. It was a bit upsetting out there. He'll handle it, don't worry. How's Helen getting on with the surprise guest?"

"I haven't the faintest idea and I am having nothing whatsoever to do with it."

A little after ten the VIP bar started to empty and they all made their way to their reserved seats high to the right of the stage. The mood in the cavernous hall was now bordering on the hysterical. The 8,000-strong audience was shrieking and bellowing for their idols. The air was thick with sweat and smoke and it seemed to throb with the sound of the music that was pounding out of the speakers which were piled twenty feet high either side of the stage. Then the tumult hit a new crescendo as the Orange Boys sauntered out onto the stage and took up station at their instruments. Cornelius smiled to himself as he compared the strutting arrogance of the young men on stage with the two shivering boys watching the video in the Caledonian Hotel. They piled through five favourite tracks as the seething mass of humanity in front of them jumped and leapt and roared out their familiar, anthem-like tunes. Malcolm Lyle said little between the tracks until the band had completed the fifth. This was fairly unusual. It was a feature of the Orange Boys that Lyle enjoyed preaching his street philosophy to his devoted brethren. At last he took the microphone and stepped forward to the front of the stage and began to shout in his strong Liverpool voice.

"You know you shouldn't be here tonight. Have you not read the papers? Have you not heard that we are the worst people on earth? We're the worst fucking people on earth you know! And you know what! We're corrupting you. YES YOU!!!" The audience bayed its glee. "Look at you all. You are the poor innocent youth of this great land and us bad fuckers from Liverpool are the great Satan and we are CORRUPTING YOU!!!!" The young fans howled with joy at the idea of being corrupted. Lyle continued. "I mean look at us will you. We don't shave. We never wear a tie. We're fucking rude to old ladies. We swear a lot. We've never done a decent day's work in our lives. We have no respect. We don't clean our teeth after eating chocolate. We can't get ourselves out of bed in the morning. We are a wart on the face of society. We deserve to be flogged.

"FLOGGED!!!"

He allowed his voice to drop a level, forcing a strained hush in the hall as his disciples hung on his every word. "You know what?

You know what's the worst of it? I don't think that the Government likes us either. Oh God, I don't think that they approve because some people say that we do some really, really naughty things. Can you believe that? CAN YOU BELIEVE THAT!!!!"

Eight thousand voices howled "NO!!"

"Honest, they do. They even think we take drugs. Can you believe it, they really think that the Orange Boys take drugs. Well you know what? You know what? You know fucking what ! WE COULDN'T GIVE A FUCKING TOSS WHAT THEY THINK!!!!!!"

Mayhem. Bedlam. Cacophony.

"Well we're going to give the authorities a bit of a treat tonight. We are going to make it easy for them. We are going to let them catch us red-handed so that they can put us away and throw away the key and protect all of you poor innocent babies out there from our wicked corrupting influence so that you will all hop off to the Job Centre on Monday morning in a nice clean shirt with your hair nicely combed and go and work IN FUCKING BUILDING SOCIETIES!!!!!" The audience yelled its support.

"Right here and now on stage and on camera we are going to introduce you all to one of our suppliers and then, in the eyes of the whole world, we are going to consume a real illegal prescribed substance. What do you reckon?"

"DO IT!!!!"

"I said what do you reckon? "

"DO IT! DO IT! DO IT! . . . "

Lyle waved to the back of the stage. Four men emerged struggling desperately to hang on to a wild-eyed six-month-old Angus bull which was bucking wildly. There was a gasp of surprise from the audience, then general laughter and whistling. Lyle turned back to the audience grinning and held up a T-bone steak for all to see. "Here you are. Know what this is? It is a real, down the line, wicked, illegal substance. This is a British T-bone steak. It is so dangerous that it is banned all over the world. And you know what, I'm going to take a hit." He took a ripping bite of the steak and hurled the remainder out into the audience. "So let's see what they are going to do about it. Because this is a symbol. Everything that we do they make illegal, everywhere we want to go they try and stop us, well here you go guys, you've caught me in the act now, come on, come and get me, come and lock me up, NOW LET'S PLAY SOME MUSIC!!!!"

Pandemonium. The band crashed into their latest hit and the roof seemed in danger of being blown clean off as the audience roared out its accompaniment. An hour later the throng spilt away into the drizzling Mancunian night. Vince and Cornelius watched the crowds drain off into the mean city centre streets from the window of the VIP lounge. Cornelius shook his head. "It's not hard to see how Hitler got on so well."

"Nope. Not hard at all. Tell you what Cornelius, I think we better make a note to remind ourselves not to invade Russia, no matter how much of a good idea it seems at the time."

"Consider it minuted Vincent. How's Helen's bull?"

"Still moaning."

"I doubt that he would ever have guessed that he would become a teen idol."

Saturday, March 4 was a big publicity day for Matador and the beef industry. The front page of the *Globe* was dominated by a dramatic photo of Malcolm Lyle brandishing his T-bone steak to the demented masses before him with the ironic accompanying headline of:

### 'STEAKHOLDER SOCIETY!!!'

Ricky's article picked up Lyle's mocking tone of the night before and mused on what action the government would take against the band. The Minister for Agriculture stared with dumb amazement at the photo, and nothing that his wife could say could either cheer him up or persuade him to eat any breakfast. His mood was not helped in the slightest by the hoots of delight that his two teenage children let out as they read the story. All over Britain breakfast-show DJs had a gleeful time talking up the story and fielding calls from their listeners.

Oliver Hamilton heard the story on the six o clock news, rang a friend to cancel their weekend away, and headed rather disconsolately for the office. By the early afternoon he had fielded umpteen calls from astonished store managers who reported a wave of teenagers demanding to buy T-bone steaks. By three he sat with his head in his hands and still his brain kept spinning and spinning. Just before the early evening news the second Matador advert hit the screens. Accompanied by jaunty 1950s music, John Cleese, wearing his famous cap and fawn raincoat buttoned to the neck, strode purposefully down a terraced street. He stopped outside a shop and carefully studied the nameplate which read 'MATADOR PETFOODS'. With an air of great determination he opened the door which caused a bell to ring. As he stepped through the door he cast a quick furtive glance down the street just in time to see a man dressed in a pin-striped suit dart into a back alley. Once inside the shop he was confronted by Eric Idle behind the counter.

**Idle.** *"Morning sir, and what can I get you today?"*

**Cleese.** *"T-bone steak please."*

**Idle.** *"Ah, T-bone steak is it? For your dog is it? Nudge nudge, wink wink."*

**A cross Cleese.** *"Course it is man. What on earth are you insinuating?"*

**Idle.** *"Oh nothing, nothing at all. I would never imagine that you would even so much as dream of eating it yourself, nudge nudge, wink wink."*

**Cleese.** *"Good. Now can I have my steak please."*

**Idle.** *"Here you are sir, nudge nudge, wink wink."*

A stiff Cleese strode out down the street to be followed by his pinstriped pursuer. A very fast sequence of events then showed him bounding in and out of buses, tubes and taxis before being seated at his 1950s kitchen table with knife and fork at the ready when the door crashed open. In marched the pin-striped figure with two policemen. At this point it became clear that the pin-striped figure bore a more than passing resemblance to the Minister for Agriculture.

**Pinstripe.** *"I take it that you are not about to consume that T-bone steak yourself sir!"*

**Cleese.** *"In that you are quite correct sir."*

With immense reluctance Cleese lifted his plate from the table and placed it on the floor where it was set upon by an eager Jack Russell Terrier. The advert ended with a voice-over extolling viewers to give their dogs a treat.

*"Buy him a T-bone steak from your local Matador Pet Shop
- and remember, it is illegal to eat it yourself."*

The next morning, most of the Sunday papers ran stories about the extraordinary set of new events that had taken the Beef Crisis to new and fascinating heights. Most highlighted the plight of the increasingly beleaguered Minister of Agriculture and speculated that if events continued to escalate, the Government could be about to face its first really difficult crisis. Two papers ran features on Sir Alistair and most carried supportive comments for his efforts from a number of prominent figures. The Minister had an utterly wretched morning as he battled his way manfully through a thoroughly uncomfortable interview on *Breakfast with Frost*. As he made his way home he ruminated on the indisputable fact that he was becoming a laughing stock.

The third Matador advert ran at 5.30.

A group of heavily armed soldiers came out of a jungle to be confronted by a savage-looking sergeant major. He yelled them to attention. *"Right! You've nearly completed your Special Services induction course. You have done the parachute jump, you've been through the minefield, you've been over the live firing range and you've just marched 80 miles through a snake-infested jungle. Now you must complete the final test. Now you must prove that you have courage. Now you must show that you have the guts to take a real risk regardless of the fact that there is a billion to one chance of danger. Yes, gentlemen, now you must eat a British steak."* At this, the battle-hardened troops backed away, halted momentarily, then fled back into the bush. The advert finished with a caption and a voice-over:

*If you've got the guts, if you are the kind of person to take a billion to one chance, then eat British Beef from Matador . . . it's worth the risk.*

After the nine o'clock news the fourth advert was shown.

This time Sir Alistair was wearing a thick coat and standing in the midst of a litter-strewn inner-city wasteland. *"Good evening. I'm afraid it is me again – Alistair McIntyre of Matador. I would like to show you something that we are doing. This, believe it or not, is the middle of one of our cities."* Winter rain had soaked Alistair's hair and an American-style police siren wailed in the distance. *"This is where a lot of our fellow countrymen live. They live in cardboard boxes and doorways. We should all be ashamed.*

*"As of last week you can now find a place like this in over fifty of our cities and towns."* As he spoke he pointed across the empty space to a cluster of portacabins with a large, neon Matador sign shining out into the rainy night. The camera followed Sir Alistair inside where a crowd of bedraggled men of all ages were sat around tables eating. Sir Alistair looked over the room then spoke into the camera. *"Beef stew. The meat comes from Matador, the vegetables come from farms all over Britain and every site is manned voluntarily by farmers' wives. Since Hitler's U-boats nearly starved us all to death half a century ago we have built a farming industry that can feed everyone on these Islands, and I mean everyone, not just those with a credit card for the supermarket. Please don't let this fine industry be destroyed. If it isn't British, don't buy it."*

The seventh item on the news show that followed gave details of a Gallup Poll which gave Sir Alistair McIntyre a 74% approval for his Matador campaign. This was the last straw for Simon Shawfield as he sat watching in the luxury of his Belgravia apartment. All weekend he had watched the media stories with a feeling of mounting panic. He now felt angry and vulnerable. He grabbed the phone and rang his secretary and demanded that an emergency Board Meeting be called for the following Wednesday morning. He poured a large whisky and drank it thoughtfully. What on earth was going on?

Vince was also watching the news that evening. Outside, the wind had got up and he could hear it howling up the valley to High Cragg like a runaway goods train. He was relishing the feeling of peace that he was always able to draw from his hilltop hideaway. Peace had been in distinctly short supply over the last couple of months.

Helen had arrived a little after seven. She had been dead on her feet but quite exhilarated having finally secured a venue for the critical May bank holiday weekend event. This meant that she had now secured all three party sites and was over halfway to achieving her target of fifty holiday sites. The work had taken her thousands of miles around the country but he had been delighted to see that her enthusiasm was quite undimmed. They had eaten and then moved onto the sofa by the fire whereupon her head had slowly sunk down to his lap and she had fallen into a deep sleep.

Vince gently stroked her hair and smiled as he absorbed the news of the Gallup Poll. He remembered Sir Alistair's abject horror when he had first insisted that he should do the adverts. It had soon become clear to all of them that the old man was as good an actor as he was good at just about everything else that he cared to turn his hand to. As the fire crackled in the grate and a flurry of rain lashed the window he allowed his mind to wander back to the evening when he and Helen had sat in the moonlight by the stream in the hills above Stirling. It had only been a week ago but it already felt like months.

He recalled the images that had had filled his head of young British soldiers waiting out the warm Picardy night before the hellish first day of the Somme. Well, the big push had been launched and, unlike the young volunteer army, they had made their breakthrough.

They had achieved total surprise with their attack. Every interview that he watched or listened to, and every article that he had read had led him to the same conclusion: that nobody had the first inkling as to what on earth was happening. He smiled as he remembered his nights alone at High Cragg after Sir Alistair had first offered them the contract. On his way home he had stopped off in Edinburgh and had bought several books about Rommel and Guderain and their breakthrough in the thick forests of the Ardennes in the spring of 1940. So much had hinged on throwing a pontoon bridge over the river Meuse before the Allies had time to collect their thoughts and organise a reinforced defensive line.

The moment had been lost and once the Panzers crossed the bridge their arrival in Paris six weeks later had more or less been an inevitability.

The concert on Friday night had been his River Meuse. He had been worrying constantly that it could easily backfire. The Orange Boys were always going to be a potent publicity weapon but there had always been a chance that it could have been a tarnished one. The events of the weekend had put paid to all his worries. Like Rommel before him, he had gambled almost everything on a hunch. His hunch had been that the Beef on the Bone Ban could easily be mocked. His gamble had been that the quickest and easiest way to the heart of the British public was by mocking something which was so plainly absurd.

He was now happy that it had worked. In a matter of five days Matador had become the talk of every bar, canteen and hairdressers in the country. Gideon had called earlier to tell him that over half of the butchers' shops had sold out the day before and that each of the fifteen pet stores had been mobbed. There wasn't a T-bone steak to be found anywhere.

He lit a cigarette and laid his head back and stared up at the ceiling. They had broken through. They had achieved their bridgehead. He knew that although the first week was always going to be the biggest gamble, it was in many ways the easiest part of the operation. It was the last time that they would be fully in control of events. Thus far they had been able to maintain complete control of the timetable. From now on the key would be to react to the unpredictable. They had already made many enemies and at this very moment he knew that these same enemies would be feverishly planning their countermeasures. They had all spent long, hard hours trying to anticipate what these countermeasures would be, but of course they really had no idea at all.

From now on the troops were going to be exposed in open country. The road to Berlin was clear but there would be many hazards along the way.

Helen stirred briefly and looked sleepily into his face.

"What are you thinking about?"

"The road to Berlin."

"How lovely." And she was asleep again.

Rearden was working his way doggedly through the Sunday papers in a hotel room when the bedside phone rang.

"Rearden."

"It's Kumalo. What is happening?"

Rearden felt the familiar prickle of fear that he experienced every time he heard Kumalo's ominous low voice. "I wish that I knew Julius. I only wish that I knew."

"Bring me up to date."

Rearden talked steadily for ten minutes as he brought Kumalo up to speed with the remarkable events of the weekend. For a moment he was convinced that the line must have been cut when he finished speaking, so great was the silence at the other end. Finally Kumalo spoke. "I cannot believe that these events can be mere coincidence. There is a planner behind all this. There is someone pulling every string though it seems difficult to understand how. We need to look into this Rearden and it needs to be done quickly."

"There has been nothing so far to suggest that our sales will be threatened . . . "

Kumalo's voice snapped down the line causing Rearden to jump. "Don't be a fool man. This is only just starting, there will be more. Much more. Whoever is co-ordinating this campaign is at some stage going to present a major threat to our success. We need to find out who is behind this and eliminate them. It is as simple as that. Have you any ideas?"

Rearden pondered this for a while. "I know of a firm of Private Investigators who specialise in corporate matters. I gather that they are pretty efficient, though by no means cheap. I could contact them tomorrow."

"Do it. Whatever it costs, do it. Now what about Hamilton?"

"He's bearing up but only just. They have called an emergency Board Meeting next week and he is scared stiff."

"Stick close Rearden. I want him out here next weekend."

"That could be difficult, what with everything . . . "

"I said I want him out here next weekend. I object to repeating myself."

"I will arrange it."

"Good. Keep me posted."

Rearden was about to say goodbye but the line was already dead.

# CHAPTER TEN

## OUT BEYOND
## THE BRIDGEHEAD

On the morning of Monday March 6 the cabinet room at 10 Downing Street was full and ready to commence its business. The Prime Minister glanced around the table and nodded. "Right, let's begin. Item number one on the agenda this morning is beef. Or should I say bloody beef." He stared at the Minister of Agriculture and raised an eyebrow for him to begin. The Minister summoned up a bright, confident smile from somewhere and started to speak.

"Although recent events have once again brought the beef issue high into the public's attention, nothing has radically changed regarding our stance on the overall problem. Our policy of strictly following the advice of our scientists, which we have consistently agreed with our colleagues in Brussels, would still appear to be the best method of . . . "

As he grimly worked his way through his presentation he was aware that his colleagues were staring doggedly down at their papers and avoiding any eye contact. He felt like a leper. After six agonising minutes he wound up his deposition.

" . . . to conclude, I feel that we must not be seen to over-react to the rather tacky publicity that the *Globe* and the new Matador company are using to bombard the public. It is important that we make a clear and firm decision as to how and when we prosecute both Matador and the Orange Boys for their deliberate and public attempts to encourage the public to ignore our ban on the consumption of beef products on the bone . . . ."

He came to a sudden halt as the Prime Minister crashed his hand down onto the leather topped table. When he spoke the Prime Minister's voice was filled with incredulity.

"Prosecute! Did I hear that correctly? Did you really say the word prosecute? My God man, have you gone absolutely barking mad!"

"No Prime Minister."

"Good. I must say that I am delighted to hear it. Now I think that it is time that we get some political home truths out in the open. This Government enjoys the largest majority that any government has known for half a century. We were voted into office by a veritable landslide because people were quite frankly fed up with having ridiculous policies pushed down their throats by wholly discredited politicians. Now I don't know about the rest of you, but as I have watched, listened and read everything that has been said over the last few days about beef, one thing has stood out very clearly to me. Do you know what that is? Well, I'll tell you what it is. They are bloody well right, that is what it is."

There was a slight intake of breath from the ministers around the table. The Prime Minister continued. "I believe that we have adopted this ludicrous ban on beef on the bone because we were so arrogant and full of ourselves that we never stopped to think for a minute how downright silly it was. I'll tell you what, I had an awful conversation with Dwight Forrester last week and when I put the phone down I reread his editorial and I could not disagree with a word of it. He is absolutely bloody right, it is both crass and ridiculous for us to condone the sale of cigarettes which are proven killers whilst banning T-bone steaks which are about as likely to be fatal as having a butterfly bite you on the nose.

"No gentlemen; enough is enough. We have made absolute fools of ourselves and we fully deserve the mockery that we are now having to endure. I will remind all of you that one of the biggest reasons that we all sit here now is the mess that the last government got themselves into over the Poll Tax issue. Well, this administration is not going to make the same mistake. We are going to get out of this mess and we are going to do it this week and that is final."

The silence that followed the Prime Minister's tirade seemed endless. The Minister for Agriculture knew with a horrible certainty that it was up to him to break it. "May I ask if you have any suggestions Prime Minister?"

"I do not have any suggestions. I have an instruction. On Thursday, before the debate on the reforms to the Common Agricultural Policy, you will make a statement to the House announcing that the Beef on the Bone Ban is lifted with immediate effect. The reason that you will give is that the scientific evidence is no longer strong enough to warrant such a measure. Yes gentlemen, we are going to do a U-Turn. I can assure you that I find it every bit as hateful as the rest of you, but I simply will not allow us to be made a laughing stock over this issue. There is however some good news. I believe that there is a very good chance that McIntyre and his new company will overcome many of the beef farmers' problems and thereby relieve us of the problem of having to throw more money into this wretched business. We should all learn a lesson from the way that he is solving a very British problem by bringing the British people together to solve it. I say best of luck to him. Now let's move on."

Ricky Myers' Brazil article appeared on the front page of the Tuesday *Globe*. Again two photos dominated the page. This time the headline read

### 'SAMBA SHAME'

The first photo showed a group of cattle grazing a patch of grass around a burnt-out shell of a house. The second showed the hollow blank faces of a woman and her three young children as they sat by a cardboard box hovel set in front of the backdrop of a sprawling shanty town.

The article followed.

*As we all count down to the big kick-off in the World Cup in June, most of us have a very particular image of Brazil. We see Pele and Zico and gorgeous bikini-clad girls on the Copacabana beach. Sadly there is another, darker side to Brazil which we have uncovered as part of our worldwide investigation into the beef that we eat. Above you can see what is left of the Vega family. A year ago Mr and Mrs Vega and their four children lived in a small village in the north of Brazil. Their family had farmed the land around the great forest of the Amazon for many generations.*

*Then a large cattle ranching company decided that it wanted to have their land to farm beef animals. They wanted everybody to move away so that they could clear the forests, sell the precious hard wood, and plant grass for livestock. The villagers refused to accept the paltry offer that the company made for their homes and refused to move away. They appealed to every politician that they could find, only to discover that they had all been bought off.*

*Yet still they refused to move.*

*Finally the company hired mercenaries to attack the village at night. Mr Vega and all the men were gunned down and the houses were burnt to the ground. The women and children were driven away with nothing other than the clothes on their backs. On the long, hard march to the shanty town on the outskirts of Sao Paulo where they now eke out an existence they suffered a further tragedy. Little Enricho, who wasn't even two, died of typhoid in a roadside ditch. The Vega family are people without hope and the murderers were never caught. They were never really hunted.*

*The company is a major exporter of beef, and over the last two years it has enjoyed record levels of sales to the UK market. It is yet another example of the British shopper unwittingly supporting murderous criminals.*

*We can only say the same thing to all of our readers that we have said many times before:*

*If it doesn't say it is British, then don't buy it.*

When the Shawfields Board met at ten the next morning the mood was a sombre one. Oliver Hamilton was acutely aware of the hostile glances that were aimed in his direction. Simon Shawfield strode in, sat down and began the meeting without pleasantries.

"You will all have guessed the reason that I have called this meeting. The recent concerted campaign to promote British beef I believe constitutes a substantial threat to our business. We made a unanimous decision to switch all of our stores into 100% Irish beef for very clear financial reasons. I have given this decision a great deal of thought over the last few days and I am happy that, considering the circumstances that prevailed at the time, the decision was a correct one. However things have moved on. I will expect individual reports in due course, but it is already clear that the fact that we are not marketing British beef is affecting not only our beef sales, but also sales of all of our other products. This downturn is already severely threatening our half-year results. I will remind you all that the reason that we adopted Irish beef in the first place was to attempt to maximise our half-year figures. I have had solicitors review our contracts with Emerald Meats and they inform me that there is no question of any get-out clause. Were we to cancel the contact we would be forced into making a provision to wipe nearly £20 million off our half year profits. I would suggest that such a course of action would precipitate a disastrous collapse in confidence in the company which would inevitably lead to collapse in our share price.

'I will remind you gentlemen that the reason we are all paid our very handsome salaries is to look after the interests of our shareholders. Well, we had better get down to doing just exactly that. We are between a rock and a hard place. Somehow we are going to have to market over 13,500 tonnes of beef which is in danger of becoming unsellable. I just thank God that it is Irish and not from some godforsaken Third World hell-hole which would be sniffed out by the *Globe*."

Oliver shuddered at this. Part of him was filled with relief that Simon Shawfield was determined to fulfil the company's contract. The other part was quaking with terror at the idea that the true identity of the beef on his company's shelves would come to light. The meeting lasted until the early evening. As he drove home he was shattered. It was clear that the company was in trouble and that there was nothing to do but to tough it out. The next few months promised to be a slow and unrelenting personal hell. As he turned off the M25 his phone rang and things got worse. Rearden told him in no uncertain terms that he was to be on the 5.00 a.m. Saturday flight to Bulawayo and that he would be back in the country by midnight on Sunday. Rearden really didn't give a shit if he would be missed at work, he suggested that he tell them that his mother was dying. It was non-negotiable. Kumalo wanted him at Clearwaters, and what Kumalo wanted, Kumalo got.

On the same afternoon the Matador team met in the waterside room at Black Loch. Their mood differed utterly from the Shawfields meeting that was proceeding at the same time. Gideon described in great detail how his model now suggested that they were 5.23% ahead of their targets. The sales teams all reported a uniformly terrific reception from the public. The shops were selling out on a regular basis. This did not cause a great problem as each shop-keeper was able to arrange for products to be delivered by the vans. Helen confirmed that she had more or less completed her job of finding her rural venues and that the decking out of the first of these would be complete by the weekend. She suggested that Sunday should be a suitable day for filming. Montgomery confirmed that work on his three buildings was more or less complete and that he had fully recruited his team. His part of the operation was on course to go active the following week, and the weekend of the March 18 would be ideal for filming. Vince outlined the plans for the covert farmers for the coming month.

Everybody was in good heart, particularly Marcus who was thriving on a rich diet of media appearances, so much so that Sir Alistair suggested that he may like to take his place in the adverts. The suggestion was thrown out unanimously.

Sir Alistair enquired if there was any other business. Dwight raised his hand with a grin. "Just a couple of points boss. Number one, the *Globe* has received over £20,000 in donations for the Vega family over the last couple of days, I am happy to top it up to £50,000. I would like to suggest that we give Victor and Ricky a couple of days off to go and sort the family out."

The motion was instantly agreed and Victor's face nearly split in two, so great was his smile.

"Second, I don't know about the rest of you, but this Potter character is really beginning to get up my nose. He is losing credibility fast, but he still seems to get himself in the news just about every day. I don't think that he is doing us too much harm, but he isn't doing us any good either. I would like to propose that you give myself and Cornelius leave to take steps to sort the smug bastard out."

Again the motion was agreed. As the meeting closed, Cornelius took Dwight by the arm. "I do believe that we are having an alarmingly bad influence on you my dear chap. I got the distinct impression that you may have something rather wicked in mind for the good professor."

Dwight's grin was full of menace. "You bloody bet on it mate. I'm going to see the pompous little prick stitched up good and proper."

The Minister for Agriculture rose to his feet a little after two on the afternoon of Thursday March 9. As he worked his way through the statement that announced the ending of the Beef on the Bone Ban, his head swam with sounds of rising hilarity that poured down from all sides. When he sat down the chamber was filled with cheers. They were hard mocking cheers which he knew effectively heralded the end of his political career. The cheers were loudest from the opposition benches, but it was the derisive cheers that came from behind him that caused him the most hurt.

The news lines soon hummed with the astounding story of a major U-turn. Political speculators barely dwelt on the threadbare scientific excuses for dropping the ban. They commented with extreme animation on how a tabloid, a pop group and a private limited company had so effectively driven a stake through government policy. The Prime Minister gave an interview for the early evening news. He displayed an unusual candour, and whilst reiterating the lack of strong scientific proof, he also admitted to the fact that recent events had caused him to look long and hard at the ban, and that he had seen the sense in many of the arguments that had been put forward. He explained that he was determined that his administration would never view the world with a closed mind, and that he saw no crime in making a U-turn if it proved to be the right thing to do.

The next day two opinion polls reported that the Prime Minister's approval level had risen to new and unprecedented heights.

The news was greeted with joy by beef farmers all over Britain. Sir Alistair immediately called Vince on his mobile phone to congratulate him. He was somewhat taken aback by Vince's low mood.

"What is it? You seem thoroughly depressed lad."

"No, not depressed. It is just a setback, that's all."

Sir Alistair was aghast. "A setback! What on earth are you talking about?"

Vince sighed. "They have just evacuated Moscow boss. They've burnt it to the ground."

"What on earth are you talking about? Evacuated Moscow?"

"In 1812 the French and the Russians fought themselves to a standstill at the battle of Borodino. It was the greatest battle that there had ever been and 40,000 lay dead and wounded at the end of the day: but nobody had won. The Russians fell back to Moscow with their army pretty well intact. Napoleon assumed that there would be another decisive battle for the city; a battle that would determine the course of the war.

"He was wrong. Instead of fighting, the Russians left the city and marched further east. When the French entered Moscow they believed that they had achieved a great triumph. The troops looted every building and loaded carts up with bounty. Then their food ran out and the winter set in. They had nowhere to go but back. Not many survived the long march home, and in the end Napoleon's armies were crushed outside Liepzig.

"I am afraid that our victory was rather too fast Sir Alistair. I was rather hoping that we would be able to keep the Beef on the Bone issue in the public eye for rather longer, that's all. Anyway not to worry, we shall learn from history; I have no intention of getting my throat cut by Cossacks."

Sir Alistair was silent for a while. "You are worth your money young man. Lateral thinking was always beyond my dull old brain. You are quite right of course. Do we need to meet up to review things?"

"No. Not at all. We don't need to change anything, we have simply lost the benefit of having the Government as the butt for our jokes. Don't worry about it."

Vince's concerns were borne out that night. The Orange Boys were playing at the NEC in Birmingham. Thousands of their fans in the audience had searched the city to buy T-bone steaks to wave over their heads at the concert. Most of the steaks were thrown into the bin; after all, there was no fun in them when they were legalised. Helen's bull did not get the chance for a further dose of the limelight. Ricky Myers watched the first twenty minutes of the concert, then left and drove back to London. As he made his way down the M1 he felt a sense of disappointment; it would have been a cracking story.

It was late on Saturday afternoon when the Mercedes car dropped a weary Oliver Hamilton at the front steps of Clearwaters. The long flight had been an unhappy one. With a heavy sense of foreboding, he had sat gazing out of the window as the hard, parched wastelands of Sudan and Ethiopia had passed beneath him. He was under no illusions that his visit was not going to be a happy one.

As Kumalo came out of the house to welcome him, his spirits lifted a little. Kumalo was smiling and his handshake was warm.

"Welcome back Oliver, it is indeed a pleasure to see you again. Come in, you must be tired. We will eat."

They ate well as Kumalo quizzed Oliver about the extraordinary events that had swept over Britain during the past weeks. He was delighted when Oliver reported the outcome of the Board Meeting and that it was the intention of the Shawfields Board to honour their contract with Emerald Meats.

"When I was fighting in the bush I learned that when things become difficult is the best time to judge a man for what he really is. You have had a very difficult time my friend and yet I see that you are still strong. This time of problems will pass. You need have no fear."

By eleven, as they sat talking quietly on the veranda, Oliver was fighting to hold his eyes open. The warm night air and the gentle sound of the crickets were lulling his chronically tired brain. Kumalo glanced at his watch and got up.

"Come Oliver. We have something to do now."

They left the house and got into the Land Rover. Kumalo headed out across the moonlit fields. Progress was slow, and it took them nearly an hour to cover ten miles. Kumalo spoke little and Oliver lolled back in his seat and gazed out as they passed clusters of silent cattle. They halted at the crest of a low hill and Kumalo flashed his headlights twice. His signal was answered by another set of headlights from a vehicle about 400 yards away. When they drew up, Oliver saw that there were two cars parked in the shelter of a shallow valley. A group of four men were sat together smoking and talking quietly. Kumalo exchanged brief words in Matabele and the men got up. Two dragged some equipment out of one of the 4x4's whilst the second pair pulled two prisoners out from the other. Both men were blindfolded and their wrists were tightly bound behind their backs. The guards pushed them with their weapons and made them kneel down.

"Oliver, these men have betrayed me. They have stolen from me. There is only one punishment for this." Kumalo pulled a revolver from his pocket, walked over to the first of the prisoners, held the gun a few inches from the side of the man's temple and fired. The impact of the bullet from such short range made the prisoner's head explode like a water melon. His twitching body sank to the floor in a kind of slow motion and his blood seemed inky black in the moonlight as it oozed into the dust.

Kumalo was quite unmoved and he quietly issued further instructions. The headlights of the three vehicles were all switched on giving the scene a film-like quality. A growing stain was spreading across the front of the second prisoner's trousers as he urinated in terror. He was muttering incoherently. One of the guards fiddled with a video camera on a tripod for a minute or two until he turned to nod to Kumalo.

"OK Oliver, now it is your turn. I need to know that I can trust you completely. You will execute this traitor for me and this will be filmed. The film will be kept with other films that I have had taken during your two stays at Clearwaters. When Shawfields have taken delivery of the very last tonne of the contract, you and I will destroy all of the films together. Furthermore, if you do this for me, I will see that a £25,000 bonus is transferred to your Geneva account on Monday. Should you refuse to do as I ask, I will know that you are not a man that I can trust. I will be forced to execute you, as well as this filthy traitor. You will be buried in this quiet place and, as far as the whole world is concerned, you will have simply disappeared. Remember, you have travelled here on a false passport. So what is it to be Oliver?"

Oliver stared down at the quivering prisoner. He felt every part of his body turn numb and cold. Without looking at Kumalo he held out his hand. Kumalo clicked off the safety catch and passed the weapon over. Oliver took it, drew in a slow breath, walked over to the prisoner and shot him through the head. He glanced down briefly at the body, then walked back to Kumalo and passed over the gun.

Already the cameraman was dismantling his equipment whilst the others brought spades and began to dig. Kumalo fixed Oliver's feverish gaze for a few seconds, then patted him lightly on the shoulder.

"Thank you Oliver. Now I can trust you. We will go back." Oliver glanced over his shoulder as they drove away. He saw the two corpses and the slow rhythm of Kumalo's men digging the graves in the light of the moon. He merely felt empty. Totally, completely, overwhelmingly empty. As empty as the moonlit plains of Matabeleland that stretched far away into the night.

As far as the mind could reach.

That weekend's edition of the *Farmers Weekly* was filled with the Matador story. Already farmers all over the country were seeking out Matador buyers at auction markets and selling their cattle to them without sending them into the ring. A wave of optimism was sweeping through the countryside as the marketing campaign went from success to success. There was a three-page profile and interview with Sir Alistair McIntyre.

On the Markets page it was noted that over the last week the price being paid for finished steers had risen by a staggering 19 pence per kilo to £1.12.

Vince tossed the magazine down and smiled quietly to himself. He closed his eyes and his imagination was filled with the picture of tanks picking their way carefully over a rickety pontoon bridge. Below, the waters of the River Meuse were placid and still and the heavily wooded riverbanks glowed in the fresh dawn light of another perfect Spring day. General Erwin Rommel cast a gaunt, dusty figure as he sat and smoked and watched his grey tanks roll their way into the history books. He too was smiling quietly to himself.

# CHAPTER ELEVEN

## SHADOW BOXING

The following week Sir Alistair made his third appearance in a Matador advert. Again the camera dwelt on beautiful countryside before panning in on a casually dressed Sir Alistair. He gave a small smile and gazed about his surroundings before turning to the camera to speak.

*"This is Mid Wales. It's beautiful isn't it? I am going to talk about young people. Like most beef farmers, I was appalled when many of our schools refused to feed British beef to our kids.*

*"I think that many of us have forgotten just what a good food beef is for children. We have got into the habit of feeding our kids the same way that we feed ourselves. But this is crazy – they are not middle aged and overweight, they don't need to worry about blood pressure or cholesterol or hardening of the arteries. Think about it. Look at the amount of energy they use. We not only have to make sure that we give them enough food to keep all that energy going, we also have to feed them enough so that they can grow.*

*"Beef has most of the things that kids need – protein, iron, lots of vitamins and lots of energy. It's a great food for kids.*

*"So what is Matador doing about this? Well, I would like to put some of our education authorities under a bit of pressure to start buying British beef again, and I am looking for a bit of help."*

The camera panned around the field. There was a selection of tents, lots of sports equipment, a large dining marquee, and a football pitch.

*"What we have here is a summer camp. As you can see, we have cashed in on the Peace Dividend and bought lots of surplus gear from the army. This camp is in the middle of Wales, and by the summer, Matador intends to have opened fifty more, enough to accommodate 5,000 visitors every week. Each will be geared up to take a hundred kids. Our young guests*

*will get lots of fresh air, see the countryside, learn a bit about farming, play lots of sport, go climbing and canoeing, all sorts.*

*"The really good news is that it will not cost either the parents or the school a penny. The costs are being shared by Matador and the farming community. However, there is a catch. Well there is always a catch.*

*"We are only offering these free holidays to schools that buy British beef. And that means Matador beef. So if you would like to see your children come to a place like this for a week AND eat the cleanest, tastiest, safest beef in the world, then all you have to do is to start exerting as much pressure as you can on your school's authorities.*

*"Just tell them this. If it isn't British – Don't buy it."*

In the days following the screening of the advert, media coverage was fairly sparse, though favourable. However the sales teams started to pick up a steady flow of new orders from schools, and the holiday camps went on to be fully booked out for the summer.

During the remainder of March and the first fortnight of April the company ran two more major adverts. In the first, Sir Alistair announced that Matador had decided to offer a 40% reduction on all of its products to old-age pensioners. This time there was a little more coverage coupled with a resounding endorsement from the Government. Finally, the company announced that it had set up its own record label which was supporting promising new bands. Every weekend there would be at least five Matador concerts held in cities up and down the country. Admission prices were kept low, but it was also possible to get in by collecting vouchers and tokens which were available with all Matador products. The new record company was launched in tandem with a string of Matador burger bars. Marcus had managed to acquire an ailing burger chain with two hundred struggling outlets.

As the weeks passed by, Montgomery's judgement was proved to be excellent as four of the new Matador groups made it into the top 30 in the charts. Sales from the burger bars soon exceeded all expectations.

The price of beef eased up steadily as the ever-increasing Matador purchases began to take the slack out of the market.

The twenty soldier farmers had been working quietly for well over a month. Two pairs had been given the job of finding out just who was importing meat, where they were importing it from, and who was buying it. All of the recent adverse publicity about imported products guaranteed that lips were well sealed. Information was gathered through a mixture of surveillance, bribery and break-ins. Slowly but surely the information painted a picture of exactly where imported products were being sold.

By the last week in March the first target had been selected. Quickshop. Quickshop was a medium sized retailer with twenty-five small superstores spread over the north west of England. It targeted the cheaper end of the grocery market, and most of its stores were to be found on the meaner side of old industrial towns. For £500 cash, a purchase ledger clerk had supplied copy invoices that showed that Quickshop had been purchasing all of its beef from two main wholesalers. Both of these companies had their premises broken into on a Sunday afternoon and a hired specialist downloaded all the information from their computers.

The paper trail showed that Quickshop had been buying a mix of British and imported meat until the Matador influence had forced up the price of the home-produced product. As soon as this happened the company had quietly switched into 100% imported meat which came from a variety of sources.

The third team had been out in the countryside recruiting more help. By the time that Quickshop had been identified as a target, there were plenty of volunteers available to launch the attack. The method of the attack was extremely simple. At nine o'clock one Tuesday morning twenty cars arrived at the Quickshop store in Stockport. They arrived along with other customers over a period of ten minutes. Each car contained a farmer's wife or daughter whose ages varied from 17 to 74. Once inside the store, the women made their way to the beef counter where they applied stickers to packs of beef. The stickers were striking and simple. They showed a union jack with a bold line through it and the words "NOT BRITISH. DON'T BUY IT". Within five minutes every pack of beef on the shelves had one of the large stickers plastered over it. Heads were shaken and scratched. The manager was summoned. He ordered that the stickers be taken off. One of the shop assistants tried, but found that it was impossible to take the sticker off without removing the cellophane wrapping. After more consultation, he ordered that the shelves should be cleared and new stock brought out to replace it.

This task was duly undertaken. Within minutes more stickers had been put on the beef. The manager ordered that a security guard should stand by the beef section to stop any more of the stickers being applied. The large guard hovered uneasily as several ladies perused the beef whilst nervously aware of his attention. Finally, a doughty woman of 69, who had driven down from her Peak District farm that morning with her two daughters, calmly paused by the beef counter and started applying stickers. For a moment the guard was totally dumbfounded, he was put off by the fact that the lady was so composed and matter of fact as she got on with her task. Soon there was a small but growing group of shoppers watching the incident unfold with undisguised interest. At last the guard decided that he simply had to take action. He marched over to the lady .

"I'm ever so sorry Madam, but I will have to escort you from the store."

"Why of course you will young man, I'm defacing your stock. Shall we go?"

As they made their way down the aisle to the exit, three ladies from the watching group calmly stepped forward and started to apply their stickers. Within minutes every item of beef had been labelled and the manager was once again summoned. He had been on the phone to head office where instructions had been issued that the shelves must be kept full at all cost. He ordered that every item once again be replaced and that three security guards should guard the counter. As he stood and watched nervously it immediately became apparent that the presence of the three large uniformed men hovering menacingly around the beef counter was proving to be a fairly major disincentive to the public. Each time a shopper stood by the counter they instantly found one if not two guards at their shoulders. In most cases they moved away hurriedly.

The manager pondered this and ordered that the guards should stand further back whilst maintaining their vigil. Ten minutes later three ladies approached the counter and started to apply stickers. The guards moved in and escorted them from the store. Once again they were immediately replaced with another four ladies and every pack was defaced within minutes.

This time the manager ordered that the shelves be left empty whilst he sought further instructions. He failed to get hold of anybody at head office. The lines to the management suite were jammed. Every store in the group was under attack.

After half an hour it became clear to Ricky Myers that there would be no more beef on the shelves that day. He purchased two cans of lager and strolled out to his car. Once inside he opened one of the cans, took a long appreciative gulp, and removed the camera that he had hidden under his jacket. He made it back to the *Globe* offices a little after eight. By half past nine he happily tossed the developed photos onto Dwight's desk. Dwight leafed through them slowly and his quiet chuckle steadily grew until it became a guffaw.

The next morning Ricky's series of photos appeared in the *Globe*. In his story he claimed to have received an anonymous tip off that things were going to happen at the Stockport branch of Quickshop. His story lightheartedly mocked the befuddled efforts of the Manager and his guards and ended with a picture of empty shelves.

All of the region's local papers picked up on the story along with several nationals. The next day, a variety of journalists flocked to the twenty-five Quickshop stores. It seemed that there was a huddle to be found around each and every beef counter. Even a few of the paparazzi had been lured by the story. Security guards stood either side of the beef counters in a state of extreme embarrassment whilst nervous store managers paced around scrutinising the face of every customer. As the morning drew on, the crowds around the beef counters grew bigger and the tension grew. It was soon obvious that no ordinary punter was going to find the nerve to buy a pound of mince whilst under such intense scrutiny. By 10.30 the tension was awful. Journalists and photographers were tense because they were worried that they might end up waiting around all day and it was more than possible that nothing at all may happen. The store management were tense to find themselves at the centre of so much media attention. Their stores were full of people, but they were sightseeing rather than buying anything.

In a slick co-ordinated move at 10.30 exactly, the next attack was launched in every one of the Quickshop stores. A group of five women marched through the waiting crowd and started to apply stickers. Within seconds a wild melée broke out as security guards pounced, cameramen jostled for position, film crews zoomed in with shoulder-held cameras and radio journalists gave breathless commentary. There was general pandemonium. Chaotic writhing groups of shoppers and journalists followed the security guards as they frog-marched the sticker women to the exits. Then a second wave of women moved in only to be met by more reinforcements. There were more ejections. There were just about enough security guards left to handle the third wave of the attack. However the fourth wave was too much to handle, and by 10.45 the battle was won and every beef package in every Quickshop store was branded with a sticker saying "NOT BRITISH. DON'T BUY IT".

At noon the Managing Director of Quickshop Ltd gave a press release announcing that his shops would not be selling beef until a further announcement was made. The Quickshop board talked until late into the night. No matter which way that they looked at the problem there was only ever one answer. At nine the next morning the company announced that in future it had decided to market only British beef.

Two restaurant chains and another small retailer chain suffered attacks over the next fortnight. In each case the result was the same and the companies soon pledged to switch to British beef. In each case they were livid to have buckled so easily under the strange pressure, but it was eminently clear that the cost and hassle of trying to stop the waves of sticker girls was nowhere near justified by the extra margins to be had from selling imported beef.

There were no fewer than three emergency board meetings held at the Shawfields Head Office during the first fortnight of April. The company became beset by a siege mentality as it braced itself for the onslaught of the dreaded sticker girls. Security was tightened dramatically at all offices and distribution centres.

These moves were made too late. Several small operations had been carried out in the weeks leading up to the attacks on Quickshop, and the reports that came in were all dominated by the intriguing name of Emerald Meats.

Vince and Gideon had met up on the morning of April 1 to go over the information that had come in about Shawfields. Ever since the onset of the Beef Crisis the company had maintained a policy of stocking a mix of British and imported beef, a mix that varied according to which product offered the best profit margins. Paid informers had divulged that a trial had been carried out in a number of stores which were converted to 100% imported meat. Sales had never wavered in these stores which had encouraged the Board to take the decision to switch to 100% imported beef throughout the whole group. Gideon had produced a financial assessment of Shawfields' recent performance. He pointed out that the City had been becoming increasingly nervous about Shawfields, and that the next set of interim figures were considered to be of paramount importance. He speculated that the decision to adopt 100% imported beef had been taken as part of a basket of measures to try and maximise profit figures for the next vital set of accounts.

Both men could understand the logic of this. What was a much greater mystery was the fact that all evidence suggested that the order for the imported beef had been placed with a single, fairly unknown Irish supplier, Emerald Meats. Following discussions with the others, it was decided that the Irish company should be carefully looked into before any further action was taken.

Donald Potter was fed up. He was sat in his university office marking essays which he found more or less terminally boring. Over the last two years, as his media career had taken off he had found it increasingly difficult to find much enthusiasm for the more tedious elements of academic life. Marking essays, he had decided, was one of the most tedious of these tasks.

As his attention once again wandered he could not help but feel that his media stardom had become something of a poisoned chalice. It had caused him to become mind-numbingly bored with the day-to-day routine of university life. It had caused him to become isolated from his colleagues who openly accused him of disregarding sober scientific principles in order to get his face on screen. And now, he found that he was coming under attack more and more as the Matador campaign gathered momentum.

The lifting of the Beef on the Bone Ban had been a personal disaster for him. He had taken interviews and gone on the offensive by accusing the Government of playing fast and loose with public health, only to find himself at the wrong end of snide comments and cheap jibes. Within days he had felt that he was being turned into a laughable crank, a figure of fun, a joke. He winced as he replayed his last two interviews in his mind. It had been humiliating and he did not seem able to come up with any answers.

Worst of all was the ill-concealed delight of his colleagues and many of his pupils. He had heard the sniggering and tittering behind his back, and worst of all, the mooing sounds as he walked down any of the corridors. He sat back from the essay and sighed deeply. Surely things couldn't get much worse.

There was a small knock on his door.

"Come."

Nothing happened. He shouted more loudly, more angrily.

"I said come in for Christ's sake."

The door opened tentatively and a diffident young woman in her late twenties cautiously came into the office. She wore jeans and an old American army jacket. Her hair was a chaotic pile of brown curls, and a large pair of glasses dominated her face. As Potter looked her, over he realised that underneath the specs and the shapeless clothes was a pretty girl with a fine figure.

She spoke nervously. "I'm really sorry if this is a bad time Professor Potter, and if it is I will go away and I won't come back at all if it isn't convenient, it was just that . . . "

He held his hands up in rather a dramatic way. "Whoaa, slow down, slow down. Now why don't you sit down, take a deep breath, and tell me who you are and what it is that you want. Why don't we start with where you have come from. What is that accent, Australian?"

She gave a small shy smile and sat rather stiffly on the very edge of one of his visitors' chairs. "It's New Zealand actually. My name is Julie Anderson and I am a reporter with the *Auckland Gazette*. I am on holiday at the moment, but my boss asked me to try and do any interviews that may be of interest to the people at home. He said that he would pay for each piece which will give me the money for my airfares.

"We have all heard a lot about you and your stand against the beef industry back at home and you are really very popular. You know how our farms are, we are more or less organic, and we don't feel that it is fair that we are always competing against the intensive farming industries in other countries.

"My father is a farmer and he has always spoken really highly about you." She then looked down and blushed a deep crimson. "I must say that you have always been something of a hero of mine."

Potter smiled happily. "Well young lady, you are lucky. My diary is not remotely demanding today so I would be delighted to grant you an interview. I must say, that it is extremely heartening to hear that my work is respected on the other side of the world."

Potter made coffee and Julie fired questions at him. Later, when she glanced at her watch she gasped in surprise. "Good grief professor, I have just seen the time. I am delaying you far too long." Again the schoolgirl blush. "I am quite sure that my boss would be quite happy for the *Auckland Gazette* to buy you dinner, that is if you want to, that is, if you don't have anything else on . . . "

Potter thought of the state of tense and silent war that had come to exist between him and his wife. He thought of the quiet emptiness of his hours at home and spoke eagerly, "That would be splendid. Thank you."

Again the shy smile. "I am staying in a little pub a few miles away. It isn't anything grand but the food is really nice. I am afraid that I don't have any smart clothes to take you anywhere that is . . . "

"Fine.Terrific. Suits me. Where and when?"

Potter arrived at the village pub on time at 8.30. He had told his wife that things had come up and she had put the phone down on him in her usual way. He scanned the small cosy bar and spotted Julie sitting in a corner. He smiled, asked her what she wanted to drink and joined her.

The food was as good as she had promised and he easily fell into drinking steadily without noticing it. She was a wonderful listener, and he was soon opening up, and bewailing the fact that all his hard work was being undone. He told her all about the cruel jibes on the television, and the mocking comments of his colleagues who all hated him, and the mooing noises that his students made when he passed them in the corridor. She gently took his hand in both of hers and expressed her deep sympathy. Behind the huge spectacles her eyes shone with concern. As he rubbed his thumb up and down the back of her hand he began to feel painfully aroused.

The old bell at the bar rang out last orders and the room began to empty. In a very, very shy voice Julie said. "Would you like to come up for a coffee in my room Donald."

As she said it he could hardly trust his voice, and when he said "Yes", it sounded croaky.

Still holding his hand, she led him up the narrow staircase and unlocked the door to her room. She took off her army jacket and plugged in the kettle. "Sit down, please." She looked around anxiously, then smiled "It will have to be the bed I suppose."

Potter sat down as nervous as a sixteen year old whilst Julie fussed over the coffee. When she had stirred the cups she turned around to look at him for a moment. She then took off her glasses, crossed over to the bed, took his face in her hands and started to kiss him fiercely.

Potter's hands were a frenzy as he pulled off her sweater and unhooked her bra. She gently pushed him back. "Wait Donald, there is something that I must tell you. I have always had, well how can I put it, it is just . . . " Once again she was blushing.

"It's OK Julie, you can tell me."

"You will probably hate me for this, but I have rather strange sexual tastes. I don't know why. The doctor said it must have come from my childhood, I can't think how."

Potter felt a tightening in his throat. "Tell me. I promise it will be alright."

She told him and he feared that his erection was about to rip clean through his tweed trousers. She said huskily. "Can I?"

"Do it. Do it now."

She peeled off her jeans and socks, then, wearing only her knickers, she peeled off Potter's clothes until he lay naked on the bed. She rooted in her rucksack and came out with four short lengths of rope. Using these she tied his wrists and ankles to the four corner posts of the bed. He lay there spread eagled and hugely aroused. She looked down at him, tut tutted, then walked to the door and opened it.

Potter's eyes opened wide with horror as the chuckling figure of Dwight Forrester marched in. He kissed Julie happily on the lips and gave her an affectionate slap on the bottom. "Great job sweetheart. Bloody great job. Now you get dressed and meet me in the car."

Julie threw on her clothes, packed her bag and left the room without so much as a glance at Potter. Dwight stared down at the bound and miserable figure. "Oh Donald, Donald, Donald, what is it that they say? There's no fool like an old fool. Just look at you Donald, what a simply dreadful sight. Yet you really thought that a lovely Kiwi girl would drop out of the sky and want more than anything in the world to bed you. You're a bloody idiot Donald and that is all that there is to it."

Tears of shame were trickling down Potter's face. When he spoke, his voice was quite broken. "You bastard Forrester. You rotten, bloody bastard."

Dwight grinned with pleasure. "If I had a tenner for every time that somebody had called me that I would be a rich man. But what the Hell, I'm a bloody rich man anyway."

"What do you want from me?"

"I'm sure that you can guess if you think hard enough Donald. You have been saying some jolly rotten things about me and my paper's campaign for British beef. Jolly rotten. Really quite hurtful I must say. Well I think that it is time that all of this stopped, don't you Donald? From now on you are going to change your tune. You're not going to do it overnight, but slowly, over the next month or so, you are going to come around to the idea that you have made a great mistake and that British beef isn't really dangerous after all. And what is more you are going to do it in public."

Potter momentarily forgot his misery and was outraged. "But that is out of the question. It is quite impossible, I could never consider compromising my scientific ethics and . . . "

"Bullshit Donald. Bullshit. Never mind compromising your precious scientific ethics. I'll tell you what will be compromising. It will be bloody compromising when I print a picture of you lying on the bed with the lovely topless Julie tying you up with a discreet 'censored' notice over your shrivelled-up dick. Now that will be bloody compromising. Donald, I have pictures of you leaving college, eating downstairs and getting tied up by the divine Julie. Face it man. You're stuffed."

Donald faced it in all its hideous reality. He *was* stuffed. "OK Forrester, you win, just like you always do. Now untie me you bastard."

"Oh I'm not going to untie you Donald. You will have to wait all night until the maid comes in tomorrow morning. And while you wait, you think about all of those farmers who have killed themselves because of what you have done. You think of the blood that you have on your hands. And why? Because you just love to see your ugly mug on the tele, that's why. You see I have you taped Donald, I know exactly where you are coming from. You deserve to suffer for the damage and the pain that you have caused by your vanity. Well you think about it all night you contemptible little git. Within six weeks you will make a public statement which will contain the words 'I made a mistake about BSE.' As soon as you make the statement I will return the photos. It is as simple as that. And believe me Donald, you are getting off much more lightly than you deserve."

With this Dwight strode out of the room and closed the door. Potter wept for hours as he waited for his morning humiliation.

As Dwight, Julie and Cornelius drove down the deserted motorway to London, Cornelius chuckled happily. "I just loved the 'contemptible little git' part. That was priceless."

"Oh, I have my moments you know."

Five weeks later Potter made his statement which caused a

brief stir. He then disappeared for ever from the public eye. He wasn't missed.

When he received a recorded delivery letter with Dwight's photos he didn't throw them away. He hid them in an old paint tin in the garage, and for many years afterwards he would gaze longingly at the pictures of the slender New Zealander who had seemed to understand him so well.

As they patiently queued to clear customs at Bulawayo airport, David Williams and Donald Atkinson were feeling rather jaded. Their task had been to try and unearth new horror stories about imported beef for the *Globe* to feature. So far they had been on the road for a month and they had come up with remarkably little for their efforts.

In Poland and Romania they had found farms which were battling manfully against a variety of problems. Despite a desperate lack of cash and the interference of appallingly corrupt bureaucracies, they found farmers who were doing the very best that they could.

In South Africa they found several examples of farms run by some pretty ghastly ex-apartheid bully boys. One had seemed particularly promising but Dwight had rejected the story. He had told them that the story was far too similar to the Haan feature. He had also pointed out that there would be little public sympathy for a campaign which was aimed to damage the economy of Mandela's new Rainbow Nation. He made the valid point that if the new Black government of South Africa was willing to forgive and forget the excesses of the old regime, it was hardly appropriate for the *Globe* to attack them.

Botswana was another disappointment. They unearthed plenty of evidence of inhumane treatment of stock as well as a chronic lack of hygiene. Once again Dwight rejected the story. He felt that it would undermine the popularity of both his paper and the Matador campaign if they were seen to pick on a poor, embattled state such as Botswana. Initially David had been livid at Dwight's holier-than-thou stance, but on reflection he had had to grudgingly admit that the newspaper man had a point.

They had talked with Vince from Gaberone the night before and he had suggested that they give it a week in Zimbabwe then return home. They checked into a small quiet hotel and made arrangements to meet Walter Evans later that evening. Walter had been a journalist on the *Globe* for several years before resigning to pursue a career as a freelance reporter in Africa. Dwight had got hold of him and asked him to assist David and Donald in any way that he could. Dwight also transferred him a sum of money which was very sorely needed indeed.

They met in the bar of the hotel and tucked into ice-cold bottles of beer.

"Dwight tells me that you guys are looking for the dirty on the Zimbabwe beef trade, that right?"

David passed him some back copies of the *Globe* and he read them through. As he completed the last piece he shook his head in amazement.

"Bloody hell. What on earth has got into the old bugger. This is a bit highbrow for the *Globe* isn't it. How is it going down?"

"I believe,"said David, "that his circulation has risen by more than 2%."

"It almost restores my faith in human nature. I would never have believed that the day would have come when the *Globe* got a circulation boost from quality journalism. Who is writing the stories, Ricky?"

"Yes."

"I thought so. We all knew that he had it in him. He must be having a ball. Anyway, where do you chaps come into all this?"

"We're farmers," beamed David.

"And?"

"And we are taking action to defend our poor beleaguered industry boy."

Walter was thoroughly bemused and shook his head. "I think that it would be best if I stop trying to fathom out what is going on here, because I can see that there is much more than meets the eye and you buggers don't look like the types to let much out."

This time Donald beamed. "Quite right too my dear chap. Let me get you another bottle of this excellent beer and you can tell us what you know."

When Donald returned with the drinks, Walter took a deep swig then started to talk. "To be honest, I am not sure how much joy you will find in Zimbabwe. By and large the country's agricultural industry has stayed in the hands of the old white community. Mugabe has often made noises about nationalisation and redistributing land to the people, but in the end he has always been far too practical to actually do it. The bottom line is that Zimbabwe is as starved of hard currency as any of the developing African nations, and agricultural produce is one of the few areas where it can be generated. He hates the fact that he has had to leave the land largely in white hands but he is sensible enough to realise the consequences to the economy of taking it away.

"The white farmers out here have always been of a pretty high calibre and I very much doubt if you could find anything bad enough about them to sell papers. However, there may just be an exception down here in Matabeleland.

"The biggest landowner in these parts is the Matabele Meat Company. It is run by a very shady character called Julius Kumalo. Kumalo was a famous freedom fighter, a big mover and shaker in Nkomo's old Zipra guerilla army. After the war of independence he emerged as one of the main leaders of the Matabele tribe. There was an almighty bust-up between Mugabe and Nkomo after the war, and to cut a long story short, Mugabe sent an outfit called the Fifth Brigade down here and they butchered the Matabele by the thousand. Kumalo disappeared for years before magically reappearing with a pot of gold to spend. He bought a huge spread called Clearwaters and set up the Matabele Meat Company. That was ten years ago. Since then they have bought up a load more farms and they are now one of the region's biggest concerns.

"It hasn't been much fun asking questions about them I can tell you. Nobody talks. To be honest I would say that they are all scared to death. It wasn't a pretty business in the War of Independence and I don't suppose that someone like Kumalo got to where he is today by kissing babies.

"I'll tell you lads, I have got the distinct feeling that I could end up in an alley with my throat cut if I say too much. That is why I feel that there may be something for you. The journalist in me wonders how this guy ran for his life, disappeared into thin air only to return with a fist full of dollars. Something tells me that he didn't earn his money by taking on a few odd jobs in his spare time.

"I think that I have one lead for you. There is a guy called Jackson who is always to be found at the bottom of a bottle in one of the local bars. His family used to own Clearwaters; they had been there ever since Cecil Rhodes and his merry men came and stole it in 1895. He got pretty badly wounded in the war and he allowed the place to go to rack and ruin. When Kumalo offered to buy it he was so broke that he had to accept. He has been drinking the proceeds ever since.

"He is probably too far gone to tell you anything, but you never know. Have a chat to him. I have heard that he starts his drinking day in the Imperial at about eleven in the morning. Try him tomorrow.

"Anyway, that's me out of this thing. It doesn't feel right at all and I suggest that you guys be very careful indeed if you start to sniff around Kumalo. Remember, you are a very long way from home out here. If you piss Mr Kumalo off, I don't think that you will be on the plane home."

They arrived at the Imperial a little before eleven the next morning and told the barman that they would give him $10 if he gave then them the nod when Alan Jackson came in. The nod came half an hour later.

They knew that Jackson was 45, but the emaciated man who shuffled to the old colonial bar and struggled onto one of the stools looked twenty years older. He ordered whisky and started another day of staring into space. David got up and sat next to him.

"Drink?"

There was no response.

"Is that a yes or a no?"

He was answered by a quiet, cracked voice. "Look at me. Do you seriously think that the answer will be 'no'?"

David nodded to the barman who duly brought a large scotch.

"What do you want?"

"Just a talk. A little talk."

"I don't like talking to strangers. I don't like talking to anyone much. Why should I talk to you? Do you think you can buy me with a lousy scotch."

David paused while the barman made his way to serve a new customer. "Maybe I would like to talk about Julius Kumalo. Maybe that would be the kind of talk that might interest you?"

A thin bony hand shot out and gripped David by the wrist. He was amazed by the wiry strength in the battered man. Jackson cast an overt glance in the direction of the barman and gave his head a small shake. When the barman stepped out of the door at the back Jackson spoke in a low urgent voice. "You bloody idiot. You don't speak out loud about Mr Julius bloody Kumalo around here, not if you don't want your dick cut off and pushed down your throat. Where are you staying?"

"The Victoria Falls."

"I'll pick you up outside at three this afternoon. Now piss off."

Jackson's old Toyota was bang on time to pick them up that afternoon. He said nothing as they passed through the long straight boulevards of Bulawayo and out into the countryside. He stopped an hour later by an isolated wooded area and led them into a small clearing. Settling himself onto a smooth rock, he pulled a small bottle of whisky from his pocket and took a hit.

"OK guys, let's make some ground rules shall we. I don't know what you know about me and Kumalo, but let's say that anything that involves him interests me. Now you might think that all of this is unnecessary cloak and dagger stuff. Well, hear this and hear it well, and remember it. Julius Kumalo is one of the most dangerous men in Africa and if you cross him he will kill you. He won't think about it. He won't worry about it. And when he has done it, he won't feel bad about it.

"Kumalo is Matabele. What is more, he is Royal Matabele. His family was part of Mzilikazi's court when they marched north to conquer these lands last century. These people are trained to become killers from the cradle. The Matabele have always been some of the most ruthless killers in Africa. My family came up here with Rhodes and took the land off them. Our two families have had a blood feud that goes back over a hundred years."

He paused and laid his bottle on the floor and unbuttoned his grimy shirt. He pulled it open to reveal a scar that ran from his sternum to below the waistband of his shorts.

"Nice, hey. Kumalo did this. It was in the war. We had tracked him and his men through the bush for three weeks. We caught them. We outnumbered them by three to one but they fought like jackals. In the end me and Kumalo fought face to face. I cut him. I nearly cut his face in half, and yet he still managed to do this to me and to escape. I was in hospital for months and when I came out we had lost. All my entrails are screwed. I have no right to be alive, especially considering the amount that I drink.

"When I came out of hospital I lost interest in everything. I got too fond of the booze, and the farm went to hell. In the end I had to sell it. There was only one buyer. Julius Kumalo.

"So as you can see guys, there is only one thing that holds any interest to me any more. Him.

"You tell me what you want of him and I may help you."

The two men looked at each other. Donald gave David the nod. He explained that they were both farmers and had been soldiers too. He explained briefly what had happened to the beef industry at home and showed Jackson back copies of the *Globe*. Without divulging too much, he outlined the fact that they were on a mission to find new stories for the paper to run. When he had finished, Jackson sat thoughtfully, slowly sipping at his bottle. Eventually he gave himself a small nod. "This paper you have shown me. Is it popular?"

"It is the third best-selling paper in the UK."

He grinned. "I guess these stories must have pissed a lot of people off."

"Just a bit."

"OK. I'm interested. Kumalo thinks that he is fire proof down here. Hell, he IS fireproof down here. The people worship him because he is Royalty. The Government hates him of course but what can they do? There was a lot of aid cut off when Mugabe sent his Fifth Brigade butchers down here after the war. If they tried to arrest Kumalo it would set it all off again. There would be another revolt and the aid would dry up. So they leave him and he does as he pleases.

"However, were he to be exposed in a big selling British paper, things might just be a little different. It would be hard for Mugabe to turn a blind eye to that." Once again he sat thoughtfully, then continued. "I can help you get your story guys. I may be an old soak but I still have friends. In the war I was in the Selous Scouts, ever heard of them?"

In response Donald let out a low whistle and nodded.

"Well the guys still stay in touch so I know what's what. When the Fifth Brigade came down, Kumalo managed to get away over the border into Botswana. Hundreds of fleeing Matabele joined him at his bush camp. They were the old Zipra guys, hard buggers, they had survived for years in the bush. They had plenty of weapons and so they were able to survive like a bandit army. To start with it was poaching and stealing. Then they got into smuggling. They were hired by all kinds of people to break the sanctions and smuggle stuff into South Africa.

"As the years went by the operation got more sophisticated and they started to move stuff all over Africa, mainly weapons and drugs. When peace came to Matabeleland, Kumalo came back. He had a stack of money in bank accounts in Geneva which he used to buy Clearwaters from me. Since then his company, The Matabele Meat Company, has bought up thousands of acres of farmland all over Matabeleland. They are the biggest farmer around now; they have over 150,000 head of cattle.

"The thing is, the ranching is still only a front. Kumalo still runs his smuggling operations. Think about it. What better way to smuggle weapons and drugs all over the world than hiding it in frozen meat carcasses?

"Now I have heard that the Company has recently landed a huge new contract. I have also heard rumours that it is the UK. An Englishman visited Clearwaters at Christmas and got the red carpet treatment. Some of the staff that work there are still loyal to me, so I get to hear snippets. I tell you, it is unheard of for Kumalo to give the red carpet treatment to any white man so it must have been big. Really big.

"A few weeks after the visit his abattoir in town was working 24 hours a day. They have been slaughtering cattle for fun for a couple of months now. It looks like Kumalo must have landed a fairish order from the Englishman.

"I heard that the same guy was back a couple of weeks ago, a real flying visit. He got in on a Saturday evening and was back on the plane home by Sunday lunchtime. I think that I know why he was here. There was an execution that night."

"An execution?" said David.

"Two of Kumalo's men. They had been skimming the take at one of his operations. When he catches them the punishment is always the same – a blindfold and a bullet in the head from short range. There is something else. It is an old Zipra trick. When they used to sign up a new recruit they would make them kill a traitor. Sometimes they made them do it with their bare hands. Sometimes it was a knife. Sometimes it was a gun. Once the new guy had made a kill, they knew that he was one of them. I believe that Kumalo got this Englishman to take part in the execution."

David was incredulous. "But surely not. Surely he would have refused."

Jackson gave him a contemptuous glare. "He wouldn't have refused. He would have been taken out onto the plains late at night. There would have been at least four of them there as well as Kumalo. He would have been given the gun and told what to do. If he had refused he would have got the bullet himself and put in a grave where nobody would ever have found him. He got on the plane the next day didn't he? That means that he didn't refuse.

"What is interesting is that Kumalo made him do it at all. For him to fly his man all the way out here to tie him in with an execution there must be a flap on. You know what? I think that it must be you guys. Think about it. If Kumalo has indeed landed a massive order to the UK you can bet your bottom dollar that he will have linked it in with something big in either drugs or weapons. Look at the facts. The Englishman comes. He gets treated like royalty. A few weeks later they start killing beef twenty-four hours a day to fill a big export order. Everything is hunky dory until you guys launch your campaign in the UK. Kumalo gets nervous. He gets nervous that his new friend is going to get cold feet and cancel the bloody contract. So what does Kumalo do? He gets the bugger out here and wraps him into an execution. He will have videotaped it you know."

The two men were shocked and silent. For a little while they stared down into the dust as a soft breeze rustled the dry branches of the trees. Eventually David spoke. "So where do we go from here?"

"You need to get hold of your bosses. If they want to run this story then I will start to dig out information. I need confirmation first and I will need £25,000. I hate Kumalo but I want paying for this. If the answer is 'Yes', walk out of the hotel tomorrow morning with a newspaper in your left hand at nine o'clock. If the answer is 'No', don't walk out at all. We will not meet again, it is too dangerous. I will send people to contact you and bring you what you need. To proceed I will want £10,000 in cash the day after tomorrow. My man will collect it. Now let's get back."

David spoke to Vince that evening. Vince spoke to Sir Alistair and Dwight then rang back. "Well guys, we're on. The money will be wired this evening so that you will be able to collect it tomorrow. There are a few things that I need to go over. First, how much does Jackson know about us?"

David thought for a moment. "Not much. All he knows is that we are farmers, that we used to be soldiers, and that we are looking to find new stories for the *Globe*."

"OK, that's cool. Keep it at that. Second, we need to know where the beef is going. That is key. We need the proof. Tell him not to worry too much about proof of the drugs and the arms. Dwight is happy to print that bit without too much evidence. It is the same as the Haan story, he's not worried about getting sued."

"That's fine."

"Thirdly, we could do with this as quick as possible. We are drying up on stories a bit. Quick as you can. Number four, for Christ's sake be careful out there. This Kumalo sounds like he is one mean son of a bitch. This story is really good, but it is not make or break for the operation. It is not worth you guys taking unnecessary risks. You got my drift David?"

"Sure Vince, we won't get too Gung Ho out here. Before you go, what's the beef price doing?"

Vince grinned. "£1.19 a kilo, we're almost there."

"£1.19 a kilo! Bloody hell Vince, we're nearly back to the good old days."

The next morning David strolled out of the hotel at nine with a copy of the local paper in his left hand. That night a small note was pushed under their hotel door giving details of a car park in the Matapos hills where they would be met to drop the money. They made the rendezvous without hitches and passed a message to tell Jackson that the most important thing was that they should know where the beef was going.

After the money was passed there was nothing to do but wait. Three days passed slowly as they waited for word from Jackson.

At one in the morning on the third day the phone in their room rang them awake.

"Hello."

"It's Walter. Pack your bags and meet me outside in five minutes."

"But why . . . "

"Don't argue, just do it. Now!!"

The line went dead. The two men did as instructed and climbed into Walter Evans' car a few minutes later.

"Have you got your passports? "

"Yes."

"Thank Christ for that."

"What the Hell . . . "

"Later. First we get out of town."

Evans was coiled with tension as he drove the car out of the quiet streets of Bulawayo. Once they were out of the city and heading south he relaxed slightly. "We've got trouble. I just heard that the police have found Jackson. He's dead. Apparently he had been tortured and executed. Now I don't know what you guys had going with Jackson but we have to assume that Kumalo knows everything."

Donald said thoughtfully. "Maybe not, he was tough bastard. Selous Scouts."

Walter's voice was quiet. "From what I can gather he was in a terrible condition. He will have talked I'm afraid. He must have hung on for a while, that's all. Poor bastard."

"So what do we do now?"

"I haven't got that far yet. As soon as I heard the news I rang you and here we are. We need to leave Zimbabwe and fast. I am afraid that everywhere will be dangerous. I don't think that we can risk the airports or the road borders. Look, has your operation got a bit of money behind it?"

"Yes."

"Good." Walter passed David his mobile phone. "Get hold of someone. We are going to need them to fix for a plane to pick us up somewhere quiet and fly us over the border into Botswana. There are plenty of guys who will do it for a few thousand dollars. We'll go into the bush and hole up until it is sorted."

David blessed the gods of the mobile phone as he got hold of a sleepy Vince on a crystal-clear line. Vince was soon wide awake and promised immediate action. Four hours later a South African contact of Sir Alistair's confirmed that a small plane would land on a quiet airfield in Eastern Zimbabwe at 2.00 p.m. the following day.

It was a six-hour drive to the small airfield, and the men decided to leave at dawn and try to stick to small country roads. The sun was not over the horizon as they eased the car out of the area of thick scrub where they had hidden through the night. As they made their way toward the road, David noticed a small finger of smoke threading its way into the sky. He stopped Walter and quickly climbed to the crest of a low hill to investigate. He came back five minutes later.

"Bloody road block. It's about a mile up. Is there a way round it?"

They studied the map and the surrounding terrain. There was no way round it. If they went back the way that they had come, they would not only be headed back towards Kumalo's heartland, but the detour would also almost certainly make them late for the rendezvous.

"OK," said David. "We'll have to hit them. Now listen up."

They all knew that the plan was a bit thin, but they agreed that it was their only option. They drove to the road and approached the road block at a quiet pace. It was manned by four armed paramilitary types dressed in the regulation denims.

"Steady now Walter." David's voice was flat and calm. He had quickly adopted the unflappable air of the veteran British Army sergeant that had soothed jumpy troops for hundreds of years. "Easy now, easy now, easy . . . GO!!!"

When the car was twenty feet from the waiting guards, Walter floored the accelerator and rammed the car into two of them. At the same moment David and Donald threw themselves out of the car, rolled, and hit the other two guards. Within a matter of seconds David had his man down and had snapped his neck. Donald was having more of a struggle. David crossed to where they were rolling on the ground and knocked out his adversary with a blow from the butt of the rifle that he had picked up. He quieted the screams of the two who had been hit by the car with similar ferocious blows. They then bound and gagged the three guards who were still alive, pushed them into the back of their Land Rover and hid the vehicle amongst a clump of trees a hundred yards off the road.

Twenty minutes later they were heading east. Walter had been shaking too badly to drive so David had taken the wheel.

"Jesus David, you killed one of them, I mean you broke his neck."

David's face was grim and he gripped the wheel fiercely. "I know I did Walter. It was necessary. That's all. Necessary. Now be a good chap and don't go on about it. We've got a long way to go today."

The drive along the quiet back roads of eastern Zimbabwe seemed endless but passed without incident. The small plane was waiting as promised and at 2.35 p.m. they passed out of Zimbabwe airspace. They were able to fly out of Gaberone the next morning and were in London the day after. Vince and Helen met them at Heathrow. As they made their way into the city, the feeling in the car was tense. "Are you OK?" asked Helen.

"We're OK." David's voice was still flat and emotionless. "It wasn't good out there. We had to break a road block to get out. I had to kill one of them. They tortured Jackson you know. It sounded bad. Really bad. What are we going to do Vince?"

Vince flinched at the question. "You are not going to like this David and I promise that I am sorry. We aren't going to do anything. To have any more involvement with this Kumalo would be madness. In the end all we are going to get out of this is another story. The operation is going well enough for us to walk away from the story. It simply isn't worth the risk. Damn it, we could have lost you guys out there."

David was angry. "But this bastard Kumalo stinks, Vince. He's a killer. We can't let him get away with it."

Vince's voice was full of patience. "David, none of us signed up to change the world. Our job is to get the price of British beef up to £1.26 per kilo. Come on, you must see that. We can't go sending our people into harm's way in Africa, no matter what kind of a bastard this Kumalo is. No David. We walk away."

They were silent as the the new industrial units that lined the M4 passed them by. Half an hour later David spoke again. "You are quite right of course Vince. Quite right. I'm sorry if I gave you a hard time over it. What do you want us to do next?"

Vince was relieved. "I think some less dangerous work is in order for you lads. You best go with Helen now and help out with the parties. Things are hotting up on that front. She could use some extra hands."

After three days Kumalo had to accept that they had got away. The Land Rover with the three bound men and their dead comrade had been discovered. He had received reports that the sound of a small plane had been heard in villages close to the Botswana border. It was obvious that they were gone.

His mind was filled with questions. It was clear that they were a part of the conspiracy that was attacking imported beef in Britain. Jackson had confessed that they were connected to the *Globe*. Yet he hadn't thought that they were employed by the paper. They were farmers and they had been soldiers. Pretty good soldiers too; despite being unarmed they had soon rolled his roadblock.

On balance he felt that he had got the best of things. He had caught Jackson before he been able to find out anything much. Jackson would have told them about the guns and the drugs but no more. They hadn't come to Zimbabwe to look for him, they had come to look for a story. After what had happened it seemed unlikely that they would come again. Not just for a story. He was confident that they could know nothing about Shawfields.

He now knew a little more about them. Only a little, it would have been so much better if he had been able to get the bastards and squeeze them dry of information. But at least he had more of a picture of the kind of people that he was up against.

He was convinced of one thing in particular. His adversaries were determined and well connected. The escape plane had proved that. He needed to find them and eliminate them before they destroyed his plans. Rearden had promised that his investigator would report in a few days.

Despite everything he couldn't help but smile. If there was one thing that Julius Kumalo loved in life it was a hunt. And this was turning out to be a real hunt.

A hunt to the death.


On the morning of April 14 Rearden arrived at the low-key offices of 'Hemp and Associates' in Hendon, North London. They were based in a brand new commercial development on the edge of a modern industrial estate where endless rows of aluminium-clad buildings created hardly any jobs. Maurice Hemp had cut his teeth in the investigating world over a period of thirty years with the Metropolitan police. For the last ten of those years he had been a senior investigator with the Fraud Squad. He had taken retirement at 50, and had used the cash to set up his own discreet investigation agency. He had specialised in corporate affairs, and a plethora of contacts from his time on the force had made sure that the business had grown rapidly and profitably.

Now, at the age of 57, he had reached the happy stage of being able to pick and choose his work as it suited him. Rearden's story had intrigued him, and he had been more than happy to take on the contract, all be it for a very healthy fee indeed.

As he was shown into Hemp's office, Rearden felt the same feeling of mild distaste as he had felt when he had first visited Hemp. Like the man himself, Hemp's office was fussy and fastidious. Everything was neatly in its place and in a disciplined order. Hemp himself was much the same. He was a rather shrivelled sort of a man with yellowy skin and tired, thin hair. His dress was immaculate to the point of being annoying and he sported a jaunty bow tie that was entirely out of step with the rest of his character. When he spoke, his voice was high pitched and quiet. He had a clipped, pronounced manner of speaking which grated at Rearden's innate laid-back Irishness.

"Good morning Mr Rearden. Would you take a seat please."

Rearden sat whilst Hemp placed all of his paperwork on his desk in an order that he was happy with.

"So Mr Hemp, do you have anything to tell us?"

"You can rest assured, Mr Rearden, that I would not have arranged this meeting had it been the case that I had discovered nothing. That would have been highly unprofessional, and I pride myself on my professionalism above all else."

Apart from winning the Hendon shiny-shoe competition you pompous little git, thought Rearden. Instead he said in an enthusiastic voice, "Splendid. Then you can bring me up to speed. Do you know who these people are yet?"

"Oh yes, I believe that I have found out precisely who they are. Unfortunately, what I have not yet managed to discover is where they are. I feel that it will be useful if I take you through my investigation step by step. That is, of course, assuming that you are not too pressed for time."

Rearden beamed a genial Irish smile. "All the time in the world sir. You just take a deep breath and fire away."

Hemp met this jocularity with a reproachful look. He then glanced at his notes and started to sum up his discoveries in the age old matter-of-fact tones of the career policeman.

"Initially, mostly for my own peace of mind, I spent some time examining every aspect of the recent campaign to promote the sale of British beef. Like you, I soon concluded that there was some kind of guiding hand behind everything that has happened. Initially I felt that I had two leads, the *Globe* and the new Matador company. Newspapers can be difficult, so I decided to look at Matador first.

"It is quite unique for a private company to be launched with such an enormous capital base. There is of course no secret as to how this has been the case. Sir Alistair Mcintyre is an extremely wealthy man, and he was able to raise the money that he required to establish his new business by accepting a take-over bid for his old company. That information is readily available from within the public domain.

"Although the new Matador company has launched itself in a highly public manner, the company has been really rather secretive about the nuts and bolts of its administration and management. I managed to discover that McIntyre hand picked twenty of his highest flying young executives and took them with him. Most of the rest of the Matador staff came with the businesses that they have acquired.

"What is very interesting indeed is the list of the company's Directors. There are only three. McIntyre himself is the Chairman which is unsurprising. His chief executive is Marcus Dalrymple. It took me a little time to find out the background of Dalrymple's appointment. I discovered that the two men served together during the war in some sort of covert operation in Yugoslavia. They have been friends ever since. There is more which I shall cover later.

"It is the third Director who is the real enigma. Gideon Rosenberg. Rosenberg is young for such a post, 37. He is the only son of Issac Rosenberg of the 'Rosenberg and Bloom' merchant bank. Rosenberg junior has a senior position at his father's bank and has been there ever since leaving university. I could find no reason why he should have ever come into contact with either McIntyre or Dalrymple. This being the case, I made the assumption that he must be involved in some way with the people who are orchestrating the campaign. Discreet enquiries at the bank yielded little. The only revelation of any interest was that it has been customary for Gideon Rosenberg to take unexplained absences of leave over the years. He seems to be a very private young man indeed. He is single and does not seem to have any kind of social life whatsoever.

"Having drawn only blanks at the bank I decided to go back further, to Cambridge, his University. Initially I felt that it was going to be much the same story. Although he won a starred First in Mathematics, Rosenberg seems to have left little mark at Cambridge. Then I had a stroke of luck. I questioned a man called Appleyard who was in the same College and year as Rosenberg. He told me that Rosenberg had fallen into a small group of friends in his second year; Their names were Vincent Allenby, Cornelius St John and Victor Gama. This information was of course quite unremarkable. However it was what Appleyard told me next which was of a much greater interest.

"Appleyard is an old Harrovian and let's say that he still moves in aristocratic circles. He told me that there has been a lot of discreet talk about Allenby and St John over the years. When they left college they set up an unusual partnership. They let it be known that they could solve people's problems, no matter how difficult, in a confidential and unorthodox way. Appleyard knew very little, but he assured me that there were strong rumours that the two men had been extremely successful in various cases where they had helped their wealthy clients to overcome a variety of personal or commercial difficulties.

"Armed with this information, I took a closer look at Dalrymple and found out something very interesting.

"I ran a routine check on the local papers in Cumbria, which is where Dalrymple lives. Last year there were a few small mentions of his name in connection with him seeking planning permission for a wind farm. In the second article there was mention of Greenpeace demonstrations at the entrance to his property.

"We talked to the local Greenpeace officer and he told us a perfectly bizarre story. Apparently they were staging their protests at the end of last year with a view to an appearance on a TV documentary. The week before the scheduled arrival of the film crew they were joined by a stranger – a large Afro-American Greenpeace operator called Marvin Hammerhead. In the middle of the night, before the dawn arrival of the Channel 4 team, Hammerhead turned up at their camp. He was violently ill and was immediately apprehended by military staff from the Sellafield Nuclear Reprocessing Plant. The activists were warned that they were in grave danger of being contaminated themselves and were ordered to report to Sellafield for tests. When they arrived at the plant, nobody had ever heard of either them nor anyone called Marvin Hammerhead.

"Their arrival at Sellafield coincided exactly with the arrival of the filmcrew at the gates of Dalrymple's property. The film was never made. The claims of the Greenpeace team were dismissed as the wild stories of cranks, and planning permission for Dalrymple's wind farm was duly granted.

"I believe that this is a typical example of one of Allenby and St John's operations and that the mysterious Marvin Hammerhead was in fact Victor Gama. It would seem to me that the success of this operation encouraged Dalrymple to tell his old friend Sir Alistair McIntyre about the exploits of the team. I believe that this was the moment that the two men hatched their plan to defend the British beef industry and that they engaged the services of Allenby and St John to make it happen.

"This then leads us onto the perplexing question of the *Globe*. I have been able to find one small connection. This time it came from an examination of the local paper from Hampshire where Dwight Forrester now lives. He is pictured at a party some months ago. The party was held by a certain Esther St John. I have found out that this lady is Cornelius St John's aunt and that she took him in following a family estrangement in his youth. Furthermore, I have established that Forrester was not usually admitted into the higher echelons of Hampshire society, and that several guests were surprised by his presence at the party.

"Once again this is pure supposition, but I believe that St John persuaded his aunt to invite Forrester to her party in order to give himself and his team the opportunity to co-opt Forrester to their cause. The first *Globe* articles appeared a matter of weeks later.

"So Mr Rearden, whilst we still lack hard evidence, I believe that we now have sufficient circumstantial evidence to be confident that we have established the identity of the people that we are seeking.

"Finding them has been an altogether different matter. These are extremely cautious men indeed. They have taken every step possible to make themselves as hard as possible to be found. It is my opinion that our best chance of locating the others is through Rosenberg.

"Unfortunately, ever since the launch of the Matador company, Rosenberg has remained hidden away at their Head Office at Black Loch. This is the Perthshire country estate of Sir Alistair McIntyre and is guarded by impressive modern security systems. Access would be possible, but both risky and difficult. However he does leave the estate on rare occasions. It is my proposal that when he next leaves we should take the opportunity to bug his car and, if possible, his mobile phone.

"It is more than likely that the team stage regular meetings. Hopefully by monitoring Rosenberg we will discover the time and venue of one of these meetings."

Hemp carefully placed his last piece of paper with the others and closed the file on his desk.

"I am impressed Mr Hemp. Very impressed. This is excellent work. I feel that your recommended course of action regarding Mr Rosenberg is wholly appropriate. Please carry out these measures and keep me informed."

Hemp nodded and Rearden made his departure with as little small talk as he had entered. Hemp made three calls.

Three days later Gideon left Black Loch and drove towards Perth. He needed a good drive to clear his mind after constant late nights staring at his computer. It was a fine bright day and he opened his window to allow the fresh crisp air to sweep into the car. After three miles he glanced in his rear mirror and cursed when he saw that a police car was on his rear bumper. He slowed down and allowed the squad car to pass him and pull up in front. The officer got out, walked to his window and invited him to get into the squad car.

Gideon then received a severe ticking off for driving recklessly on country roads. Had he not considered the dangers of slow-moving farm vehicles or cycling children. In future he should remember to slow down as he approached blind corners. However the officer informed him that it was going to be his lucky day and that he was being let off with a caution. The telling off took five minutes which was time enough for a man to quietly slip into Gideon's car and fit his listening devices.

Vince joined Victor in Ireland on April 22. Victor and his old Marine sergeant major Bill Atkins had spent a week watching Emerald Meats. The company occupied a quiet rural site four miles outside Cork. The storage shed, abattoir and office block were all very new and the site was located two miles down a narrow road. The two men had monitored the comings and goings of traffic from a clump of bushes on a low hill 400 yards from the perimeter fence. They were able to watch almost everything that went on in the yard below through high-powered binoculars.

On the first two nights they had made a slow circuit of the half-acre site. There had been no expense spared on security. A ten-foot-high razor fence ran all the way round. Access could only be made through the automatic gate which was controlled by a small guardhouse which was manned 24 hours a day. At night the perimeter fence was patrolled constantly by a guard and a large Alsatian.

They had already learned a great deal. They had logged all incoming and outgoing vehicle traffic. During the six days of their vigil there had only been two wagon loads of live cattle delivered to the abattoir. During a period of two days, there had been 128 wagons carrying chilled containers to be unloaded into the storage depot. The majority of these had arrived in the hours between midnight and four in the morning. Thirty chilled distribution wagons had left the site. Victor had spent a day by the gates of Cork Docks and had eventually been able to identify the vessel that was the source of the late-night deliveries. He had phoned its identity through to Vince.

There had been three other highly suspicious late-night visits to the site – two from cars and one from a van. Using his night vision enhancer, Victor had been able to note the registration numbers of the vehicles, which all came and went between the hours of two and four in the morning. These he had also given to Vince for checking.

Bill Atkins was manning the lookout point whilst Vince and Victor met up at a small country hotel twenty miles to the north of Cork. They went to their room and Victor made coffee.

"What do you know Vince?"

His friend was solemn. "It is all beginning to have a pretty bad smell about it. First, the boat. The *Alto Parva* is a Liberian registered vessel and has made stops in Lisbon and Le Havre en route to Cork. Guess where it was loaded? Mozambique and the Republic of South Africa."

"The two main outlets for Zimbabwe exports yeah?"

"On the button big fellow. We also managed to get a read on the number plates. One of the cars was from Dublin. The other car was from Londonderry and the van was from Belfast."

Victor was grim. "You're right. It stinks. When a van from Belfast turns up at two in the morning it only tends to suggest one thing. So much for the bloody peace talks. You reckon that Emerald Meats is Kumalo's big new customer?"

"Yes I do."

They sipped their coffee quietly for a moment. Victor spoke. "So what is the plan? I figure that it is best that we walk away, don't you? It is the same scene as the lads faced down in Africa. Sure, the story is getting better all the time, but I don't think it is worth our messing about with these boys just for the sake of a story. After all, the way that the beef price is going we could have the whole job wrapped up in a month or so."

Vince was troubled. "You're right of course, but I'm bothered. Really bothered."

"Go on."

"OK, let's assume that Emerald Meats, the Matabele Meat Company and Shawfields are indeed all connected. Let us also assume that Jackson's information about Kumalo's drugs and arms operations is correct. If these facts are correct we can also assume that Kumalo will have set up some pretty big-time smuggling deals on the back of the Shawfields contract. OK so far?"

Victor nodded.

"Right. The key fact is that every one of these deals hinges on the crucial fact that Shawfields simply have to fulfil their contract. To start with everything was going fine, and then we started to do our stuff. This seems to have worried Kumalo, and if Jackson was right, he summoned his man from England and forced him to kill someone. Then what happens? He finds out that David and

Donald are in Zimbabwe sniffing around for information about Zimbabwean beef. Again, he doesn't take any half-measures. He pulls in Jackson, tortures the poor bastard and executes him. He also throws a security net around Bulawayo to try and catch our lads. They slip the net and kill one of his men in the process.

"I think that we can assume that this will have seriously pissed him off. However at the end of it all, he may not have got David and Donald, but he will have learnt enough to suspect that people like us must be involved.

"Kumalo isn't running a ten-bob operation here. We are talking about multi-million pound deals. I think that he will go to more or less any lengths to find out what is going on. And that means that he is out there looking for us. He's resourceful, he's ruthless and he's rich. I have a horrible feeling that if he looks hard enough he will find us in the end. And if he does, we will never get the chance to spend our twenty million quid."

Again Victor nodded. "I'm with you Vince. I suppose that your reading of the situation is that we will have to get to him before he gets to us."

"Dead straight we do."

"How?"

Vince lit a cigarette and sucked hard. "There's no point trying to get to the bastard in Zimbabwe. He owns the bloody place. He'd sniff us out and top us before we got out of the airport. No. We have to get to him here. We have to find out the complete facts of the Shawfields story. If we can get enough information quickly enough, we can tip off the authorities and expose the whole facade in the *Globe*. We'll attack Shawfields to boot. I reckon that this would land Kumalo in such a tonne of shit that the last thing on his mind would be getting back at us. By the time the dust settles we will be gone and far away."

"So we need to get into Emerald Meats."

"We need to get into Emerald Meats."

The big Nigerian chuckled. "How did I know that you were going to say that?"

Vince smiled. "Like I always say Victor, life's a bitch and then you die. Can we do it?"

"Not easily. The damn place is like Fort Knox. But we can give it our best shot. Come on, I've drawn out some plans, let's have a look."

A little after three in the morning two nights later a team of five men hid in the long grass fifty metres from the perimeter fence at the back of the Emerald Meats complex. Vince, Victor and Bill Atkins were accompanied by Billy Hutchinson, the ex-Wormwood Scrubs burglar who had helped at the training camp, and a young Londoner known as Elf who was a computer hacker.

The guard and his dog passed level with where they were hiding and then started on another circuit of the site. When man and dog were 75 yards away, Victor and Bill slithered forward and cut a hole in the wire large enough to crawl through. Once they reached the other side they sprinted forty yards to the cover of deep shadow that the moonlight cast from the rear storage shed. They both wore night vision goggles. They waited for seven minutes until the guard and his dog once again approached. When they were thirty yards away, Bill and Victor dropped them with simultaneous shots from silenced dart rifles. Their targets dropped softly to the ground and Bill and Victor pulled them into the shadows.

The others crawled through the fence and joined them. Bill headed for the guard room whilst the others skirted the outside wall of the storage block and headed for the offices. Bill quietly entered the back of the guard house at the gate, and rendered the guard unconscious with a belt across the back of the head with a sand-filled sock.

He stripped him, tied him up, and put on his uniform which was rather tight across the shoulders. He assumed his seat at the reception window and waited.

Billy Hutchinson got through the front door of the offices and disabled the alarm in a time that was a personal record: 43 seconds. Once inside they moved quickly to Rearden's office. Elf removed the hard disk of the computer whilst the others rifled his desk. They then moved to the main administration office and removed a further three hard disks. After six minutes they were once again in the corridor and heading for the exit.

A soft Irish voice stopped them in their tracks.

"Now then lads, I don't think that it is time for you to be leaving just yet. Mr Rearden seemed to expect that you might be going to honour us with a visit and, bless me, well here you are. Now I would like you to turn around really slowly and lift your arms in the air, again, really slowly. Now let's see who we have here. I figure that this big dark man must be Mr Gama. To be sure he is a hell of a big fellow like they said, and you . . . "

For Vince the world entered the realm of weird slow motion. One minute he was slowly turning to face two hard-faced men covering them with automatic weapons. The next minute he was floating on air. Somehow his legs had disappeared. Although it only took a split second for him to realise that Victor had kicked his ankles from under him, it seemed to take about half an hour. As he fell to the floor of the corridor he saw Victor pull a revolver out from somewhere behind his neck. He then hit the deck as the air all around him erupted into sound. The exchange of gunfire only lasted for three seconds but again it seemed like a great deal longer. He could feel the disturbance in the air above where he lay as a cluster of bullets streaked by to smash through the glass front door of the offices and out into the night. Then there was silence.

Vince lifted his head to see that the two men were lying in an untidy heap in the middle of the corridor. Victor was stood frozen like a statue in the classic pose of the marksman. Hutchinson and Elf were picking themselves gingerly from the floor.

The gun seemed somehow like a silly little toy in Victor's massive hands. It seemed almost comical. Vince fought back the urge to laugh. A growing pool of blood was slowly spreading out from where the head of one of the Irishmen was resting on the polished floor. Vince fought hard to try and restore a sense of reality to the situation. Slowly, like an ancient mummy coming back to life in some black and white B movie, Victor was relaxing his firing stance.

The sound of the shattered office door swinging open brought them all back to their senses. Victor swung round in a blur of speed only to relax again as he saw Bill Atkins at the end of his sights. In turn the ex-sergeant major was staring at Victor down the sights of his gun. The old soldier quickly took in the scene in the corridor and then said in a mild voice, "If you have finished up here, I think that it may be time for us to leave."

They slipped through the fence and jogged to where they had parked their car. They left Ireland early that afternoon on the Seacat catamaran to Holyhead.

Vince and Victor called at Elf's flat in Islington the following afternoon. It had taken some time to break the Emerald codes but in the end the hacker had got in. Vince pored through the documents for twenty minutes them got up and kicked a litter bin across the room in a fury. Victor took him gently by the arm.

"Hey, cool it man. Easy. What's the problem?"

"I'll tell you the problem, the whole thing was a waste of bastard time, that is the bloody problem. Emerald Meats has been making large purchases of imported beef all right, and do you know where from? The Matabele Meat Company? Like hell it is. It has been buying from a certain V. Henninger of bloody Luxembourg. I should have bloody guessed it. They have another link in the bloody chain. Bastards."

Vince was shaking uncontrollably as he sat unsteadily on Elf's threadbare settee. Victor joined him and put his arm around his shoulder. Vince allowed his head to sink into Victor's chest and he started to sob helplessly. Elf said, in a rather embarrassed voice, "I'll get some coffee together shall I?"

Victor smiled at him. "Yeah, that would be great."

When Elf had left the room Victor spoke to Vince in a soft, soothing voice. "Come on Vince, don't worry, it's cool. You're suffering from shock, that's all. I've seen it lots of times. It just creeps up and gets you. Don't fight it. Just let it out. That's the way."

He rocked Vince like a baby for nearly ten minutes until his friend slowly regained his composure. For a while he was silent, then he spoke in a sombre voice. "I am in blood so far stepped that returning were as tedious as go o'er."

Victor clapped him on the back with delight. "That's more like it. Macbeth no less. A part that I have always aspired to, though Othello is probably more my line of work. Now then, on your feet you bastard and turn around three times. You should know better than to quote the Scottish play at a time like this. It's bad luck. So turn around boy and drive away the demons."

Vince reluctantly got up and allowed himself to be turned around three times. As he completed his last circle he found to his surprise that he was smiling. Elf came in with the coffee. "You OK mate?"

"Fine," said Vince.

"I'll just pop out for a while and leave you lads to it."

"Hang on a sec." Vince reached into his pocket and tossed an envelope across. "There's double what we agreed, what with all the hassle and that."

Elf caught the envelope and pocketed it. "Sound as a pound Vince. Sound as a pound." He gave a quick thumbs-up and left the flat.

Victor got up from the settee and started to pace. "Well I reckon you have it right with the Shakespearean bit. Basically, we are in it right up to our necks and there is no turning back. The fact that they were expecting us and that they knew my name simply bears out what we suspected anyway. Nothing has changed. We still need more proof and there is only one place that we are going to find it: V. Henninger of Luxembourg. So me and Bill will get over there this afternoon and case it out whilst you get on with other things. However we need to make some changes. We have to be treble careful about security now. None of us must ever stay anywhere that they might suspect. We certainly need to stay clear of Black Loch. I'll leave you to get hold of the others. Be really clear on this Vince. Mr Julius Kumalo is going to be one seriously pissed-off individual."

Julius Kumalo was indeed a seriously pissed off individual. Rearden winced as wave after wave of rage poured down the phone line from Matabeleland. Kumalo's vaulting anger made him feel almost liquidised with fear. At last the African became calmer and his voice assumed the consistency of ice. Rearden decided that he preferred the rage.

"OK now listen. I have had enough of you and your fools. I am coming over personally. I will bring a team of eight men with me. We will arrive at the end of the week over a period of three days at different entry points. I will give you details tomorrow. I want you to rent a house somewhere secluded in the south of Scotland which can accommodate ten. I repeat that it must be extremely secluded. Now I need you to get out some of the weapons from the last consignment. I will give you a list. Inform our clients that there will be a fortnight's delay on their delivery. A fortnight will be enough.

"We will give Hemp's listening devices another four days. If nothing comes up in that time, we will lift Rosenberg and question him. Now am I understood?"

"Perfectly."

"What have you done with the bodies?"

"They are buried somewhere safe."

"And the rest of the staff at Emerald?"

"They know the score."

"They better. That's all for now."

"Julius, one more thing."

"What?"

"What about the Henninger offices. What if they try to get in there."

"I am not a fool Rearden. I have replaced the local security firm with four of my own men. God help the bastards if they try and get in there. Anyway, it is immaterial really. These men are not fools. They will know who we all are by now. They don't need to get into Henningers to find out."

"OK Julius. See you in a few days."

The line was already dead. Rearden rubbed his dry, tired eyes with his finger and thumb. What the hell had he got himself into?

That Friday's edition of the *Farmers Weekly* was yet again dominated by the Matador story and the extraordinary rise in the beef price. The actions of the sticker girls in Quickshop and other retailers had provoked a wave of fear through those purchasing imported beef. Import companies were plunged into deep financial trouble as retailers refused to honour contracts, so great was their terror of being exposed. Cash flows became intolerably stretched and by the third week of April the first meat importer had put itself under administrative receivership. Retailers were beginning to struggle to find supplies of beef as the farmers increasingly refused to sell to anyone other than the Matador buyers. A major supermarket at last agreed to stock Matador's own branded products. Others seemed set to follow. Overall sales at Shawfields continued to be hit and the rumblings in the City caused their share price to drift down.

The price of finished steers had risen to £1.23.

The Met Office promised that the May Bank Holiday weekend was going to herald the start of Spring as unusually hot and sunny weather was confidently forecast. For the Matador team the weekend promised to be vital. All over the country final plans were being put into place.

Vince and Cornelius sat in the cafe of a motorway service station near Birmingham to go over several final details. Vince was tired and drawn. Cornelius's voice hid none of his concern as he spoke to his friend.

"Bear up old chap. We're almost there."

"Of course. I know that. It is just . . . well, well men are dead Cornelius. Men are dead. We never expected this."

"Whether we expected it or not, it is the case, and we can't turn the clock back. We just have to see it through. There is simply nothing else to do. Here, I've bought you a present. I've persuaded Helen to come and see you tonight. You can watch it together."

Vince smiled as he looked into the carrier bag. Inside was the video of *High Noon* and a bag of popcorn.

"What would I do without you daft bastard?"

"Starve, I should think. Without giving too much away, you will find that the chaps in the white hats win. Just remember that is who we are. We are the chaps in the white hats. And, just like them, we will win. See you at the party then."

"Yes of course. Take care."

As Cornelius marched out of the cafe, Vince gazed at the determined face of Gary Cooper under his white hat and chortled.

# CHAPTER TWELVE

## IN THE SHADOW OF BRANDENBURG GATE

As dawn broke on the morning of May 1, 1998, the skies over Britain were blue and clear from Land's End to John O'Groats. Out in the fields, skylarks rediscovered voices that had been forgotten during the hard, wet months of winter. All over the countryside there was a sense of new life as grass and corn grew and the buds in the trees started to explode into impossibly clean shades of green. All over the country alarm clocks were sounding to meet the dawn. The growing numbers of the Matador volunteer army got out of bed with a new sense of spirit and purpose. Breakfasts were eaten amidst lively, upbeat conversation. Car doors were banged closed and ignition keys turned with an air of adventure.

Vince woke without the aid of his alarm clock. Through the window of his hotel room the sky was already an electric blue. Helen stirred next to him and he embraced her sleeping body to him. As he watched a cluster of crows flapping busily across the area of sky framed by his window he allowed his mind to wander.

A lazy smile played on his lips as he once again caught himself indulging in odd visions of a war that had been done and dusted many years before he had been born. Marcus and Sir Alistair had a lot to answer for. This time his half-awake brain swam back to the spring of 1945. He pictured the endless ranks of hard-faced Soviet troops receiving their final orders for their final battle. Over a million road-weary Russians were massed in every field and pasture around the outskirts of Berlin. They had become the unstoppable force. From the near nemesis of Leningrad and the very gates of Moscow they had slowly grown into an irresistible juggernaut that had rolled the previously undefeated German Armies a thousand miles back to their capital.

At last they were poised for the final push into what was likely to be the most vicious and bloody battle of all. None of them would have had any illusions about what was going to happen. They all knew that the Germans would defend their capital to the last half-acre before calling it a day for history's most total of all wars. And yet they were focused. Focused by the chance to avenge all the terrible wrongs that had been done to their vast homeland and its peoples. They were focused on one goal; the total destruction of Berlin and the end of Adolf Hitler.

Vince shook his head a little and glanced down at Helen's sleeping face, thankful that she couldn't read his childish thoughts. He smiled as he thought of his own army which was massing at that very moment. It was an army of over twenty thousand now. Twenty thousand women young and old. Like the Red Army at the gates of Berlin all those years ago, his army was united by a sense of purpose. They had all suffered. They had all seen their men come in at night shattered and bewildered and depressed. They had all faced the prospect of years of hard, backbreaking work being thrown away. They had all looked at their children and grandchildren and wondered if there would ever be a farm left for them to inherit and tend. And through all these dark days, they would get into their cars and do their shopping at the very supermarkets who were so cynically easing them towards bankruptcy.

At last the day had arrived when they had the chance to strike back. The chance to deliver a crippling blow and to avenge all the pain that they had endured.

Their Berlin was the 1,547 stores of the Shawfields supermarket chain.

Their Adolf Hitler was Simon Shawfield who had made his endless millions on the back of their suffering. Vince enjoyed the thought of Shawfield lying blissfully unaware in his bed whilst an army of 20,000 angry women were slowly massing to destroy his cosy little world.

"What on earth are you dreaming about now?"

"About being within sight of the Brandenburg Gate."

Helen smiled fondly and rubbed his hair. "Sometimes, Vincent

Allenby, you are like a lost, dreaming child. Whatever shall I do with you?"

The attack started at every one of the 1,547 Shawfield stores at exactly nine that morning. In a way it came as a blessed relief to the security men who had stood watch over the beef counters for over a fortnight. The company had planned its tactics well in advance. Within minutes of the attack Simon Shawfield was informed and he raced to Head Office to head up the war room.

The decision had been made to keep stocks of beef on the shelves as low as possible. Therefore the first wave of sticker girls soon had every package covered. It came as no surprise to them when the guards took no action, the Shawfield plan of battle had been sold to Matador by an informer several days before. As more beef was loaded onto trolleys in the store rooms, phone calls were placed to bring many extra security men into every store. Once these men were in place the new packages of beef were brought out and put on the shelves.

Soon the second wave of sticker girls came forward and started their task. They were promptly removed from the store. As in previous attacks a second, third and fourth wave then moved in. However this time there were plenty of guards to evict them before they could blanket cover the products. As the fourth wave was escorted out, a sense of triumph began to sweep through the Shawfield Empire. Then came a fifth wave, then a sixth, then a seventh.

It soon became clear that the ejected women were simply returning to their cars and altering their appearance by donning a different coat or hat. The guards on the doors found it quite impossible to recognise who had been ejected and who was a *bona fide* customer. A grinding battle of attrition ensued and the nerves of the security men were stretched taught.

In the Head Office war room all heads slowly turned to Simon Shawfield who was now chewing his knuckles with anxiety. By three in the afternoon the onslaught was still continuing. At last Shawfield smashed his open hand down on the table.

"OK, if that is the way the bitches want to play it, then that is the way they can have it. Do it. We move to plan B."

Every one of the volunteer women had been made aware of Plan B and its consequences. Every one of them had accepted these consequences. Now as they trudged in and out of the stores on ever-tiring legs, it came as something of a blessed relief when Plan B was at last put into action. The word was passed to the security men and, instead of ushering the women out of the stores, they escorted them into the small rooms that were reserved for shoplifters.

Police stations were telephoned, and informed by the Shawfields management that they required the presence of their officers. In every store between fifteen and twenty sticker girls were escorted to the shoplifter's room to be detained until the police arrived. It was made known to them that the Shawfields company had made the decision to prosecute them for committing acts of criminal damage against their property.

Ricky Myers breathed a sigh of relief when his mobile phone rang to inform him that Plan B was in operation. He had begun to despair if they would ever do it as the hours had drifted by. He had waited all day on the car park of the Buxton branch of Shawfields and had begun to worry. Once he had received his call he leaned into the Land Rover that was parked next to his car. Inside was Emily Shaw. Emily was a gentle, smiling 72-year-old farmer's wife from the hills above Macclesfield. She was disabled, and she needed assistance from Ricky to climb into her wheelchair. When Ricky slowly marched her up the aisle to the beef counter, the security guard's face registered huge misery.

"Good afternoon young man" said Emily brightly as she reached into her handbag to find a sticker. The young guard stood back politely as Emily carefully applied her sticker to a small packet of rump steak. She looked at her work with great satisfaction and said "There now. That's better isn't it?"

"Madam, I really am very sorry but . . . "

"No young man, there is no need to be sorry. I am quite aware that you are only doing your job. Now where is it that you require me to go?"

The guard led them to the door at the back of the store with acute embarrassment as other shoppers jeered and hissed.

Once inside the holding room Emily greeted her fellow offenders with great cheeriness. "My goodness, isn't this all ever so exiting?"

Ricky was grinning boyishly as he arranged the sixteen detainees around Emily's wheelchair and took several photos. Giving them the thumbs-up he said, "Sorry girls, but I really have to dash. Look after Emily for me won't you?" He bent down and kissed Emily on the cheek and said "I'll see you soon." and darted out of the room.

By the early evening, police stations the length and breadth of Britain had processed 21,332 cases of criminal damage on behalf of the Shawfields supermarket chain. Hot, harassed desk sergeants cursed the company roundly as they battled their way through the mountain of paperwork.

Simon Shawfield consented to give an interview for the six o'clock news. When asked if he was happy to justify his company's decision to order the arrest of 21,332 otherwise blameless citizens on the charge of criminal damage he gave the camera a thoughtful look then said, "I am more than happy with our decision. There are some who claim that farmers have had a difficult time and that they are fully justified in carrying out actions such as those that we have seen today. I totally disagree with this. There is a very important issue at stake here: the issue of free trade. My company has made the decision to stock beef from Ireland. Ireland of course is a fellow member of the EC and we have conducted exhaustive investigations that have categorically shown that Irish beef is some of the best in the world.

"Furthermore, it also offers our customers exceptional value for money. My company refuses to be bullied into stocking over-priced goods simply because it upsets a particular interest group. Farmers would do well to stop moaning and get on with being more efficient in order to compete with their colleagues within the EC. It is highly unfortunate that my company has had to adopt the measures that we have taken today, but we believe that we are making a stand for the rights of our customers to buy excellent goods for the very best value for money."

As the news moved on to the next item Dwight Forrester clapped his hands together with joy. He was sat in Esther St John's drawing room where the pair of them had happily killed the afternoon over a bottle of gin.

Esther smiled meekly. "I gather Dwight that you feel that Mr Shawfield has rather walked into whatever dreadful plot that you and my cousin have planned for him."

"Oh you gather right sweetheart" chuckled Dwight. "You gather absolutely bloody right. By Tuesday I will made that jumped up, pompous Pommie git wish that he had never been born. Jesus, I'm going to crucify the bastard."

"How simply charming. Another gin dear?"

"You keep pouring, and I'll keep drinking."

"Then we could well be here for a while."

"You know," mused Dwight, "I'm beginning to come round to the idea that you Poms aren't so bad after all."

Esther grinned. "And I must say that you colonials are not entirely insufferable either."

# CHAPTER THIRTEEN

## SUNLIGHT ON A
## BROKEN COLUMN

By 5.00 p.m. that Saturday afternoon the Chief Constable of Greater Manchester was beginning to get very hot under the collar indeed. He had been bothered at home several times as he received a number of calls from officers complaining that police stations right across the region were clogged up with otherwise law-abiding citizens queuing up to be booked for criminal damage to Shawfields' property. The whole fiasco angered him immensely, but he had had to inform each caller that there was nothing that he could do.

If the flood-like influx of farming women wasn't problem enough, he was now receiving reports of appalling, and wholly unexplained traffic jams building up in the West Pennine Moors.

At last he could stand it no more. He bade his long-suffering wife a moody farewell and drove to the station. Once he arrived he demanded to be briefed. He was told that there was increasing gridlock on roads leading out of Bolton, Horwich, Blackburn and several other towns. Huge tailbacks were reported on three of the region's motorways and it was clear that the situation was rapidly deteriorating.

When he studied a map it was clear that the huge volumes of traffic were circling a seemingly nondescript area of the Pennine Hills. It was totally inexplicable. The Chief Constable hated things that were totally inexplicable. Even more, he hated these things happening on his patch. His temper worsened a few notches and he loudly demanded that somebody better find out what on earth was happening.

Reports started to come in over the next hour. Officers had been questioning the motorists in the many queues. They had found most of the cars to be filled with young people in high spirits. In every case they had told the confused police that they were on their way to Peggy's Party. What party? Her birthday party of course. Where is it? At her house. They managed to collect two copies of invitations which were promptly driven back to the station.

The Chief Constable read with open amazement.

### PEGGY HOLGATE INVITES
### YOU TO HER 17th BIRTHDAY BASH

### 1 May / 2 May 1998

*At Higher Clough Farm,*
*Higher Clough, Nr Bolton*

He looked around his officers. "And where may I ask is Higher Clough?"

One of the officers cleared his throat awkwardly. "It's a small village up on the moors, about ten miles out of Bolton. The farm is three miles out of the village."

"And who may I ask is Peggy Holgate?"

"We gather that she lives there."

"Oh that is what you gather is it? Well how splendid, that's clear as day then. So you gather that a certain Peggy Holgate does indeed live at Higher Clough Farm and she may even be 17 today. May I suggest that those two facts don't entirely explain why we seem to have about 50,000 people trying to get to her party, or does it? Am I missing something?"

"No sir."

The Chief rocked back in his chair and stared wearily at the ceiling. "Get me Bill Thorn. Get him now. I don't give a damn if he is off duty. I also want the copper who patrols the Higher Clough area in my office within an hour."

Bill Thorn was Greater Manchester's Chief Community Liaison Officer. He didn't look much like a policeman. He wore his hair long and dressed casually in kickers, jeans and a sweatshirt.

"What do you know Bill?"

"It's all in my report boss."

"What report?"

"The one I wrote two weeks ago. You obviously didn't read it. Here, have a copy."

The Chief indeed had never seen the report which was now tossed on his desk. He skimmed through its eight pages quickly. Over the last month Thorn and his opposite number on the forces of several other big cities had heard about a big party coming off. Included in the document was an invitation the same as the one that the Chief had already seen. The report concluded that there was going to be a major rave staged on the Bank Holiday weekend up in the hills above Bolton. However, unlike other raves, it was rumoured that there was to be live music and that the Orange Boys would be playing. The Chief wearily dropped the report onto his desk.

"My apologies Bill. I never saw this."

Thorn lit a cigarette. "Doesn't surprise me boss. Everyone I talked to told me I was daft. If you aren't close to these things I suppose it is easy to dismiss them as fantasy."

"So what is happening?"

"The word was put out about a month ago that there was going to be a massive do up in the hills. The birthday party scam has been used before once or twice. If you label up a rave as a birthday party you don't need any planning permission or anything. So long as nobody is charged for admission, then there is nothing illegal and nothing that we can do to stop it. What is different this time is that everybody was adamant that there was going to be live music and that the Orange Boys will be playing. Have you heard of the Orange Boys Chief?"

"Of course I bloody have. I don't listen to them in the car but I know who they are. They are very popular I believe."

Thorn chuckled. "Popular would be something of an understatement boss. They are massive – biggest band on the scene at the moment by a bloody mile."

The Chief became even more thoughtful. "If it is indeed the case that these people will be playing up in the hills at this party, and if it is also the case that there is no admission charge, in your opinion, how many people will want to go and see them?"

"How long is a piece of string boss? I really couldn't be accurate, but if you want a ball park figure, I would guess that there will be between 80,000 and 120,000 people on their way to Bolton."

"What!!! You ARE kidding me Bill, please tell me that you are kidding me."

"Nope. That is my realistic estimate and I promise it will be pretty close."

There was a knock on the door and the Chief's secretary ushered in a beefy uniformed policeman in his early fifties. He cleared his throat nervously and introduced himself. "PC Duckworth sir. Higher Clough is on my beat."

The Chief smiled to put his man at ease and waved him to a chair. "Duckworth, this is Bill Thorn, he tells me that Peggy Holgate is having a 17th birthday party and about 100,000 guests are on their way up to your patch to help her celebrate. Is this correct?"

"Apparently so sir."

"The fact that you use the word 'apparently' strongly suggests to me that you didn't know that this was about to happen."

"Not really sir." Duckworth's genial, ruddy face was a picture of misery. "I mean sir, well, there were some strange things happening, but, well . . . "

"Strange things like what Duckworth?"

"Well there have been a lot of big wagons going up to the Holgate farm over the last couple of weeks, especially big bales of straw, he has been taking tonnes and tonnes of straw."

The Chief rolled his eyes in exasperation. "What may I ask is a big bale of straw, and why is it so unusual for a farmer to buy it?"

Duckworth swallowed. "A big bale of straw is exactly what it sounds like. It is like a normal bale of straw except that it weighs about half a tonne. Farmers buy straw for feeding and bedding their cattle. Holgate always buys it of course, that is quite normal, but the amount that he has been buying would feed about 1,000 beef cattle and he has only got about 50 . . . "

Duckworth stopped as the Chief let out a long and miserable groan. He could think of nothing to say other than a timid "Sir?"

The Chief spoke with resignation. "Do you not realise what you have just said Duckworth? You have just spoken the magic word. 'Beef'. Bloody, sodding, bastard beef. Right at this minute, every one of my stations in the region is clogged up with women who are being booked for putting stickers on packets of beef in the Shawfields supermarkets. Right at this minute I have a major, major traffic jam taking thousands of young people to an ill-disguised rave up in the moors, and, surprise surprise, it is being staged at a beef farm. And guess what, the band who are drawing all of these people up into the dark, satanic moors is the same band that brought a bull onto the stage at the Nynex Arena a few bloody weeks ago. Now don't you dare try to tell me that this is just a coincidence."

The two men stared down anxiously.

The Chief carried on. "I suppose that it is quite impossible to drive up to this farm because all the bloody roads are clogged. Well, that's fine. Duckworth, you and me are going for a little ride in a helicopter and we will have a cosy little chat with Mr Holgate and try and get some sort of a clue as to what the bloody hell is going on here. Wait outside for me will you. Bill, you can go. I apologise for the fact that I did not get to see your report earlier, some bastard will suffer because of it." He banged the button on his intercom. "Get me the traffic people in here now."

When the three traffic control officers came into the office a few minutes later he briefed them as to what was happening. "Now listen. I am not happy about this. I am not happy that we have been caught with our trousers down looking like a bunch of tossers. But that can't be helped now. However, I am not willing to write this business off as good, innocent fun. No bloody way. I want all the roads leading up to this farm blocking and the traffic turned back. I don't care what excuse that you use but I want it doing. There is nothing that we can do about the people that have already arrived, I am certainly not going to incite a riot by sending officers in to try and clear the site. But I want no more, you hear, no more. Now go and get on with it."

When the door closed on the three traffic officers the Chief reached into his desk drawer, pulled out a bottle of scotch and poured a generous measure. As he drank it he allowed himself to calm down. He drained the tumbler and shook his head. "Bloody beef."

As the helicopter pulled up into the clear evening sky, the Chief nudged Duckworth who had immersed himself in the spectacular view of the Greater Manchester conurbation which was sprawled below in the light of the weakening sun. "Tell me about Mr Holgate."

"He's a good bloke really boss. Bit of a character. Likes a pint. He's been hit pretty hard by the Beef Crisis they say. I've heard rumours that he may even lose his farm. I've never had any bother with him."

"Until now."

"Yes sir, until now."

The chopper swooped over the M62 and over the town of Bolton. Before them the Pennine Hills looked stunningly beautiful in the rich, orange evening light. They could see now that every road heading into the hills was jammed solid with cars. As they came over the top of one of the moors they saw Higher Clough. Already there were thousands of cars parked in the fields, and a stream of people were heading into a small valley. At the end of the valley was a towering construction.

The Chief pointed at it. "There you are Duckworth, that is where all the big bales of straw went."

The bales had been used like giant pieces of Lego to create a huge stage. At the side of the stage speakers were piled high and plugged into three large generators at the back. The sides were built up with scaffolding which held a myriad of colourful lights. Already the valley sides and bottom were teaming with people. The pilot swung the helicopter round and landed in a field by the farm. It was not alone. There was another chopper in the field which was disgorging people and equipment which was being loaded onto a tractor and trailer.

The Chief couldn't help but smile as he read the logo on the side of the second chopper. "Matador".

They found Arthur Holgate in the kitchen with his wife and daughter and a distinguished-looking man who the chief thought was very familiar.

Holgate beamed as Duckworth entered. "Now then, it's Jack Duckworth here to see us Eileen. Going up in world a bit aren't we Jack? Helicopters now is it? Who've you got with you?"

Duckworth felt consumed with embarrassment. "This is William Spencer, Chief Constable of Greater Manchester."

"Bloody Hell Jack, top brass hey, better watch our P's and Q's then hadn't we. Well, sit yourself down William, your timing's good, kettle's just boiled. This is my wife Eileen and my daughter Peggy. She's the birthday girl. And this is Sir Alistair McIntyre, an old friend of the family."

Of course, thought the Chief, the man on the tele. Everybody's favourite uncle. He forced a smile and sat. Holgate glanced out of the window and noted the deep red hue of the sky. "Tell you what William, I reckon the sun's about over the yardarm. How about somat wi' a bit more pep."

The Chief knew that he really should decline, but all of a sudden the idea of somat wi' a bit more pep seemed a hell of a good idea. "That would be grand. No water please. Go on Duckworth, don't be shy, have drink if you want one. It's Saturday night." He took a steadying sip. "Now, I wonder if any of you could tell me what is happening here?"

Holgate was more than happy to do so.

"I thought you would have known by now. It's our Peggy's birthday. She's 17. Things have been a bit tight over the last few years and we haven't been able to run to a party. Well, job's started to perk up a bit since we started selling to Matador, so we thought we'd push boat out a bit and have a proper bash. We thought it would be nice if we invited a few town folk up to get a bit of a breath of fresh air. That's when Sir Alistair got involved. His outfit is all for town and country getting together, and he was happy to help us out a bit."

The Chief turned to Sir Alistair. "And what bit of help have you given may I ask?"

Sir Alistair smiled amiably. "Oh nothing much. We have a record label, so we were able to get a few of our bands to come and play. I got in touch with the Orange Boys since they seem to be quite keen on beef, and they were happy to come. We've chipped in a bit here and there to help, you know the kind of thing, machinery, lighting, speakers, generators, nothing much really."

The Chief was almost speechless. He drained his glass as he gathered his wits. He didn't think to complain when it was refilled.

"Do you realise that there are thick end of 100,000 people heading up here?"

Holgate grinned. "Our Peggy has always been a popular girl."

The Chief continued. "Did it never occur to you to apply for planning permission?"

"Course not. It's a free country isn't it? You don't need planning permission to give a birthday party."

"What about safety? You can't just have 100,000 people turn up with no thoughts about safety."

"Why of course not, " said Sir Alistair easily. "We have engaged a couple of chaps who have lots of experience in running large festivals and we have over a thousand volunteers on site who have full St John's Ambulance training. We have been more than responsible I can assure you."

The Chief realised that these people would have an answer for anything he tried to say. It was pointless even trying. "Well I can see that you have run everything by your lawyers so I am clearly wasting my time here. I am not happy. Not happy at all. I have instructed that all approach roads be blocked. There is nothing we can do to get rid of the people who are already here, but I am putting a stop on any more."

Sir Alistair said in a very mild voice. "May I ask, on what grounds you are stopping people using public highways in a perfectly legal manner?"

"I'll think of something, don't you worry. Come on Duckworth. We're going. Thank you for the drink Mr Holgate."

As the door closed on the two policemen they all burst into laughter.

Vince, Cornelius, Montgomery and Helen all stepped in from the adjacent pantry. They too were laughing.

"Well Sir Alistair," said Cornelius, "how does it feel to be such an anti-establishment figure. A septuagenarian Mick Jagger/"

"It feels bloody marvellous young Cornelius. I should have done it years ago. They've been a bit slow with the road blocks don't you think."

"Nor particularly," said Vince. "They must be stretched to the limit with having to book all the girls from Shawfields. I reckon we should give them half an hour before we open up the second phase."

In fact it took the police nearly an hour to block the approach roads and it soon became apparent that the queues were dying down anyway. Motorcycle officers soon found the reason why. Along all of the approach roads signs appeared saying "Party Car Park". Cars were waved into fields and parked up. The partygoers then waited patiently to be collected by a convoy of tractors and trailers which ran them cross country to Higher Clough. By the early hours of the morning well over 90,000 visitors were erecting their tents all over the moors of Higher Clough farm. Over a hundred Matador stalls served an endless supply of burgers and sausages all night.

The first of Montgomery's bands started playing a little after midnight and soon the night air was thumping with the deep base boom of the speakers. The weather was unbelievably kind and a bright moon lit up the surrounding moors. There were remarkably few incidents and the well-staffed medical tents had to deal with nothing worse than a steady stream of sprained ankles and bad LSD trips.

The excitement gradually rose to fever pitch. A little after four in the morning Sir Alistair took the stage to near-hysterical acclaim. He raised his arms and patted the air in a gesture to request silence. As Helen stood arm in arm with Vince in the wings of the straw stage she shook her head in disbelief. "Just look at him Vince, can you believe it! That's my dad!"

At last the tumult died down a little. Sir Alistair took the microphone. "Good evening."

Thousands of voices reciprocated. He smiled. "I have been to many birthday parties over the years but none quite like this. Do you know, I had quite a ticking off from the Chief Constable of Greater Manchester earlier . . . " Rolling cheers of delight. " . . . I can't see his problem. All I can see is people having a good time. Anyway, I am not going to bore you. I would just like to say that I am delighted that Matador has been able to help in making this such a special night for Peggy. Make sure you all eat British beef and lots of it, and now I'm going to hand over to two young men that I think that you are all familiar with, ladies and gentlemen, I give you the Orange Boys!!"

The valley seemed to erupt as Malcolm Lyle and Pete Swan took the stage.

Lyle gestured to where Sir Alistair had joined Vince and Helen. "He's great isn't he?" Roared agreement. "Now, I reckon that we all better sing 'Happy Birthday' for Peggy. Come here will you." A deeply blushing Peggy Holgate joined Lyle and nearly died of embarrassment as 90,000 people sang to her. When they finished, the drums started to thunder and the Orange Boys exploded into their first song.

Matador went on to sell over half a million videos of the set that followed, a number that guaranteed that Matador made a handsome profit from Peggy Holgate's seventeenth birthday party. They went on to be involved in three more massive parties that spring and summer, but everyone agreed that none of them had quite the magic of the warm May night high in the Lancashire moors.

At 7.30 Sir Alistair, Vince and Helen were finishing off a huge cooked breakfast in the kitchen. Cornelius and Montgomery were snuggled together on the old sofa and completely dead to the world.

Sir Alistair looked at them fondly. "Quite a night."

Helen managed a tired smile. "A wonderful night, don't you agree Vince?"

Vince was far away. "Pardon?"

"We were saying it was a wonderful night."

"Oh, yes, fabulous."

Helen frowned. "You don't seem too enthused."

"Oh, sorry. I am, of course I am, how could I not be. I was just thinking, that's all."

Sir Alistair chuckled. "Always thinking Vincent. Always thinking."

Vince smiled back. "I suppose I just can't help it."

"Well you won't have to be thinking for much longer. I would hazard a guess that the beef price in next week's paper will have hopped over £1.26. Marcus and Gideon tell me that their biggest problem now is finding enough animals. Retailers are all scared stiff of the sticker girls. They just don't dare stock any imported beef at all. The fact is that the damage done to the industry means that there just is not enough beef in the country to supply the demand. Even before this weekend's actions Gideon was positive that the price was set to go into the £1.30's."

Vince nodded reflectively but still seemed glum.

Sir Alistair clapped him on the shoulder. "Come on man, cheer up. I'm going to be writing you lads a cheque for £20 million next Friday night. Surely that's a reason for good cheer?"

"Of course it is Sir Alistair. But we are not there yet. Helen, have you got the energy to fly me to the Airport. I'd really better go and join Victor in Luxembourg."

Helen was aghast. "Oh Vince, surely not. What does it matter now? Surely we can drop this story. We've won. We don't need it anymore."

Vince was very quiet. At last he spoke. "I wish that was the case Helen. I really do. But it isn't. I have bad vibes about this. I can feel him out there, and as long as he is out there, none of us are safe. It doesn't matter whether or not the beef price goes up to £1.50, so long as Julius Kumalo is out there we will never be able to feel safe. We need to finish it."

Helen was about to speak again but her father gently took her hand. "No Helen, Vince is right. Kumalo is a highly dangerous man. We have disturbed the leopard in his lair. We can't pretend that it never happened. We don't know for certain, but we have to assume that he will come for us. We have to stop him first, and to stop him we must have the proof from the Henninger office. Now, are you too tired or can you fly?"

"I can fly Daddy. I just don't want to."

When she dropped Vince at Ringway Airport she held him tight for a long time. "Please be safe."

He smiled down at the top of her head. "Course I'll be safe. I'll be with Victor."

He pretended not to hear her muffled sobs.

Vince met Victor at Luxembourg airport at 3 o'clock that afternoon. As they drove into the city in a taxi, Vince told his friend all about the party in the hills. A thin drizzle had started and the quiet Sunday streets seemed lonely and dismal. Vince felt worn out and a little depressed. "So how have you guys got on?"

"Not great," said Victor. "We have found a pretty good lookout point. There is a three-storey terrace on the other side of the street to the Henninger offices and we have managed to lay up on the roof. We've done three days. There isn't much moving. The office never opened for business on Friday so there isn't much coming and going. One thing is for certain though, we're on the right track."

"How come?"

"The only people that seem to be in the offices are four black guys. They are big, black as coal, and they sure don't look much like office clerks. What's more, they seem to have very suspiciously bulging jackets, they may just be carrying big fat calculators but I reckon that hand guns are more likely. If you want my opinion, these boys are fresh in from Bulawayo. After the Emerald Meats job I figure that we have to assume that Mr Kumalo is expecting us."

Vince sighed. "Well, it was only what we thought I suppose. Take me there. I'll have a look. Have you any ideas how we could get in?"

"Not really. These guys seem to know what they are doing. It could soon turn into another gun battle."

"We can't have that. We were bloody lucky in Ireland. We need to find another way."

They sat on the roof in the rain for most of the evening. As the hours drifted by, they only got a couple of quick glimpses of Kumalo's men. What he saw soon convinced Vince that Victor's appraisal had been correct. He sat back against the stone parapet and smoked thoughtfully. Then, suddenly, he sat up and grinned. Victor noticed this new energy and grinned back. "Looks to me like you've just had a brainstorm."

Vince pushed his sodden hair back over his head and said "Maybe. Maybe I have. Have you got the phone?"

"Sure." Victor handed him the mobile phone and he dialled. "Hi, that you Dwight?"

"Yeah, who's this?"

"Vince."

Dwight glanced at his bedside clock. "Bloody hell mate, it's two in the morning. Where are you?"

"Sat in the rain on a rooftop in Luxembourg."

Dwight laughed. "Jesus, do you blokes never sleep?"

"Seems not," said Vince. "I could use a favour Dwight."

"Ask away."

"What is the lovely Julie up to at the moment, you know, Donald Potter's dream Kiwi."

"Dunno mate," said Dwight. "I should think she'll be around. Why, do you want her for something?"

"Yes, I think so."

"Well go on then, tell me."

Vince quickly outlined his plan which left both Dwight and Victor chortling with delight. When he had finished Dwight said, "OK mate, give me an hour or so and I'll get back to you."

They climbed down the fire escape and joined Bill Atkins at a small hotel a few streets away. The ex-sergeant major pulled himself awake as they came into the room.

"Hi Vince. How's tricks?"

"Never better Bill – and you?"

"Not so bad. This is going to be a tough nut to crack though."

Victor's deep laugh boomed. "Not any more. Vince here has it taped. Go on, tell him, you're going to love this Bill."

Like the others, Bill was delighted when he heard the plan. Though he never would have admitted it to Victor, he had been dreading having to tackle the tough-looking Matabele guards. The phone rang just as Vince came out of the shower and Dwight informed him that Julie would be at Luxembourg airport at eleven in the morning.

Vince called Elf in London and was not surprised to find him wide awake. He agreed to make the trip once he was convinced that there was unlikely to be any more shooting.

By six the next evening they were all together in the hotel room and had agreed on the plan.

Julie had exchanged the casual student look that had so beguiled the unfortunate Potter for a slick Italian business suit and a cashmere polo neck sweater. Her hair was neatly tied back and the over-sized goofy glasses had been replaced by a designer pair. With her expensive briefcase she looked every inch the young Euro executive. She looked at the sheepish men who were eyeing her nervously. "Oh come on lads, let's get on with it shall we?"

Vince, Victor and Bill looked at each other helplessly. Vince said "Bill, you're . . . "

"Oh piss off Vince."

"Victor?" The big man looked down at the carpet and shrugged. Elf sat in the corner and played with his Gameboy.

Julie sighed with annoyance. "OK, I'll decide then. Whose idea was this?"

Vince shrugged and said "Mine."

She smiled. "You get the vote then."

She stepped forward and walloped him across the face and then kicked him hard in the shin. He grabbed at his shin and howled with pain. She tore at his hair and yelled at him. "Come on for Christ's sake, hit me will you."

Vince took a step back, breathed deeply, and gave her a vicious slap across the cheek. She gasped, then belted him again. "Harder you bastard."

This time he thumped her with a closed fist and she crashed to the floor. "Oh Jesus Julie, I'm sorry, I . . . "

"Don't be bloody sorry. Come on, fight me, tear the clothes man."

She leapt onto him and the pair of them fell into a heap on the floor as he ripped at her expensive clothes. At last she stood up and perused herself in the mirror, breathing deeply. "Fine. That's better. Just one more thing." Again she leapt at Vince and kissed him fiercely. When she pulled away, her lipstick was smeared. Once again she studied herself in the mirror. Her clothes were torn and ripped, her makeup was completely haywire and her left eye was beginning to close and colour. She nodded to herself then turned around. "OK chaps, I think that I will do. Let's boogie shall we?"

"OK" said a thoroughly miserable Vince. She walked over to him and kissed him again, this time a great deal more tenderly. "Don't worry about it matey. Us Kiwi girls are tough as teak."

Ten minutes later the desk sergeant at the local police station nearly jumped out of his skin as the front door crashed open. His eyes widened as a completely hysterical Julie staggered in screaming uncontrollably. She collapsed against his desk and spoke in fast, breathless sentences. His English was nowhere near good enough to understand her so he summoned help. Within minutes she was surrounded by a cluster of concerned policemen whilst a female officer held her shaking body. At last they managed to calm her enough to understand her babbling story.

"I had to go and see someone . . . at Henningers . . . they have an office just down the road . . . number 18, Rue de Antoine . . . they let me in . . . then they locked the door . . . I asked to see Mr Henninger but they just laughed . . . there were four of them . . . big. Big black men. They just laughed. Then one of them grabbed me . . . I tried to fight but they were too strong . . . they held me down on the desk . . . I fought but it was no good . . . " Tears of shame poured down her smudged cheeks. Her voice dropped to a mere whisper. "They raped me. The bastards raped me. All of them. One after the other."

She clammed up then. She sat like stone staring at the floor. A murmur of anger spread through the policemen and within minutes two squad cars screeched to a halt outside 18 Rue d'Antoine. Vince, Victor, Bill and Elf watched from their car as the police beat at the door. A voice from inside replied, but the door did not open. The police then smashed the door down, and a little while later the four Matabele guards were frog-marched to a waiting van whilst the police brandished their captured weapons in triumph.

Language was a major problem at the police station as the enraged Matabele men roared their anger. It was almost inevitable that one of them would lose his cool, and when he did, he smashed an unfortunate policeman's nose into a pulp. After this, all four men were hurled into cells until the morning. Charges were prepared for rape, illegal entry into Luxembourg and the possession of illegal firearms. The distraught Julie was escorted back to her hotel and asked to report back to the station at her leisure the next morning.

The police searched the Henninger offices thoroughly before locking up and leaving a little after 11 pm. Vince waited for an hour, then broke into the offices via the back door. Within twenty minutes Elf had stripped all information from the computers and they were back on the road. They collected Julie from the front of her hotel and drove through the night to Paris. They caught the morning train to London and were back in Elf's flat by 11.00 a.m. Vince had dosed off when Victor shook his shoulder a couple of hours later.

"Wakey, wakey. Rise and shine."

Vince opened his eyes to see every one of the big Nigerian's teeth shining in a beaming smile. Victor tossed him a pile of computer printouts. "There you go boy. We've got them. Hook, line and sinker. It's all there in every detail. The Matabele Meat Company sells to Henningers and Henningers sell to Emerald Meats. We've e-mailed the whole lot over to Ricky Myers and Dwight is going to run the story tomorrow. Sir Alistair is on his way to town and he is going to have a word with a couple of old pals at the Foreign Office. They will pass everything on to the Irish and Zimbabwe governments. By this time tomorrow Mr Kumalo will be hopping about like a toad in a frying pan. We've done for him Vince. He'll have to scoot back into the bush again."

Vince laid his head back and sighed with contentment. Victor was right. Kumalo was about to be hit by a tidal wave of trouble. There was no way that he would find time to come after them now. It was over.

*The Globe* would plunge Shawfields into a total catastrophe and no retailer would dare stock imported meat for a very long time.

It was over.

He pictured the old black and white images of the Russian soldiers as they hung the Hammer and Sickle flag from the Brandenberg Gate as the last of the German defences of Berlin crumbled to defeat.

It was over and all he wanted to do was to sleep for about seven years. He opened his eyes and smiled up at Victor.

"I think we've done it. I think that we've actually done it." He grabbed a can of lager and opened it. "Well, I think that with regard to a sense of symmetry, we should all meet up at my place tomorrow night to have a bit of a celebration. What do you say?"

"Sounds good to me," said Victor.

Gideon was taking an afternoon drive to clear the cobwebs when his mobile phone rang.

"Hello?"

"Gideon, it's Vince. How the hell are you?"

"Fine. No problems. And you?"

"Floating on air mate, floating on air. We've got him Gideon. We got into Henningers and we've got it all, the Matabele Meat Company, Emerald Meats, Shawfields, the bloody lot. We're going to nail him Gideon. We've done it! We've won. So listen. We're all meeting up at my place tomorrow night to celebrate so get yourself there, OK?"

Gideon smiled with delight. "No problems Vince. I'll be there. See you tomorrow."

"Great. Take care." Gideon laughed out loud as he sped through the Perthshire countryside. It had been their greatest-ever operation and they had won. He looked forward happily to the drive down the next day and the celebration that would follow.

A few minutes later Hemp called Rearden on his mobile.

"Rearden."

"It's Hemp. We've just recorded a call on Rosenberg's mobile. It was Allenby. Apparently they have found out some highly damning information. There was mention of a break-in to a place called Henningers."

Rearden snapped angrily. "Yes I know about that."

Hemp was quite unperturbed. "They are meeting up at Allenby's place tomorrow evening for a celebration. As you know, we have never located Allenby's property, but we do have a tracking device in place in Rosenberg's car."

Rearden was silent for a while. "OK Hemp. This is good. I will collect the tracking device from you this evening and pay you in full for your services. You can consider our contract to be complete. Please prepare my invoice. I will call at about six."

"Very well," said Hemp.

Kumalo was standing at the hotel window staring down at the muddy waters of the River Thames. Without turning round he said "What did he have to say?"

Rearden repeated what Hemp had told him. Kumalo digested the information then smiled slowly. Rearden felt the cold chill of fear run through his bones at the sight of the twisted smile. "This is good news indeed," said Kumalo. "We will go to the Scottish house tonight. Bring Hamilton. Now go."

Rearden left and Kumalo continued to gaze out of the window. He sensed the smell of his prey. Soon the hunt would meet its destined end. Tomorrow he would kill his quarry. Tomorrow he would find his revenge.

Simon Shawfield was awoken by his alarm clock at 7.00 a.m. on the morning of Tuesday, May 4. Before getting out of his bed, he lay for a while with his hands behind his head. The bedroom window was being quietly buffeted by the hard, rainy wind outside. He decided that he was safe to view the day with cautious optimism. The two days since the onslaught of the sticker girls had without doubt been bad, but not entirely catastrophic. Overall the media had served up publicity which had been unkind rather than scathing. Junior Government ministers had made comments which were broadly noncommittal. They had condemned the sticker girls for flouting the law whilst not exactly condoning the draconian actions taken by Shawfields. They had offered mild support for Simon's comments on farmers needing to keep up with their European colleagues. The good news had been that there had been no coverage in the *Globe*. For two mornings he had picked up the tabloid with gut wrenching trepidation, fully expecting a horribly damning story: there had been none.

*The Globe* had concentrated on joyous coverage of the Pennine Party and had taken great delight in the fumbling antics of the police. The Monday morning front page had been dominated by a huge photo of a beaming Sir Alistair receiving the acclaim of the

90,000 crowd alongside the Orange Boys.

The bad news had been sales. Every store had reported a collapse in beef sales. If this were not bad enough, even worse news was that almost every store reported that overall turnover was down by over 10%. It was painfully obvious that the great British public was voting with its feet.

Once again, an emergency Board Meeting had been held the previous day. The drop in sales had led to a split in opinion around the table. Some were confident that it would be a three-day wonder and therefore not a reason for panic. Others were gravely worried that the weekend's events had put a serious dent in Shawfields' public reputation, and that the damage would take months to repair. Everyone unanimously agreed that it was critical that the slump in sales was hidden from the City for as long as possible.

Shawfields shares had lost 3% of their value when the Stock Exchange opened following the weekend break. Every director knew that the slide could easily become a crash.

As he watched the rivulets of rain make their haphazard way down the glass of his window, Shawfield felt that things might just start going their way. It would not take too long for the story of the sticker girls to fizzle and die. The public were fickle, and their notoriously limited attention span would soon be diverted by the exposure of some soap star's sexual antics. If Shawfields could just avoid the glare of further bad press for another week there was a chance that the situation could normalise.

He got up and showered. He forced himself to hum as he shaved. He dressed carefully and admired his well-groomed, expensively attired figure in the mirror with some appreciation. As he made his way down the stairs to the kitchen he told himself that things really weren't all that bad after all.

This upbeat mood died as soon as he entered the kitchen. It was as if somebody had died. His two teenage daughters had ignored their cereal and were staring down at the table. His wife sat at the head of the table with her head in her hands. When she looked up her face was streaked with tears. Her eyes were quite desperate. When she spoke, her frayed voice was little more than a whisper.

"Oh God Simon, what are we going to do?"

He felt his stomach collapsing down through his thighs. He felt fear wash through his soul. His own voice held a tremble when he spoke. "Why? What? What on earth is the matter?"

By way of a reply his wife tossed a copy of the *Globe* to him. As he sat down heavily, he found his first glance at the front page a confusing one. The headline was easy, it read in big black letters

## 'SHAWFIELD SHAME'

The words immediately made his heart sink. So much for the hopes of a week free of publicity. What confused him were the three pictures. In the middle was a photo of himself. It must have been taken at some banquet or another. He was wearing his dinner suit and he was brandishing a cigar and a glass of champagne. He looked arrogant and smug. It wasn't a very nice picture at all. Bastards.

It was the other two pictures that made no sense to him whatsoever. On the left there was a photo of an old lady in a wheelchair. She was sitting by a gravestone whilst staring into the lens with a perfectly calm expression. Who on earth was she?

On the right was an even more bizarre photo. It was a tall black man in jungle fatigues. He was armed to the teeth with two bandoleers of ammunition, a number of grenades in his belt and a murderous-looking machine gun. Behind him, the countryside was arid and desert-like. He stared into the camera with a hard, fathomless glare. He looked every inch a killer. Who in God's name was he?

Feeling like a man who was about to sit in the electric chair, Simon Shawfield began to read with terrified fascination. The story, which had been jointly penned by Dwight and Ricky Myers, went on to become something of a legend amongst media circles. Old hands all agreed that they had never before or after seen such a piece of journalistic hatchet work. The story was not designed to hurt and embarrass Shawfields. It was designed to destroy, to annihilate, to obliterate.

*Dear Simon Shawfield,*

*We do hope that you have enjoyed your breakfast, because it is the last thing that you are going to enjoy today. We hope that it will be the last thing that you enjoy for a long time.*

*This newspaper is going to expose your shame. We are going to lay out the details of your lies and your endless greed for all of our readers to see. And when they have finished, we will leave it to them to decide if they ever want to shop with you again.*

*Last weekend you ordered the arrest of over 20,000 ladies who were trying to defend their livelihoods. You appeared on TV. You showed no sign of regret, no sign of remorse, in fact you seemed petty pleased with your tough-guy stance.*

*You told us all that you were quite happy to sell us Irish beef. You said, "Farmers would do well to stop moaning and get on with being more efficient in order to compete with their colleagues in the EC." That is what you you said, isn't it?*

*Let us have a look at those two statements and introduce the people whose pictures appear either side of your own.*

*One of those farmers who you say would do well not to moan is Emily Shaw. Emily was born on her farm in the Peak District seventy-three years ago. She started helping on the farm when she was five. In all her life she has never had a moment's trouble with the police until you had her arrested last Saturday. You say Emily would do well not to moan. What after all has she got to moan about?*

*Well, Simon, we will tell you.*

*Eight months ago the bank informed Emily and her husband Jack that they were going to repossess her farm – the farm where she was born. Of course they had never had a single case of BSE but their income from beef cattle had collapsed by 50%. Fifty-four years ago Jack Shaw landed on the D-Day beaches and marched with Montgomery all the way to Berlin. He took everything that Hitler could throw at him. But he couldn't take the despair of having his farm taken away. Instead he took his shotgun into the barn and killed himself.*

*Emily's protest was to put a sticker on a package of your beef and you had her arrested. Of course you did. What right has Emily Shaw got to moan?*

*The other thing that you told us on Saturday, Simon, was that you* were proud to sell good, clean, traceable Irish beef. The trouble is Simon, is that it isn't Irish at all, is it? You just thought that we wouldn't find out, didn't you? Oh dear Simon, you should have known not to underestimate the Globe.

The fact is that we have discovered the truth. The truth is that you have been buying your beef from the man in the other picture.

Who is this dangerous-looking man? His name is Julius Kumalo and he is an ex-terrorist who now farms thousands of cattle in Zimbabwe. He rules his lands with a reign of terror. Those who cross him end up in a shallow grave out in the wilderness.

Oh of course your beef has been coming from Ireland. It comes from a company called Emerald Meats. They import it from Zimbabwe and simply put a nice Irish label on it.

Did you ever wonder why they were willing to sell you the beef so cheap? It certainly did not concern you. You are an endlessly greedy man running an endlessly greedy company. We will tell you why it was so cheap. Julius Kumalo doesn't really care about making money from selling beef. He uses the carcasses to smuggle drugs and weapons into Europe. When you buy his beef you provide the transport for his smuggling racket. When you pay him for his beef you are helping to launder his money.

Next time you hear about another teenager dying of a heroin overdose or another victim being gunned down on the streets of Belfast you can take your own share of the blame.

This appalling scandal has happened for one reason and one reason only.

Greed.

Your greed is so great that you will turn a blind eye to anything so long as it inflates your already criminal profits. How dare you criticise Emily Shaw for putting a sticker on a packet of your blood-soaked beef?

We look forward to hearing from you Simon. Have a nice day.

'Best regards,
'Everyone at the Globe.'

Shawfield laid the paper down on the table and gazed blankly into space. His wife was talking to him but he didn't hear a word that she said. After a few moments he got up and walked out of the kitchen as if he were in a trance. He put on his coat and left the house. A cluster of journalists were waiting for him on the pavement outside. They were screaming questions at him but he couldn't really hear them either. A slight smile played on his lips as he passed through the reporters like a zombie. He couldn't help but think of the song, 'Everybody's talking at me, I don't hear a word they're saying, only the echoes of my mind . . . '

Once in the car he was on auto pilot all the way to Head Office. As he made his way down the shiny corridors to the Boardroom people made way for him like they would a leper. 'People stop and stare, I can't see their faces, only the shadows of their eyes . . . '

Unbelievably as he approached the impressive oak door of the Boardroom he found that he was softly singing to himself, "I'm going where the sun keeps shining, through the pouring rain, going where the weather suits my clothes. Banking off a north-east wind, sailing on a summer breeze, skipping over the ocean like a storm."

He was singing as he sat down at the table. Haggard faces regarded him with open astonishment. For an endless two minutes he was silent, quietly contemplating the words of his song. He then looked slowly round his shattered colleagues.

"Where is Hamilton?"

At first nobody seemed to want to answer. Eventually a timid voice said quietly, "We don't know Simon. We can't find him. He seems to have vanished."

Shawfield chuckled at this. "Well, well. Surprise, surprise. Over the hills and far away is he? Oh well, I can't blame him really. Best place to be at the moment." For a brief moment some of his old clarity and command came into his voice and face. His voice was suddenly crisp and businesslike. Some of the worried directors began to feel a sense of relief. It did not last long as they digested his words.

"I am dreadfully sorry that this regrettable business has happened. I truly am. My own position of course is quite untenable. I could fight it out but I have absolutely no wish to. I am not going to do the decent thing and go down with my ship with all guns blazing. I am going to take the quickest and easiest way out. I will issue a statement announcing my resignation within the hour. I apologise for leaving you fellows in the shit like this but that is how it is going to be. I wish each and every one of you all the luck in the world. My God you are going to need it."

Without any further ceremony Shawfield stood up and left the room whistling to himself.

The article on its own would have guaranteed a steep drop in the Shawfields share price. However when Simon Shawfield put every bit of his 31% stake in the company on the market early that afternoon, the slide became a freefall. Trading in the doomed shares was suspended the next day. The Shawfield brand name was irredeemably doomed. Six months later the company met with its inevitable end as it was taken over by another supermarket chain.

In the midst of the hurricane of crises that blew around the beleaguered Shawfield directors, thankfully one problem did go away. Emerald Meats simply ceased to exist and therefore so did the Shawfields contract.

Two weeks later the shelves of the Shawfields stores were filled with British beef and Union Jacks. But of course it was too late.

Far, far too late.

By the time that his old company was swallowed up Simon Shawfield had emigrated to the Natal region of South Africa. He became reclusive and interested only in his vineyards. No matter how much money his wife paid to a host of high-flying therapists nothing ever worked. He withdrew into a sunny dream world where there were only grapes.

His wife stuck it for two years then divorced him and returned to England with their two daughters. Shawfield barely noticed their departure, and, against all the odds, he went on to live happily ever after.

Sir Alistair's Foreign Office contacts wasted little time. Initially as he imparted his information they took it with a casual, laid-back air. However, as soon as they realised that the whole story was going to be spread all over the Tuesday edition of the *Globe* they leapt into action like men possessed.

It did not take a great deal of coaxing to get the Irish Government into gear. For some time they had been increasingly alarmed about the corruption at Cork Docks, and the name of Emerald Meats had come to their notice on several occasions.

The police raided the Emerald Meats site at 3 a.m. on Tuesday morning as copies of the *Globe* were being distributed all over Britain by night delivery vans. They found the site deserted. The offices had been cleaned out of all paperwork and the guardhouse was unattended. There was plenty of meat. Carcasses hung in their hundreds, seeming rather forlorn amidst the deserted surroundings. It took some time to find evidence of any criminal activity. After three days' careful searching, one of the forensic teams found unmistakable traces of gun oil in four of the carcasses.

They had rather more luck with the registration plates which Victor had noted down. The Dublin car led directly to a major cannabis haul and the successful conviction of two drug dealers that the police had been chasing for several years.

By cross referencing a variety of reports from surveillance teams, road checks and pictures from surveillance cameras, the police in Northern Ireland eventually tracked down the transit van. It was the first piece of a new jigsaw. The whole puzzle was completed some four months later when the authorities arrested a semi-psychotic splinter group of the IRA who were hell-bent on scuppering the peace talks. A large cache of East European automatic rifles, grenades and ammunition was unearthed. It was established that the weapons had originally been part of an arms consignment supplied by the Soviet Union to Mozambique in the late 1970s.

The Ambassador for Zimbabwe was not remotely amused when he was invited to visit the Foreign Office well after midnight. He put on an act of studied grumpiness when he was guided into a panelled room with leather furniture. Twenty minutes later he was beaming like a man who had won the Lottery. After a high-speed dash back to the Embassy he had no qualms about waking the Minister for the Interior at his home in Harare. The Minister's reaction was similarly ecstatic. Late-night phone calls buzzed around the sleeping African capital. It took very little time indeed for a course of action to be decided on. Kumalo's growing power and influence in Matabeleland had been causing the Harare Government mounting concern for many years. The Mashona Ministers had been itching for an excuse to cut him down to size without provoking a wholesale revolt. At last, care of the British Foreign Office, the excuse had been handed to them on a silver platter. Three trucks of soldiers from a local base surrounded, entered and took control of the Matabele Meat Company site a little before six that morning. At the same time, two helicopters carrying members of the Zimbabwe Special Forces landed at Clearwaters. In the absence of Kumalo and his most trusted lieutenants there was no resistance. The extent of the operation emerged over the following days and weeks. Large caches of arms and drugs were discovered both at the factory and on the farms. Assets were seized and the Matabele Meat Company was closed down. For a while the farms were allowed to go to seed. There was no great rush of prospective buyers. Six months later the lands and the factory were purchased at a rock-bottom price by Matador. The business was converted into a Co-op where all the farm and factory workers became members. Matador leased the land and factory to the co-op at a discounted rate and helped the young business to market its products.

As the years passed the co-op thrived and became something of a model African enterprise.

As a grey dawn slowly broke over southern Scotland, Julius Kumalo, Oliver Hamilton, and nine Matabele soldiers were playing a waiting game in an isolated farmhouse in Lanarkshire.

Nobody spoke much and everyone's attention kept being drawn to the electrical box on the kitchen table. This was the tracking device that they had collected from Hemp which would tell them when Gideon Rosenberg had set off from Black Loch.

Kumalo was standing at the window watching the rain lash down on the wet fields. His mobile phone had rung several times and he now knew the full extent of the Government sweeps in Matabeleland. The kitchen door opened and Rearden came in looking grave. He passed a copy of the *Globe* to Kumalo.

"You better read this Julius."

Kumalo read the article through twice very slowly. His face twisted into its strange smile. He held out the paper towards Rearden and pointed to his picture on the front page.

"This was 1977. I was rather a handsome chap before Jackson did his stuff to my face. They took this picture for some Russian newspaper. They wanted to show the revolutionary heroes who they were supplying arms to. It seems a very long time ago."

He gently laid the paper down on the table and addressed his men in Matabele. He told them of the raids back at home and he translated the article in the *Globe*. He then turned to Oliver and Rearden. "I have explained everything. All of our sites at home have been raided by government forces. They will find plenty of evidence against us. Once again we are exiles."

He paused and resumed his vigil at the window. "I have told them that they are all free to go. I can offer them plenty of money and they should have a fair chance of making a new life for themselves outside of Zimbabwe."

He turned to the two Europeans. "Of course the same applies to both of you. You have both done well. None of us could ever have anticipated the Matador factor. These people have outwitted us from beginning to end. I believe that you both have sufficient funds to disappear and start a new life. You should go now."

"What about you Julius?" Asked Rearden.

"I am a Kumalo. My family sat at the thrones of Mzilikazi and Lobengula. I must see this through to the end. I will find these people and they will pay for what they have done."

One of the Matabele soldiers emerged from the huddle that they had gone into and waited to address Kumalo. Five of the younger men had decided to try and get away. Four of Kumalo's old Zipra colleagues had elected to stay and to follow Kumalo wherever he may lead them. Kumalo nodded slowly. He gave his sombre blessing to each of the departing young warriors and then they picked up their bags and drove away in one of the hired cars.

"Well, I'd better be on my way too Julius." Said Rearden. "I'm only sorry that things have turned out this way. Come on Oliver, I'll give you a lift."

Hamilton looked at him blankly. "No thank you. I think that I will stay."

Kumalo raised an eyebrow. "Why?"

Hamilton's face was abnormally bland. "Because there really isn't anything else left to do. Well is there?"

Kumalo studied the face carefully. He had seen it before many times. He had seen how stress and the pressure of combat caused young men to mentally dismantle themselves. The world which had once been so complex and diverse would become utterly simple. Their diminished brains would merely focus on the single goal of killing. In his Zipra days Kumalo had used many of these young men as cannon fodder. He had sent them off on missions from which there was almost no hope of return. As he looked deep into Oliver's face he experienced a wave of immense sadness. It had all gone on for far too long. His endlessly brutal life at last had begun to seem tiresome. He said, "This isn't your fight Oliver. You should go."

Hamilton responded with a faraway smile. "It is my fight Julius. I want it to be my fight. I want to stay."

Kumalo shrugged. He shook Rearden by the hand and the Irishman departed.

With an effort, Kumalo forced some energy into his body.

"Come. We will drive up to Perth and park a few miles from Black Loch. When Rosenberg sets off it will be easier to follow him."

The six men loaded all their gear into the double-wheelbased Land Rover that they had hired and set off to Perthshire.

# CHAPTER FOURTEEN

## THE CROW MAKES WING

The tracking device went active with a beeping sound a little after four in the afternoon. They were able to follow Gideon from a distance of two to three miles as he wound his way south. If anything the weather was getting worse. The Land Rover was buffeted alarmingly as they crossed the Forth Road Bridge. By the time they passed through Kelso at six o'clock the skies had closed right in. A near gale force wind blew the driving rain in soaking horizontal waves over the sodden fields. The roads were getting much narrower and Kumalo told his driver to speed up so that they could get closer.

When they turned into a single-tracked road which was marked with a cul-de-sac sign, Kumalo ordered that they pull right up behind Gideon's car. The driver struggled to pick up speed as the narrow road wound its way into the Cheviot hills. The sky was almost black and the rain made the windscreen wipers constantly struggle to keep visibility clear. At last they sighted the red glow of Gideon's tail lights two hundred yards ahead.

"OK," said Kumalo. "Pull right behind him. When he turns in we will stop him and find out how the land lies ahead."

Gideon was alarmed when he saw headlights on his rear bumper. He reached for his mobile phone and dialled Vince.

"Vince, it's Gideon. I think that I am being followed. I am about three miles from the gate and I have lights right behind me." He was livid with himself as he heard the tremble of fear in his voice.

Vince closed his eyes for a moment. Inside he had known it all along. For days he had been consumed with a sense of foreboding. Every instinct had told him that it was inevitable that Kumalo would find them. And now he was here. Now he would have to be faced. "Hang on a sec Gideon." With his hand over the receiver he said, "Victor. It's Gideon. He's about three miles from the gate and he thinks that he is being followed."

Victor grabbed the phone. "Gideon. It's Victor. Keep going. Don't try anything, just keep going. Try and get up here. We'll be ready OK?"

"OK Victor, I'll try."

Victor turned to Vince. "What time are Helen, Marcus and Sir Alistair due in the chopper?"

"It should be any time now."

"Good. Let's get them on the phone."

Marcus answered. "Listen up Marcus," said Victor. "We have a problem. Gideon has just called. He is about three miles out and he thinks that he is being followed. Are you close?"

"About two minutes away."

"Excellent. Take up position over the gateway and report what you see. That's it for now. Ring Vince's phone when you have anything to report."

Victor dropped the phone into his pocket and gestured Vince to follow him. They crossed the yard in the driving rain to the outhouse where Vince stored his vegetables. Victor hurled packing cases to one side to reveal two wooden crates which Vince had never seen before.

"Take this." He heaved out the first of the crates and Vince could barely lift it. Vince half-dragged his crate back into the house whilst Victor used his great strength to shoulder his burden. Once they were back in the kitchen Victor ripped open the cases. Inside were two Israeli Uzi machine guns, a sniper's rifle, a shoulder-held rocket launcher and night vision equipment.

"Jesus Victor, when the hell did you get all this gear?"

"As soon as I heard about Kumalo." Victor did not look up from pulling the weapons out of the cases. "There is a similar stash up at Black Loch."

Montgomery had started to shake uncontrollably and Cornelius did his best to calm him down. "Oh Jesus Cornelius, he's coming, he's coming for us, oh Jesus, we're going to die, he's going to kill us . . . "

Victor strode across the room and slapped Montgomery hard. "Quiet." His voice was murderous. "Button it Montgomery. Nobody is going to get killed if we stay calm and keep our wits. Now get a bloody grip man."

Tears of fear and shame poured down Montgomery's cheeks as Victor resumed his work on the weapons.

The phone rang. "Victor. It's Marcus. OK, we're in place. We've sighted both vehicles, this is what is happening . . . "

Gideon took the turn into the gate too fast and his car ripped along the side of the stone post. He leaned forward and squinted to try and get a clear view through the pouring rain. He tried to go fast but it was impossible. Visibility was appalling and the road was treacherous. Behind him the headlights were slowly gaining. He forced himself to take deep breaths to calm himself and allow full concentration on the road. He threw his car around a tight corner and he lost control. He began to skid and a granite outcrop lurched towards him through the rain. The car hammered into it and for a moment he was dazed as his chest ripped into the seatbelt.

Quickly he regained his wits. He unstrapped himself, leapt out and started to run up the steeply climbing track. As he glanced behind he saw that the headlights were only 100 yards short of his crashed car. He forced himself not to look and to run.

A hundred feet above, the passengers of the helicopter watched the scene unfold. They could see the desperate, scrambling figure of Gideon as he fled up the track. The Land Rover had to stop when it met the crashed car. One man leapt out and started loping after Gideon with easy athletic strides. Five other men started to try and push the wrecked car aside.

Sir Alistair assessed the situation quickly. Gideon had a three hundred yard start on his pursuer but it was still more than two miles to High Cragg. He would never make it. He shouted to Helen over the noise of the rotor blades. "Go down! We need to pick him up."

"We can't. It's impossible. The helicopter will not take the weight of three passengers. I'd never get it back in the air."

"I know that. I am going to get out."

Helen turned to her father with a horrified expression. "No daddy, you mustn't, you can't . . . "

Sir Alistair's voice was harsh. "Don't you dare argue with me. Just get this machine down. I am an old dying man and I will not see Gideon taken by that murderer. NOW DO IT!!"

Gideon became aware of a further noise that could be heard above the howling of the wind. His head was pounding as his blood vessels throbbed with the effort of running. His breath was coming in shallow gasps and despair was beginning to set in.

The sound then merged into a remarkable picture as a helicopter appeared out of the mist and landed on the road fifty yards ahead of him. A figure climbed out and waved to him urgently. He found new reserves of energy and sprinted forward.

"Get in!!!" shouted Sir Alistair. Gideon did not need asking twice. He clambered inside and immediately he felt the helicopter start to lift. He closed his eyes with a surging sense of relief as they climbed into the mist. When he opened his eyes he realised that Sir Alistair was not with them.

"Helen!! Your father, where is he?"

Her voice was tight with emotion. "He had to stay back on the road. The chopper can't carry more than two passengers."

Kumalo heard the chopper too. As he ran he shook his head slightly. Everything he tried to do seemed to be doomed. Who would ever have thought that they would have a helicopter? His skin prickled with a superstitious awe. He was beginning to feel the inevitability of his fate. He knew that he was entering his last battle. All that there was left was to die like a man.

As he ran round a corner he was just in time to see the belly of the helicopter as it lifted up into the swirling mist.

A man stood in the middle of the road about forty yards ahead of him. Kumalo slowed to walking pace, slipped the safety catch off his weapon and approached.

Sir Alistair McIntyre waited quite calmly as the big Matabele came up to him. His white hair was plastered over his forehead and his face was pale and stretched. When Kumalo paused a few yards short he gave him a laconic smile.

"Julius Kumalo, I presume?"

Kumalo shouldered his weapon and took Sir Alistair's proffered hand. "And you are Sir Alistair McIntyre. I gather that your helicopter would only carry two passengers?"

"Correct."

"So you got out so that Rosenberg could get away. You are a fine man McIntyre. I salute you."

"Thank you."

They eyed each other as the rain ran down their faces.

Kumalo said, "I was going to question Rosenberg about who was up there. Of course they know that we are here now. We have lost the luxury of surprise. I would like to ask you some questions. How many of them are there? Are they armed? But you won't tell me will you?"

"No."

"And if I resort to vigorous methods of questioning I doubt if you would tell me even then. No, I have seen men like you. You wouldn't talk." His eyes had a slightly lost look. "Besides, I'm not sure if I have the stomach for torture any more. Not any more."

"Why don't you leave it and walk away Kumalo? What is to be gained? You must know that it is over."

Kumalo smiled. "You are right of course. It is over and we have lost. Unfortunately my people are not very good at walking away from lost causes. When Rhodes and his men invaded Matabeleland a hundred years ago we fought them. They had machine guns which we had never seen before. Wave after wave of our finest warriors were cut down as they charged the spitting guns. We knew it was hopeless after the first attack, but we kept up assault after assault until the sun set. That is the people that we are McIntyre. I am of those people. I know only one way. I cannot stop now."

He gently nudged Sir Alistair with his weapon and walked him to the side of the track. He bound his wrists and ankles, and then tied the wrist binding to more rope which he tied to a sturdy fencing post. As he finished, the Land Rover pulled up alongside. Before he climbed in, he cast a last regretful glance toward Sir Alistair. The old man was sat up ramrod straight and his eyes blazed with defiance.

Kumalo gave him a nod of respect then climbed on board.

The helicopter touched down in the small field by the house. Marcus, Helen and Gideon darted inside. For a brief moment everyone started to talk at once.

"Shut up, all of you. NOW!!" Victor's voice was like a pistol shot and provoked immediate silence. "Better. We have no time, so listen. Helen, you take Marcus and Gideon out. Fly a few miles and find somewhere to land. Don't call the police yet, they can't help us. Cornelius and Montgomery; you two need to start walking right now. Head up over the fell. Walk as hard as you can for forty minutes, then find a ditch and hide. Switch on your phone every half-hour. When it is safe I will call you. Whatever you do, don't move once you have hidden. It is going dark now. If you don't move you will be safe. Now, all of you go: go now."

"Wait Victor," said Marcus. "You want Vince to stay. Why?"

Victor told him quickly. Marcus nodded. "I thought as much. Look, Vince has no training for this kind of thing. I have been a soldier and I still shoot regularly. I will stay. Besides, I am much more expendable."

Victor thought for about five seconds. "OK, you're right. Vince, you go in the helicopter and co-ordinate things from there. Do not ring us under any circumstances. I will call you. Now go."

Seconds later the helicopter lifted off and disappeared into the thickening light. Cornelius and Montgomery donned waterproofs and headed up the side of the fell.

Victor handed the sniper's rifle to Marcus and pointed to a spot on the skyline. "There. Make it up there as fast as you can. Hopefully I will take a few of them out with the rocket. When they come out of the vehicle, you fire. They will probably take cover. Keep firing, but fire wild. Don't give away the fact that you have a night scope. When they come for you they will use the horns of the bull. The Zulu and The Matabele always attack like the horns of the bull. The horns strike first and then the head comes forward to finish the job. I will wait on the right-hand flank, you watch out for the left-hand flank. When you have a certain target, you shoot. That will be my signal. With luck when we have taken out the horns I will be able to deal with the head. Good luck."

They shook hands, then Marcus headed out into the rain and started to climb towards the distant ridge.

As the Land Rover approached the crest of the track Kumalo ordered a halt. He cautiously crawled to the brow of the hill and surveyed the scene. The main house and the out-buildings were sixty yards away. He watched patiently for several minutes then returned to the vehicle.

"We are at the house. I don't think that they are there. I think that they have fled into the hills." He gestured to his driver. "You take the Land Rover forward. We will follow behind."

Victor lay on his stomach a hundred yards behind the house. Even at such a short distance it was getting harder to see clearly in the rain. At first he almost sensed it, then the shape of the crawling Land Rover slowly became visible as it came over the brow of the hill. He kneeled up, pulled the stock of the rocket launcher to his shoulder and eased the trigger. The rocket lanced across the tussocky ground and erupted into the Land Rover. The driver was killed instantly. Those behind were thrown to the ground by the blast, but escaped with little more than cuts and ringing ears.

Victor cursed when he realised that Kumalo had deployed his men behind the vehicle. He had only taken out one of them. Five left. He moved quickly in a doubled-up trot and started to climb up the side of the fell. As he moved he was pleased to hear the crackle of Marcus's rifle as he laid down covering fire.

Kumalo laid back on the wet grass and breathed deeply. A rocket! They had fired a rocket! When would the surprises end? He brought his men around him under the shelter of the brow of the hill. Above them, bullets occasionally fizzed and pinged. Kumalo once again slithered to the top of the brow and soon located the source of the firing. He smiled grimly.

"OK, they are holed up at the top of the cliff. It is a pretty tough position. We will have to approach with caution. Two pairs will come in from each side and I will take the centre. Go carefully and quietly. With all of this wind and rain we should be able to surprise them."

It took Marcus a little while to get the hang of the night scope. Eventually he mastered it and started to scan the ridge that ran away to his right. It took him several minutes, but at last he detected movement. It was really quite dark now and he marvelled as the ghostly green image of a man emerged from the cover of a rock. He waited, and then a second figure emerged, and carefully started to pick its way up the hill. They were still several hundred yards away. He did some mental calculations and reckoned that at their current speed it would be six or seven minutes before the men were in decent range.

He felt hugely tempted to try and locate the other attackers but was fearful of losing his excellent view of his prime targets.

Five hundred yards away, Victor had crammed himself into a cluster of tussocky grass. Using his night vision goggles he was able to check on the progress of the men that made up the left-hand prong of Kumalo's horns. The lead man moved well. He was fast without being reckless. His movements were decisive and economical. Victor recognised an experienced bush fighter. The second man demonstrated no such skill. His movements were clumsy and careless. Who was he? Victor found it impossible to believe that this was one of Kumalo's best men.

Marcus forced himself to breathe evenly. The two men had ducked behind a large rock. When they came out they would have to cross at least fifteen yards of open ground before they could reach the cover of the next rock. When they came out they would be little more than fifty yards away. It was time.

Strangely his mind was drifting back to the hills of Yugoslavia where he and Alistair had fought together all those years before. He blinked with annoyance and refocused his concentration.

Then they came. It seemed that the glowing green figure stepped out from behind the rock in a weird slow motion. Marcus was not even conscious of gently squeezing the trigger. He was only fully aware that he had fired when the butt of the rifle recoiled into his shoulder. The green figure collapsed, and once again he squeezed the trigger out of pure instinct. Either the second or third shot must

# THE CROW MAKES WING

have hit, because he heard a piercing shriek before the figure disappeared back behind the rock. As the gale howled over the top of the fell he could hear the plaintive cries of the wounded man. He cried out in Matabele as his life ebbed away from a shot in the guts. Marcus felt suddenly bitterly sorry for the dying man who was so very far from home.

Victor's nerves were stretched to breaking point. At the moment that Marcus fired, the two men were no more than a dozen yards from his hiding place. Both their heads snapped round automatically to the sound of the gunshots. Victor dropped the first man with a short burst from his Uzi which lifted the top of his skull clean off. He dropped his aim and raked the second man's legs with a second burst. The bullets ripped through the legs just above the level of the knees and the man collapsed in a screaming heap. Victor leapt forward and wrenched his weapon away from him. As he leaned close he saw that this was a white man. His eyes were peeled wide with pain and terror. Victor laid his knife across his throat and whispered into his face. "How many in the middle? How many?"

He allowed the blade to break the skin which brought another shrill shriek of pain. The man gasped out the words "Only one. Only Kumalo."

Victor let him drop and had started to crawl away when the man started to yell, "Julius!! JULIUS!!! They know where you are!!! THEY HAVE NIGHT VISION GLASSES!!!!"

Victor turned and put out the light in Oliver Hamilton's eyes with three bullets through the temple. Oliver slowly slumped back until his shattered skull lay in a fast bubbling stream.

Kumalo paused as the shooting started. First he saw tracers heading over to his left. His men did not reply with any fire of their own. He heard the shriek followed by the agonised moans in Matabele.

Whoever had fired from the top of the ridge had hit both of his men with three shots. It meant two things. The rifleman was clearly a real marksman and he obviously was using night vision gear.

307

This assumption was verified quickly as Kumalo listened to the last words that Oliver Hamilton was ever to speak.

He lay close to the ground and considered his situation. It was poor but he had known worse. He would probably make it if he decided to beat a fast retreat. That is what he would have done in the days of the War of Independence. Retreat, exfiltrate, live wild in the bush for weeks on end before finally returning to one of the camps in Zambia.

But this time it was different. He had nowhere to retreat to. If he had wanted to retreat he would never have followed Rosenberg in the first place.

Somehow he had to maintain his attack. Of course everything had changed now. He was outnumbered, out gunned and at a huge disadvantage without the benefit of night vision. He screwed his eyes closed and forced himself to think. At last he smiled as the solution came to him. He remembered the wounded buffalo. A wounded buffalo would hide itself deep in the very most impenetrable of thorn bushes. Though it had no hope of survival, it would force its pursuers to come far too close in order to find it. Once they were close it would use every last ounce of its energy to explode out of the bush and to charge them.

He glanced about in the hopelessly murky light until he located a stream. He crawled slowly along the stream until he found a pool deep enough for him to sit in up to his neck. He closed his mind to the cold and waited for the hunter to come.

As the minutes passed Victor started to become increasingly anxious. He kept stopping to scan the ground at the base of the crag. Every time he searched he found nothing. Where could Kumalo have gone? Surely he could not have made it to the top of the crag, and yet he felt certain that he would have definitely spotted him if he had retreated.

He shook his head with annoyance and continued his stealthy search. He stopped as he came to a small stream and once again scanned the ground ahead.

Again, nothing. Nothing but the moaning of the wind and the ceaseless dripping of the rain. He eased his way across the stream and was about to crawl up the bank when he was frozen by the sound of someone tut-tutting behind him.

"Good evening Victor Gama. We meet at last. Please throw your weapon away, put your hands on your head and turn around slowly."

Victor did as instructed. As he turned he noted with disappointment that Kumalo had chosen his spot well. The deep pool where he had hidden was sat at the base of a ten-foot waterfall which would ensure that they would be hidden from Marcus.

"Please relax Victor. I have had time to think in this wretched cold pool. I have had enough of killing. It has gone on for too long. I just want it to end now. I have waited for you because I would like a warrior like you to send me on my way. Here. Catch this."

Kumalo pulled a necklace from his neck and tossed it to Victor. "This is a sacred thing to me. In return for your life I will ask you to take this to the Matapos Hills in Matabeleland. My soul will go with the charm and it will be able to rest at last. I ask this of you Victor Gama as a fellow African. Now end it. And make it clean."

He passed his weapon over to Victor. "Tell me Kumalo, what did you do to Sir Alistair?"

"He is fine. I tied him to a post on the road. He will be a little wet, no more. Now please . . . "

Victor allowed his mind no thoughts. He raised gun and put a whole magazine into Kumalo's chest. It took Kumalo a long time to fall. At last he slumped down into the pool. When Victor came close he saw that the strange scarred face was smiling. Julius Kumalo had been ready for his death.

Victor made the calls as he walked back to the house. Helen immediately took off and headed back to High Cragg. Cornelius felt an overwhelming relief when the call had come through. He and Montgomery had found a ditch and had hidden as instructed. As the minutes had passed he found it almost impossible to keep his friend calm. Montgomery had become almost mad with panic. He was shaking from head to toe and his eyes were overflowing with stark terror. Victor managed to get his Land Rover past the burned-out vehicle that he had blown up with the rocket. Ten minutes later he had loaded Sir Alistair on board and was headed back to the house. When he arrived the others were all there. They were all subdued, even more so when they saw the condition of Sir Alistair. He was as pale as death and soaked through.

Victor was matter of fact. "Helen, get him changed, then we'd best drive him straight to hospital." He studied the hunched figure of Montgomery. "I think Monty here needs to go as well. Are you OK Marcus?"

"Fine Victor. Don't worry about me."

Victor seemed to sag visibly. "I suppose we had better call the police now. We'll have some fun explaining this little lot . . . "

"No!! No police." It was Sir Alistair. He swallowed hard to find the strength to speak. "There is no need. If they get involved now you will all be in a world of trouble. No, I forbid it absolutely. You must not . . . " He collapsed into a fit of agonised coughing.

Vince spoke to him gently. "If we don't tell the police, then what exactly do we do?"

Sir Alistair managed to bring his breathing under control. "Now listen. There is no evidence anywhere that could tell the police that these men came here. They didn't even know where they were going themselves remember – they had to follow Gideon. These men came to murder us. It is as simple as that. We owe them no favours. You must bury the bodies and bury them deep. Destroy all of the evidence. These men will simply have disappeared and nobody will ever know where to find them. Please Vince. You must do this. All of this is my responsibility. I cannot allow you all to be drawn into a nightmarish investigation by the authorities. Please, promise that you will do as I say."

Vince considered Sir Alistair's words. They certainly carried great sense. He hadn't much stomach for having to go over the events of the past months with the police. He nodded and said, "OK, you're right. We'll do it. We'll do it tomorrow. But now you are going to hospital. No arguments."

Sir Alistair sagged back with relief. As they looked down on his drawn, pale face it became obvious to all of them that he was not going to be with them for long.

The next day was an extended misery. The rain continued to lash down and it never seemed to get properly light. In the morning Victor, Vince and Cornelius buried the six corpses whilst Gideon started to cut up the wrecked Land Rover with a blow torch. This was the longest job. After Cornelius had left to go and see Montgomery, it took the others several more hours until the job was done. However, by nightfall all of the evidence was safely buried. They ate a miserable meal and spoke little.

Cornelius returned at eight that evening. His cheeks were streaked with tears. Vince asked with concern, "Is is bad?"

"Awful. Bloody awful. Sir Alistair is really bad. They think that it is pneumonia. He looks terrible. And Montgomery . . . I just don't know. He won't say anything. He just stares into nothing and shakes. I felt terrible. The doctors kept giving me a hard time, saying that he must have had some kind of shock, grilling me about it, and all that I did was tell lie after lie. Oh Jesus Vince.."

He sagged forward and Vince took him in his arms. Outside, the wind was still howling over the fells and the rain lashed the windows. For a while the four of them remained cocooned in a silence that was broken only by the wind, the crackling of the logs on the fire, and the deep, despairing sobbing of Cornelius.

# CHAPTER FIFTEEN

## FALLOUT

The next days passed slowly. Marcus and Gideon had to head back to Black Loch to field the flood of questions about Sir Alistair's health. Vince, Victor and Cornelius spent their time moping about the house and hanging around the hospital. The passage of time brought little in the way of good news. Sir Alistair was either delirious or sleeping. Nothing that anyone could either do or say seemed to be able to drag Montgomery back. His mind had fled to a secret hideaway world and nobody knew the phone number. Helen refused to move from her father's room. Occasionally she dozed in the armchair by his bed but otherwise she more or less went without sleep. When Vince tried to talk to her she brushed him away gently and shook her head.

Their evenings at High Cragg were equally strained. Cornelius constantly walked a stretched tightrope of emotion. He paced the room endlessly. Victor was quite the opposite. He sat in a corner for hours turning Kumalo's charm over and over in his big hands. Vince often could stand it no more and headed out into the rain for long aimless walks over the hills.

On Friday afternoon the phone rang. It was Helen. "Hello Vincent, it's me. Daddy has come round and he would like everyone to come and see him this evening. I have talked to Marcus and he will come down with Gideon. Would you ring Dwight please?"

"Of course."

"Then we'll see you later."

Her tired sad voice squeezed at Vince's heart. Everybody but Montgomery met up in Sir Alistair's hospital room that evening. The mood was sombre. The old man had ordered that he should be dressed and he sat looking impossibly frail in an armchair. When he spoke, his voice carried a mere fraction of its former strength. "Good God, look at you all. It's like a bloody wake, I'm not dead yet I'll have you know. Come on Marcus, sort this out, pop the champagne, we are going to celebrate."

The confusion on their faces told him that they really didn't know.

He smiled. "Here. You obviously haven't seen this." He opened that morning's copy of the *Farmers Weekly* and held it up.

"£1.28. That is today's price gentlemen. The price for finished steers in this magazine is reported to be £1.28. Gentlemen, we have done it. You have done it. Gideon here has already received a bank transfer for £20 million which I presume he is already fizzing around the world money markets."

Marcus distributed glasses of champagne but the mood didn't lift. Sir Alistair shook his head sadly.

"Come on chaps, you are all as bad as my wretched moping daughter. If it wasn't for what has happened to me and Montgomery you would all be celebrating as if there were no tomorrow. Don't worry yourselves too much about Montgomery. Marcus and I saw many similar cases in the war, Victor, you must have seen this kind of thing too?"

Victor nodded. "Some men cannot bear the stress of combat and they deal with it by finding a safe place for the mind to hide. Time and care almost always allow the mind to be coaxed out of its secret cupboard. You wait and see. Montgomery will be fine, I promise. I have made enquiries and I have found a superb clinic that specialises in this kind of thing. We will send him there for a while and you just see how quickly he snaps out of it."

He took a tiny sip of champagne and suppressed a cough.

"Then there is me. Well, I can't hide the fact that I am pretty well done for. But I would like to remind you of the situation that prevailed when we entered into our contract. I was quite open and honest and I told you all that I had cancer and that I had little time left. Since then I have had the best few months of my life. I have had an absolute ball. As things turn out, I am going to have marginally less time than I may of hoped for." He looked at them all with a mellow smile. "Do any of you seriously believe that I would have swapped any of what has happened for a few extra lousy months? Now come on. Let's celebrate."

The mood lifted marginally and they downed four bottles of Marcus's champagne. When the time came to leave they all bade their farewells to Sir Alistair and headed out into the night. He died a little after four the next morning with his daughter at his bedside holding his hand.

The true success of the Matador campaign only really came to light with the death of its leader. His death was featured on the front pages of all the papers and and was the subject of several editorials. Some thoughtful commentaries suggested that Sir Alistair's campaign had opened up a new era in retailing. The British public had no real love for the faceless multi corporations that had come to dominate the High Street, and they had voted resoundingly with their feet by supporting Matador so wholeheartedly. His funeral was a vast occasion which was attended by the great and the good in impressive numbers.

Vince barely had time to say a word to Helen all day as she tore around supervising every detail. Close to the end of the evening he managed to take her to one side. She was uncomfortable and ill at ease. She could not look him in the eye. Her voice was flat.

"Please Vincent, not now. I don't know when. I don't even know if there will be a when. Maybe you should just forget about me. You are a rich man now Vincent, go and enjoy it. There is so much to do. I just have no time. No time to think. No time to come to terms with things. Please, just leave me alone."

Before he could say anything she turned and walked away. With a brittle smile she helped the last guests to find their coats and their cars. Vince watched sadly, then left by the back door. As he stepped out into the night and stood by the inky waters of the loch he remembered how he and Cornelius had walked along the same path a few weeks before. It had seemed like the ultimate challenge and they had taken it on.

Now that it was all over there seemed to be only emptiness.

Cornelius left the next day for London so that he could be close to Montgomery. Victor was more mysterious and told them that he would be away for a while.

Vince withdrew into the cocoon of High Cragg for eight weeks. He spent his days walking and reading and trying not to wait for the phone to ring. Gideon and Marcus stayed in regular contact. Matador was going from strength to strength. After desperate pleading from a variety of farmers, they had decided to add British milk, cheese, butter, lamb, chicken, pork and eggs to their portfolio. Cornelius rang every few days but there was no change in Montgomery. Victor came to visit after a fortnight.

He told Vince about the charm that Kumalo had entrusted to his care. He had flown to Zimbabwe and had hiked the Matapos Hills for several days. He told of the strange haunted atmosphere that he had found there. He had camped out under the stars and had walked and walked until he found the right place for the charm. He had spotted a ledge high on a cliff where an eagle had made its nest. It had taken him two hours to make the dangerous climb. From the ledge he had gazed down onto the majestic spread of the plains of Matabeleland. He had hung the charm from the branches of a young tree that had managed to root in the shallow soil against all odds.

When he had stood at the bottom of the cliff and looked back, he had been filled with the sensation that the air was buzzing with the soul of Julius Kumalo. He shook his head as he spoke. "It is a part of Africa that has always confused me. The superstition and the magic and the witch doctors. I have never really believed it but it is always there. I'm glad that I went, Vince. I needed the time. I needed to come to terms with the fact that I have killed six people. The Matapos Hills were what I needed. They brought out the African in me. You kill to protect. If that is the reason for killing, then the gods will never be harsh in their judgement. I'm fine now. How is everyone else?"

Vince brought him up to speed. The next day they travelled down to London and visited the clinic. Cornelius gave them a thin smile as they entered Montgomery's room. Montgomery was out of bed and sitting in the sunshine on a small veranda. He didn't acknowledge them when they spoke. He didn't seem to be aware of anything at all. He just stared out across the manicured lawns and rubbed his hands together over and over.

In London Victor asked if Vince wanted him to stay with him up at High Cragg.

"Thanks Victor, but no. I think that I am better on my own. I'll be in touch."

As he walked down the platform at Kings Cross station he heard Victor shout. He turned and the big man yelled over the heads of hundreds of commuters, "She'll ring, Vince!! She will."

Towards the end of June, Vince was lying on his back staring up into the shimmering heat of a clear blue summer sky. He was watching the spectacular tumbling and falling of a pair of skylarks. He had been lying in the meadow all day pondering on what on earth he was going to do with his life.

His phone rang and his heart jumped.

"Hi Vincent it's Cornelius." He could sense some of the old joy in his friend's voice. "Great news. Montgomery is starting to come out of it. He spoke a little today. The quacks are over the moon."

"Oh that's brilliant news," said Vince.

"Fantastic. Now there is something else. I had a call last week from Aunt Esther. A friend of hers has a farm down in Hampshire. Apparently she is wanting to open a farm shop to sell her Jersey ice cream to the tourists. She was telling Aunt Esther all about it. The thing is, there is some git of a London lawyer who has bought a fancy house nearby and he is hell bent on trying to stop her getting planning permission. Well, Aunt Esther was livid and she said that she might just know of some people who could help . . . "

Vince smiled. "Help solve the problem."

"That's it," agreed Cornelius enthusiastically. "Help solve the problem."

"May I gather from this that you don't feel that we should be considering retirement just yet?"

"Good Lord no. After all Vincent, you don't seriously consider that a paltry £20 million is enough for us to live our lives in the way that we have become accustomed to?"

"Absolutely not,"laughed Vince. "Absolutely not. Count me in. I'll see you in a few days."

For the first time in ages he felt happier as he made his way over the hills towards the house. It had become his habit always to walk back past the place on the ridge where Marcus had fired the sniper's rifle to such good effect. As he reached the cluster of weathered rocks he frowned. There was a truck parked by the gate to the small paddock by the house.

Fighting back waves of optimism, he raced down the crag. When he walked round to the back of the truck the tailgate was down. Inside Helen was coaxing out a stubborn Aberdeen Angus cow. Two young calves huddled fearfully at the rear of the straw-filled box.

"Thank goodness you are here. She is being a real stubborn bitch. Come on. Lend a hand."

With a deal of shouting and slapping they pushed the cow and her two calves into the small meadow. They soon settled down to their new surroundings and the calves started to suckle their mother hungrily.

Vince put his arm around Helen as they watched the cattle settle in. She laid her head on his shoulder. "It seemed a shame to have a place like this and no livestock. They'll like it here. The one on the right could be a champion you know. He's got wonderful breeding. I expect to see you show him at Kelso Show in a couple of years."

She was silent for a while, then she looked up into his face. "I do hope that I haven't blown it. Will you still have me?"

He grinned back. "Don't be so bloody daft. Come on, let's go get a drink. Now listen, I've just had Cornelius on the phone, there is this lady down in Hampshire and she . . . "

It was dawn on the plains of Matabeleland. The young boy had sat huddled in his blanket all night. He had waited patiently for the fine brown cow to have her calf. She had given birth a little before dawn and he rejoiced as there were no complications. The infant was now unsteadily trying to find its feet. A wizened old man crossed the plain to join the boy.

"I see you grandfather."

"I see you too."

"He is a beautiful strong calf grandfather."

The old man examined the leggy calf critically then nodded sagely. "This is true. He will grow up to be a king of bulls."

He gazed across the burnt grasslands to where a blood-red sun was climbing over the misty horizon.

"We will call him Julius."

**THE END**